THE GRAFT

THE
GRAFT

Martina Cole

headline

First published in 2004
by HEADLINE BOOK PUBLISHING

10 9 8 7 6 5 4 3 2 1

Cataloguing in Publication Data is available from the British Library

ISBN 0 7472 6969 6 (hardback)
ISBN 0 7472 6970 X (trade paperback)

Typeset in Galliard by Avon DataSet Ltd,
Bidford-on-Avon, Warwickshire

Printed and bound in Great Britain by
Mackays of Chatham plc, Chatham, Kent

HEADLINE BOOK PUBLISHING
A division of Hodder Headline
338 Euston Road
London NW1 3BH

www.headline.co.uk
www.hodderheadline.com

For Christopher Wheatley.
It's an honour and a privilege to be your friend.

For Ricky and Maria.
Remembering when we were kids.

Prologue

It was so hot in the room, like an oven. He could feel the sweat trickling down his face and wiped it away carelessly. He wished that it would rain, that the storm would break and everything would finally be over.

The thought brought a smile to Nick Leary's handsome face.

He was restless, tired but far from sleep. Unable to sleep. He had too much to think about.

His wife was sleeping soundly beside him, her faint snoring loud in the quiet room. She was as usual curled up in a ball, her face devoid of the frown lines that daybreak inevitably brought with it. Her blond hair was still immaculate even as she slept. Tammy never looked untidy, it was part of her personality. He believed that if she had a head-on crash in her 4 × 4 she would die with every hair in place and her make-up untouched, like film stars did in the movies. She broke wind gently and it made him grin in the dimness of the room. She would be mortified when he told her. Tammy hated any reference to bodily functions and would go to great lengths to hide the fact that she burped, farted and crapped just like everyone else. She snuggled down and he smiled in the dimness.

He was lying on his back, one forearm thrown casually across his eyes. Nick Leary was a big man. Big in stature, and with a big personality to match. He had a reputation as a shrewd businessman and loyal friend. He cultivated this image carefully because it was important to him.

He rarely did anything without it being of some benefit to himself, which was why he had an eight-bedroomed farmhouse, enough money to do what he wanted, and a lifestyle envied by most of his peers. But Nick had grafted for it, had pulled himself and his family up by the proverbial bootstraps – and pulled them up as high as they could go.

He heard a distant rumble of thunder and felt his whole body finally relax. A few seconds later the insistent drumming of the rain hit the windows and he almost cried out with joy. He had prayed for this rain, known that it was coming and dreaded that it might not arrive. He had a tension headache. He always got them when it was stormy but this time he had a lot on his mind as well. He moved restlessly around in the bed once more.

'Keep still, Nick, for Christ's sake.'

Tammy's voice was muffled but he could hear the impatience in it.

'Sorry, Tam.'

He willed his body to be still. All he needed now on top of everything else was her up and ranting her head off.

Tammy Leary liked her Sooty and Sweep and no one interfered with that – not if they valued their own hearing anyway. Her nasal twang he could cope with in the day, he loved her dearly after all. But at night her voice sounded like a banshee wailing, and that banshee had a toothache and a temper on it. Best leave her to sleep, especially tonight with the storm well on its way overhead and his neck and shoulders stiff with pain and the trepidation that was surrounding him.

He closed his eyes once more, but knew he would not sleep.

Then he heard it.

He opened his eyes and lay motionless. Sweat still covered his body when he felt the first chill hit him. He was straining

2

to hear now, every fibre of his being on red alert. Thunder clapped loudly overhead and a flash of lightning lit up the room. He slid quietly from bed and tiptoed across the wooden floor of the bedroom. The en-suite light was on and there was a crack of light coming from underneath the door. It was enough for him to see by.

Nick slipped out on to the landing.

The rain was heavier now; he could hear it surrounding the house.

He stopped dead as he heard the muffled movements once more. Someone was moving around downstairs. He could hear the sounds of drawers opening and closing. His heart was thundering in his chest, so loud he wondered if anyone else could hear it. He passed his sons' bedrooms and was relieved to see that their doors were shut tight.

At the top of the staircase he paused and listened once more before descending the staircase as quietly as he could. At the bottom he felt inside the large umbrella pot and located the baseball bat he'd left there for just such an occasion as this.

The house was large, set in seven acres and not easily accessible. You gained entry through electric gates and you never turned up at the Learys' without first letting them know you were coming.

He glanced around the entrance hall. There were three sets of double doors. These led to the large front room, the television room and dining room. Another staircase led down to the cellar and two more doors to the kitchen and study. Off the study was a well-stocked library. But it was the study that the noise was coming from.

It was inside the study that Nick kept his safe.

He crept across the entrance hall. His heart was in his mouth now. He swallowed with difficulty. The storm had quietened momentarily but was picking up in intensity once more. The wind was whistling round the house now and it was an eerie sound, a frightening sound, and God knew Nick was frightened. More frightened than he had ever been in his life before.

He thought of Tammy and the boys to stop the fear from making him turn back and run away.

The study door was open a crack. He looked through it, then pushed it further open. There was someone standing by the fireplace, his back to the door. He was wearing a ski mask and was dressed all in black. He was holding a weapon, a large hand gun, but it was dangling by his side.

He turned as Nick leaped across the room, raising the hand with the gun in it. Nick caught him with the baseball bat on the raised arm and heard the crunch of bone. The man crumpled to the floor and Nick hit him over and over again, on the head and the body, putting all his considerable strength behind the blows. This fucker was not getting up again, he would make sure of that. He was panting with exertion when he finally stopped.

In the dimness he saw that the intruder was still and breathed a sigh of relief. He turned to put on a lamp and then saw Tammy in the doorway, silent and terrified, the two boys standing to either side of her, their little faces white with fear and shock. Even in his terror at what he had done he noted how handsome they both were. He went over to them, dropping the bloody baseball bat as he ran, and gathered them up, all three of them, into his bear-like embrace.

'It's OK. Everything will be OK.'

He said it over and over like a mantra, his voice quavering with reaction to what he had just done, the violence of his attack. Then he ushered them from the room and across the entrance hall to the kitchen, turning on all the lights as he went. They needed light now.

The sudden glare made the boys squint and Nick smiled at them as best he could.

'It's all right, boys, Daddy's here. You're OK now.'

He hugged the two blond heads to him, felt their fear in the tremor of their narrow shoulders.

'What's happened *now*, Nick? What the fuck is all this about?'

Tammy grabbed her sons from him, holding them to her, all the time looking at the door, clearly wondering if the intruder was coming after them. The shock was making her teeth chatter.

'A burglar, sweetheart. I caught him . . .'

Nick's voice trailed off and he picked up the phone from the wall.

'What you doing?'

'I'm phoning the police, love.'

Tammy stared at the doorway again.

'What if he gets up . . .'

The boys started really crying then.

Nick shook his head, trying his best to calm them all down.

'He won't. I promise you, he ain't going nowhere, darlin'.'

He held up a hand to them all for quiet as he heard Emergency Services replying.

'Police, please, we've been burgled. I caught the fucker . . .'

He was babbling into the receiver now. Aware of it, he passed the phone to his wife.

'You tell them, I'll check on him.'

'No!'

It was a scream. Tammy dropped the phone on to the floor and started to shout in absolute terror.

'He had a gun, Nick, I saw a gun . . . He'll shoot us all!'

She was hysterical. By the time he had calmed her down they could already hear police sirens in the distance.

'Oh, thank God, thank God!'

His wife ran out of the house and on to the wide driveway with her sons to greet the police and ambulances.

'He's got a gun . . . He's got a gun . . .'

She was shouting it over and over again.

5

The police quickly moved her and the boys away from the front door and tried to calm her down. They needed to know if the intruder was still armed, if he was going to try and fight his way out of the house. They wanted to know where her husband was, if he was OK or being held hostage.

But she was past any sensible conversation and they realised it. They handed her over to the paramedics.

It was the eldest boy, Nick Junior, who filled them in on all the details they needed.

Nick Senior meanwhile returned to the study and stared at the body sprawled on the floor. Blood had pooled all around the head. He could smell its sickly sweetness. He backed away and out of the room, finally dropping down on to the small loveseat in the entrance hall when his legs wouldn't function any more.

The police found him there with his head in his hands, muttering over and over, 'What have I done? Dear God, what have I done tonight?'

Book One

No beast so fierce but knows some touch of pity.

– William Shakespeare
Richard III (Act I, scene ii)

Protection is not a principle but an expedient.

– Benjamin Disraeli, 1804–1881

Chapter One

Tammy was finally asleep, the paramedics had seen to that, and the boys were with their nanny in the playroom. Nick could feel the silence hanging over the house and he hated it. Dawn had come and gone and somehow the day had passed. The police had talked to him, over and over, until eventually his doctor had told them he needed breathing space. He was after all in shock. Not that the police had taken that into consideration, of course.

But once they had ascertained the intruder's identity they seemed to go easier with Nick somehow. Were softer, more inclined to believe in his fear for his family. He had worried for a while that they would see him as the villain of the story and not the boy who'd been burgling his house. The world had gone mad that way lately.

His mother Angela watched the changing expressions on her son's face and said stoutly, 'You'll be all right, Nick. No one in their right mind would give you a capture for this, son. You was defending your own.'

His mother's voice was harsh, its cockney twang seeming out of place in these palatial surroundings. She had slept through it all thanks to her penchant for a bedtime whisky.

'Let it go, Mum, eh? Make a nice cuppa.'

She plugged in the kettle but he could see the anger in her stiff shoulders and the set of her back.

He smiled gently then.

She was game, his mother, a right little firebrand. He adored her with all his being. But her mouth had often got her into trouble, not just with her family but with others who came into her orbit. Angela Leary never knew when to leave well alone.

'That little fucker was going to get a slap eventually.'

Her voice rose with her anger and her animosity at what had occurred. To enter her son's home armed! It was the gun that frightened her most, that and the fact the boy turned out to have been a known drug user and all-round thief. When the paramedic had removed his balaclava the investigating officers had instantly identified him. In fact, he was well known to all the police round about. He was in short a little fucker, and a dangerous little fucker at that.

Ignoring her son's need for peace, Angela Leary carried on talking.

'Who do these people think they are? Coming in other people's houses to rob them, *harm* them. Creeping around while decent people sleep in their beds . . . beds paid for with graft, not thievery. And he had a gun! Jesus Christ, when I think of what might have happened, I feel ill with the fright of it all. Shot in your beds, you could have been . . .'

Nick felt as if his head was going to explode at any moment.

'All right, Mum, we get the picture.'

He was shouting at her now.

She instantly came towards him, all concern. She looked old and frail and he wanted to cry with the love he felt for her then. Angela Leary had fought all her life, first to get money from the drunken sot she had married, then to put a roof over her family's heads and food in their bellies. She'd been up and out at four in the morning cleaning other people's houses, scrubbing and polishing for strangers. Then home to get her kids off to school before she was out again to work in the plastics factory in Romford. Nick adored her and never raised his voice to her but today he was on edge. He couldn't listen to her any longer.

'I'm sorry, Mum, but it's still all so raw . . .'

His voice trailed off.

'No, I'm sorry, son, I should know when to shut me trap. But I can't believe anyone would do that to me or mine. If I'd have got my hands on him . . .' She shrugged. 'Let's hope he don't die anyway. Let him live and go to prison. Though they don't put them in prison now, do they? He'll probably end up on holiday in bleeding Africa or somewhere. You know what them bleeding bleeding hearts are like!'

Nick would have laughed if he'd had a laugh left in him. Angela made the tea and carried on ranting and raving at the world but he had tuned her out now.

The boy was alive.

That was all Nick could think about.

The boy was still alive.

'Your son is very ill, Mrs Hatcher.'

The doctor's voice was quiet and she looked into his face steadily.

'I ain't surprised, are you? His head was caved in with a baseball bat.'

She laughed, a nervous high sound, and the doctor's heart went out to her.

'You really should think about what I said. Organ donation can be very comforting to some relatives. It's as if a part of a person lives on . . .'

She turned on the doctor then, her eyes bright and her voice harsh with emotion.

'I ain't turning nothing off! He'll be all right. A fighter, my Sonny, a strong boy.' The tears spilled over on to her cheeks. 'He'll be all right, love him. He just needs a bit of sleep, that's all.'

11

The doctor shook his head at the nurse sitting beside the distraught woman and sighed.

She grabbed her son's hand once more and said gaily, 'My Sonny Boy will be awake soon. He's only seventeen. They never get up before five in the afternoon, do they, teenagers?'

She nodded at the nurse for confirmation of what she'd said. The absolute misery in the woman's eyes made the nurse feel like crying herself.

'I'll get you some more tea.'

She left the room with the doctor. Both of them knew that Sonny Hatcher would never open his eyes again. He was brain dead.

Judy Hatcher closed her eyes and tried to stem the tears. Her face was haggard, but these days it always was. Drink and drugs had seen to that. Her blond hair was greasy and scraped back off her face. Her blue eyes were listless, almost as dead as her son's, and her naturally slim body emaciated from too much vodka and a liking for weekends devoted to cocaine and amphetamines though heroin was her drug of choice. She was supposed to be trying to get off it but methadone didn't have the same kick, the same way of obliterating all her troubles and thoughts.

She leaned over and opened her bag, taking out the photos once more.

'Here, look at this one, Sonny, you and me in Yarmouth. You was only two, remember that?'

There was hope in her voice, but in truth she hardly remembered it herself; she had been drunk and stoned for most of that holiday. Tyrell, Sonny's dad, had still been around then. He'd been so handsome; still was. She gazed sadly at the photo. Sonny was the image of him except his skin wasn't as dark.

She had left a message with Tyrell's mother and hoped he would come to see Sonny before . . . She wouldn't think about it. She wasn't turning nothing off, no matter what they said. Deep inside she wanted Tyrell to come and make the decision for her. But he was in Jamaica with his second wife and their two kids, so he had a long journey back.

Tyrell's mother was in a right state, bless her. She loved this boy but was housebound now, too scared to leave it. Jude would ring her again soon, let her know how he was. She was a good woman, old Verbena, a star really. She was the nearest thing to a mother Jude had ever had, and she adored her eldest grandson. But then she would. She had practically brought him up.

Verbena had been good to his mother as well. She had always made sure Jude ate and tried to help her take care of herself. In fact, over the years Jude did not know what she would have done without this help.

Verbena was someone she could go to. No matter what Jude did, or more to the point didn't do, Verbena was always there for her, the only constant in her constantly changing world. She had never judged the mother of her beloved grandson, instead she had tried to understand her.

Which was no mean feat as Jude Hatcher had never really understood herself.

She wished Verbena was here now, wished Tyrell was here, wished someone, anyone, would come and take this burden from her shoulders. She had never been very good at decisions; she always made the wrong ones.

Jude rested her head on the pillow next to Sonny's and cried. She didn't know what else to do.

'He's a little bastard, it was bound to happen to him sometime.'

Detective Inspector Rudde's voice was bored-sounding. Once they had realised it was Sonny Hatcher lying broken on the study floor police interest had waned. He was a known creeper, with a string of offences as long as his arm, and was also a mouthy, uneducated little fucker who had been done for practically everything you could be done for bar murder. And by the looks of it, if Nick Leary hadn't jobbed him he would be up for that now and all.

'He is still a human being, and there's nothing to say he was actually going to harm anyone . . .'

Peter Rudde rolled his eyes to the ceiling in annoyance, his big fat face incredulous at the inanity of what he was hearing.

'A loaded fucking gun, a farmhouse with more antiques in it than Sotheby's, and *you* think he had it for a laugh? Use your fucking loaf! No, I'm recommending to the CPS that no action be taken. Sonny Hatcher was an accident waiting to happen. Fuck me, that geezer Leary just cut our crime rate by forty per cent. They should give him a fucking medal.'

DC Ibbotson sighed. It was a waste of time trying to reason with his boss who didn't know the meaning of the word.

'What, I ask you, would Sonny Boy know about antiques?' he tried, changing tack.

'Fuck all, I should imagine. Knowing him, he would just have nicked the ashtrays. But that ain't the point. He thought there was swag there and that would be good enough for him.'

Ibbotson persisted.

'Maybe someone else sent him to the house . . . someone who knew what was in there?'

Rudde shrugged his enormous shoulders.

'I don't give a flying fuck, I ain't taking this no further. As far as I am concerned he done us a right favour. If, and it's a big if, he was sent in there, we'll never get to the bottom of it, though I would like to know where he got that gun from. That would be worth knowing anyway. But when I present this case to the CPS I'm going to make it plain it's a waste of police resources chasing this up. We can only wait and see if they agree with me, though I think they will. Sonny Boy Hatcher was on the road to destruction sooner rather than later, unfortunately. As it happens, he picked on the wrong person tonight.'

He pointed a finger in the younger man's face.

'You tell me why an otherwise law-abiding citizen should pay for the sins of that little cretin? If Hatcher hadn't been on those premises with intent to rob he'd be in the pub now as usual, scoring a bit of blow, instead of lying in hospital with his head caved in.'

Rudde didn't wait for an answer.

'It's the law of the jungle, mate. Survival of the fittest. Supposing Leary had been a frail old lady living alone. Wouldn't you feel sorry about it then? Wouldn't that make all the difference? It'd be wrong to break into her gaff, wouldn't it? Yeah, make all the difference to you, that would – but it's the same bloody crime.'

He laughed sarcastically.

'*Then* you'd be baying for Hatcher's blood along with everyone else. Well, fuck *him*, and fuck all the creepers we deal with. Personally, I am sick of them.'

It was quite a harangue and Rudde knew it but he couldn't stop. He was arguing for every person who had ever been ripped off, attacked or greased by a worthless criminal. He was on a roll and enjoying it.

'Sonny Hatcher mugged an old man as he was drawing his pension. He was also up in court for threatening an elderly neighbour. This paragon of virtue beat up a pregnant woman, so you tell me why I should cut him some slack?'

Ibbotson couldn't answer him, he didn't know what to say.

'He knew the law. No one knew it like Sonny did,' Rudde steamrollered on. 'He knew when he walked in that house armed that he was all but fucked. That if he had a capture he would be looking at an eighteen at least. So fuck him. He came up against someone with more savvy than himself, and not before time neither if I might say. Now get the statements sorted and stop annoying me, OK?'

Ibbotson nodded.

This conversation was closed. He only hoped the CPS would see it differently, but didn't hold out much hope. His boss's attitude reflected the whole station house's. But as Ibbotson had argued earlier on in the canteen, should a boy's life really be forfeit just because he turned to petty crime? Apparently the local consensus was it should.

The DC left the room sheepishly, aware that everyone thought he was a prize prat and for the first time feeling they just might be right.

Tammy was wide-eyed with shock.

'Are you having me on?'

Nick shook his head.

'Honest, they want me for GMTV in the morning, to get my side of the story.'

As shaken as she was, Tammy unconsciously tidied her hair.

'Oh, my God! You are going to go, I take it?'

Her voice brooked no refusal and he sighed once more.

'Because you put your side across, right? You could have been killed, Nick. If they want to charge you, the best thing to do is make sure everyone hears your side of the story.'

'I don't know, Tams. I ain't that kind of person, I hate being in the limelight.'

'Well, don't you worry, *I'll* be right beside you.'

Even in the midst of her shock and horror at what had occurred Tammy was already deciding what she was going to wear and wondering if she could fit in a quick sun bed to take some of the pallor from her skin.

At the end of the day this was for her husband. She wanted them to come across as respectable people with a few quid but a down-to-earth lifestyle.

In her own way, she was doing what she thought was best.

* * *

Tyrell Hatcher sat on the plane in silence. He was a good-looking man and he knew it, could see the looks he attracted and ignored them. His looks and his personality had always been at odds with each other. His second wife Sally accepted that women liked him but trusted him implicitly. He wasn't in fact averse to a bit of strange but it was a rare occurrence and usually only happened after they had had a row or some such crisis in their lives.

Sally was a chocolate-coloured queen and he adored her, but sometimes Tyrell needed the anonymity of a strange body. He pondered that thought now, wondering if this kink in his make up had been passed on to his eldest son. Tyrell had nearly destroyed his life for a quick fuck. Sally knew nothing about that. But he had still done it, enjoyed the fear of being caught, enjoyed the danger of it. Had this flair for risk-taking been passed on to his eldest boy?

His two other children were stable, industrious and hard-working, so what exactly was the score with Sonny Boy? Why was he beaten to a pulp inside someone's home while apparently trying to rob them?

Tyrell wiped a hand across his face. He was so tired but he knew sleep would be a long time coming.

He didn't want to blame his former wife Jude for their son's life-style but it was hard not to. Tyrell was suddenly remembering the times he had been called out at all hours of the day and night to bail out Sonny or his mother at the local nick. And the times he had bailed Jude out of bad situations as well as police stations. But whatever she was, Jude was also to be pitied. He must remember that now, must not blame her for what had happened. Sonny had always been a handful, always had a chip on his shoulder. Yet he had loved his young half-brothers. Had looked out for them, always asked after them and been pleased to see them.

Now Tyrell had to break the news to them as well, had to brave everyone with the announcement that his first-born, the son he had loved the best, was as good as dead, was a thief. He knew Jude was just waiting for him to give the word to turn off life support. She would never get her head round that. He was expected to shoulder that burden too and he would, he had no other choice.

But it was how Sonny had died that was going to be the hardest part, telling everyone that his son was a gun-carrying thief. That he was everything they were not. Tyrell's mother would be the hardest hit. She had practically brought the boy up, had always been there for both him and Jude. For some unknown reason Tyrell's church-going, Jesus-loving mother had taken to poor Jude from the first time she had clapped eyes on her, and the feeling had been mutual. She had seen some need in Jude that had appealed to her motherly instincts. He often thought it was because she was so troubled. Jude was the most troubled person he had ever met. It was also the neediness of her; Verbena needed to be needed, and unfortunately for her none of her own children needed looking after any more. She had brought them up to take good care of themselves, even though she had not left her house for over twenty years.

He wished he could close his eyes and then everything would be back as it was. But he knew that was impossible.

He wished he had taken the boy to Jamaica with them, but that had not really been an option. Sally had tried her best with Sonny but they didn't exactly hit it off, and four weeks in Jamaica together would have been stronging it for both of them.

Tyrell shook his head angrily, making his dreads slap against his cheek; the stinging sensation was welcome. It brought him back to the present.

He would have given Sonny anything within reason, he had only to ask. But then, Tyrell had been telling him that all his life and the boy had still turned to crime. He'd enjoyed being with the kind of people anyone else would have crossed the road to avoid. He had almost seemed to revel in his growing notoriety. Drugs, drinking, fighting. Nothing was sacred to Sonny. He swore whenever he spoke, would argue relentlessly about nothing, and was almost always fighting the world for what he saw as slights against him, both real and imagined.

Yet through it all, the meetings with the school, the sitting in courts and the helping with paying the fines, Tyrell had never stopped loving this troubled boy who carried his name. And for all his faults he would never have put him down for this, never in a million years. Armed robbery? Because that was what it amounted to. He'd been armed and inside someone's home.

Their home.

Tyrell imagined what it must have been like to see him standing there with a gun, and shuddered once more.

The terror of it must have been overwhelming. His heart went out to the man who had fought back so furiously. He was sure he would have reacted in much the same way in that position.

But why did his boy do it? That was what Tyrell wanted to know. Why?

Sonny had been a little sod in the past, but this was big-time skulduggery and Tyrell would have laid money that his son was not so far gone he would do something like this.

It seemed he would have been wrong.

And if he was wrong about this, what else was he wrong about? How could he trust his instincts any more? How was he going to switch off the ventilator and then bury his eldest son? How was he to cope with it all once the plane landed and he was back on solid ground?

He was questioning his whole life now, and finding it lacking.

Distinctly lacking.

Verbena Hatcher was tired, but knew she wouldn't sleep. Instead she picked up her Bible and, clasping it tightly, she prayed for her grandson. All around the room were pictures of her loved ones. Her children, her parents, even her grandparents. Every inch of space on wall or table was covered with smiling faces, and important events in her life and the lives of her family. Christenings, weddings – hers as well as her children's – graduation photos . . . smiling children and grinning adults. They amounted to a life well lived.

And among all those smiling faces stood a small photograph in a silver frame. It was of Verbena and Jude, with a tiny Sonny Boy asleep on his mother's lap. It was Jude's expression that Verbena most loved in that photo, rarely looking at her grandson when she glanced at it. For once Jude looked happy, completely and utterly happy, and Verbena had known it was because at last she had a family of her own in that little boy. Her own arm was around Jude's shoulders. It looked almost protective, as if she was shielding the girl from the world. She knew Jude kept the same photo in her purse. And in her own way Verbena still tried to protect her, as she had tried to protect her grandson.

Her lips moved silently in the Lord's Prayer and then she beseeched Him to watch over her grandson. Begged him to make Jude's grief easier to bear, and offered her own life in exchange for that of the boy she loved more than anyone else in the world.

Her daughter Maureen came in then with a small black rum for her mother.

'Drink this, you need it.'

Verbena shook her head. She rarely touched alcohol.

'Please, Mummy.'

She knew then it was not good news and duly took the glass and drank it down. The burn felt surprisingly good and the taste was as she had remembered it. It brought back the smell of new-mown grass, the aroma of sunlight on polished windows, and relay radios playing along the street. It brought back the sounds of summer, hearing the cricket results and listening to Barrington Levy. It brought back the taste of Akee and salt fish, and the laughter of her father when he would allow her a small sip of dark rum from his heavy glass on a Friday night. The sounds of the cicadas and laughter, the sounds of happiness, were replaced by her feeling of dawning despair.

It had been good remembering, but it was ruined forever now, replaced by the bad news she was sure was to come. Why else anaesthetise her?

'Maureen, has Jude rung?'

The young woman shook her head.

'Not a word. I am going to the hospital in a minute, Mummy.'

Verbena nodded absently.

She knew it was a lie, a kindly one but a lie all the same. The news had arrived by one of those text things, she guessed, having heard the noise earlier on. The incessant beeping that told the young people of the world they were attached in some way to the rest of their peer group. The rum would give her heartburn, she knew, so she took a couple of Tums. But her heart was heavier now than it had ever been. Her boy, her Sonny Boy, was dying and there was nothing she could do about it.

She looked around the room and pictured him there, lying on the sofa listening to Beenie Man or Bob Marley, singing along to the music, his eyes dancing with happiness and his body flourishing from her love and good cooking. All wasted now. But forever in her mind's eye, no matter what anyone else thought, he was her heart and always would be.

Verbena braced herself for the bad news she was sure was going to come.

Judy Hatcher was holding on to Tyrell. She could smell the distinctive mix of cigarettes, grass and deodorant. He looked as good as he smelled. She was shaking with sadness and hurt and he held her to him gently as they watched their comatose son.

'All right, Jude, everything will be all right.'

It was just something to say, crap, because they both knew nothing would ever be all right for her or him again.

21

*   *   *

Nick Leary looked at the policeman's face on the monitor and buzzed him in. It seemed an age before the man had driven up the drive and reached the front door. Tammy put the kettle on and smiled half-heartedly at her husband. For the first time in ages she felt protective of him. It was usually Nick protecting her. But seeing the whiteness of his face and the shaking of his hands she wanted to cry for him. In twenty-four hours their lives had been turned upside down, and all because some kid had decided he wanted to take what they had. What they had worked for all their lives.

It was wrong, all wrong, that they might have to fight to defend themselves in court. Their brief had already warned them about that.

Nick was not a saint, she knew that. But he did not deserve all this. He had ducked and dived, but that was for his family, his wife, his kids.

As Tammy poured water into the teapot the policeman entered the kitchen with her husband. Detective Inspector Rudde was sound. She knew he was on their side.

'Mr Leary.'

He nodded his head respectfully.

'Mrs Leary.'

She smiled back at him and raised her perfectly plucked eyebrows.

'Can I get you a cup of tea? A Scotch?'

'Both, if you don't mind.'

They all grinned, the ice broken but the fear still tangible; still there between them all like a pane of glass.

'I've got a good malt in the study, twenty years old.'

Nick left the kitchen as fast as his legs could carry him. He could feel his own heartbeat, hear it roaring in his ears. He hoped that this would all come to a head. He was even at the stage where if they were going to nick him, he hoped it would happen soon. Anything was better than this limbo, this endless waiting.

In the kitchen Tammy stared into Rudde's eyes.

'What's going to happen to Nick?'

He smiled gently.

'If it's left to me he's in the clear, but obviously I can't speak for the CPS. My recommendation is that the whole thing is dropped, forgotten about.'

'And the boy?'

'They are going to turn off the life support.'

She nodded. After swallowing deeply she asked, 'So it could be a murder charge?'

Rudde nodded.

'But I doubt that very much. Manslaughter, maybe.'

She busied herself with the tea, her fear of losing Nick overwhelming her once more.

'What a waste of a life.'

The detective didn't answer her, he didn't know what to say. He saw a lot of wasted lives in his line of work and had given up worrying about them.

'Me and Nick, we came from fuck all, us two. Council house kids us. But we *grafted*. We worked. Still do. We made the life we've got, and it was fucking hard work sometimes. But we pay our dues and we live our lives. Why should we have this hanging over our heads because that thug decided to come in our home and steal from us?'

Tammy Leary beseeched him with her eyes to answer her question.

'Why do I feel we've done something wrong? That we are the bad people in all this? Because we're not! We are good, law-abiding people, and now our lives are ruined over that worthless little bastard.'

She started to cry.

'He should never have been here in the first place. We didn't invite him, he invited himself! This is *our* house, we paid for it fair and square, why should we feel bad because he forced himself in here? My husband was looking out for us, for me and the kids. He's a good man, a decent man. Ask anyone who knows us.'

She was crying now, sobbing with fear.

Rudde stared at her for long moments, not knowing what to say to her. This was part and parcel of his job. He had had to tell people their daughter was not coming home because she had been murdered. He had told people their son had died in a fight in a pub over the most obscure reason ever. Had often explained that people had lost loved ones in car crashes and train wrecks. And it never got any easier, no matter how often he had had to do it. Now this family were decimated because the husband had tried to defend what was rightfully his.

Rudde would have done the same, given the circumstances, but he wouldn't say that, of course. Instead he drank the tea and the Scotch and tried silently to convey his solidarity with them both.

But the tea was like piss and the Scotch went straight to his head. On top of all that he realised he was getting old.

He didn't know which depressed him more.

Chapter Two

The interview on GMTV had gone better than anyone had expected. Tammy was in her element visiting the studio. Now that the shock had worn off and the imminent danger of prosecution had receded into the background, she was finding their newfound celebrity status quite enjoyable.

Plus, they were in the right. The more she thought about it, they *were* in the right. That boy had been robbing them, he was armed and he was dangerous. Her Nick had only been protecting his own. It seemed GMTV had never had so many calls and emails regarding a guest and the consensus seemed to be that Nick was only doing what anyone else would do in the same predicament.

She was proud of him, proud that he had taken the stance he had taken and glad that it had worked out well.

Because Nick could have been shot and killed. They all could.

That was what frightened her most in the dead of night, when her veneer of hardness was stripped away and she felt once more the shock of fear the sight of a gun can bring to the uninitiated. That boy was a thug, a young thug but a thug nevertheless. He had to have expected to pay some kind of price for his behaviour. Unfortunately it was the ultimate price but that was not their concern.

He should *never* have been there in the first place, and then he would still be all right. On the plus side, they now had offers coming in from all angles, the TV and the newspapers. It seemed their lives were up for public scrutiny and Tammy couldn't get enough of the attention.

As she meticulously applied her make-up she imagined the reaction down at the country club where she was meeting a few friends for lunch later. She almost hugged herself. In forty-eight hours their lives had been turned around, and excitement was now officially the order of the day. It would give her new Jimmy Choos an outing as well. She had been going to save them for a more formal occasion but she must look her best these days, the photographers were everywhere.

In her heart of hearts she knew that a boy was dying and her mood of elation was out of place. But Tammy was the kind of person who made the best of everything, took any opportunity that came her way and didn't give a toss who she trampled on in the process. She wasn't cruel or unkind, saw herself more as a realist, someone who looked out for her own.

And notoriety was fun, she would not deny that.

Tyrell was staring down into his son's face. Sonny was a good-looking boy still but now, with all the tubes attached to him and the ventilator noisily breathing for him, he looked so very vulnerable.

He remembered when Sonny was a baby how he would fetch him for the weekend. As much as he had wanted his son with him, he knew the weekends gave Jude the time and space to get out of her nut and so those occasions had been spoiled for him, like so much else. Jude took every opportunity she could to obliterate the present and both the men in her life had suffered because of it. Yet his son had loved her, adored her. When Tyrell later broached the subject of Sonny's living with him full-time the boy had smiled and said, 'But what about me mum?'

It had been more of a statement than a question. It had been the reason for his whole existence. No one else had ever been able to cope with Jude like Sonny had, everyone else became worn out one way or another. Heroin addicts wore everyone out in the end. They lied, cheated, cried and fought to get what they wanted.

It was the nature of the beast.

Jude had tried, he would never take that away from her, she had tried so hard to be a better person, but somehow the world in general had never been kind to her and it showed: in her eyes, in her stance, in everything about her. She looked ten years older than she was, and that was on a good day. Smack did that to people. But what she had going for her, what people rarely saw, was the kindness of her, and the bigness of her when it came to her son.

She had tried for Sonny when she wouldn't even try for herself, and Tyrell had stood beside her and tried to help her on her way.

But that was in the past now.

Sonny had always looked out for her after that, had tried to be the man who finally took care of her. Like Tyrell had tried all those years before until he had realised he was wasting his time. Jude was a junkie. They even called her Junkie Jude on the estate where she lived. It was as if her mother had picked her Christian name out in advance.

Junkie Jude. Jude the Junkie.

Sonny Boy had lived with that stigma all his life.

Be happy in thy own self.

Where did that come from? Tyrell's mother probably. Well, Jude had never been happy, it was beyond her. It was as alien to her as voting or living in the real world. She had lived her whole life on the periphery of happiness, frightened to embrace it in case it kicked her in the teeth.

And now her son was dying after trying to pull off an armed robbery.

Sonny Boy was only seventeen years old and for all the trouble he had been, and he *had* been big trouble over the years, Tyrell still had difficulty believing his son was capable of that.

He had spoken to the police but there was no doubting the boy's intentions, apparently. The gun had been loaded and was so far untraceable, though it had been used in an armed robbery before.

But for all Sonny's faults, and they were legion, Tyrell still could not for the life of him see his son with a gun.

Someone else had to have been behind this robbery. Sonny couldn't work out the day of the week for himself without a piece of paper and a pen. It was ludicrous for anyone to think he'd dreamed up and executed a crime like this on his own.

Jude crept into the side ward. She crept everywhere it seemed. Tyrell looked into her haggard face and his heart went out to her. He knew she had gone out for a drink or a lift of some sort, probably both, knowing her. But Sonny was all she had. Was all she had ever had. And Sonny had adored her. It was why he had never tried to take him away from her. Sonny had tried in his own way to take care of her always, first and foremost, as she had never been able to take care of herself.

'Sit down, Jude. Take the weight off, eh?'

She smiled at him, as usual glad of a kind word from this man who had left her because she couldn't go from one hour to the next without some kind of chemical enhancement.

In fact she didn't know what the real world felt like any more, it was years since she had faced the day like normal people.

But none of that had bothered Sonny Boy; he had taken care of her as if she was his child instead of the other way round. He was a kind boy, always had been, one who loved his half-brothers dearly. Who had had to live with his mother and her lifestyle because he was frightened to leave her alone. It was the main reason he had skipped school: he had been frightened of what he might come home to if he didn't watch over her. For years she had speedballed, smoked dope and injected herself with anything she could get her hands on. Jellies were everywhere around the house. She had even injected Mogadons in the past. Oblivion was all Jude craved, and she would crave it even more now.

Tyrell closed his eyes and his heart to the trauma she would experience once the machines were turned off, as turned off they would be.

Sonny, their Sonny, was already gone. It was all about picking up the pieces now, clearing up the mess.

Jude looked at him with haunted eyes. They had once been a dazzling blue, but were so faded now as to be almost colourless.

She turned on him suddenly.

'You want to turn it off, don't you? Get rid of him once and for all.'

Tyrell didn't answer her.

When Jude went into one of her rants he always kept quiet even when he felt like telling her exactly what he thought. She was hurting. Better she took it out on him than the police or the doctors.

She was shaking her head as if she somehow felt enormous pity for him, which of course she didn't. It was all gestures with Jude when she was out of it. Elaborate gestures she wouldn't remember twenty-four hours after the event. He could feel her hurt as if it was his own.

He saw her then as she was when he had first laid eyes on her. It was at a party. She was stoned, everybody was, all puffing away and listening to Curtis Mayfield. She still had the same vacant look in her eyes she had had then, only nowadays it troubled him. Where once it had attracted him, now it scared him because he had no idea what she was on and neither did Jude most of the time. Tyrell had sussed her out, that was what hurt her. She knew it and he knew it. He could almost smell her fear.

He wondered if she could smell his.

*   *   *

Tammy walked into the country club as if she was a movie star. She was even wearing sunglasses. She stood for a few seconds in the doorway to make sure everyone saw her before removing them and walking towards the restaurant. She looked good and she knew it. Always immaculate, she had taken extra care with her grooming this morning.

She waved to other friends as she made her way over to the table that held her band of closest cronies. That was what her husband always called them and Tammy protested, but to call them all close friends would have been pushing it, she knew that.

None of this lot would know a friend if they fell out of a tree and hit them on the head. What they all had was something in common: husbands who bankrolled them, a nice life, big houses and top-of-the-range cars. And Tammy was queen of them all because her husband could buy and sell the lot of theirs.

She wore her crown well and they respected that.

'All right, Tam?'

This from Melanie Darby. She was second fiddle to Tammy and actually a nice person. Out of them all it was Melanie she would call the closest to her. Melanie's husband Ray was into all sorts and no one asked her about any of it.

Tammy sat down and sighed dramatically.

'It's been a nightmare, girls.'

Fiona Thomson pushed a glass of champagne into her hand. Tammy noticed it was a very expensive label and realised she was paying for this lunch. Nick would go mad but she would cross that bridge when she came to it. Some of her girls' lunches came to nearly a grand and even though they were well heeled it sent Nick off the deep end; he was mean in some respects.

But he didn't understand, she had a front to keep up and giving expensive lunches was part of that front. Ordering expensive wine gave Tammy a buzz, and she loved the looks on her friends' faces when they realised what it was all costing. They were the elite of their crowd and she was the queen. And being queen didn't come cheap, whatever her husband thought.

She was just finishing her tale of woe when Fiona said gently, 'So they ain't going to do Nick then?'

Tammy placed her glass of champagne on the table and gave her a look that would have floored most women. Fiona, though, was made of sterner stuff than most.

'I beg your pardon?'

'Look, Tams, all I am saying is, my old man said Nick could get done for manslaughter . . .'

Tammy, however, was one glass of champagne away from fighting her and it showed. The other women all tried to shut Fiona up with looks and waves of their hands.

'And your old man would know all about that, wouldn't he? Being a bank robber and all that.'

Fiona laughed.

'It's hardly a secret, Tams. He done his time, love, so yeah, he would know what he's talking about. And he said that if Nick had any brains he should get himself a good brief.'

'My Nick's got brains, love, he knows the score. So tell your old man not to worry about him, all right? If he had any sense he'd worry about himself, love, or that's what my Nick says anyway.'

This statement was loaded and Fiona sighed.

'Whatever you say, Tams. I was just saying, that's all.'

'Yeah, well, don't. My Nick was only defending his family. That ponce had a fucking loaded gun. You remember that, won't you, when you're gossiping about it? He wasn't holding up his local Tesco's, like some I could mention.'

All the women fell quiet now. Tammy had gone too far and she knew it. She waved over the waiter and ordered two more bottles of champagne. At nearly four hundred quid a pop it was one of her most expensive lunches yet. But Tammy, who'd been on the verge of leaving before this contretemps, was now going to sit it out to the death.

Her husband had his faults and they were legion, but she was fucked if Fiona was going to get the better of her. Or, more to the point, hers.

She smiled nastily as she said, 'Better get on the phone, Fiona. See if your mum can pick up the kids. After all, you don't have a nanny, do you, and time's moving on.'

Fiona grinned happily. Nothing fazed her, which was another thing that annoyed the life out of Tammy.

'It's half-term, ain't it? They're in Spain with me mother-in-law.'

The knives were well and truly out now and the other women sat back to enjoy the spectacle.

They were not disappointed.

Nick was at the police station with his golfing buddy, DI Rudde. The two men had been acquaintances for years. Now they were almost bosom pals, though they didn't let that on to anyone else, another unwritten law.

'So what's the score, Peter?'

Rudde sighed.

'You're home and dry, more or less. I've said I do not feel there are any reasonable grounds for a prosecution against you. Sonny Boy was a known face, a little villain, and he had a loaded gun. I said I had no doubt he would have used it if necessary. He was a suspect in a stabbing a few months ago. I can't see the CPS making any case against you.'

Nick visibly relaxed.

'I still feel bad, Pete.'

'I know, mate, but that's because you're a decent person – more than could be said for that little fucker. He had no chance, did he? Mother's a junkie, his life's been one long round of trouble and aggravation. This was bound to happen one day, it just happened sooner rather than later.

'I see them all coming through here, Nick, the no hopers. I feel sorry for some of them, but, at the end of the day, they're all accidents waiting to happen. You have the law on your side as far as I am concerned. It says you can use *reasonable* force to eject an intruder from your home. If that intruder has a gun then you are within your rights to disarm him, as you did.'

'I didn't just disarm him, I disabled him! He's going to die, ain't he?'

Peter Rudde didn't answer him.

'Ain't he!'

Nick was shouting now.

'I need to know, Peter. When are they going to turn the machine off?'

He patted Nick's arm.

'As far as I know, his dad is back from Jamaica and he's taking over. The mother couldn't decide what shoes to wear without a fix of some sort.'

The detective watched his friend relax back into his chair.

'Come on, let's go and have a beer, eh?'

Nick nodded sadly.

'You'll let me know as soon as . . .'

' 'Course I will. Now come on, a large Scotch and you'll be right as rain.'

It was a stupid thing to say and they both knew it.

'Mum, can we go back to school tomorrow?'

Tammy looked at her eldest son but she wasn't seeing him. She was still reliving the insult she had received earlier in the day from one of her so-called friends.

'You what, son?'

Nicholas Leary Junior sighed heavily.

'I said, can we go back to school tomorrow?'

Tammy nodded absently.

'Wait till your dad gets in, he'll tell you.'

'It's boring, Mum, we need to get back into a routine . . .'

'Let your dad sort it out, OK?'

Nicholas looked at her once more and said flatly, 'We need to get back to normal sooner rather than later.'

'I thought it was half-term?'

In her drink-addled brain Tammy dimly remembered what Fiona had said.

'Not for private schools, Mum. We were off all last week, remember?'

It was said sarcastically and this annoyed Tammy as her son knew it would.

She shouted at him then.

'Who are you, Nicky, fucking Stephen Hawking? Mr fucking Know All?'

He sighed once more.

'Oh, forget it!'

His complete dismissal of her sent Tammy into a frenzy of anger.

'Your father could be done for fucking murder, you selfish little fucker!'

Nicholas Leary Junior at twelve years old was already a force to be reckoned with in this house. He had all his mother's acerbic wit and his paternal grandfather's utter disregard for others' feelings. Tammy's mother adored him. His own mother gravitated between wanting to kiss him and wanting to kick him all day long.

Today she was upset after learning that her husband could still be done for manslaughter. This had scared her, especially as she knew she couldn't cope without Nick around even though she had spent her whole married life pretending he was nothing more than an albatross round her neck.

But her friends had sounded as if they knew what they were talking about and suddenly the thought of losing her husband was scaring Tammy all over again. He had done what he thought was right; could they really lock him away for protecting his family? According to her so-called friends they could. They could do exactly that.

For the first time in years Tammy really saw her home and it was beautiful. Her Nick had given them the best there was and she had never really appreciated it until now. Nick drove her mad. He was a flirt, he was a fucker, he was a drinker – but he was a grafter, and he had grafted for her and her kids. For the first time ever she envisioned life without him and the picture in her mind was bleak.

Nicholas Junior left the room and went back to his brother James. The nanny had already gone home. Nick Senior would not let her live in, said if she did it would be too easy to leave the boys, and he had been proved right.

Nicholas Junior knew that as much as his mother loved him and his brother, she would go out at the drop of a hat. Tammy would go to the opening of an envelope as his father always pointed out when they rowed.

Now, though, it wasn't such a problem. At twelve he felt he was adult enough to take care of his little brother. So his mother left the house without a backward glance these days. Years before, though, when she would leave them with their granny, Dad would go mad and tear out of the house in search of her, his own mother admonishing him as he wheel-spinned off the drive, ranting and raving about his lazy mare of a wife.

Nicholas Junior sighed.

He wished his parents could be happy, reach a compromise of some sort. But he knew that the way they carried on was more from habit these days, and it saddened him sometimes.

He knew they loved one another dearly, but they talked to each other as if they were mortal enemies. It was awful to watch and to listen to; they scored points off each other constantly. You could almost feel the despair coming from his mother sometimes, and the complete and utter bafflement of his father. He gave his wife everything except his time.

His granny had explained to Nicholas Junior her thoughts on the subject, confided in him even. She said she worried that, when married couples started to ridicule one another, they would eventually lose respect for one another. Once gone it was hard to get that respect back apparently. Granny Leary thought his mother and father had spent so long taking the piss out of each other in a good-natured way that they didn't take each other seriously any more. It made sense to Nicholas Junior. He had watched them, observed them really, deliberately spied on them in fact. There was love there, he knew that, but not the kind of love that married people should feel. They were more like brother and sister.

His granny said that happened in lots of marriages, it was the day to day that killed romance, but one day something would happen to make them realise that all you had in life *was* your family. Your children, and the years you had shared.

He hoped she was right.

He hoped this tragedy would make them see the error of their ways, appreciate what they had in each other. Because the worst of it all was, they actually thought they were set like a jelly, that they were happy.

It was almost painful to watch them being happy sometimes.

His brother James was asleep and Nicholas automatically covered him up with a blanket even though the night was warm.

He thought of the boy who had died and pushed it from his mind instantly. They had enough to contend with as it was.

'So basically, what you are saying is, an Englishman's home is his castle?'

Nick nodded sadly.

'I suppose so. The fact that the boy was black had nothing to do with it. I didn't know anything about him until after the event. When the paramedics removed his balaclava . . .'

He was paranoid about anything in his story appearing suspect. The girl nodded sympathetically, but he was on to the press by then. What you said and what was actually printed were often completely different things.

'How do you feel about the boy now?'

It was how she said 'boy' that really rankled. It made Sonny Hatcher sound like a ten year old.

Nick sighed.

'I am sorry from the heart for his condition, but at the end of the day he was armed and I wasn't . . .'

The girl grinned at him quizzically and pointed one well-manicured finger at him as she said in her ultra-posh voice: 'But actually you *were* armed, weren't you?'

Her voice was harsher now. Challenging him.

'You had a baseball bat.'

He stared into her pretty blue eyes. Shame she was half the size of a house, she could be good-looking otherwise. But he made himself calm down, bit back the retort that sprang to his lips.

'Well, all I can say is, love, my baseball bat wasn't loaded with bullets like his gun was.'

He stood up abruptly.

'Now, if you'll excuse me . . .'

He had annoyed her and he knew it but he was past caring. They were all carrion only he had never realised that before.

As he sat in his lounge now and watched the tape he wondered what on earth had made him do those interviews with the press. He saw his own guilt reflected in his face as the reporter spoke to him. Yet when it had hit the news it had all looked so different. They had cut and chopped the interview about so that he looked like a fine upstanding citizen, only doing what anyone would have done faced with the same circumstances.

Even the gutter press were on his side, it seemed.

His brief had advised him to tape every interview himself, and now Nick was glad he had done just that.

He was pleased he had covered himself because some of the press had asked one question and then answered it in words he had used in response to a totally different query. He was living and learning all right.

Tammy came into the room and he smiled at her.

'You all right, girl?'

She sat down on the sofa beside him and snuggled into his arms.

'I'm scared, Nick.'

'Don't be.'

He kissed the top of her head, smelling expensive shampoo and perfumes.

'But Fiona said they could nick you . . .'

'Fuck Fiona, Tams. They won't. I spoke to Peter Rudde, he said he didn't think the CPS would pursue it.'

Nick's mobile rang then. He didn't answer it but instead rejected the call.

'Who was that?'

'No one, love.'

She sighed heavily and he kissed her once more.

'Was it a bird?'

He laughed then but it was more of a groan.

'Oh, Tammy, give me some credit, will you?'

She didn't answer him but the mood between them was broken and they both knew it.

Chapter Three

'Jude, listen to me, will you?'

She was staring at him and Tyrell knew she was high. He knew they were giving her methadone on prescription but he had a feeling she was on the real McCoy today. It was the way she looked at him. The way her eyes wouldn't focus. The expression of sheer nothing on her face.

As he looked at her, holding his son's hand, it occurred to him for the first time how alike they looked.

'I ain't turning nothing off.'

Tyrell sighed then.

'Let him go, Jude, please. It's terrible to see him like this . . .'

She glanced at him then. He could almost feel her pain and once more was overcome with sorrow for this woman who had given birth to his son and then set out to destroy him along with herself.

Sonny had been born an addict. Jude had tried to stay clean before the birth but it was impossible for her to go from one day to the next without some kind of chemical cosh. There was a theory about heroin addicts, that most of them were deeply troubled people, but a few like Jude seemed to grow more dependent on H the better their lives were going. A doctor had explained to Tyrell it was from fear of losing everything or everyone. They were always too frightened to be happy because in the past it had never lasted. Consequently, they destroyed everyone around them.

Well, she had certainly tried to destroy him. Eventually he had backed off because he just got sick and tired of picking up the pieces.

Now he was back in the driving seat once more. Trying to sort out another mess, only this time there was no way to resolve it happily.

If they could get Sonny buried it might make her move on with her life. He was brain dead and without any vital functions, kept barely alive by the machines they'd hooked him up to. And now they needed those machines for another patient, one with a chance of living their life again. Unlike their poor son.

'If they take him from me I will have nothing, Tyrell. It's all right for you, you have other kids, your wife, family . . .'

'You've got nothing now, haven't you? Come on, Jude, what've you really got? A boy who can never speak to you, hug you, help you when it all falls out of bed. I loved him, Jude, he was my first-born and I never turned my back on him, or you either for that matter. So don't give me your bullshit now, please.'

She knew he was right, but it was so hard to take it all on board. What would happen to her when Sonny was gone? Who would take care of *her*, make sure she ate, made sure she bathed? It was only now that she realised just how much she'd relied on him. Sonny Boy was her all. He had taken care of her since he was old enough to bring over her kit so she could have a blast while she lay on the sofa, laughing at his antics. It was why she had never let Tyrell have custody, even when he had begged for it.

Sonny had been her passport to his father's money, and the only person who had loved her, *really* loved her no matter what she did.

She lost people like others lost jobs, they all got fed up with her. But not her Sonny Boy. Like most addicts she stole, lied and cheated to get what she wanted and he was the only person who always forgave her, no matter what she did. He was the only constant in her rotten life.

'I've told them they can harvest his organs. Maybe some good can come out of all this, eh?'

'You think it was his fault, don't you, Tyrell? You think he was bad . . .'

He shook his head.

'He was good, Jude, the kindest boy I ever knew. He had a heart as big as the world. But that Sonny Boy is gone now. He is dead. Let him rest in peace.'

'But what about *me*? If he goes, what will *I* do?'

Tyrell sighed once more.

The selfishness of her addiction was always the overriding factor that drove Jude. No wonder Sonny had come to this.

'But this isn't about you, is it? For once, this isn't about you at all. It's about Sonny Boy and his needs now. I'll take care of you. I always have, haven't I?'

Jude looked at him, considering. He'd left her but it was true he'd always looked out for her. Tyrell always was a soft touch, Sonny had to have inherited it from somewhere.

'All right,' she mumbled. 'Do it then. But don't expect me to stick around. He's my baby, it's too hard for me to watch.'

And too long since her last fix, he could tell from her anxious eyes. But at least she'd agreed. Sonny Boy could depart in peace.

Tammy heard her husband before she saw him. Lying in bed, sipping her coffee and flicking through the *Daily Mail*, she heard his feet thundering up the stairs and his voice bellowing. All she could make out was that he was going to murder her when he got his hands on her.

He burst through the bedroom door with the bill from the country club clutched in his hand.

'What is this?'

41

He thrust the piece of paper into her face.

She moved away from him silently, carefully placing the coffee on the night table by the bed in case it stained the Jacquard bedding that had cost a small fortune and made her smile every time she looked at it.

'I'm not joking, Tammy, me and you are going to fall out bigtime over this.'

Nick was fuming, really angry. He was so angry he was actually shaking and this sight affected her more than she would have thought possible. For the first time ever Tammy was afraid of him.

He had come after her many times over her spending, it was a family joke, but this was different. Even she knew she had gone over the top this time. The fact that she secretly felt guilty made her even angrier than her husband.

She was his *wife*, surely she was *entitled* to spend his money? Anyone would think they were all on the breadline, the way Nick carried on. She would brave it out as she had in the past.

'You can afford it, what's the matter with you!'

She was shouting back now through sheer force of habit. As Nick drew himself up to his full height and bellowed back at her she was reminded of just how big he was.

'Eighteen hundred fucking quid on booze for that crowd of fucking leeches you call mates?'

He was spitting with anger now, his face close enough to hers that she could smell his breath.

'Three hundred sobs on food for that load of anorexic cunts! None of them has eaten a meal since their last pregnancy. Are you having a fucking laugh or what!'

Tammy was annoyed now and bellowed back.

'Who the fuck do you think you are talking to, eh? I am your *wife*!'

Nick was staring down at her in utter disbelief.

'Ain't I got enough on my plate without you bankrupting us at every opportunity? Is it an illness with you, an overwhelming urge to use the credit cards that you can't fucking resist for even one day!'

She sighed to antagonise him even further. It was a bored sound, guaranteed to aggravate the life out of him. She had perfected it over the years and now she knew just how to imply *someone* was stupid in their relationship and it certainly wasn't her.

It worked. He was beside himself now.

'Two grand on one lunch! That is a car to some people, or a fucking foreign holiday. Ain't you got no concept of the real world at all?'

Tammy was ashamed, but she wouldn't show it. It wasn't even as if the lunch had been a resounding success. In fact, she regretted going at all. But she wasn't going to tell him that. Give him ammunition for the future when she next wanted a spend up.

'Oh, fuck off. We can afford it, you know we can. What am I suddenly married to – the long-lost Marx Brother fucking Cheapo! So I spent a few quid. So what? Big fucking deal.'

She dragged herself from the bed, pushing him out of her way as she went.

'The way you carry on, Nick, anyone would think we were on our uppers. Money is for spending . . .'

He lowered his voice as he snarled, 'Do you know what it would look like if the papers got hold of this bill, eh?'

He shoved it none too gently into her face.

'That boy dying in hospital and his poor mother going back to her council flat, and *you* are dropping more on a lunch than they could spend on his funeral?'

It pulled her up short. What people said about her was always foremost in Tammy's mind. He watched with a satisfied expression on his face as the fear gradually took hold. She was sorry now, he could see it on her face, and as usual when he had won the argument with Tammy, he felt bad. He had only said that to frighten her and he had achieved his end.

Nevertheless he pushed the point home.

'This has got to stop, Tammy. You have to cease with the spending, love. It looks bad. I mean, by the time you had got your hair and nails done, bought new clothes and all the rest of it . . . I found the Lakeside receipts as well by the way . . . you had dropped over three grand yesterday. In a few hours you spent more than many people earn in a month.'

He was finally getting through to her and he knew it.

'I'm sorry, Nick, but you know what I'm like, I can't help it.'

He sighed.

'I'll have that credit card removed surgically if necessary. This is your last chance. One more spending spree like that, Tams, and I will cancel it. Do you hear me?'

She nodded sheepishly.

'I'm taking the boys back to school today. I've arranged for them to sleep there for the next few weeks until all this blows over, OK?'

She nodded, annoyed with herself that she was pleased the boys would be gone for the rest of the term. She loved them but they drove her mad with their continual wanting when all she wanted was a bit of peace.

As Nick left the room he looked back and smiled at her.

'I'm sorry I shouted.'

'Me too. Nick!'

He faced her once more.

'Are you OK?'

She shrugged.

'I'll survive, I always do.'

He left her then and she climbed back into bed and for the first time in years cried for her mother.

Her mother wasn't actually dead, lived in Spain with her toy boy in fact, but she might as well have been for all the use she had ever been to Tammy.

* * *

44

Verbena was upset. She made herself a cup of tea as she listened to the radio. The house smelled of perfume. Tyrell's wife always put on too much. Now she had gone shopping with the boys and the house still stank of her. She liked the girl, what was there not to like? She was pretty, kind, loved her sons and adored the man she was married to.

But she irritated Verbena. It was her voice. Her ways. Everything the girl did grated on her. And she knew it wasn't Sally's fault. It was because every time Verbena looked at her she saw Jude.

She blamed her son for the way Jude was. Believed that he should have stuck his first marriage out. God himself knew he had fought hard enough to marry the girl in the first place.

Tyrell's father had taken one look at her and decided she was definitely not the woman for his son, and he had said as much.

Which had not gone down too well with Verbena or Tyrell.

But she had taken to Jude, she didn't know why. That girl had been pulled from pillar to post all her life. Meeting her mother had told Verbena everything she had needed to know. That woman, or girl – she had after all only been seventeen when Jude was born – was the most selfish individual Verbena had ever clapped eyes on. And Jude had inherited that selfishness. That belief that you looked out for yourself first, even before your children.

When Verbena had phoned Jude's mother about her grandson, she had replied that he'd got exactly what he had asked for. It seemed everyone thought like that. Even her own neighbours and friends from church thought Sonny Boy had finally got what he had been asking for. Verbena understood it. If it had not been her own grandson who had died she would have felt the same, she was honest enough about that.

But it was much easier when it was someone else's family in the frame and not your own. It was simple to make sweeping judgements when it didn't really affect you personally.

Sonny Boy had always ruined everything for himself and there had been nothing she could do about it. He had stolen from a young age, even from her. He had lied, cheated, taken whatever he had wanted. She knew all that, no one knew it better than she did. But there was also kindness in him, real goodness.

Her husband Solomon said Verbena had been taken in by Sonny's big eyes and poor-little-me act, but she knew she had connected with that boy like no one else had. And Jude's lifestyle had affected him. How could it not? He was always smoking dope, the scourge of the young people today. He had seen it all his life with his own mother. Got a problem? Pop a pill, inject some happiness into your arm, smoke yourself happy.

Verbena hated drugs, yet somehow she understood Jude's reliance on them. Jude used them as a crutch and she always felt that if Jude had let herself be herself she would not have found the world such a scary place, and neither would her son.

But that was in the past, and the past was best left where it was.

She sipped her tea and waited for the call that would tell her Sonny Boy was finally gone. She wouldn't cry, not until she was completely alone.

Verbena prided herself on her strength. If only everyone else could live their lives properly, how different the world would be.

James and Nicholas Junior were settled into school and Nick was back in Essex. He drove off a narrow country lane in Dunton, bumping slowly along an unmade track until he came to a building site.

Getting out of the car, he stood for a while observing the frenetic scene around him. Nick was behind this development of six large detached executive properties containing everything from hot tubs to gyms. They were to be on a private gated estate and had all been sold off plan. They were at least a year away from completion but already the houses looked good.

His ganger Joey Miles walked over to him.

'Didn't expect to see you.'

Nick smiled.

'Well, here I am. I had to get away for a while . . .'

Two of the brickies saw him and waved. One shouted, 'Good on yer, Mr Leary. That little bastard got all he asked for.'

Nick didn't answer.

Joey saw the expression on his boss's face and felt angry with the boy who had caused it.

'Everyone's on your side, Nick. I mean, you never asked him to rob you, did you? If I got up in the middle of the night and some bastard was in my house robbing me, I'd have done the same. Anyone would.'

Nick looked down at the stocky balding man who had worked for him for years and said, 'But you didn't do it, did you? I did.'

Joey patted him on the back.

'Look, it was on the cards with him. Someone was going to aim him out of it one day, he was scum. A burglar and a creeper from a kid. It's been all over the papers about him, little fucker, he was. No matter what his family say about him being a nice boy, he wasn't fucking robbing them, was he? It would have been a different story if he was, I bet ya. Thieving little bastard . . .'

Nick closed his eyes.

'Leave it out, Joey, eh? Just tell me what's going on with the houses and then I'll get off.'

Joey walked with him to his car and told him all the relevant news. As Nick was getting in his Mercedes he said, 'I mean it, Nick, you can't hold yourself responsible. You did what any decent man would have done. You protected your own. Get over it.'

Nick nodded.

As he drove away Joey watched him sadly. Nick Leary was a good bloke. Now thanks to that boy's stupidity he was paying a terrible price for looking out for his own family.

The world had gone mad.

* * *

Jude Hatcher walked into her flat and sank down on to the sofa in the living room. It was so quiet without her son.

She closed her eyes and pictured Sonny Boy as he lay dying in her arms. She would have held him all day and night if the urge had not taken hold of her. She opened her bag and took out her kit.

She laid it on her lap and stared at the small tin that held all she needed for oblivion. She heard Tyrell come in just after she had boiled her fix on a spoon. He watched her from the doorway as she injected it slowly into her left arm. Her veins had collapsed and the bruising was vicious.

The smell of it was sweet in the air. Sighing, he went through to the chaos that passed for a kitchen and put the kettle on. He opened the window and tried to air the place before going through the lounge and down the hallway towards his son's bedroom. This room always amazed him. It was small, but usually spotlessly clean. Today, though, the drawers had been turned out and the whole place was a mess. He guessed rightly that at some point Jude had searched it for money or valuables. Tyrell tidied it all up without thinking.

As he looked into the drawers in the scratched dressing table he saw his son's whole life and felt the urge to cry once more. Designer underwear when they rarely had any food in the house. Expensive tops hanging in the narrow wardrobe, which told him Jude had not looked in there yet or it would have been empty except for a few wire coat hangers. She always sold off anything of value they possessed. It had hurt her son that even his clothes weren't safe from her and her constant quest for money.

Tyrell wondered what his boy had wanted from that large house in the country, wondered when the urge to rob it had taken him over. He had thought about it so much, but still could not work out what had made his son choose that place to rob.

Sonny had always been strictly small-time; he had been a hustler, a kiter. He wasn't into heavy-duty robbery. Unless he had progressed over the last year from a young tearaway into a hardened criminal. He was just seventeen, for fuck's sake!

Tyrell went back to the kitchen and made the tea, scrubbing two mugs back to cleanliness before filling them. The whole place was filthy.

He went into the lounge once more with the tea, but Jude was gone from him. She was lying back in the chair, staring into space.

'Like old times, eh, Jude?'

The sarcasm was completely lost on her, as he knew it would be.

Tammy wandered round her house aimlessly. She saw the expensive curtains, the hand-made carpets and carefully chosen antiques.

She remembered her home when she was a kid. A council flat with coats on the bed, the constant smell of fried food and a father who would shout the house down when he got back from the pub. He still did that except he owned the pub now, thanks to Nick, and was slowly drinking himself to death in it.

Her mother had always been running off with someone, it was how she was, yet Dad always wanted her back. She had been round the turf more times than a Grand National winner and still he wanted her.

Nick had bought the pub for him. He had been so good to them all. He had come from the same road as them, gone to the same school as Tammy, had started courting her when they had been twelve and thirteen respectively.

He had worked like a demon all his life. Even then he had had a paper round, a milk round, and worked the market stalls. It was the markets that had got them the first real money they had ever possessed. Her Nick could sell a fridge to an Eskimo. He had the gab all right, and she had loved being the girl he had chosen.

Now, as she looked around her home, she was aware of just how much he had done for them all. The kitchen alone had cost over sixty grand. It had everything a kitchen could have, and was also the size of most people's houses. It had a family area built round an inglenook fireplace that was twenty-five feet by eighteen alone. And that was without the actual kitchen itself or the utility areas.

There was an indoor as well as an outdoor pool, and stabling for ten horses. The whole place was huge and it was tasteful and it was hers. She wondered why she had never really appreciated it before. Nick's old mum ran the place for her, and Tammy was glad to let her get on with it. It was too big for her to worry about, and she was out more often than not.

Now she was trying to imagine what it would be like to be without it, wondering for the first time if that boy had tried to rob them through envy, because they had it all and he didn't.

But he didn't know that they had come from nothing themselves. How hard the road had been before they had finally cracked it. And her Nick, whatever his faults, had worked day and night to get them all a better life. She should appreciate him more, she knew that. She meant to, but somehow when they were alone it all deteriorated because they didn't know how to be alone any more. Those days were gone, the days when they'd waited with bated breath for each other. Not that Nick had ever been much of a one for sex anyway. He was always too busy. It wasn't until her first affair that Tammy had realised what she had been missing.

It had blown her mind, what that first fella had done to her, and she had loved it. Had finally realised what her mates had been hammering on about for all those years. If she was honest with herself that was when her dissatisfaction with everything at home had set in. Suddenly having the biggest house and the newest car meant nothing, because she had quickly realised that that kind of sex kept people together even when they hated one another. She had tried the new tricks she had learned on Nick and he had gone

50

ballistic, wanting to know where she had got them. She had told him from women's magazines and such like, but she thought he knew.

That was what hurt. She suspected he had sussed her out but, instead of giving her a clump, he had ignored her even more.

Perhaps it was because the big I am, the big womaniser, knew he was useless in the kip. Not that Tammy had ever told him that, of course, she wasn't that stupid. Yet she still loved him. In her own way adored him.

He was lying on the chaise-longue in the dressing room off their bedroom and he had had a drink, that much was obvious.

'You all right, Nick? I didn't hear you come in.'

'They turned the machine off, Tams, the boy's gone.'

She knelt beside him then and took his hand.

'No one can blame you, Nick, you only did what any man would have done.' She was surprised to see he had been crying. 'No one can blame you, darlin'.'

She could smell the beer and whisky on his breath and guessed he had started out in the pub before coming home to finish the job properly.

She knew him so well.

He pushed her away gently and sat up. Putting his head into his hands, he groaned, 'I can blame myself though, Tams. And I will, until the day I die.'

He was sobbing now, his huge shoulders quaking with emotion. She hugged him to her, the big man, the big I am, reduced to crying like a baby. For some reason this disturbed her more than the boy's death.

Chapter Four

'Given the facts of the night in question, we at the Crown Prosecution Service have decided that we shall take no action against Mr Nicholas Leary. It is not in the public interest. We feel that he was a victim of circumstances beyond his control and we offer our sympathies to the family of Sonny Hatcher. Thank you.'

The spokeswoman walked off camera. It was obvious she'd been nervous. Her voice had quavered and her hands clutched her papers until the knuckles were white. Sky News put the statement out live and Tammy watched it with relief. It was over then.

Suddenly the screen was filled with a picture of Judy Hatcher and her shrill voice burst out of it.

'Murderers! You're all murderers. You owe me, Leary. You owe me for my boy's life.'

The screen was filled with the image of the grieving woman and her grey screaming mouth. Tammy sat up abruptly in the bath, causing the water to wash all over the marble flooring. Although they had been told what action was going to be taken the night before, until she had seen it with her own eyes she was not inclined to believe it. Now this woman was spoiling it all.

'My son was murdered, he wasn't doing any harm to anyone. He never owned a gun in his life.'

Jude sounded lucid for once. Only those who knew her well realised just how capable she could be when the fancy took her. Shame it never lasted for any length of time. She was being hustled from the room by two policemen as if she was the one in trouble. Tammy could see the toll the death of her son had taken on the woman and felt a reluctant twinge of sympathy for her.

She soon pushed it away.

The Sky reporter was saying that Judy Hatcher was under the care of a psychiatrist and that she was an ardent advocate of her son's innocence. He said it in such a way as to make it apparent to anyone listening that Sonny Hatcher was a dangerous young man and only his mother was unaware of that fact.

Tammy couldn't listen to it a second longer.

She lay back in her enormous bath and switched over to ITV 2 for the lunchtime edition of *Emmerdale*. She wasn't watching it, but the sound of the voices was soothing. She took a large gulp of her Chardonnay and a long drag on her cigarette.

Sod that woman! What did they owe her? From what Tammy had heard she was a heroin addict, had brought her son up on her own and made him into the thief he had become. Tammy's eyes strayed to the small mirror compact full of cocaine she kept near her at all times. Her own hypocrisy didn't faze her at all.

Instead she consoled herself with the thought that even though she might have a few lines on a long lunch or a night out with the girls, hers was just *recreational* drug use. It wasn't as if she was addicted. It was just the Essex way of keeping the night going. Whereas that woman was a *real* addict, she *injected* herself. Which was a different ball game altogether.

Mainlining meant you were hooked, everyone knew that.

Her line of thought reminded Tammy she was due for her Botox injections that afternoon and Christ himself knew, she could do with them. All the worry of the last few weeks had really begun to show on her face and that bothered Tammy.

It had been her idea to put a TV in the bathroom. Even though she rarely watched it, lately it had been a Godsend.

Until today, of course.

She pushed the Hatcher woman from her mind once more. At the end of the day she was just a mother protecting her own. Tammy would have done the same herself. Not that her boys would have been caught up in crap like that, of course, but it was the same principle.

She gulped down the glass of wine and poured herself another. It was over.

That was the main thing, she had to remember that.

Nick could go back to his daily grind now and no one would think badly of him and, if she was really honest with herself, she would be glad to get him out from under her feet.

The strange thing was everyone was on their side yet the way Nick was carrying on you'd think everyone was against him. Still, it must be strange to know you were the reason some-one had died even if it was a little thief who only got what he deserved.

Sonny Hatcher should never have been in their home in the first place. Tammy reminded her husband of that at every available opportunity. No matter how hard she tried, she could summon up no sympathy for the boy. He should have stayed home that night instead of turning their world upside down.

Detective Inspector Peter Rudde was drinking a large brandy in the company of his DC, Frank Ibbotson. The junior officer raised his glass and then downed his drink in one gulp.

'So that's it, sir, it's all over?'

Rudde nodded.

'Best outcome. Leary wasn't doing anything I wouldn't have done. Did you see that boy's form? Jesus, he'd been up for everything at some point.'

He pushed his glass at Ibbotson for a refill and the younger man duly made his way to the bar. The news came up on the wide-screen TV and the outcome of the Leary case was broadcast yet again. Once more a cheer went up in the crowded bar and Rudde guessed that the same thing was happening in pubs all over the country.

You couldn't pick up a paper but it was the main story. Was an Englishman's home really his castle? It seemed it was this time and he for one was glad of that fact. Sonny Hatcher was a violent little bastard. Rudde knew just how violent he could be. The papers didn't know the half of it because most of Sonny Boy's skulduggery had been when he was a minor. He had stabbed a neighbour and walked away from that one because of his home life. But how long could you blame everything on where or how a young thug lived? Plenty of people lived in terrible conditions and they were all right. Rudde himself had come from one of the roughest council estates in East London and look at him now, he was a law enforcer.

He didn't thieve or lie or attack people.

Well, he conceded, he lied sometimes. But then, didn't everyone if they were honest? Ibbotson came back with the brandy and Rudde was gratified to see it was a double. The boy was learning at last.

'Good lad.'

He sipped this one, savouring the taste.

'It should all die down now and we can get back to normal. We wasted too much time on that case.'

Ibbotson nodded.

He sipped his pint daintily and this, for some reason, annoyed the life out of Rudde.

There was a lock-in at the Fox and Ferret even though it was only three in the afternoon. Nick had bought the pub a few years earlier, it was another of his little investments. Today the raucous sound of his friends cheering inside was depressing him.

One of his workmen, Danny Power, the local wag and joke merchant, shouted out: 'Here, Nick, I heard the Catholic Church has said that kid has got to be buried thirty foot down . . . because deep down niggers are nice people!'

The laughter was long and loud until Nick's fist connected with Danny's chin then the place went deathly quiet in seconds.

'Get out.'

Nick Leary's eyes were wild with grief and anger.

Danny pulled himself from the floor in shock.

'Here, Nick, I was only joking . . .'

Nick grabbed him by his shirt and started to drag him to the door. He was aware of all his friends watching, wondering what was wrong with him, but he didn't care. That was too much, it was going too far.

'Open the fucking door, Jimmy, or I'll smash this cunt through it.'

He was more than capable of it and they all knew that. Nick could have a row. He needed to be able to protect himself in his businesses and was a legend in some quarters.

Jimmy Barr who ran the pub quickly unlocked the door and they all watched as Nick threw his long-time friend out into the car park.

'You're sacked. I don't ever want to see you around here again, right?' Nick was shaking with temper and upset.

Jimmy Barr quickly brought him inside and relocked the door. He knew Danny was better off away from Nick for the time being.

'Calm down now, Nick, he was drunk, that's all.'

He poked his face against his friend's.

'I don't give a fuck! That boy is dead and gone. And you lot think it's fucking funny? Well, I don't. I don't care what colour he was or what religion. He was a boy, a seventeen-year-old boy.'

'A seventeen-year-old boy with a gun, Nick.'

This from Anthony Sissons, one of his oldest mates. They went back to infant school together and that gave him the clout to speak his mind.

Nick stared at him for long seconds before he smiled.

'All right, Ant, but I never liked those kind of jokes at the best of times. You know that.'

The talking started up again then but the atmosphere had soured and they all knew it.

One of the men at the bar, a new workman of Nick's, said to the man beside him: 'What was all that about? It was only a joke.'

Joey Miles replied gently, 'Nick's sister Hannah is married to a West Indian bloke called Dixon. Nick's really close to her.'

'I didn't know that.'

Joey laughed because he could hear the surprise in the other man's voice.

'Most people don't, and if you want to stay in your job, you'll keep it to yourself. Now I'm too drunk, me mouth's running away with me. Time I went home.'

He pulled himself off the barstool with difficulty, slapped Nick on the back and left.

Verbena was inconsolable. Her eldest daughter Hettie had come all the way from Birmingham to hold her hand. Verbena didn't want her there; she didn't want anyone. She wanted to grieve on her own. Hettie was aware of how her mother felt.

'Mummy, for God's sake, eat something at least, eh?'

All her daughters called her 'Mummy', but coming from Hettie it was more like a nickname. There was no feeling in it. Since the onset of her agoraphobia her eldest daughter had lost all respect for her mother and it hurt. She was trying to feed her chicken but Verbena had no appetite for it.

'When are you going home, Hettie?'

It was a loaded question and they both knew it.

Her daughter sighed.

'Don't start, Mummy. You know how I felt about Sonny. He stole from me, he stole from us all. Unlike you I don't have the spirit of Christian forgiveness.'

Verbena sighed again. Her daughter was very like her in looks. She was big, Caribbean big, with the ample hips and breasts inherited from a long line of Jamaican women. But she didn't have the kindness that usually went with them. Her whole life was a fight or an argument of some sort. Yet she had loved this child more than the others until Sonny had arrived. Maybe Hettie knew that. Had sensed it? Verbena couldn't think about it now.

'I just meant the kids are probably missing you, that's all. I know how you felt about Sonny. You don't need to come to his funeral. Anyway, we don't know when they will release the body.'

Verbena was talking so normally, it was eerie to listen to herself. But she only wanted people at the funeral who'd cared about Sonny, and this daughter of hers hadn't. Though who could blame her? Sonny had robbed her, stolen a ring from her one Christmas when she had visited her mother, and he'd sold it. The worst of it all was it was her husband's mother's ring, worth nothing in money terms but priceless in other ways.

But it had been for his mother, it had always been for his mother. He was dead because of his mother but Verbena would never say that out loud. Poor Jude had enough to contend with as it was.

She pushed away the food and stared out of the window again, watching the children as they hung around the estate while she waited for more news. Any news was welcome at this moment. She had already heard the worst anyone could hear. Nothing else could ever hurt her in quite the same way.

Tyrell was in a drinking club in Brixton Heights, the Railton Road to the uninitiated. He knew he should not have gone out but he could not sit there at his mother's and listen to his son being dismissed like so much garbage by everyone but her. He wasn't ready for that yet even though he knew he should be. Poor Sonny had got what he deserved after all, if anyone really deserved to die for trying to nick a video or a DVD recorder. It was the gun that still troubled Tyrell most. Where would his son have got a gun? No one seemed to know but he was going to make it his mission in life to find that out.

He had been doing security around London for years; now he had his own company. He had no shortage of cronies and employees to sit with him while he got drunk. He wasn't a rum drinker by nature but it was a good drink to get drunk on. Anyone who tried it once would understand that.

Tyrell laughed at his own thoughts, and smiled at his friend, Paxton Regis.

'Do you know, when he read the autopsy the Coroner said that the geezer had used excessive force on my boy. Excessive . . . that sounds a lot when you say it out loud, don't it?'

He coughed loudly before he continued, 'He carried on hitting Sonny even after he was unconscious.'

Tyrell gulped at his drink.

'Fear, see. He was frightened. Guns do that to people, don't they? They scare me, I can tell you. Once we had an incident on a door in Ilford. We ejected some little bullyboys and they came back with a gun. Little fuckers! I was so angry when I saw it, so angry. So I know what that bloke saw, you know?'

Paxton nodded sadly.

'I could understand his fear because I have felt it too, you know. But even though I understand how he reacted, I can't forgive him for taking my Sonny. If he had known my boy, he would have seen what he was really like because he wasn't a bad kid.'

Tyrell was really drunk now and Paxton was wondering when it would be time to take him home.

'Now we have to bury him, bury that child, and it's all wrong. All fucking wrong.'

He was rambling and Paxton nodded at the barman for another rum. Hopefully his friend would drink himself unconscious. Tyrell was in the wrong job, the wrong life. He was just too nice, that was his trouble.

He gulped at his drink once more. Tyrell wasn't really a drinker so it hadn't taken much for him to get drunk. But the club was quiet today, quieter than usual, as if everyone was grieving with him even though every man there quietly admitted they would have done the same as Nick Leary. You protected your own, especially your kids and your woman.

Sonny had crossed the line.

But no one said that out loud, of course. Tyrell was far too well respected and liked for that.

'All right, Jude?'

She heard the voice and tried to focus her eyes but it was hard.

Sally Hatcher smiled at her even as she tried not to wrinkle her nose at the smell around her. She had promised Tyrell she would pop in and see how Jude was doing. By the looks of it, not very well.

Tyrell had said that he had to go to work. She knew he didn't want to deal with the business today but anything was better than watching this woman destroy herself, apparently. Or watching his mother's heart break all over again.

'Get your coat on and I'll take you to Verbena's house, she wants you with her.'

'Go away.'

Sally sighed. Her short hair sat perfectly on her finely shaped head, and her slim athletic body brimmed over with health and well-being, making Jude look even older and more haggard than she actually was.

'Come on, Jude, Verbena needs you.'

'No one *needs* me, Sally. Never did, never will. Now do me a favour and fuck off.'

There was no insult intended in the words, swearing was as normal to Jude as breathing. She was already building herself a joint, only this one would hold heroin. She smoked it sometimes. Once Sally left she would mainline and get properly floating.

Sally watched her in disgust. No matter how many photos she saw of a younger, prettier Jude, and there were plenty of them in Verbena's house, she could not equate them with this excuse for a woman before her.

Sonny would have known what to do with her in this state. She'd been like a job to him. Now Jude was going to have to get used to taking care of herself.

The front door opened abruptly and three young men walked in without knocking. They were all white with styled and cropped hair. One had the logo of West Ham Utd shaved into the side of his head, two crossed hammers.

Sally stared at them incredulously.

'How did you get in?'

The tallest boy looked her over and obviously found her lacking.

'I might ask you the same thing?'

'They're friends of Sonny's,' Jude said testily. 'Now go *home*, Sally, for fuck's sake. I can't cope with you here and all.'

Sally picked up her bag and said gently, 'If you're sure?'

Jude looked at her slyly, guessing the other woman was glad of an excuse to leave her.

'Oh, I'm sure.'

Sally left her to it. There wasn't really anything else she could do.

It was ten o'clock when Nick finally strolled through the front door. Tammy was in the television room watching a film. She had a large glass of wine beside her and a cigarette in her hand. He stumbled into the room and flopped down beside her. She smiled at him briefly before her gaze turned back to the TV.

He looked around him. It was a nice room, a comfortable room. It was a room many people would love to possess. Yet to them it was the dossing room. The curling up and watching TV room.

He moved closer to his wife; he needed her tonight, needed to feel loved. Wanted. He had never felt so low in his life. The guilt was weighing on him heavily. Every time he closed his eyes he saw that boy's face.

He clasped Tammy's hand and she squeezed his back affectionately.

'Tam . . .'

'It's over, Nick.'

He nodded.

'But, Tam . . .'

'You're pissed.'

She said this without taking her eyes off the TV.

He nodded once more.

'I need to talk to you, Tam.'

She looked at him.

'In a minute, wait till this ends.'

Her voice was warmer now, softer. He looked at the screen. Richard Burton and Genevieve Bujold were fighting.

'What is it?'

She sighed in annoyance.

'*Anne of the Thousand Days.* It's about Henry VIII and Anne Boleyn. He's just dinged her in the Tower of London and he's offering her an annulment if she shuts her trap and don't ask for nothing from him. But she knocks him back so he has her nutted.'

'Sounds good to me.'

Tammy laughed despite herself.

'Look, let me see her die then I'll make you a drink and we can talk all night if you want.'

He watched the screen, amazed by his wife's passion for history. Whatever else she was, Tammy was without doubt a mine of information about royalty. She had loved Diana and cried for three days after her untimely death. She had more feeling for a woman who had been beheaded centuries before than she did for the boy who had died at her own husband's hands.

But that was Tammy all over.

Nothing ever bothered her unless it affected her personally. And she had taken the threat to Nick's liberty personally. In Tammy's mind the fact that her husband could have got into trouble for defending his own family was tantamount to two fingers up at her from the British legal system. At her, Tammy, who adored royalty – except for Prince Charlie, of course. Who saw herself as British through and through. Who even made remarks sometimes about Nick's Irish heritage. She had been devastated when he had nearly been arrested for doing what he had done. She'd even slagged the Queen off on more than one occasion recently. And all this from a woman who would normally defend the monarchy to the death.

He had loved her loyalty, though, even if it had always been tinged with selfishness. Tammy saw anything he or the boys did as a reflection on her.

He glanced at the screen once more. Anne Boleyn was walking sedately to the scaffold. Nick watched her, wondering briefly how it must have felt, leaving her young child in the care of the man who was in effect murdering her.

He could hear soft crying from Tammy and hugged her close to him. She was a nightmare in some respects, but he had to admire her consistency. Anne Boleyn was her idol. Tammy knew everything there was to know about her. She huddled into Nick's arms, and allowed him to comfort her.

It did not occur to her that she should be comforting him. As far as she was concerned it was all over.

And not before time either.

*   *   *

Tyrell lay on his mother's sofa, drunker than he had ever been in his life. Though Verbena had never liked alcohol she understood his need to obliterate the last few days.

She sat studying the pictures all around the room of Sonny Boy and his mother. He had been a handsome child. Sally came into the room with two mugs of tea, made just how Verbena liked it with plenty of sugar and a healthy dollop of condensed milk. The sweet warmth eased her for a moment.

'Was she really bad?'

Sally sat on the edge of the sofa and shrugged.

'The usual.'

Verbena sighed.

'You shouldn't hold a grudge against her, you know, Sally. She is to be pitied.'

Her daughter-in-law didn't answer, just smiled tightly. She had been hearing that for so long it had absolutely no effect any more. As she looked into Verbena's sad eyes she felt the pity she always did for the older woman's distress at what had befallen her family. It just annoyed Sally that no one blamed Jude Hatcher for any of it. It was always poor Jude, unfortunate Jude. Never selfish, drug-addicted Jude who had systematically ruined everyone around her.

'Can I get you something to eat?'

Sally was deft now at changing the subject.

Before Verbena could answer the glass of the living-room window shattered and a brick landed on the coffee table. The unexpected noise made both women scream. Tyrell opened his eyes and sat bolt upright on the sofa, obviously terrified by it as well.

'What the fuck . . .'

It was as if everything was moving in slow motion. Verbena watched her son as he ran to the broken window, his voice loud as he cursed whoever had thrown the brick. Glass lay everywhere. It was a few seconds before she realised it was all over her lap, and that a few small pieces had cut her legs and face. At first she had thought it was tears she could feel. It wasn't until Sally screamed that Verbena realised it was actually blood.

Jude was floating now. In her mind Sonny Boy was home with her once more. He was young again, but not too young. Old enough to help her out with things. He had been such a good kid. He had scored for her since he was old enough to ask for a five-pound bag.

She pulled the tourniquet off the top of her arm with her teeth. Jude still went through the ritual as she had always done. Pumping the muscle was like a part of the high for her. The whole process was a major part of the high.

She liked this bit best, when the main high was being replaced by a feeling of complete well-being. This was what she liked to call her thinking time. This was the time when she'd liked to chat to Sonny Boy for hours. He would make her laugh or smile about things. Would roll her a joint to soften the edges once the heroin had worn off and its magic was replaced with the urge to do the whole thing again.

He had never judged her, never tired of her like everyone else. She had been like his baby, like his child.

A big fat tear escaped from her eye then. For the first time Jude cried quietly. It was only when she was alone that she could really grieve. She pulled herself up from the sofa and negotiated the chaos of the room, finally stumbling into her son's bedroom. She sat on the bed, breathing deeply, and opened the drawer of his dressing table. In a tobacco tin was his signet ring. His father had bought it for him and she had made sure the hospital had given it back to her after his death.

Now Jude weighed it in her hand. It was quite heavy with a small diamond chip set in a plain gold square. It had the letter S written neatly in old italic script on the left-hand corner.

She remembered his face as he had opened the box on the morning of his fifteenth birthday. He had been so pleased with it. Over the years it had been in and out of Uncle's when money was tight and Jude had needed her sustenance. Sonny would always move heaven and earth to retrieve it, to have it back on his finger, even thieving to get the money.

It was all she had left of him, she had already sold almost everything else. But as she looked at it, glinting in the half-light, she knew her Sonny Boy would understand what she was going to do.

If she hurried Big Ellie would still be up and she could get her money and score some gear ready for the morning. Jude got up off the bed with difficulty, but she clutched the ring tightly in her hand.

At the end of the day Sonny had known her better than anyone. Until she sorted out a regular supply of money, this would have to go. He would have seen the logic of that. He knew her need and also understood why she had the need in the first place.

He had been a good kid, her Sonny Boy, and his death would not be in vain. She would make sure she got something out of it if it was the last thing she did.

Chapter Five

Tyrell had no interest in what the police had to say about the attack on his mother's and went off to work with a frown on his face. He was sick to death of it all. He just wanted to grieve in peace.

No one was surprised by the events of the night before. The police seemed sorry for the boy's mother but not unduly bothered about the broken window. Sonny had been a legend in his own lunchtime around the estate and people had little sympathy for him personally. He had robbed enough of them over the years to cause widespread offence.

Tyrell's mother, though, was a different kettle of fish altogether. She was respected and liked even though she never left the house now. Everyone came to her and she dispensed advice and sympathy, so to think that anyone would take it out on her like this was making Tyrell feel capable of murder himself.

The paramedics had stitched her eyebrow in the house. Realising she would not leave, they had had to calm her down before they had been able to take care of her wound. Verbena had been more worried about leaving her home than she had been about the attack. But Tyrell understood that. He understood her fear even better than she did.

His mother had not left the house for over twenty years, and he knew that she would never leave it now. Her nerves had got to her long before his brother's death, but that had been the catalyst that had caused all their lives to change so dramatically.

His mother had taken so much in her lifetime, and she had taken it all on the chin in true Jamaican fashion. She had seen her adopted country as the salvation of her family, as the means to give them all a better life. She had worked every hour that the good Lord had sent, and she had dressed her children in fine clothes, fed them the best foods. She had sent her children to school, and made sure they had arrived there and, more importantly, stayed there.

Unlike their contemporaries, they had been too fearful to play truant, too frightened to let her down, and make her feel ashamed of them.

She had taken them to church and taught them the goodness of Christ and of a life well lived. Her job had been as a care assistant in a hospital, and it had involved shifts, and she had taken every shift she could, never missing one. Like her husband, she had understood that without money they could not further themselves or their children.

When her last baby had arrived, it had been Hettie and Maureen to whom she had entrusted him, and it had been Hettie and Maureen who had taken him to school one day and who had watched in horror as he had run into the road and been mown down by a nice man who had been surprised and terrified by the fact that a young boy had run out in front of his car and had died within seconds.

It had been no one's fault, but Verbena, already under too much pressure, had taken the death so badly she had gradually lost the urge to do even the most mundane of things. Her children and husband had watched their strongest supporter wither away under the weight of her grief. First the job had gone, then the visits to the shops. Day by day, she had sat indoors reading the Bible, looking for a reason for her son's death. Going out less and less, until finally even her church had not been enough to make her leave the house, her world had come to her. Until now, her illness was accepted as an intrinsic part of her and not as something strange or alien. It almost seemed normal to her family and friends.

Yet there were no photos of her last-born in the house, and there was never any mention of him. Samuel Hatcher had been obliterated from their lives, because Verbena had never been able to cope with his death, or with her own guilt.

Yet Tyrell knew she thought of him constantly and went over and over in her mind the morning she had sent him off with his sisters to his death, while she had tumbled into bed exhausted from her night's work, glad to see the back of them.

Tyrell often wondered if that was why she had taken Jude under her wing the way she had; she had needed someone to love and Jude had come along at the right time. She had never seen Jude for the user she was, had never believed that Jude was capable of manipulating her.

But Jude, knowing his mother's weaknesses, had played on them, had used them to make herself into what his mother had wanted.

It was why he had never gone for custody of his son. His mother had always talked him out of it and he had tried to please her in any way he could. Tried to make up for what had happened to her, tried to assuage the hurt inside her in any way he could.

Then Sally had come along and it had been easier to leave Sonny where he was. Now he had to live with that, and, like his mother before him, his child was dead and gone, and there was nothing he could do to change that.

Except wish that he had done things differently, as she did.

For the first time ever he really understood what made her tick. Understood the gaping hole inside her that no one or nothing would ever fill. *Could* ever fill.

Her last-born and his first-born had died senselessly, and now he knew how hard it was to come to terms with such a tragedy. To make some kind of sense of it all, when there wasn't any kind of sense to be made.

He pushed these thoughts from his mind. His hangover was making his head pound, he had an upset stomach and felt he would die of grief. All in all he was completely and utterly drained.

Everywhere he looked were young men with bright smiles and their whole lives ahead of them. All around him were young men travelling to work or school, busily going about their lives, unaware that his son was cold and dead. As he got out of his car in Tulse Hill he wondered when they would be able to bury his boy.

Dinny White, his gofer and sidekick, was waiting patiently for him. Dinny was light-skinned with a lightning grin and long relaxed hair. He knew how good-looking he was, he didn't need reminding. He smoked dope constantly, was always in a good mood and was an exceptionally good listener. They strolled into a nearby house together, chatting about nothing.

Dinny loved life and it was hard seeing his friend and boss so obviously unhappy. But he kept his own counsel. If Tyrell wanted to talk, he would.

Inside the house Johnny Marks, a large white man with thick black hair and a pristine vest, was busy making tea. This house was the hub of Tyrell's business. It was where he interviewed his doormen and where he paid them out. It was where he kept his different cell phones and where he conducted his other businesses – the ones his wife and mother had no knowledge of.

Johnny Marks answered the door to them both.

'All right, Tyrell? Sorry about Sonny Boy, but he had it coming.'

Only from Johnny would Tyrell have taken that statement.

He shrugged.

'Let it drop, eh, Johnny?'

The other man opened his arms wide in a gesture of helplessness.

'You better get used to hearing remarks like that because it's the general consensus, mate. He was a pain in the arse and you know he was.'

'He was still my boy.'

Johnny smiled then, a wide white-toothed smile that made him look much nicer than he actually was.

'How's poor old Judy?'

'How'd you think?'

'Off her nut?'

'Got it in one.'

'Well, understandable, ain't it? Now, shall we get down to business? Coffee or tea?'

He made the coffee and brought the mugs through to the lounge on a tray. Tyrell envied Johnny his easiness with the world. Nothing fazed him. It was all either black or white.

They started the business of the day.

Angela Leary was tired, she had not slept much the night before. As she tidied up the spacious kitchen of her son's home she couldn't help envying his wife the luxury that was afforded her. This was all a far cry from Nick's home when he was growing up. He had really made something of himself and Angela was proud of him, so very proud.

She would defend him to the death, no matter what anyone else said. Not that anyone had said anything, of course, but if they did . . . well, she would be waiting for them.

Her daughter-in-law was the bane of her life. Tammy had everything a woman could possibly want and yet still she wasn't happy. She was man mad that one, and then she wondered why her husband didn't have any time for her.

The kids had been bundled off to that posh school and no one saw them from one end of the year to the other. And even when they came home Madam, as Angela secretly referred to Tammy, was never around. The poor nanny, an insipid-looking bitch if ever there was one, did all the donkey work with the kids.

Sometimes Angela daydreamed that Tammy was gone. She was never specific as to how but occasionally a sumptuous funeral was included in the dream. After all, she was Nick's wife and she deserved a good send off. And then Angela saw herself ruling the roost without interference.

As she cleaned she listened to Radio 1 and sang snippets of the songs to herself. The kitchen was her domain. Madam never came in here unless she had to and yet it was gorgeous. A large Aga heated the place so it was warm as toast all the time. There were two double ovens and a large American fridge as well as countless other gadgets. It was a dream of a kitchen but Madam hated it with a vengeance.

Still, that suited Angela. Sometimes she sat here until the early hours of the morning, knitting and listening to her radio. Sometimes she would have a drop of something to keep the cold out. There was a TV in here but she listened to the Sky music channels on it. Radio was so much more satisfying than television. With television you had to keep looking at the thing. She just liked to listen, liked the company it afforded her.

Angela made herself a cup of tea and settled herself into the easy chair her son had provided for her against his wife's wishes. It was old, and he had rescued it from her flat when she had moved in. Much to the annoyance of Tammy. Even though it had been re-covered she still thought it was riddled with fleas from Angela's poor dead cat.

She had nursed her son in this very chair, bared her breast and fed him his fill. Another thing Madam did not like to be reminded about.

So Angela made a point of reminding her. Often. It was little things like that which made life worth living.

As if her mother-in-law's thoughts had conjured her up, Tammy burst into the kitchen like a gale-force wind.

'I'm going out. Will you see to the dinner? I might be late.'

It was a game they played, as if she was doing them a special favour by feeding them. Like it wasn't what she did every day of the week.

'Of course.'

Angela let her eyes stray to the vegetables already peeled and the meat already seasoned and trussed ready to be cooked later in the day. She made eye contact and Tammy was the first to look away.

'See you then.'

Her voice was cheery and Angela smiled slowly and said quietly, 'See you then.'

Round one to her if she wasn't mistaken. The slamming of the front door told her she was right about that much anyway and she smiled again.

Nick was inside his site office. He noticed that all the newspapers except for the sporting ones were missing. Usually they started the day with a discussion of the assets of the various women featured in the tabloids. Jordan was usually voted tops, though a few were die-hard natural tit men. Nick assumed, rightly, that he was still news.

He sat at his desk and pondered the girlie pictures plastered everywhere. They did nothing to arouse him, he found them in your face and tacky. But he couldn't say that. Not unless he wanted to come over as less than a man. His blokes' whole lives revolved around a bit of strange and making sure the wife never found out. The wives did, of course, and then all hell would be let loose. He had seen them have stand-up fights with their men as well as the girlfriends. It was wearing at times.

Lynn Starkey came in and he smiled at her. She was a big girl and she was fun enough. She ran the site like a military operation and he didn't know what he would do without her.

Round her desk were pictures of young men in various stages of undress. It was her way of getting back at her colleagues and Nick laughed at her when she pretended to drool over them to annoy the blokes on site. None of them was very good-looking and the women they talked so freely about would in fact give them a wide berth. But they didn't like being reminded of their middle-aged spread and their less-than-perfect profiles.

Lynn called the pin-ups her Himbos, and the expression always made Nick smile. It was a good office really, had a good atmosphere, and when the trouble had started they had all been behind him. They had all seen it as representing the right to retaliate of the common man.

Now he made Lynn a cup of tea and took it over to her.

'How are you, girl?'

She gazed up into his eyes. He knew she had a crush on him but he could live with it.

'OK. You?'

Nick shrugged.

'Getting there. How's it been going anyway?'

He changed the subject quickly because he could hear the men coming into their offices, could hear their talk and banter, and wasn't sure if he could cope with it all today. Would his life ever be the same again?

He doubted it.

All he knew was, he needed a drink.

Jude Hatcher was sipping a black coffee and listening once more to the boys telling her about Sonny. She was nodding and smiling as they recounted stories about him, stretching the tales and exaggerating them until they were complete lies, but well intentioned nonetheless. Eventually they would all believe them and Sonny would be a part of urban legend.

The front door opened and his best friend Gino came in. He passed Jude a small bag of brown and she smiled her thanks at him.

The other three lads sat in stunned silence as they watched her burn her fix. Even though they fancied themselves men of the world she was the only adult they knew who was a heroin addict. They had mates who used, but it was only snorting. All their parents were straight, alcohol and cigarettes being the only drugs allowed in their houses.

Alcohol had in fact caused more than enough trouble for Gino especially as his errant father couldn't get through the day without it. But if his mother had known he was in Jude Hatcher's flat she would have gone ballistic. Gino saw the hypocrisy of that even if she didn't.

The local boys had always been impressed by Sonny's way of life. Jude's flat was a haven for truants, the dispossessed and runaways. She'd always had an open door. Now that her Sonny was gone she needed the youngsters more than ever.

Gino had promised to help her out in place of Sonny and he intended to do just that. It was the least he could do in memory of his friend.

At six Sonny had walked the estate looking for whatever dealer Jude owed less money to and then he would score and bring back her precious cargo and bask in her cuddles and kisses and her exaltations about what a big boy he was for his mummy.

Once she had injected, though, he'd been as far from her mind as the moon. He had soon realised that as well and had taken what she offered when he could.

In fact, it was amazing that he'd never indulged himself. He had a puff with his mates and dropped Es of a weekend but the brown had never interested him. In a funny way she had been proud of that much; it wouldn't have done to have two addicts in the same house. She had robbed him, stolen his birthday money and presents from his father, even sold his clothes, and he had always forgiven her, understanding her need better than she did herself.

He had robbed for her, getting off because of his home life. That was until he hit sixteen, of course, then it wasn't so easy to walk away from it all any more. No one listened to his pleas about his mother being unable to exist without her drugs. He had even held his hand up to stuff that had nothing to do with him over the years for a money gift, when he couldn't be nicked on account of his age. And people had used him for that without a thought.

Sonny would have done anything for her, yet she could not do the one thing he asked of her.

To get herself clean.

He had even tried locking her up in the house, but her pleas and eventually her aggression had made him score for her once more and then the whole cycle would start all over again.

As she lay back with a glazed expression the youngsters all gradually left the flat. Jude was gone now, in her secret place. They drifted away gradually without bothering to say goodbye.

Nick was in the pub, knocking back shorts at an alarming rate, when his mobile rang. He glanced at the display and rejected the call before turning it off altogether. It was Tammy, and he had no interest in talking to her. Joey Miles watched his friend sadly. He had taken it bad. No matter how many people told him he had done the right thing, it made no difference.

'Come on, Nick, let's go and get some food, eh?'

He shook his head.

Nick Leary was a big man and because he generally had such a nice way with him people forgot that he could also be a hard bastard when the fancy took him. It was this that had got him where he was in life. He had sailed close to the wind more than a few times, but hadn't they all in pursuit of a better life?

A tall blonde with high breasts and a perma-grin walked towards them.

'Hello, Nick, long time no see.'

She was the girlfriend of a business acquaintance but she always had her radar tuned for a better alternative. The business acquaintance was also married so she wasn't bothered about Tammy. In fact, it was *what* she had heard about Nick's wife that made her think she might be on to a much better thing with Nick than she had first thought. He was also a bit of all right so the sex part wouldn't be such a trial either. Her current squeeze was short, bald and had a belly that could accommodate triplets and still leave room for a West Ham footballer.

He also had an open wallet of Olympic standards, so at least he had that going for him if nothing else.

Nick had not answered her and she tried again.

'Hello, Nick, remember me?'

He stared at her for long seconds before shaking his head.

'Sorry, no, I don't.'

He sounded completely uninterested, something that rarely happened to her when men were around. She was nonplussed for a moment and Joey closed his eyes in distress. The blonde was shocked and it showed on her face. *Everyone* remembered her, she was Des Carter's bird, that court case must have turned Nick's mind. She would not even contemplate the thought that he could be blanking her.

'Des's girlfriend?'

She was still the coquette, deciding to give him the benefit of the doubt. Joey gave her points for perseverance anyway.

'Where is Des then?'

Nick gave a good impression of a sailor looking out to sea. His hand over his eyes, he peered around the bar for a few seconds. He saw the humiliation burn in her eyes and told himself to let it go, but he couldn't. Instead he turned his back on her and started to order himself another drink. As he owned the pub that wasn't hard.

Joey tried to ease her embarrassment.

'Leave it, love. Get a drink on me, OK?'

'Des won't like this when I tell him . . .'

Des was a local hard case, but not that hard a case he would take on Nick. But she obviously wasn't thinking when she spoke.

79

Nick turned round and said nastily, 'Oh, I'm quaking in me boots, love.'

He passed her his mobile.

'Get him on the blower and I'll talk to him now, eh?'

Joey pushed the phone away from the stricken girl.

'All right, Nick.'

Joey's voice was low, annoyed, people were already looking at them. The girl's friends were thrilled with this turn of events and she knew it.

'He's drunk, love . . .'

Nick poked a finger at her and said loudly, 'Not that drunk though, eh? I wouldn't touch you with a barge pole.'

She walked away humiliated and Joey waited a beat before he said, 'She didn't deserve that, Nick.'

He laughed.

'Didn't she? Des's wife is a good woman. She's given him five kids and she's stood by him through every bit of shit he ever got himself into. And what does he do? He takes up with *that*. Even paid for her fucking tits! She sees me as an alternative pay packet, nothing more, nothing less. Well, she can fuck off. I have enough trouble trying to stop Tammy bankrupting me on a daily basis. Her and all I don't need.'

He wiped a hand across his face, he was sweating again. Since the boy's death he had felt like this a lot. He shook for no reason and got panic attacks. Felt sick, couldn't sleep, eat or think properly. All he thought about was the boy.

He had enjoyed taking it out on that girl; she was a slapper as far as he was concerned. His mate's bird. No more and no less. He knew she would be on her mobile in nano-seconds, telling him all about the insult. Well, good luck to her. Des wouldn't say a dicky-bird to Nick, but she would find that out soon enough.

He looked at the barmaid then and shouted out, 'What the fuck am I paying you for, Candice? Get me a bloody drink, will you!'

Candice sighed. Taking down the brandy optic, she slammed it on the bar in front of him. Pushing a clean glass towards him, she said acidly, 'Now you can pour your own drinks, can't you?'

Nick finally laughed then. He had always liked Candice, she was a tough little cookie.

The woman walked towards her car slowly. The shopping bags she held were heavy and she stopped to change hands. The plastic Tesco carrier bags were digging into her palms. Her toddler was wandering off in all directions and she called to her affectionately.

Gino watched her. She was slightly built with long dark hair. She looked exactly what she was, a nice respectable woman. He had been watching her for the last hour although she didn't know that, being too preoccupied with her child and the shopping. She looked and acted like one of those people who always assume nothing bad can happen to them. It was a miracle but there were still people around like that in this day and age. It amazed Gino, even as young as he was. He had learned a long time ago that you trusted no one unless you knew them well, and even then you kept a sceptical eye out. She was just what he was looking for. She had pulled out money from the cash point before making her way to the car and he was pleased about that. Her cards he could sell on but there was no substitute for cash itself.

He waited until she had opened the boot and dropped in the shopping bags before he made his move.

As she opened the back door of her Renault Clio to put the child in its car seat he sneaked up behind her and pushed the blade of the knife into her side, just nicking the skin enough to make her feel it without actually hurting her.

She still had her bag over her shoulder and he whispered in her ear, 'Drop your bag and don't look back at me. If I see you looking I'll come back and do you and the baby, OK?'

81

She nodded and dropped the bag from her shoulder immediately.

The little girl was smiling quizzically, understanding suddenly that none of this was a game.

'Pretty baby, lady, you want to watch out for her.'

Gino picked up the bag slowly and then punched the woman in the side of the head for good measure. She fell into the car as he knew she would and he was off with the bag, sprinting out of the car park and into the warren of houses that made up his estate in seconds. He bolted to a piece of waste ground and then searched the bag eagerly. He was amazed at what people kept in their bags. The usual array of Tampax and birth control pills, headache tablets, lipsticks and baby wipes competed with letters and gas bills – all addressed to her, of course. Even a bank letter with her statement inside and a chequebook.

Would people never learn?

He had enough here to remortgage her house or open a moody bank account in her name.

The purse inside the bag now held no secrets from him. It was jam packed with the usual female paraphernalia: photos of home and the kids. Her house looked really nice with a big garden and a wide-screen TV set in the corner of the lounge, up-to-the-minute DVD player – she might as well have put an advert out to get burgled. There were also her credit cards, debit cards, her Tesco clubcard, Boots loyalty card, even her membership to Blockbuster Video. Her whole life was in that one leather shoulder bag. And now it was his to do with as he pleased.

Gino grinned as he took out the three hundred pounds in cash and removed the cards. Then he searched the side pockets of the bag. So many women slipped off their jewellery and placed it in their bag without a second's thought. He was not disappointed. There was a small pair of gold earrings there together with a diamond tennis bracelet.

A good haul. Gino was pleased with himself.

As an afterthought he took the letters. Her address might be useful to whoever he sold the stuff to.

Whistling, Gino left the waste ground. He had achieved his objective and was one happy little bunny.

Tammy heard about the débâcle in the pub over a long lunch in Brentwood. They were celebrating her life getting back to normal, which meant she was picking up the bill as per usual.

She basked in the pleasure of knowing that her husband was always faithful to her. He might chat up birds, have a joke at times, but basically he had no real interest in them. All her friends – and she used the term loosely – had trouble keeping their blokes indoors; she had trouble getting hers out of the house. Nick was happy these days to come home, slip off his shoes, eat his food and watch the box. All that poke and he never left the house now unless it was to earn more money, or get drunk. Not that she was knocking him for that.

If only he would take her out occasionally. Unlike her mates whose husbands were out trumping anything with a pulse, her old man lived like a hermit. She guessed he had the occasional bat away from home, she wasn't stupid, but in fairness to him he had never shoved her face in it like so many of his mates did with their wives.

For that much at least she was grateful.

Now he had knocked back Des's bird Tammy was happier than she had been in ages. How people perceived her was important. Being seen to be in control was important. Her friends couldn't understand how she kept Nick in his place because she was not a woman to be faithful herself. In fact, she spent her whole life on the chat up and everyone including Nick knew that.

No one could believe the way she got away with it. Only Tammy knew the price she had paid for her lifestyle and she would never tell anyone what that was.

She nodded to the waiter for more wine, aware that she was

giving them all food for thought and basking in their utter astonishment that Nick Leary didn't feel the urge to play away. Tammy knew that jealousy was rife around the table and enjoyed the moment while it lasted. Sipping daintily at her white wine, she winked at the good-looking young waiter and was gratified to see her friends roll their eyes at the ceiling in amazement.

They all wished Nick was theirs, while wondering if they could be woman enough to keep him as faithful as Tammy did.

And that was exactly what she wanted them to think.

In fact, Nick had not come near her in that way for years. He cuddled her, and he hugged her, and the other night they had fallen asleep together. She had felt his need for closeness and had responded to it. But the truth was, he had no sexual interest in her whatsoever. Thankfully, he had no interest in anyone else either.

Impotence he called it, and it was that very thing that kept Tammy in gold cards and Mercedes sports. Kept her kids in private school and gave her licence to do whatever she wanted.

But she would never let on to anyone.

If he managed to get it up now and again with someone else as she suspected from the occasional absence on unspecified 'business' then that was OK as far as she was concerned. As long as it wasn't serious, she couldn't give the proverbial flying fuck. At least that was what she told herself.

Tammy pushed the thoughts from her mind once more. Her biggest fear was that her husband would fall in love with someone else, one of his one-night stands. But Tammy being Tammy had already worked out a nice little earner for herself should that befall her and hers.

Nick Leary would pay, and pay big-time.

Her macho husband's biggest fear was that his reluctance in the marital bed would be broadcast to the world, or more specifically, to their circle of friends. He had always had trouble keeping it up, as *she* so nicely put it, now he couldn't even raise a smile as *he* so nicely put it.

But she played the game, pretended that they were at it morning, noon and night, and even though she would shag a table leg if it bought her a drink, her friends all thought Nick didn't know about her affairs and she kept the pretence up. It was part of her street cred now and she knew that and she used it.

Even though her husband had the reputation of a womaniser, she could honestly say that even in her most jealous rages she had never been able to find out anything concrete to throw at him. But that was Nick all over, if he was using brasses again, she would never know about it and, in a way, she respected him for that, even as the thought drove her mad.

She had found a pack of condoms in his jacket pocket and it had thrown her whole world off-kilter. When she had confronted him, he had told her he was trying out brasses to see if he could sort himself out.

Her jealousy, as usual, had got the better of her. That a nameless, faceless tart could get her leg over with her husband when she could not even raise his interest made her self-esteem hit the floor once more. It had taken an affair with a young guy who cleaned their pool to get her over that one.

Yet her sensible side told her to be pleased that at least Nick wasn't sleeping with someone he cared about, it wasn't with an actual *bird*. Most of her friends' husbands had birds that were an open secret. At least Nick had never humiliated her in that way. If he had a bird, she would have heard about it from one of her so-called friends. They would have *enjoyed* telling her about it.

She had often been out with Nick and seen her friends' husbands with their birds. Younger women, far beneath their wives in the food chain, but with full breasts and firm skin that no matter how much money you acquired you couldn't emulate. They were all too stupid to see that they would be traded-in eventually for younger versions of themselves even if they gave the men kids, which was often the mistake their wives had made. A belly full of stretch marks and a crying baby turned them from sex objects to mother figures overnight. It was how their world worked, and even when the men hit their fifties there would always be someone new to step into the girlfriend's shoes and, in some cases, even the flat they had lived in.

This was why Tammy had made a point of knowing all there was to know about her husband's businesses. She knew what Nick was worth down to his last penny, and his last euro. He had to be getting it from somewhere and he was most certainly not getting it from her, and if he ever surprised her with a twenty-to-one shot she would be ready and waiting to turn him over good and proper. As her old mum used to say, 'don't get mad get even.' Hit a man in the pocket, it's the only place, other than in his balls, where you can bring tears to his eyes.

Well, he would lose his money and his nuts if he ever did the dirty on her and he knew it.

Gary Proctor and her husband just worked, and that was it, according to Nick, but her name was not Gilly Hunt and she was not changing it now. If he took her for a cunt she would be ready and waiting for him and even though his bosom pal Gary Proctor was not exactly the answer to a maiden's prayer, she knew there were birds out there who would gladly overlook that fact.

She was watching out for herself, and it annoyed her that most women she knew did not make provisions for the rainy days that were bound to come. He could take everything she had, but she'd still have her pride and he was never going to take that from her.

Gino stood in the small alleyway near his flats and waited for Big Ellie. As she walked towards him he smiled.

'All right?'

She nodded.

Ellie was big, powerfully big, with arms like meat cleavers. But she had a lovely face that belied the nastiness underneath the make-up. She came from a large family noted mainly for their fighting skills and their belligerence. She scored drugs for people, never seeing herself as a dealer, but touched only alcohol herself. She saw drugs as a mug's game. She also did little favours for people when she could. For money, of course.

'You got it?'

He handed her the three hundred pounds cash, which she counted quickly. Then she opened her fake Burberry bag and gave him a small plastic bank bag full of brown and a phone number written on a piece of paper.

'You never got that number from me, right?'

He nodded.

' 'Course not. What? So you think I'm stupid.'

'My brother would kill me if he knew, so you can imagine what would happen to you, can't you?'

The threat was unmistakable and he nodded his agreement.

Gino had had a good day. He had got one hundred and fifty for the cards and chequebook so he was still quids in. Now all he had to do was unload the jewellery and he would be laughing.

'You got it then?'

Jude's face was so open and trusting it made Gino feel good. She took the bank bag from him and grinned.

'Fucking hell! This is like Christmas, Gino.'

He felt six feet taller from her admiration.

'I'll see you all right, Jude, don't you worry.'

It was an idle boast but it felt good. He would try and keep her sorted, it was the least he could do for his friend.

'I got the number you wanted and all.'

He saw the light leave her face. It was wiped clean of any expression; she had paled even more than usual if that were possible.

'You're joking?'

He shook his head and passed it to her carefully. It was written on a scrap of newspaper and as she gazed at it she felt her heart lift. Mobile numbers changed, but land lines stayed the same.

'Oh, you are good, Gino! Fucking good.'

She placed a grubby hand to her mouth, as if stopping herself from saying something else. As Gino watched her he felt omnipotent.

'Oh, Gino son, you don't know what you've given me,' she said eventually.

He knew exactly what he had given her but he didn't say that, of course, he just basked in her praise.

When he produced the bottle of vodka Jude was speechless, but it showed him just how good you could feel helping out someone less fortunate than yourself.

Chapter Six

It was a crisp morning. Even though the house was warm the frost was still white on the roofs of the outhouses. Nick Leary had woken with the thought already uppermost in his head: Sonny Hatcher was being buried today.

It was burning Nick up inside. No matter how much he drank or how long he slept he couldn't rid himself of that thought. Seventeen and he was being buried today. A boy, only a boy. A stupid little thief but just a boy, a handsome one who should by rights have had his whole life ahead of him.

Nick looked out of the bedroom window and watched the birds going about their business. Even in his troubled state he marvelled that this wonderful view was all his. And it was some view; field after field until finally in the distance you could see the estuary. It was beautiful, with no other habitation in the distance to spoil it. Of a night he would watch the lights of ships in the distance and wish he were on one of them. Today in an early-October frost the view from the window was like a Christmas card.

Tammy breezed into the bedroom from the en-suite bathroom, all white towels and Versace perfume.

'Morning!'

She was chirpy and for some reason that annoyed Nick. He lay in bed and studied her. She was still a good-looking woman, he couldn't take that away from her, and she could still make him laugh which had always been her greatest asset in his eyes – though she didn't know that, of course. She thought it was her fascinating conversation and firm body.

'It's the funeral today.'

He didn't know why he had said it.

Tammy shrugged her slim shoulders in bewilderment.

'Yeah? And?'

It was all over as far as she was concerned.

'Look, Nick, you got to let this go, mate. It happened and nothing we say or do will change that.' She shrugged. 'You were looking out for your own. He should never have been here in our home in the first place. He should never have been out thieving.'

She spoke it like a mantra, she'd said it so often. She wished she could make it all better for him but she knew she couldn't. Nick was fighting this alone as he had fought everything he had overcome in his life.

She came to the bed and sat beside him, slipping off the towel. Her huge breasts were probably enough to set most men's blood racing to their loins. Unfortunately they didn't do anything for Nick. Physically she had never done anything for him and the thought saddened Nick even as it maddened her. She never had. She had not been his type, if that was the right expression.

Tammy caressed his thigh through the bedclothes.

He thanked her for the thought if nothing else.

He knew it wasn't fair on her the way he was, but it was hard for him to focus on sex with her at the best of times. She always seemed like a bitch on heat. Eager . . . so eager. There was never any finesse to it. Straight sex, no kissing, that was his lovely Tams.

He was almost getting himself into the mood for what she wanted when she inadvertently ruined it.

'Shall I jump back in with you, babe?'

It was that 'babe' that killed any hope they'd had but she didn't know that and he wasn't going to tell her.

How many other blokes had she said it to over the years?

Nick pulled the quilt back. Smirking at her, he said nastily, 'If you can get it hard then it's all yours, darlin'. And let's face it, Tams, you've had enough practice with everyone else.'

Her face, that had been so open and soft, hardened.

'Oh, fuck you!'

'Not this morning you won't, love. I couldn't raise a smile, Tams, let alone anything else.'

He laughed at his own wit even as he felt desperately sorry for hurting her. Why did he do this to her? She didn't deserve this treatment. He grabbed her arm before she could storm away from him.

'I'm sorry, Tams. Honestly, darlin', it's nothing personal, you know that.'

She could hear the sorrow in his voice and knew that he never set out to hurt her even though that was what he always ended up doing. She pulled away from him. Grabbing the towel from the floor, she covered herself up once more. Feeling ashamed of her nakedness now, sorry she had started it all up again.

'Ain't it? Well, it feels like it is.'

She picked up a hairbrush from the dressing table and started to drag it through her hair angrily, the hurt and embarrassment making her feel hot with shame.

'You better see someone and you better see someone soon. This is starting to drive me mad, Nick.'

She stared at him through the dressing-table mirror.

'Are you seeing anyone else, Nick?'

He could see the fear in her eyes and sighed heavily.

' 'Course not. There's no one, I swear that to you, Tams.'

He was telling her the truth and they both knew it.

'Not even prostitutes?'

'*Especially* not fucking prostitutes.'

Though that had been the case in the past.

He walked to the bathroom and locked the door. The sound of the bolt being driven home was loud in the silence of the room.

Tammy looked at herself critically in the bedroom mirror. She was still looking good so it wasn't her fault. As she looked around the beautiful room, at the Italian furniture and the expensive drapes, she wondered about other women all over the country who were getting the rogering of a lifetime from their old men in surroundings far less salubrious than this. Lucky them. She wondered not for the first time whether marriage to Nick was worth it.

Yet the strangest thing of all was she loved him.

She always had and she always would.

Jude was dressed and ready to go. In her black suit and with her hair done 'specially by a neighbour's daughter she looked almost lovely. Even her make-up was correctly applied. Tyrell knew she could only have done it if she'd stayed off the brown. It must have taken a lot for her not to use on this black day.

She looked almost like the girl she had once been; the slim shoulders, the long legs. Her hair, freshly coloured and cut, looked thick and lustrous. She had never known just how lovely she was. Even his mother, a harsh critic of white girls at the best of times, had been enamoured of her. Still was, in fact. Jude was like a daughter to Verbena. An errant daughter admittedly, but a daughter all the same.

Verbena looked into the sad eyes of Jude Hatcher and felt the tears rolling down her own face. This quiet crying had been going on for the best part of the night. She would not go to the funeral, could not bring herself to leave the house even for her Sonny Boy. But she would be with them in spirit and they knew that.

Sally watched them all looking at Jude and felt the usual resentment welling up inside her. She swallowed it down as she always had.

Reverend Williams held on to Verbena's trembling hand. She was a staunch supporter of his church and he respected and admired her for the way she had fought to bring her family up in the ways of God.

They were a credit to her – all except Sonny Boy who had been a disgrace since he had first learned to listen to his mother instead of the rest of the world. Reverend Williams felt ashamed of the feelings he had for Jude Hatcher but even his Christian spirit was stretched to the limit where she was concerned.

She had taught her child nothing of any value in his short life. All she had taught him was how to lie and cheat. She was as much to blame for that boy's death as if she had bludgeoned him herself. It was no mystery where the money was to have gone once he had robbed that poor family.

The man who had been responsible for taking Sonny's life had looked shell-shocked on television even as he defended his actions. To take a life must be a terrible thing, and for that boy to lose his because his mother couldn't function without drugs was also a terrible thing. But no matter how hard he tried to feel sorry for Jude Hatcher, the feeling just wouldn't come.

But he kept his own counsel, there was nothing else he could do. When the grieving mother smiled wanly at him he forced himself to smile back. She was carrion as far as he was concerned. She'd leeched off her son just as she had leeched off society all her life.

'The cars are here.'

He stood up abruptly, glad to be leaving the house at last, pleased the day was officially beginning. Once the boy was interred they were all coming back here and poor Verbena would have her family around her and could grieve in peace at last. He knew that the people round about had no real sympathy for Sonny Boy, saw his death as something that was going to happen sooner rather than later. But he also knew people cared about poor Verbena and was glad of that fact. She deserved to be cared about; she was a good kind person. Her only mistake in life was believing that she could redeem her grandson, even though he had let her down time and time again.

Now he couldn't ever let her down again.

Nick was in the pub again, only this time he was in the small office he kept beside the cellar. This was where he sorted out his less salubrious business dealings. Joey Jones brought him a large Scotch and said cheerily, 'Bit early even for you.'

It didn't stop him pouring himself one.

'What's the score?'

Nick's tone of voice was strictly business. Joey understood his friend's feelings without anything being said. He would leave all that to the mouthy fools in the pub above, who he just knew would mention the boy's funeral at every possible opportunity.

Joey knocked back his Scotch in one gulp.

'A rave. Little Bobby Spiers wants to use the land in Bishops Stortford. It's a proper venue, good DJs, plenty of advertising, Kiss 100, etc. He's got it sewn up. He'll get the licence himself so all we do is cream it off.'

'What did you say to him?'

Joey poured himself another drink.

'I OK'd it, of course. Why? You got any worries about it?'

Nick shrugged.

Joey grinned as he said, 'Plenty of young crumpet bombing around. Might give it a look see meself.'

Nick groaned.

'Not you and all. It's like Shagland round here.'

'Wendy's pregnant again. I won't get nothing from her for fucking months, you know what she's like.'

'Go for it. What else is happening?'

Nick's voice was bored-sounding now.

Joey looked through his notebook. It was the same kind that women used for shopping lists; in it was everything he needed to know to run his side of the businesses. It was long, slim and perfect for hiding away.

It was also easily disposed of which was its main attraction as far as he was concerned. All the legal stuff was well documented; this was for the other stuff, the semi-legal stuff Nick Leary did so well.

'Time-shares are doing all right. The flats are all paid up. The clubs are all paid up. Nothing really to worry about. I can sort it all out . . .'

He looked at his friend.

'Why don't you go home, mate?'

Nick was holding his head in his hands and crying quietly. Joey didn't know what to do. In all the years he had known Nick he had never seen such a display of emotion before. On one level he understood it. After all, he had killed the kid. But on another level he felt that Nick should let it go now. 'What's done is done,' as his old mum used to say. You couldn't undo anything no matter how much you might want to.

She also used to say: 'Count to five before you answer anyone in anger. It stops you saying things you can't take back.' That advice had kept his marriage going longer than anyone had ever thought it could last.

Eventually, after what seemed an age, he went over to his friend and put one arm warily across his shoulder. Nick grabbed at the arm and hugged it, crying even harder. Eventually he pushed his face into his friend's stomach and held him around the waist tightly. While he cried his heart out Joey stroked his back, hoping against hope that no one came looking for them.

He would hate to have to try and explain this one away.

If he had wanted raw emotion he could quite easily have stayed home and had a ding-dong with his wife. Screaming and crying was, after all, her forte.

'Come on, Nick mate, pull yourself together, eh?'

He could hear the embarrassment in his own voice and was ashamed.

'I should never have done it, Joey. He was so young . . . so fucking young . . . but I had no choice, see? I had no fucking choice . . .'

' 'Course you didn't, mate, any man would have done the same thing.'

He pulled away from his friend gently.

'Go home, mate. You're in no fit state . . .' But he knew that going home was the last thing Nick Leary wanted to do. 'Get your coat,' he said decisively. 'We're going into town and me and you are going on it.'

Nick wiped his eyes.

'I ain't in the mood, Joey, honestly.'

'Neither am I, but we'll get in the mood, right?'

Nick grinned then.

'Spearmint Rhino?'

Joey laughed loudly.

'Eventually. Let's just see what the day brings, shall we?'

Nick nodded once more.

Anything was better than sitting here thinking about Sonny Hatcher's imminent burial. Even a pole-dancing club.

Tyrell listened as the Reverend Williams said good things about his son. He especially noted how kind Sonny had been to his mother, how he had always taken care of her with love.

He glanced at Jude. She had her eyes closed and he could see the film of sweat over her face. He sighed heavily, wishing the day over.

In his mind's eye he saw his Sonny Boy when he had been a baby. How did that dear little boy turn into the little fucker they were now burying?

Anger was getting the better of him again. No matter how often he told himself that this Nick Leary had only done what any man would have done, Tyrell still wanted to tear him limb from limb.

He stood up as he saw Jude walking unsteadily from the church. Glad of an excuse to leave, he followed her. This hypocrisy was killing him. He would have had more respect for the Reverend if he had spoken truthfully about the boy Tyrell had loved.

It had been hard to admit that his son was not the good boy he had been expecting, but at least Tyrell had accepted a long time ago that Sonny was flawed. And it was all because of this woman, now huddled on a bench and scrabbling in her bag for something, anything, to make her high.

'Come on, Jude.'

He walked her through the graveyard to his car. Inside he opened the armrest and passed her a small bag of H. She took it from him gratefully, her eyes expressing her thanks even as she struggled to open it properly because of the shaking of her hands. Five minutes later she was lying back in the front seat of his BMW, her eyes finally peaceful and her arm dangling beside her. She'd obliterated today as she had obliterated every day of her life since he could remember.

He pressed a button and the CD player came to life. The Supremes were singing that the world was empty without their babe. And the strangest thing of all was, the way he felt inside, at that moment he could have written the song himself.

As bad as Jude was he still cared about her. She was the only woman ever to have affected him in that way. Like his son he felt the urge to take care of her. It was a knack she had.

Jude played the victim so well because she really was one.

Her own biggest victim.

There was something about her eyes that would always attract him. When she was high they looked so deep and lost, she was so totally gone, that he wanted to hold her and bring her back and make it all better.

But you could never make Jude any better because she had never really known that what she did was wrong.

Nick was in a club in Rupert Street. It was a private club owned by a mate. A young girl with bright eyes brought on by an influx of Colombian marching gear and a short skirt that just covered her punani was smiling at him. It was a *bought* smile; he had bought her with a bit of gear and a few drinks. The knowledge depressed him.

He went to the toilet and snorted another line; at least on coke he felt that he was alive. It was good gear, it had already given him the rushes. He was only sorry it was the drugs that had given him the racing heart and not the girl.

He was off sex. If he never had another shag as long as he lived it would be too soon. He laughed at his own thoughts then stared at himself in the mirror of the plush and expensive room.

A young man had followed him in. He was in his twenties, good-looking with thick blond hair and piercing blue eyes. He looked like a young Steve McQueen and he knew it. Nick watched him closely: the fluid movements of his body, the arrogance of youth when it knew just how lovely it was.

He felt an urge to tell him to be careful, warn him that: 'One day, in the not too distant future, you, my son, will be me.'

He wanted to laugh at his thoughts then because he knew this boy, like the girl outside, was wasting the best part of his life selling himself to the highest bidder. He locked eyes with the boy in the mirror. The boy smiled lazily at him before putting his hand leisurely down his trousers. It was the ultimate come-on for queers.

Everything was sex with people these days; all it was now was a commodity. There was no real feeling left with anyone, not even his own wife. Nick glared at the boy and mimed sticking his fingers down his throat and vomiting. The boy's eyes widened in shock, then he shrugged before walking into one of the cubicles.

Nick glanced down at his hands; they were gripping the basin so hard his knuckles were aching. He waited for the boy to emerge once more before he took back his fist and slammed it with all the force he could muster into the young lad's perfect face.

Walking from the toilet at an unhurried pace, he caught Joey's eye and they left the club, laughing. The boy's jaw was broken and Nick knew it. The knowledge gave him no satisfaction whatsoever but he had made his point. Or at least he felt that he had anyway.

Time enough to be sorry tomorrow.

Sally had seen Tyrell leaving the church and her heart had sunk down to her boots. She knew he was going to look after Jude but stood her ground and made a point of not following him. She knew he loved her, but he loved Jude differently. They all loved Jude differently. Poor Jude, as she was always called.

Well, Sally couldn't find it in her heart to feel sorry for her like Tyrell did. She saw Jude as a selfish, manipulative bitch. But of course she rarely said that, having learned her lesson over the years.

It still galled her that even Verbena could see no wrong in her. Sally felt she would always come second. Yet here she was, Tyrell's wife, a good mother, a good daughter-in-law, and a good decent person, but it still wasn't enough.

It would *never* be enough.

She couldn't compete with Jude's neediness and that would always be her downfall. She fantasised sometimes about taking to the bottle so she could compete on the 'poor little me' stakes.

Yet she knew this was unfair because in fact Jude just wanted them all to leave her alone so she could get on with whatever shit she happened to be wrapped up in at the time. Jude wanted shot almost as much as Sally did. But only when it suited her. It didn't stop Sally from hating the woman who had been like a third person in her marriage from day one.

She herself had cared about Sonny Boy after her fashion; he was her sons' half-brother after all. But she would have been a liar if she didn't admit deep in her heart that his death had given her a moment or two's vicarious pleasure because she'd felt that once he was gone, Jude would be gone too.

Now, though, she wasn't so sure.

Jude would be there still, like the spectre at the feast, as she had always been; only now she really was *poor* Jude who had lost her only child.

Sally prayed that her bitterness would vanish, but feared that it wouldn't. A dead lover she could have coped with, but Jude was a different kettle of fish altogether. She was the living dead and she wasn't going anywhere.

Spearmint Rhino was packed out. In the VIP bar Nick had been drinking steadily for hours. The coke and the whisky were taking their toll and he felt completely and utterly out of it. His head was starting to ache and his eyes had stopped focusing an hour earlier.

He had also lost Joey.

Nick sat on a sofa and watched the goings on around him. He tried unsuccessfully to find his mate but he was nowhere to be seen. Getting up, Nick lurched into a big man who, suited and booted, was very obviously a City gent.

Nick mumbled an apology as he tried to pass him. But the man, by day a respectable accountant, was as worse for wear as he was. He followed Nick outside.

As he flagged down a cab the man started swearing at him. It took a few moments before Nick even realised this was aimed at him. He actually looked around to see who had annoyed the man.

He watched as the City type came towards him, face screwed up in anger, and felt the urge to laugh. This guy was flabby, a typical desk boy, not an ounce of muscle to be seen. But big enough to be a problem if you didn't know how to handle yourself.

Nick put up his hand in a friendly fashion.

'Oh, come on now, you don't want to fight with me.'

Paul Cross wanted to fight anyone and everyone, that much was evident by his demeanour.

'You taking the fucking piss?'

It was a fair question, Nick supposed.

'I don't know, mate, you tell me.'

It was as good as a battle cry, said with enough disdain to cause a fight or to prevent one, depending how the other man decided to take it.

Paul Cross, much to Nick's chagrin, decided he wanted a fight. Nick sighed as he planted his feet more firmly on the pavement. He could have a row, had *always* been able to have a row. It was what had got him where he was in life.

He had been the best fighter in his year as a teenager, and eventually the best fighter in his whole school. His skills were legendary where he came from and now, in his drink- and drug-fuelled state, he was quite looking forward to taking on this man who had probably never, in all his life, had a fight that wasn't driven by anger. Well, Nick had fought without anger all his life, just to prove a point or to get a little bit further in his chosen profession. This prat would not know what the fuck had hit him.

In reality this was the best thing to have happened to Nick all day long. He had been looking for scapegoats since he had left his house and here was a big burly one just waiting to be burned. And Nick would burn him all right. This ponce would be drinking through a straw for the next six months of his fat, stupid and pointless life.

Paul Cross saw the change in his antagonist then. It showed first in his eyes. He looked more closely at Nick and something in his stance told him that this man really wanted to hurt him. He also realised with an even bigger sense of shock that the other man was genuinely capable of doing it.

It was a revelation.

Paul Cross had fights as a matter of course, had made himself the big man with his mates by always being ready to rumble. But never before had he felt in actual danger of his life.

Now for the first time he realised what fear actually was.

He had always been careful to pick on people he knew he could beat, people who were not capable of real fighting in the same way as he wasn't really capable of it. He was nothing but a bully, and this guy had looked drunk enough to have taken a smack and gone down leaving Paul the victor as usual. It would have been something to talk about the next day. Something to brag about.

Now Nick was walking towards him, fists clenched and eyes dead. He was menace incarnate in a red shirt, looking more scary at that moment than the devil himself.

'Come on then, you cunt, I fucking dare ya.'

There was something in the man's voice. It was as if he was looking forward to hurting his opponent, and hurting him badly.

Nick enjoyed taunting his victims like this, it was all part of the game.

'Come on, big boy. You wanted it, now you've fucking got it.'

Paul Cross was sobering up faster than a dealer at a blues. He stepped backwards, trying to get away from the man before him. The club bouncers watched the proceedings but kept their distance. This alone told Paul Cross that he was dealing with someone well out of his league.

The black cab Nick had stopped had waited, and the driver, a big man with a false smile and too many tattoos, watched them squaring up to one another. He put his money on red shirt; that was one aggravated fucker.

Paul was cornered now. He was up against the wall and he was panicking. He could feel the sweat of fear pouring down his back. It was the first time anyone had intimidated him to this extent.

Nick pushed his face close to Paul's as he whispered, 'What's the matter, City boy, lost your fucking bottle?'

He was smiling now.

'Do you want to die?'

He laughed quietly, staring into the man's face.

'You see, I've killed once before and I could easily do it again.'

It was said matter-of-factly but Paul believed him. He vaguely recognised the man before him but wasn't sure where from.

He held his arms up in a gesture of supplication.

'Come on, mate, I was out of order . . .'

He was trying to talk himself out of the situation, as humiliated as he was terrified.

Nick looked at the man in disgust.

'You're all fucking mouth, ain't ya? All fucking mouth and no trousers, as my old mum would say.'

The words made him laugh.

He put a hand on the wall, effectively trapping the man in front of him. Paul Cross could smell his coke breath, horribly rancid and heavy.

'You give me one good reason why I shouldn't smack you all around fucking Kings Cross and I'll let you go home, all right?' He laughed once more and said quietly, 'Because, you see, I *want* to hurt you. I'll rephrase that – I really want to hurt *someone* and you'll do.'

Paul Cross knew that the bouncers were waiting with bated breath for his answer. They had moved closer, knowing they were all out of range of the CCTV cameras and happy that anything that happened would not be down to them. He took another breath before he said placatingly and in obvious terror, 'I've got kids, mate. Look, I was out of order, out of my depth . . .'

Nick grinned once more. He was shaking his head in sorrow now.

'See, you mate, *you* are the cancer that is blighting society. You go out with your mates and you pick a fight, and I bet normally, in all fairness, you fucking win it. The big I am, eh? Well, I ain't never lost a fucking fight yet, and I have fought the best. Now you want me to leave you alone because you got kids?'

He laughed once more.

'Well, tough shit, because tonight you picked on the wrong person. You inadvertently came across your Nemesis because ten of you wouldn't fucking scare me, right? No one in the world scares me. And I feel this terrible urge to wipe you all around this pavement just to teach you a lesson.'

Nick poked him hard in the chest as he spoke.

'Because, you see, I don't like you very much. But then, today I don't fucking like *no one*!'

It was delivered with so much hatred even the bouncers stepped back in case they themselves inadvertently antagonised the enraged man.

Paul Cross felt urine running down his legs and the utter humiliation was too much for him. Pushing past Nick, he ran off as fast as he could. Nick watched him go without a word. As he had witnessed the other man's fear he had felt all the anger leave him as quickly as it had arrived.

He looked down at the pool of steaming urine on the pavement and, turning to the bouncers who were still watching him warily, bowed theatrically.

'Was it something I said, lads?'

Nick walked back inside the club, suddenly sober again and ready once more for a night on the town.

* * *

Joey saw Lance Walker across the bar and felt his heart stop in his chest.

Lance had a reputation for causing trouble, even though his countenance belied this. A big man, heavyset and muscular, he had been blessed with a bullet-shaped head and a neck like a bull's. He also had huge, blue eyes that made him look easy-going and kind. His thick, black hair was streaked with grey and this just added to his look of amiability. People assumed he was a nice man, a friendly soul. In fact, Lance was one of the most dangerous individuals to ever walk the earth, and if no one else was aware of that fact, Lance himself was.

He also loathed Nick Leary, and Joey knew that if Nick saw him the Third World War would erupt.

Nick and Lance had fallen out a few years before and no one knew why. Nick had never offered any explanation and neither had Lance. Joey knew though that Nick was still out to harm him and felt the nervousness wash over his body. He put his drink on the bar and then walked away trying to find Nick.

Ten minutes later he went into the toilet and saw the two men chatting to each other as though they were lifelong buddies. Smiling, to hide the fear in his heart, Joey had a quick line and prayed that whatever had gone down between them was now sorted.

He could see though that there was still an atmosphere and Joey wondered when it would all go off.

Lance was a handful, but Nick was already in overdrive and Joey had watched him getting more and more uptight as the weeks had gone on. Nick was looking for a scapegoat to vent his pent-up feelings and Lance could be exactly what he was looking for.

Joey decided that his money was on Nick if it went off now.

Both men ignored his presence as Joey slipped away from the room. He knew when he was not wanted.

Chapter Seven

Tyrell woke up to a dingy light that told him he was not at home. He closed his eyes and winced as he remembered the night before, then opened them again to see Jude lying beside him. She was gone, completely unconscious, and he knew that if his marriage to Sally survived this it would survive anything.

He remembered leaving the cemetery with her and taking her back to her flat. He also vaguely remembered going out to buy more white rum when they had finished the bottle she had already had. He was quite sure he had not had sex with her.

Sally would think he had, of course. She was like all women in that respect. She thought that his caring about Jude was because he still wanted her. Yet he had not wanted Jude sexually for years. Why would he? Thanks to the heroin, Jude was now asexual as far as he was concerned. As far as she was concerned too. Sex had never really meant anything to her other than a means to an end. She had, however, always been more sexually active than he had. In fact, by the time he had taken up with her she had had more sexual encounters than Bill Clinton, and Tyrell used the expression advisedly because she had been doling out blow jobs for years. Jude, as a good working girl, honestly didn't see oral sex as any kind of betrayal and had nearly convinced Tyrell of that. But only nearly.

He closed his eyes once more at the humiliation of finding himself back with her.

He remembered how even when he had found all that out, about her extra-curricular activities, he had still wanted her. She had held an attraction for him he had never fully understood. She had been like a hidden cancer to him, he had never realised until later what she had done to him and her son.

She had been his world once, and therefore his world had become as small and petty as hers.

As time went by the sexual favours she traded in to finance her habit had become more and more outlandish and she was getting paid accordingly, seeing it as something funny, something so hilarious she would try and laugh about it with him. And because at the time he had been obsessed with her he had laughed, or tried to laugh at least. What had she done to him that had made him forgive her so much? What did she have that made him overlook so much?

Whatever it was, it had made him take whatever she decided to dole out to him and be grateful for it. Consequently anything she had done, and she had done things that would make most prostitutes blanch, had not really seemed important in the big scheme of things. Jude had become all in all to him. It had taken him years really to see the big picture. See the world beyond her and her needs.

Jude would do anything to get what she wanted out of life, and that meant literally *anything*. Sonny had had to come to terms with that at an early age and had actually coped with the knowledge much better than his father ever had.

Sally, when he had met her, had been like a breath of fresh air. Yet Tyrell knew that if he learned she had done half the things Jude had done, he would blank her completely and walk away from her without a second's thought.

But he also knew that if Sally ever did that to him, slept around like that, then it would have been *meant*, she would have done it *deliberately*. Whereas with Jude it was nothing, all that really mattered was satisfying her craving for drugs.

Sally would never hurt him, not like Jude had. She wouldn't stand there and look him in the face as if he was the one with the problem. Yet Jude had done just that, so many times, and he had overlooked what she had done, overlooked what he had heard about her, because she was an addict and addicts were not responsible for their actions.

Or were they? Was his sister Hettie right? She always maintained that Jude only did what she did because he let her and in a tiny part of his mind Tyrell had always agreed with her, though he had never said it out loud.

Jude was like a disease, and he and his mother had ignored that fact because once you accepted it you would have to do something about it and they both knew there was nothing anyone could do about her.

Only Jude could help herself, they all knew the truth of that, but the guilt he felt for leaving her was still raw. Probably because of it he could not have left her last night if his own life had depended on it. He had missed his own son's wake for her, and in a way he was glad about that. It had been hard enough facing up to Sonny's death without the funeral as well. He imagined everyone trying to find nice things to say about his son and failing. Saw his poor mother surrounded by her family all busily pretending to her that Sonny's death was a tragedy when to everyone else it wasn't, it was just a foregone conclusion.

Tyrell wiped his hand across his face. The feeling of being out of control was familiar in these surroundings. Jude had always affected him like that. He realised now she had probably made Sonny feel the same way too. He closed his eyes once more. Sally was going to kill him and she had every right. At this moment he didn't care.

He slipped from the bed and stared down at Jude. She was snuffling in her sleep, her face harsh in the early-morning light. He thought briefly again about his Sal. She looked wonderful in the morning, but then she had no reason not to. If Sally had a drink you got the fireworks out. He pushed the uncharitable thought from his head, but how he wished he could find a happy medium with his women.

Tyrell walked quietly along the hallway to the kitchen. Putting on the kettle, he lit one of Jude's Bensons. He had not smoked a cigarette in years but he needed one this morning. It was funny but when he had been with Jude he had smoked like the proverbial chimney and since he had left her he had rarely touched them. He only smoked these days when he was stressed, and usually the stress was caused by the woman lying asleep not ten feet away from him or by the son he had buried the day before.

It was still early, dawn was just breaking. He watched the lights going on in the other flats, could see TV screens flickering in the distance, and wondered at the fact that his son would never see anything like this again. Seventeen years old and he was gone forever. Never to be held again, never to be loved again. Not that his mother had held him for years.

God certainly was a hard task-master.

His own mother was always talking about a vengeful God, and at this moment Tyrell hated Him, almost as much as he hated himself for never being there for his son. His boy was dead and the world was still carrying on. The sun still came up and the clouds still gathered for rain. It felt wrong somehow. There should be more than this to mark the loss of a young life.

Tyrell pulled deeply on his cigarette once more. The clouds were growing darker and he knew it was going to pour down. Somehow the estate always looked storm-laden; it was as if this place attracted bad weather.

He wondered if Sally was awake, and if so whether she was contemplating his demise. Not that he'd have blamed her if she was.

He made coffee and listened as Jude moved around the bedroom. He heard her go into the bathroom, heard her coughing her guts up. He actually heard her passing water. He had forgotten how thin the walls were in these flats. There was literally no privacy here. You could hear baths emptying, toilets flushing, people having sex. Could hear fighting, laughing, babies crying, children being beaten or tickled depending on which flat the noise was coming from.

Once he had lain beside Jude and listened to it all, laughing or frowning depending on what was going on. Now he just found it depressing. This was Jude's life as it had been his life, then his son's. Maybe if he had stayed things might have turned out differently. But no, he was fooling himself. When he had finally sussed Jude out for the leech she was, sucking the life from everyone around her, he had run a mile and waited patiently for his eldest son to do the same. Confident that Sonny would run out on her eventually.

Only now it was too late. He had left his boy here to pick up the pieces of Jude's wasted life and this was the result.

Sally was awake. Instead of jumping out of bed and making breakfast for her sons she just stayed there alone, wondering where her husband was and how she could physically maim him when he finally showed up.

The utter humiliation of the day before still stung: the pitying looks of his family, the questions from the boys about their daddy's whereabouts. The sadness in Verbena's eyes as she had realised what had happened. Poor Verbena, always trying to explain about Jude, and her needs.

Fuck Jude and fuck her needs.

It felt good cursing in her head. Sally did it sometimes to relieve the pressure, and the pressure was building up now to dangerous levels. If Tyrell didn't get his arse back home within the hour she was leaving him. Once and for all she was going to go, and as her mother would be sure to point out, not before time.

Her mother had never understood or liked the fact that Jude was still everybody's darling. Had seen it as a slight on her own daughter that a drug addict took precedence over a woman who was educated and beautiful and far too good for the Rastaman who had swept her off her size four feet. From the moment her mother had found out about Sonny Boy and learned of his reputation, she had warned Sally it would end badly.

Sally had liked Sonny Boy to begin with, in her own way even cared for him, but as time had gone on and Sonny Boy had grown up and his mother had still been a big part of their lives, she had started to resent him herself.

Why couldn't it have been Jude who died?

All the famous junkies died young, so why was it that Jude seemed immune to death? She jacked up, was always out of her skull, and yet she looked OK. If she had died, life would have been so much easier for everyone.

Sally was ashamed of her own thoughts now, for wishing Jude dead. But the truth was, she had wished her dead for years. She thought back to all the times Tyrell had left her to go and see to Jude, poor Jude, wonderful, bleached-blonde Jude. Jude the mother of his first-born son. Jude the woman who still had the power to drag *Sally's* husband across London on a whim.

Finally she started to cry.

The boys burst through the door. Seeing her distress, they hugged and kissed her and she could see the fear on their little faces as she cried bitter tears. She was crying for herself and for her boys who, no matter what they did, would never be able to take the place of the brother they had buried the day before.

Sonny Boy was dead and gone and consequently no one would ever be able to live up to him. It had been bad enough when he had been alive, now that he was dead they had no chance.

Once more she felt the urge to hurt Tyrell, but even more she wanted to hurt Jude. Now Sonny was dead, she'd decided that if her husband went near that woman once more she would divorce him and take the kids. There was no reason for him to run over there any more. Sonny was gone, that part of his life was over and done with.

Sally was smiling now, the tears drying as she realised she finally had a stick to beat her husband with, as beat him she would.

'Come on, boys, let's get you breakfast, shall we?'

'Where's Daddy?'

She looked down into her son's face.

'He had some unfinished business, sweetheart. It should be all over by now.'

Her mobile rang and she picked it up off the dressing table. It was Tyrell. Still smiling widely at her sons she rejected the call.

Let him sweat, she was sick to death of the lot of it.

Tammy could see the evidence of her husband's night out written clearly all over his face. The stubble, the heavy red jowls and bloodshot eyes told her he had been on a drinking marathon again.

It was happening a lot lately.

She hoped now that the boy's funeral was over it would finally put an end to it all. Even though she had liked the notoriety at first, it had begun to interfere with her sex life. Everywhere she went people recognised her, and if she wanted to carry on her liaison with the little Greek waiter she had been cultivating then the sooner they drew a line under this the better.

The boys had been getting grief at school as well, but for the money they paid the place they could sort it out for her. Then when her sons came home she would get the names of the kids involved from them and give the mothers a piece of her mind.

If only Nick could sort things out like she did. He dwelt on

113

everything, whereas she just got on with it all. She smiled to herself. That was women for you. The power behind the throne and the real reason men made it in life. 'From mother to wife,' as her auntie used to say. She didn't finish the saying which ended, 'from the wife to a bird.'

As Tammy sipped her tea she felt an urge to punch her husband square in the face. She was so lonely at times. Even now, while they sat at breakfast together, he didn't have a word to throw at her. Even a row would be better than this total silence.

Nick looked so lost, so sad, that it annoyed her. She had felt like that for years, for all the good it had ever done her. Now he was a national hero, had the world at his feet as far as she was concerned, and all he could do was sit and feel sorry for himself.

'Oh, for crying out loud, Nick, get a grip!'

Her husband's miserable face was killing her. In fact she couldn't for the life of her understand why he wasn't celebrating. He ignored her as he flicked through the local paper. He had found over the years that if you blanked Tammy often enough she shut up naturally. She was like a kid in that respect. If you didn't take any notice, she went off in a huff and picked on someone else. When he saw her pick up her mobile he smiled inwardly. One of her friends would now be the recipient of her venom.

When she walked from the kitchen he gave up any pretence of reading and sipped at his now lukewarm coffee. It was over, finally it was all over and he was still a free man, able to go about his business and live his life.

In one way this knowledge excited him. His background and environment made him hate Old Bill so in a way he relished the fact he had got one over on them. But in another way he hated the fact he had got away with murder.

Because when all was said and done that was exactly what it was. It didn't matter how much his wife and friends twittered on about the circumstances, he had taken that boy's life. Now he was having to live with that knowledge and he had a feeling it was going to be harder than any prison sentence.

He saw Sonny Boy Hatcher's face first thing in the morning and last thing at night. He wondered what the boy would be doing if he was still alive; wondered if he might even have become a fully functioning member of society.

Nick doubted that very much, but stranger things happened at sea. He wished he had someone he could confide in, someone he could talk to about the feelings bottled up inside him. He reminded himself of the night before, the fights he had tried to have and the one he had managed to orchestrate.

At times he felt like he was having a breakdown. His heart would race and his stomach constantly ached. He felt as if he was going to die himself. And the crying . . . He cried like a baby, unable to stem the tears, feeling such fear and revulsion for what he had done.

It was terrible to have all that weighing him down. It was as if Sonny Hatcher hadn't died at all but lived on in Nick's mind, a constant presence that filled his thoughts and pricked his guilty conscience.

'Don't go, Tyrell, please.'

Jude's voice was quiet and for once it sounded genuinely sorrowful. He could see fear in her eyes at the thought of being alone, truly alone, for the first time in years. He knew it would be a daunting prospect for her but he also knew the sooner she got used to it the better. The night before he had not had it in him to deny her his company, they had just buried their child after all, but now the fear of what he would be going home to was uppermost in his mind. Sally was not answering the phone, and that was worrying him.

'I can't hack it on me own yet.'

He looked into Jude's blue eyes and saw real emotion in them.

'I gotta go, Jude. I am sorry, man, but Sally is pissed off with me big-time.'

Jude looked into his handsome face and felt her fingers curl into talons. She would get her way. She would keep him near her if it was the last thing she ever did.

Tyrell was reading her mind all the time, but she was unaware of that. He knew her better than she knew herself.

He picked up his suit jacket and slipped it on. It felt incongruous to be dressed in a black suit and crumpled white shirt in the disarray of Jude's home. For the first time ever he had smelt the underlying air of decay that surrounded her. It was in her bedding, in the towels, in the bathroom, in the fridge and cupboards. Why had he never noticed it before? As he had wiped his face on a grubby towel the stench had hit him like never before.

He'd realised then that what he was really experiencing was his son's life. His two younger boys with Sally as their mother wiped their faces on towels that smelt of flowers, slept in bedding that was crisp and clean. They ate good nutritious food that didn't fight for space alongside cans of Tennant's Super in the fridge.

Jude had failed their boy, but he had failed Sonny worse than that even. He had left him here. Tyrell had told himself it was because a boy needed his mother, that it was because Jude had nothing else so how could he take her son from her, when in reality he had left the boy here to cope with her when he'd finally tired of it himself.

He shook his head and said loudly, 'I'm going, Jude. I'll pop in another time and see how you are, OK?'

He wanted to get home and wash the smell of this place from his body. His breath was sour from the white rum of the night before but nothing would induce him to use any of the toothbrushes in that bathroom. He had cleaned them with water and his finger. He just wanted to run away from all this now, it was too distressing to see the squalid reminders of his son's life now that Sonny was dead.

Looking around him at this dump that passed for a human habitation Tyrell was beginning to panic at the thought of staying here a second longer. He could see Jude working herself up to laying a massive guilt trip on him with every passing second.

'You can't leave me, Tyrell, not like this, not with my baby still warm in the ground.'

She was starting to cry now. She was good at crying, though only once or twice had she managed to shed tears of real emotion. This time was not one of them.

'Stop it, Jude, come on.'

'It's all right for you. You can waltz out of here and back to your nice normal life with Sally and your boys. And what am I left with, eh? Fuck all as usual . . .'

She lit a cigarette. After coughing heavily she shrieked, 'Just leave me! Just fuck off out of it, why don't you? We never mattered anyway. Not to you.'

'Don't say that, Jude. You know the trouble you've caused me with Sal over the years . . .'

'Oh, Sal, marvellous Sal! What about this family, Tyrell? Me and Sonny, what about us?' She was poking herself none too gently in the chest as she spoke with nicotine-stained fingers.

'What about you, Jude? I stayed with you last night. I can't stay all day as well, that would really cause ructions.'

He was trying to reason with her even though he knew he was wasting his time.

She changed tack then, seeing her chance.

'I suppose I'd better get used to being on me own, get used to being without me boy. It's all right for you, ain't it? You've got two more.'

She sat on the edge of the sofa and he could see the varicose veins in her ankles and the pitted skin between her toes where she sometimes injected herself. Her feet were a disgrace. The nails were dirty and the hard skin was yellowed and looked as if it was decaying.

Those feet had rested on his calves the night before and he felt the bile rising inside him at the thought. It was as if he was seeing Jude for the first time. Really seeing her, and the life she led.

'I am going, Jude, and nothing you say will change that. I'll pop back in the week.'

He took a wad of money from his pocket and thrust it towards her. He could see a couple of fifty-pound notes among the fivers and expected her to snatch it from his hand as usual but for once she didn't. It was a calculated gesture and they both knew it.

'I don't need money, I need company.'

He shook his head sadly.

'What you need, sweetheart, is someone to get stoned with and it ain't going to be me.'

Jude saw the determination in his eyes. Sighing, she turned from him, stabbing the cigarette out in the saucer that passed for an ashtray.

'You walk out of here now and that is it, Tyrell, I mean it.'

Her voice was low. When she looked up at him again he could see the determination on her face. It was the look she always wore when she was out of gear or needed money for something, the look that said she would get what she wanted. As she invariably did. She was stronger at such times than anyone realised, even herself.

'I'm not joking, Tyrell. If you walk out on me now, you'll regret it.'

'Why? What are you going to do, Jude, kill yourself?'

He knew she had used that one on their son, knew she had made him toe the line with that threat on many occasions, especially Christmasses and birthdays when he had been due to be with his father and his brothers. Unless she had a bloke or a new dealer who would allow her plenty of credit. Then she couldn't wait to get him out of the door.

She nodded then.

'What else is there for me now?'

Her voice was low and hurt. She sounded completely serious.

Tyrell sighed and said sarcastically, 'You could pick that money up from the floor and get yourself some gear. That's what you usually do, ain't it? That's what you would be doing if Sonny was still alive.'

He could not believe what he had just said and neither could Jude. All those years of trying to stop her from killing herself with drugs and now he was actually advising her to take them?

'You bastard!'

He shrugged.

'I just can't do this any more, Jude. Don't you realise that I have lost a child as well? My first-born son was buried yesterday and I really don't have to listen to all this shit any more. As you so rightly pointed out, I have two other boys who, incidentally, really loved their brother and will miss him. I think they might need me as well today. The world, believe it or not, Jude, does not revolve solely around you.'

In a part of her brain she knew he was right, but she wasn't one to listen to the voice of her conscience. Jude only ever did what she wanted and only understood what she allowed herself to.

Tyrell saw her as she came towards him and put his hands up to defend himself, but her nails caught his face anyway before he grabbed her by the wrists. He struggled with her for a few seconds before she sagged at the knees. He kept hold of her wrists as she dropped on to the floor. She was crying once more.

'I can't cope without him, not today, Tyrell. I can't go on without him, I can't.'

He pulled her up gently and hugged her to him. He was nearly crying himself as he pleaded with her. 'Please stop this, Jude. Please give me a fucking break. I can't police you all the time, girl, like poor Sonny did. I have got to get home, can't you understand that? My family need me as well.'

They were both startled by the front door opening then and turned to look towards the doorway of the living room. Three young men walked in. Tyrell recognised them as friends of Sonny's. They had been at the funeral the day before.

'How the fuck did you lot get in?'

His voice was harsh. He wasn't sure he wanted these youngsters walking in and out as it pleased them. Didn't Jude have any idea at all about the real world? He pushed her away from him gently and she slumped back on to the couch, leaning forward awkwardly to pick up the money lying on the floor.

'What are you? Fucking deaf? How did you get in?'

'Through the front door.'

His demand was answered by the tallest boy who spoke to Tyrell with no respect whatsoever.

'You want me to mash your face, boy?'

The boy blanched at the annoyance in the large Rasta's voice. He knew that Sonny's father could be a handful and wished he had remembered that before he had spoken. But the urge to show off in front of his friends was paramount in his life and he was now paying the price.

'Leave them alone, Tyrell. Anyway, I thought you were leaving.'

Jude's voice was dismissive and he felt an urge to slap her face but calmed himself down enough to say almost normally, 'Of course. You were just seeing me out, weren't you, when we were so rudely interrupted.'

Even Jude managed a smile at the tone of his voice.

Tyrell looked the boys over and sighed inwardly. These were his son's friends and he had no interest in them whatsoever. You could see what they were just by looking at them. The small blond one was already stoned out of his nut.

'Were you good friends with Sonny Boy?'

The question was directed to the tall boy with the surly face and short cropped hair.

Gino nodded.

'You knew everything about him, I expect?'

120

' 'Course.'

The words conveyed the message 'more than you did'.

'Then where did he get the gun, clever bollocks?'

Tyrell turned to a white-faced Jude as he said, 'Put the kettle on, I think I might stay for a while after all.'

Chapter Eight

'For fuck's sake, Nick, you're starting early even for you.'

He swallowed down his vodka and burped loudly.

'Who are you, me mum?'

He pushed himself up from the table and wandered towards the bar. The head barmaid Candice was watching him warily. She could feel the anger coming off him and sighed heavily. It was going to be another one of those days.

There had been plenty of them lately. It was as if Nick had moved into the pub. He was there when she went home and there when she arrived in the morning. It was getting wearing. She had her own little scams afoot and didn't need the added pressure.

'I feel like I am, having to keep reminding you about your drinking and not eating and the fact that you keep starting fights with the customers . . .'

She watched his reflection in the bar mirror. He rolled his eyes and she felt a moment's anger.

'Shag off, Candice, for fuck's sake. Give me a break from your poxy voice. I might as well be at home with Tammy.'

Candice grinned at him as she said seriously, 'Now come on, Nick, I ain't that bad.'

He was chuckling as he replied, 'If she heard you say that, you'd be spitting teeth for a week.'

'You seem to forget me and Tammy go way back. She wouldn't pick a fight with me.'

He knew it was true. No one in their right mind would pick a fight with Candice; she was like a bloke in the aggression stakes. In fact it was one of the reasons she ran the bar so well. No one would willingly take her on now. Too many had tried over the years. He liked her, always had. She was friendly without the usual female fluttering. What you saw was what you got, and she was a good-looking woman.

'Lovely tits' was something he had heard said of her many times over the years. He had also heard her favourite answer to anyone who had the gall to say it to her face. Unrepeatable though the answer often was it had always made him smile.

'Come on, have a cup of coffee with me, eh?'

He shook his head.

'Have a vodka with me instead.'

She sighed again, pulling down her cropped top and then hitching up her skin-tight jeans. She yawned loudly as she said: 'Fuck off. Unlike you, Nick, I have to do a day's work.'

'Come out the back and have a shag then.'

Candice grinned.

'You'd get a shock if I said yes, wouldn't you?'

'Too right I would. After what I just put away, I couldn't get it up if you paid me, love.'

She touched him gently on the arm as she said, 'Come on, have a coffee with me then get yourself down to the site office.'

As she spoke George Michael came over the bar courtesy of the new sound system. He was singing 'Careless Whisper' and Nick suddenly felt the urge to cry.

That was happening a lot lately.

Shaking her head, Candice walked back behind the bar. Taking out her handbag, she cut two smooth lines of top-grade cocaine expertly.

'Come on, Nick, snort this. It'll sort your head out and sober you up a bit.'

He minced behind the bar like a woman and she laughed out loud. After he'd snorted both lines he said loudly in an American accent, 'I have an eighth in me pocket. You can have it, sweetheart, for being employee of the month.'

Candice wiped the excess from around his nostril and laughed: 'Go home, go to work, just fucking *go* somewhere!'

As he put his jacket on she sang along to the music. He was opening the door to leave when she shouted, 'Ain't you forgotten something?'

Nick raised an eyebrow quizzically.

'Employee of the month?'

She held her hand out to him and he placed the small package in it. Candice grinned. It was a heavy eighth, exactly what she needed for a day in the bar.

It was strange seeing Nick snort. Usually he hated it around him, but she guessed rightly that he was feeling things still and in that way she felt sorry for him. He had been through the mill lately, but he was also rich and respected. You couldn't have it all ways as Nick Leary would eventually find out.

When she heard his car pull away she picked up her mobile and tapped in a number. 'He's on his way and he's half cut again.'

She turned the phone off without even bothering to wait for an answer. She cut herself a line and snorted it quickly. Once the regulars arrived it would be like a mad house and she would have to talk twenty to the dozen and serve three people at once. Just as she wiped her nose and rubbed her lips together to moisten her lipstick the first customer arrived.

Candice smiled at him and poured him his usual drink. It was a good job she had here and she knew it, but if the word on the street was true then Nick was pissing it all away.

She hoped he got it sorted sooner rather than later. He was starting to get on her nerves.

*   *   *

'I mean, who would give my Sonny a gun?'

'Oh, leave it out, Tyrell! And you call yourself a fucking Rasta? You can buy a gun in the local pub for a fucking score.'

'Not that kind of gun you couldn't, Jude. It was top quality merchandise, and it had been used in an armed robbery. I think we can safely assume the police believe our son was involved in that too. It's one of the reasons the CPS wouldn't prosecute. So don't talk to me about guns that cost a fucking score!'

Jude was sick of the whole conversation.

'What good would it even do finding out where the gun come from, eh? You want to sort someone out, you go and see Leary. He's the one who killed Sonny.'

'Not that fucking tune again, Jude. You can't blame the man for protecting his own! How many times . . . The gun was high-velocity. If Sonny had shot it he would have sprayed the fucking place with enough bullets to wipe out this block of flats!'

Jude rolled her eyes to the ceiling.

'Precisely. So why didn't he then?'

Tyrell shook his head so hard his dreads slapped his face.

'Are you telling me that Sonny should have shot the man? Is that what you're saying?'

Jude sat down, defeated.

'Of course not . . . I don't know what I mean, Tyrell. Just fuck off, will you? All you're doing is depressing me.'

He took a deep breath to calm the rapid beating of his heart.

'So none of you has any idea where he got the gun from?'

The tall boy left the room. Tyrell could hear him passing water in the bathroom in short staccato bursts. He wondered where the boy got the money for the crack he was so obviously on.

He waited for the boy to come back. Instead he walked from the flat, his footsteps loud as he thumped heavily down the flights of stairs.

'Where's he gone then?'

No one answered.

'This is a fucking joke, Jude, but I will find out what the score is, and believe me, when I do you had better be ready for fireworks.'

'Oh, piss off.'

Tyrell was annoyed.

'You know more than you are letting on, Jude, but I'll find out the score in the end.'

'Go home to your family, Tyrell, I don't need all this now. I can't cope with any more today, I need a breather.'

Her voice was harsh and he knew she was telling the truth as she saw it. The two young men who remained would be company enough for her. He wondered briefly which of the three boys scored for her and guessed rightly that it was probably the one who had just had it on his toes.

So much for the earlier dramatics.

He walked from the flat quickly. It was only when he was outside that he realised he didn't have any money left for a cab and couldn't remember where he had left his car.

Gary Proctor was looking over the warehouse with interest. It would be well worth the money and the commitment required to turn it into a grafting place. They needed somewhere to keep all the equipment they used for the raves and the private parties. This was ideal. It was well equipped, had a blinding alarm system and was also centrally placed for the people who would ultimately use it.

He phoned Nick to OK the purchase and was not surprised to find that his phone was turned off as usual. Gary left a message for him to ring back and then rolled himself a joint as he glanced around once more at the enormous space, picturing its potential.

Nick was a pain lately, but everyone hoped that now he could draw a line under things and they could all get back down to business.

A young man with dyed blond hair and a lisp asked him if he was finished yet. Gary smiled lazily as he told him to come inside and shut the door. The boy was nervous and had every reason to be. Gary Proctor knew his own rep and he knew it worked for him.

This boy was driving him for the day so he felt he had the right to ask a favour of him. After all, he was going to pay him a hefty wedge and they were alone, so why not take advantage of it?

'Want a puff?'

'What is it, black?'

'Nah, scuff. Me mate brings it over from Amsterdam.'

The boy shook his head vigorously.

'Don't touch it.'

'Really, what do you touch?'

The boy shrugged, his slim athletic body shown off to best advantage in the tight-fitting T-shirt and jeans he wore.

'Skunk, Es, a bit of coke now and again . . . mushrooms.'

He was bragging in that inane way seventeen year olds inevitably did when talking to anyone over thirty.

Gary toyed with the idea of telling him that he had grown his own mushrooms years before and that he was responsible for most of the Es that hit the clubs in the south east. Especially his own clubs. He took a cut from every dealer in there, plus selling them the gear in the first place.

Instead he smiled at the boy.

'You think you could do a good set for me tonight?'

The boy nodded eagerly.

'Yeah, man. Fuck! I mean, 'course I could.'

'Come here then.'

The boy edged towards him, slowly picking up the nuance in his voice.

'Come on, son, you ain't silly, are you? You know what I want.'

Gary knew that if Nick found out about this he would kill him, but he was past caring. Anyway the boy would be too scared to say anything, he would make sure of that. The kid's name was Jerome and he wanted to be a DJ. Gary had just offered him a spot in one of the clubs he managed. He might act as if the clubs were his, sometimes even thought they were the amount of time he put in seeing to them all, but in fact they were Nick Leary's. Gary chose to forget that for the moment.

Jerome wasn't queer, Gary would lay money on it. Which, unfortunately for him, was the boy's chief attraction. Gary lazily unbuttoned his trousers, watching the boy's eyes. He saw the pupils dilate as Jerome realised what was expected of him.

Gary laughed in anticipation. This was the bit he really liked, the bit that turned him on.

'Get your laughing gear around that.'

The boy was stepping backwards now, shaking his head and waving him away with his hands as if Gary had just offered him a sandwich and he was trying to say he was full up.

'Leave it out, man, I ain't into all that queer shit.'

Gary grinned once more. He had two gold teeth. They glinted in the harsh sunlight coming through the roof panels. He was a big-set man, barrel-chested, with short legs that were now planted firmly on the ground.

'Get over here now, boy. I ain't in the mood for no girly shite. Get your mouth round that.'

'You can fuck off, Gary, I ain't going near it.'

The boy turned to leave and Gary struck him a blinding blow to the side of his head. He punched him three more times, each harder than the last, then when Jerome was on the floor, dragged him to his knees by his hair.

'You have two choices, son. You can do this with your teeth still intact or with them scattered round this floor, but either way, son, you are doing it. Do you get my drift?'

The boy was crying now, sobbing.

Gary, however, was laughing his head off. He liked it like this, liked the fear, it added to his excitement. Unfortunately for Jerome he decided there and then that he would not be doing the favour for anything.

So Gary had to be far more persuasive than usual.

Lance Walker was lying on a cold floor and he was trussed up like a chicken. His head was throbbing and his mouth was dry. He knew he had been taken and the knowledge annoyed him.

His arms were burning with pain from being tied tightly behind his back for so long, and he knew that even if he were untied he would not be able to use them. He looked around him and in the dimness he could make out machinery, but what sort he couldn't tell.

The place stank of mildew and he guessed rightly that he was in a basement. It was so quiet though, he knew he was in an empty property. The place had the neglected feel of a disused house and he wondered briefly whether he would walk out of there. Somehow he very much doubted it.

His personality did not make him fearful often, but now he was uneasy at the thought of being at someone else's mercy. People were usually at *his* mercy and he knew that the irony of his situation would please a lot of his contemporaries.

'You are awake at last then?'

The voice made him jump and he turned over with difficulty to see Nick walking out of the shadows, a cigarette in his hand and a smile on his face. 'You fucking piece of shit, Leary. Let me up and fight me like a man. But you ain't a fucking man, are you?'

The words were delivered with enough hatred to start an average war.

Nick laughed, he had to admire the man. He was tied up and helpless yet he still had the front to mouth him off.

'You never learn, do you, Lance? Anyone else would have the

nous to try to placate the man who had drugged and trussed them up like a kipper. You was a thicko at school and you're still a fucking Dumbo all these years later. Now where's my money?'

Lance stared up at Nick and his eyes burned with hatred.

'Everyone lost their money, Nick, you know that. We all lost out, the puff was delivered and dropped into the sea and the fucking bastard plod were waiting for us. You were there, you know what happened.'

Nick dropped his cigarette by the man's head and watched as the smoke curled upwards. He put it out gently with his shoe and then lit another one. Then he said in a quiet voice, 'All I know is, Lance, we all paid you a fucking hefty wedge and then like a crowd of cunts we waited by the sea in pissing fucking rain for the drop and as we saw the bales being dumped over the edge of the boat we all got out of our nice warm motors to collect and the next thing we knew fucking plod was all over the place.'

Lance shrugged with difficulty.

'It happens. You know the score, we've all been there before and no doubt we'll all be there again. It's the nature of drug dealing, unfortunately it's illegal, and the filth do tend to try and stop the bigger operations. Annoying, true, but also a fact of our fucking lives. You can't win every time, Nick.'

Nick knelt down and said loudly now, 'I have it on good authority, that the puff that was dumped over the side of the boat was in fact straw, and that filth had been alerted days before. When they finally stopped chasing us and looked in the plastic sacks they realised that we had *all* been had over. Now, I wonder who could have set that up? You, by any chance?'

'Who told you that load of old pony?' The man's voice was high with indignation and also with a trace of fear.

Nick grinned once more and Lance knew it was over.

'Wouldn't you like to know? Now, for the last time, where the *fuck* is my money?'

Lance's biggest problem was the fact he would happily cut off his own nose to spite his face. Any other man would have tried to placate the person who was willing and happy to remove him from the earth. Not Lance. It had now become a battle of wits and instead of putting his hands up to the capture he closed his eyes and said in a slow guttural voice, 'Bollocks to you and bollocks to your fucking money. You think you are so hard, don't you, but I know all about you, Leary, *everything*. You would do well to remember that.'

Nick did laugh then and it was loud, heavy laughter. Lance knew that no matter how much he screamed no one was going to hear him.

He wondered once more where he was but knew that Nick was not going to tell him. Standing over the man, Nick brought his foot down with all the force he could muster on to Lance's face, then he ground the heel of his shoe into the man's bloody and bleeding nose.

'You are really fucking me off, Lance, now for the last fucking time, where is my poke?'

Tammy was shopping in Brentwood. She was wearing clothes that cost enough to fund a year's missionary work in a Third World country, and she was starving. Only not for food. Her favourite sustenance came from young men.

She punched Costas's number into her mobile and when she got no answer just stopped herself from leaving a message. She wasn't stupid. She never left messages or texts, nothing that could put her in the frame should it all fall out of bed with her current squeeze.

The first time she had almost been blackmailed it had hit her hard. She had believed it was her sparkling personality and humungous breasts that had been the attraction. It had never occurred to her that it was also her seemingly inexhaustible credit cards. So now she didn't buy many presents for her amours, and then only if they serviced her according to her wants and not theirs.

But it had been a learning curve and Tammy was always open to new experiences. It was, she thought, part of her charm.

If only she could get her husband out of her head for longer than five minutes at a time, she would be all right.

She walked inside a small boutique, her eye having been caught by a black Fendi radio bag. As she examined it and caressed the luxury of the leather she decided to treat herself. At only six hundred quid, she reasoned, it was in fact a snip.

She handed it to the pretty assistant and smiled.

'I'll take it, sweetheart.'

The assistant, a tall blonde in her twenties, smiled back happily as she began the elaborate packaging of the handbag. It was like a work of art when she had finished and Tammy happily passed her one of her gold cards. She sat on the suede chair awaiting her credit card slip, planning the outfit she would wear to show the bag off to its best advantage and who to invite to the bag's debut outing. She always treated her purchases as if they were life-changing events – which for Tammy they often were.

'I'm sorry, Mrs Leary, but the card has been declined.'

Tammy stared at the girl for long moments, before she said quietly, 'I beg your pardon?'

'The card. It's been declined.'

The girl was more embarrassed than she was and for some reason this made it all the worse for Tammy. She had shopped here regularly for years but this would be her last visit, she was convinced of that already.

'There must be some mistake, love, try it again.'

'I did, Mrs Leary, and it was declined a second time. Maybe another card?'

The girl was still smiling but it was forced.

Five credit cards later Tammy was walking from the shop empty-handed. Her face was still burning from the humiliation as she climbed behind the wheel of her Mercedes sports.

She would kill Nick. If it was the last thing she ever did she would kill that bastard stone dead.

Sally was sitting with the boys watching a video when Tyrell arrived home. She did not acknowledge his presence and neither did the boys other than by quick smiles in his direction when he came into the lounge. They had always picked up on atmospheres and Sally, love her, could cause atmospheres that would not look out of place on the moon.

This was a lovely room, and after his night at Jude's Tyrell appreciated it more than ever before. It was painted pale green with white woodwork and a cherrywood floor. To his mind it was beautiful. Sally had a way with rooms. She made them all light and airy, but today it was the smell he liked most – the smell of cleanliness and pot pourri, something that had annoyed him in the past, reminding him a bit too much of his mother's house. Today, though, this room was everything he wanted from a home. It was funny but Sonny Boy had loved this house too. Had always boasted to his friends about his dad's home. It was the only place the boy had ever really relaxed in.

Like his father before him, Jude had stressed him out. It was only here in this calm environment that he totally chilled. He would smooch down on the sofa with his little brothers and watch TV, laughing and joking with them, watching their antics and enjoying the feeling of belonging.

Who was he kidding?

Tyrell was still standing in the doorway trying to convince himself when Sally's words hit him.

'Are you coming in or not?'

Her voice was more of a bark. She was talking to him as if he was one of the kids and this annoyed him. Ever a believer in attack as the best form of defence he took the bait willingly.

'You talking to me, Sal?'

The boys dragged their eyes from the screen at the sound of his voice. This was not the way their father talked to their mother and it shocked them. Both of them sat watching with wide eyes as their father stared his wife down.

'You know something, Sal, you'd better give me a break, girl, because you are starting to get on my nerves.'

Sally just stopped her mouth from dropping open in shock.

'Excuse me?'

Her own voice was high and this annoyed her.

Tyrell was on a roll now. He laughed as he said: 'You heard me. You talking to me now, not one of the kids or one of their little friends. It's me, Tyrell, your husband, the man who buried his child yesterday and had to spend the night placating a woman who has *nothing* left in the world. You hear what I'm saying? *Nothing*.'

He knew he was deliberately making her feel bad but didn't care any more, he was not in the mood for any of this. He was tired, he wanted a bath and something to eat. He also wanted to throw his suit in the trash because he knew he would never wear it again.

And he felt an overpowering urge to slap his wife's scornful face. He wasn't sure why he wanted to do that but the urge was getting stronger by the second.

'Upstairs.'

The boys scrambled from the sofa and Tyrell watched them run from the room. His wife's voice could be very cold at times, he had never really noticed that before. Her hands were on her hips now as she stood up and looked at him dangerously.

'You come in here, into *my* home, and you try and put *me* down in front of *my* children when you spent the night with another woman? I can smell her on you, Tyrell. I can smell the dirt and the stench of that woman and her life, it's still clinging to you after all these years. Now you can go upstairs and you can pack your bags and you can get out and go back where you came from. I don't need you. *We* don't need you.'

She didn't know who was the more shocked by her words, her husband or herself. But he had asked for it. He had been asking for it for years. Well, this time it was finally over for them. Jude Hatcher had got what she wanted. Sally only wondered if it was what the man in front of her wanted.

'You don't care about my Sonny, do you? You never did.'

'Oh, don't be stupid, Tyrell, of course I cared about him. Why wouldn't I? He was a nice kid in his own way. But it's over now, and I am not living with Jude in our lives any more. I can't. If his death means you have to be there for her from now on, then that is it. I've had it.'

It was a fair comment, Tyrell knew that in his heart.

'I'm sorry, Sally, but it's been so up in the air lately, and Jude was in bits yesterday. . .'

' 'Course she was.'

'Don't be sarcastic, Sal. Her son's . . .'

Sally sighed.

'I know her son's dead, but she is always in bits about something, Tyrell. She plays you and you can't see it. If it hadn't have been Sonny's funeral yesterday it would have been something else. You spend more time over there than you do here, and it's because of her, not poor Sonny. I could have understood it if it was Sonny.'

She was talking through clenched teeth now and forced herself to relax.

Tyrell slumped into a chair. It was so comfortable he could quite easily have sat back and dropped off into a nice dreamless sleep.

'This has to stop. You are either here with me and the boys now or it's over, I mean it, Tyrell. You have to keep away from Jude. She is not your responsibility any more.'

He started laughing then, really laughing, it was almost tinged with hysteria.

'Oh, is that right? I am sorry, Sally, I was under the mistaken impression that I was a grown man. I didn't realise I had exchanged one mummy for another.'

He leaped from his seat then and was gratified to see his wife jump in fright.

'Oh, have I raised my voice to you, Sal? Forgive me. Shall I get on the floor and kiss the hallowed ground you walk on? Or better still, how about I write out fifty times, "I shall not fuck off said wife".'

'Don't be so bloody childish. Anyone would think you'd never been hurt before. Sonny is dead but what about us? We're all still alive, if you'd bother to take any notice.'

He stared at her in disgust and all his real feelings, his suppressed feelings, spilled over.

'You could never compete with Sonny, so don't even try. You made it your mission in life to keep him an outsider. I would watch him trying to get into your good books, trying to make you like him. He was a kid, for fuck's sake, and you made him nervous with all your tidying up and your constant fucking correcting him about how he ate, how he sat, how he spoke. Yet he had more life in his little finger than you have in your whole body!'

Sally was hurting now, really hurting. Whatever she had expected today this was not part of it. Yet she knew what he said was true, she had resented the boy. It was only human nature, but the guilt was there nevertheless.

'If I'm that bad then why don't you leave, Tyrell? It sounds to me as if you're only looking for a reason to go. Well, you go, boy, I don't need you.'

She waved him away from her.

'I did everything for your son, everything I could, and it wasn't easy, I can tell you. Jude made sure he didn't feel comfortable with decent people. He robbed you, robbed your family, robbed me. Yet you would put him above me and mine? He took the boys' money on many occasions and they covered up for him. So you go, Tyrell.

137

Go and live with that piece of dirt who mothered your darling Sonny Boy and leave me and my sons to get on with our lives in peace.'

He knew she had every right to say what she was saying but it still felt all wrong to him. She should respect the fact that the boy was dead. Now was not the time to pull Sonny to pieces. She should be helping him through his grief, not making it worse.

He poked a finger in her face.

'You listen to me, Sal, and you listen good. I am that far . . .' he opened his right finger and thumb about half an inch '. . . from topping myself over my boy. I dream of him. I think of him all the time. The guilt I feel is so bad I can't breathe sometimes with the thought of his life and how it turned out. So don't you dare fucking try and give me the bum's rush in me own back yard. Because it won't work. This time it won't work.'

He rifled his pockets for his cigarettes. As he lit one she shrieked, 'Oh, no, you don't! You're not tainting my air with your cigarette smoke. Another of Jude's filthy habits that you've taken up once more.'

He walked from the room, drawing on the cigarette to make as much smoke as possible. As he stamped up the stairs he made loud puffing noises to annoy her. Then in the bathroom he sat on the toilet as the bath ran and cried like a baby.

'Where did he get the gun, God? Just tell me that.'

Tyrell shouted the words over the rushing of the water then he lit another cigarette and lay back in the bath. It wasn't until the water was stone cold that he stopped crying. The boys were playing Sean Paul and Blu Cantrell and the words made him want to cry once more. The track was called 'Breathe' and Sonny Boy had loved it.

Tyrell wondered briefly if he was having a breakdown.

Then he got out of the bath and, still dripping wet, packed a bag. With his wife's eagle eye on him all the time he dressed himself and walked from the house without another word. He didn't know where he was going, but one thing he did know: he could never stay under that roof again.

In his BMW he lit another cigarette and as he drew its smoke into his lungs realised that for the first time in years he felt free.

Angela Leary ran into the hallway as her son's key went into the lock. She had heard his car coming up the drive and was waiting for him as he fell through the front door.

'She is like a lunatic, Nick! She's wrecked the bedroom and the en-suite . . .'

He nodded wearily.

'Good. Can I have a cup of tea, Mum?'

He was not bothered in the least.

' 'Course you can, son, but don't you think you ought to talk to Tammy first?'

He shook his head.

'No.'

Nick laughed.

'Why would I want to talk to her? Anyway, we'll see her soon enough.'

Tammy was tearing down the stairs as he spoke and he looked at his mother as if to say: See.

'Hello, darlin'. What's the matter with you today?'

'You're drunk!'

'And you're ugly but I'll be sober in the morning.'

As a good Irishman his father always maintained that was the only sensible thing Churchill ever said.

Nick pushed Tammy out of his way.

'Make the tea, Mum, I am parched.'

'You bastard, Nick! You'd humiliate me by cancelling me cards . . .'

He laughed once more.

'Oh, they did it then? I thought it would take longer than this.'

Angela watched the two of them gleefully. If he had cancelled Tammy's credit cards then this was going to be a fight. And she for one wanted a ringside seat.

She decided on the kitchen for the venue as there were not too many breakables easily within reach there and she knew that Tammy would be going for anything within arm's reach. But Tammy, for once, just stood there and looked at her husband as if she had never seen him before.

He saw how pretty she was when she wasn't plastered in make-up, saw the cut of her curvaceous figure and the defeated look in her eyes, red-rimmed from crying yet still the same deep blue that had attracted him all those years ago at school.

'You'd really do this to me, Nick?'

He nodded, but even through his drink-fuelled state realised he had done something terrible. Maybe not in other people's book, but what he had done to Tammy was unforgivable in her eyes.

And the worst thing was, he had done it for pure spite.

He opened his arms wide and Tammy threw herself into them. As she cried he rubbed her back and kissed her hair, murmuring endearments.

'I'm sorry, babe, but it was only to teach you a lesson. This spending has got to stop, right?'

She nodded. With tears still running down her face, she made herself smile.

'I love you, Nick. I know you don't love me back, but I do love you, I do!'

'I know that, Tams. God love you, I've always known that.'

Angela walked back into the kitchen disappointed and put the kettle on.

Chapter Nine

Verbena was not surprised at her son staying away from home, it had been on the cards for a long time. But she was surprised by the fact her daughter-in-law seemed to blame her.

Tyrell had been away from Sally for a week now, staying at a friend's, and didn't seem to have any plans for going home. He didn't look too bad on it either, which had been the case on past occasions. But Sal was one of those women who demanded total attention and anyone would eventually find that wearing, Verbena knew.

Now, as Tyrell sat and drank coffee with her, she asked the question she had been aching to ask all week.

'Are you going home, son?'

He sighed.

'I very much doubt it, Mum.'

'You can't just walk away from your marriage. Life is about making compromises, doing things you sometimes don't want to do . . .'

He shook his head impatiently.

'I know what you're going to say but you might as well save your breath.'

'What was it all about?'

She knew, and he knew she knew. But she looked so old sitting there in her chair, her grey hair tamed now but still with tendrils escaping around her wide open face, that he didn't have the heart to hurt her any further. He loved this woman, loved her so much. Yet all he seemed to do was disappoint her.

'Mum, please, I can either do what she wants twenty-four hours a day and lose meself, or I can show her I can live without her.'

'That is fine for you but what about the boys?'

Verbena's voice was clipped now, annoyance coming to the fore.

'They'll survive. I would always look after my kids. What, do you really think I would abandon them?'

She pursed her lips and crossed her arms over her chest, a sure sign she was upset.

'Is that really what you think of me?'

The hurt was in his voice, even in his stance. For the first time ever he felt the urge to slap her face. Not to hurt her, but to snap her back into the real world. She had been stuck in this house for too long.

Verbena picked up on his mood and said quietly, 'Don't blame me if you mess this up. You only have yourself to blame this time. Those two boys need you more than ever now. You should get back home and take care of them. They lost their brother, you know.'

'And I lost my eldest son.'

'Those boys need you to take care of them.'

'I'll take care of them, I always have.'

She shook her head sadly.

'See that you do, boy.'

She said it as if he needed a reminder of his fatherly duties and this made Tyrell angry even though he knew she didn't mean the half of it. It was just the Jamaican mother coming out in her.

He looked her in the eye as he said coldly, 'Look after my boys? Are you joking with me, Mum? I looked after Sonny, didn't I?'

The words hung on the air.

His mother's eyes seemed to be saying, 'And look what happened to him.' She had always believed he should have stayed with Jude for the sake of Sonny Boy. She believed that boys needed their fathers, needed strong male role models, especially if the mother was not up to much which was obviously the case with Jude. But he had refused to sacrifice himself, had felt he could do more for his son by getting him out of a drugs environment and giving him a glimpse of a different way of life.

He had been wrong, he realised that now. But at least his son had known some interludes of normality, some happy times, in his father's company. Tyrell had to believe that or he would go mad. He had at least to hope he had made some difference in his son's life or what would it all have been for?

'Thanks a lot, Mum. I feel so much better for that.'

'He got in with the wrong crowd, didn't have any chance with his mother and her lifestyle. That is why boys need their fathers. Your boys will need you now more than ever, can't you see that?'

She was almost pleading with him.

'That wasn't a boyish prank gone wrong, Mum. Sonny's gun was a top-of-the-range model. He had to have been into some pretty heavy stuff even to have got a sniff of one. This might have Jude written all over it in some ways – maybe he was working for one of her dealers, I don't know – but what I do know is I have to find out if I am ever to know any peace. So don't try and make me out as the villain here, I did my best with Sonny.'

'I am not saying anything to you, son, except that I think you give up on people too easily.'

Tyrell picked up his coat and sports bag, too tired to argue with her. He had only been away from Sal a week but already he felt like a different man. As sad as he was over his son, he could deal with his feelings much better when he was away from his wife. Every time he had tried to grieve at home Sal had made him feel as if he was doing it to spite her and the boys. And he still resented the way she had treated Sonny in the past.

'Don't go stirring up a whole heap of trouble for yourself,' Verbena warned.

He laughed despite himself.

'When I find out what happened maybe I'll be able to sleep again at night.'

'Where you going?'

There was fear in her voice at his leaving her. He smiled, trying his hardest to keep a lid on his feelings.

'I am going to find out where my Sonny got a gun, and who or what made him want to use it.'

Jude looked at the phone number scrawled on the scrap of newspaper and wondered if she dared to use it yet. She had promised herself that she would not until the dust had had plenty of time to settle. Then she would go for the jackpot. Sonny had told her everything but she knew she had to play this one close to her chest. Bide her time.

There was plenty of gear around at the moment and because of the way Sonny had died she was also getting quite a few freebies and mercy wraps. She had never been so well off for drugs in her life.

As she sat in her flat she felt a wave of peace come over her due to the fact that she had enough drugs to see her through the next few days. She would leave the phone number until she wasn't in such a good position. Then the person on the end of the line would pay.

She glanced at a photo of Sonny and poked her tongue out at it. Then, smiling, she blew him a kiss. She was getting used to his being gone. It was funny but lately she felt as if she had been let out of school. She could take what she wanted now, drink what she wanted, and there was no one constantly trying to modify her behaviour. His friends had been so good to her as well, making sure she was taken care of. They loved having somewhere to hang out and she liked the company.

Especially Gino's. If she wasn't mistaken he would be on the brown in no time. He had the temperament for it, the natural laziness combined with carelessness that made a heroin addict.

People who had never tried it didn't understand the feeling it gave you, the complete and utter peacefulness of the high. It was an acquired taste. The first few times you jacked up your body rejected it and the nausea was awful. But it was like anything else: you had to keep at it and then eventually it would all be worth it.

In a way she envied Gino his first taste. That first high was what you tried to re-create day after day, but you never, ever managed to feel that good again.

She was playing Canned Heat. 'On the Road Again' was her favourite track, it mellowed her out. She missed Sonny's music, enjoyed hearing the boys playing it while they puffed. It occurred to her she had not opened the curtains in the flat again but she couldn't gather up the energy to do anything about it. She would get one of the boys to open a window when they came round.

Gino's mother was giving him grief about the amount of time he spent round here apparently and she knew it was hard for him. But he would arrive, he always did.

She leaned back and sank into the broken springs of her sofa. She would blast in a few minutes and set herself up for the rest of the day. But first she would listen to her music. When Sonny had been small, they had sung along with the music. It had made them both laugh for some reason.

She couldn't remember now what the reason was. Like most of her life it was just a blur, a few fleeting memories that, cobbled together, made up some kind of existence.

* * *

'Is Nick about?'

The man's voice sounded disjointed coming over the intercom and Angela said loudly, 'Who wants to know?'

She knew the score in this house. You never let anyone in who you didn't know.

'Tell him it's Stevie D, he'll know me, love.'

She went into the television room.

'There's a man at the gate for you, son. Stevie D. He said you'd know him.'

Nick jumped from the sofa, smiling.

'Let him in! I ain't seen him since we were kids.'

He grinned.

'You remember him, Mum? Steven Daly. He done a fifteen for armed robbery, I used to knock about with him when I was young, before he got a lump.'

She nodded happily, remembering.

'Oh, yes. His mother was a lovely woman, Katherine Daly, died of cancer a few years back. I went to the funeral.'

Steven Daly drove up the impressive drive and marvelled at how well his friend had done since their days as schoolboys together. Though in fairness when he had got his lump Nick had made sure he had a few quid to spend on the inside and also sorted him out a single cell through a friend in the prison service.

Stevie really didn't want to be driving up this drive today, having to do what he had come to do. But Nick would understand, he was sure of that.

Nick stood just inside the front door, calming down the dogs he had recently acquired. This house was something else and Stevie wished he had brought his wife. She would have loved to have seen it. Maybe another time, when the business in hand had been taken care of.

As he parked Nick came outside to greet him, smiling warmly.

'All right, my son? Long time no see.'

Stevie gripped his hand and they held each other's forearm as they shook hands. Nick walked his old friend inside the house, glad for once that his wife was out shagging her current amour.

Angela made a fuss of Stevie and he made all the right noises, telling her about his mother and how he missed her and how he had bought her a Mass that very Sunday. He thanked her for coming to the funeral and commiserated with her on the loss of so many of her friends.

Nick finally rescued him and took him into the library. Even in his evident agitation Stevie was impressed. Nick poured them both large Scotches.

'I'm driving, Nick.'

'Get a fucking cab, you nonce. Remember the old days when you could fill your boots and still drive home in peace?'

Stevie laughed.

'I do. But thank God those days are gone, eh?'

Nick laughed too and nodded.

Stevie saw that his friend was still powerful-looking but noted the way his eyes were sad once again. Sadder even than they had been when he was a kid and had had to live around his father's moods.

And Nick Senior's moods had been legendary.

'Sorry about your recent troubles.'

Nick shrugged, making a show of not really being bothered.

'Shit happens.'

'They'll all think twice before they try and have you over again, eh?'

He nodded but didn't answer directly.

'How's the wife and kids, Stevie?'

'OK. She found it hard at first, me being home after such a long stretch, but we're gradually getting back to normal, you know.'

Nick knew how hard it was for couples when they had been apart for so long to get back into the swing of things. He had

147

always seen Bernice all right for a few quid over the years, it had been expected. But when Stevie had been banged up they had still been young and in love. She had waited for him, with three young kids and a broken heart, no sign of another man. She had done him proud by their standards. He only hoped the wait had been worth it for both of them.

'So how are you, Stevie? There's no way you drove all this way just to wish me well. What's going on?'

He sat down opposite Nick in one of the large leather chairs placed to either side of the fireplace and looked around him at the book-lined walls before answering his friend.

'This is some fucking drum, Nick.'

Stevie's admiration was evident, and also the fact he didn't begrudge his friend his good luck one bit.

Nick nodded, embarrassed.

'It was Tams, weren't it? She has trouble just leafing through an Argos catalogue. We had to have the real McCoy in here.'

He didn't add this room alone had cost over one hundred grand, and that a lot of the first editions on display were his, books he had tracked down and purchased for himself. It would hardly have fitted in with his image, he knew that. It would have sounded as if he was bragging. He always played the house down even as he loved the fact it was his.

Or had loved it once, before Sonny Hatcher made his way inside and died in it.

He topped up his friend's glass as they chatted about nothing, catching up on each other's life. Nick knew Stevie would get to the point in his own good time. Meanwhile he was enjoying having some male company.

'I don't know how to tell you this, Nick, but I have to,' Stevie broached the subject eventually. 'And I have to have some kind of retribution.'

Nick stared at his friend for a few moments before saying in a neutral voice, 'Heavy words, Stevie. Have I offended you, mate?'

The threat was there if you cared to see it.

Stevie shook his head as he answered him.

'Nah, Nick. Give over, mate. This is to do with one of your employees – Gary Proctor.'

Nick sighed.

'What's he done now?'

'I don't know how to say it, Nick. It's fucking totally out of fucking order and I have to spank him – and I mean *spank* him.'

Nick looked at his old friend. His hair was still thick and red though now it was peppered with grey. He had the look of a man not long out of prison: the hesitancy was there, the fine-tuned muscles and the pallor that seemed to cling to a body for a while. He was also very nervous, but he had his rep and Nick knew that Stevie was not scared of him in any way. He was more worried about what he had to say.

Nick got up from the chair and poured them both another drink.

'So come on, spit it out, mate.'

Stevie sighed heavily as if he had the weight of the world on his shoulders.

'You know my sister Laetitia?'

Nick nodded, puzzled.

'Surely someone ain't got her in the club? She must be forty if she's a day.'

Stevie forced a laugh.

'It weren't me, Stevie. She's a bit long in the tooth for me, my son!'

Stevie was laughing now and the sound was pleasant in the quiet of the room.

'Nah, nothing like that. But it is about her son. He's seventeen and a right nice kid. Wants to be a DJ . . . at least, he did until he had a run in with Gary Proctor.'

Nick frowned.

149

'Tell me what Gary has done and what you want from me. If it's a chance in one of the clubs for the kid to show his talent then it's his, I'll see to it meself. If Gary fucked him off I'll put him wise, don't worry.'

Stevie shook his head once more.

'I wish it was that simple. This is so fucking hard, Nick, harder than the time I done in stir.' He swallowed audibly. 'The boy was assaulted by Gary. Jerome put up a fight, bless him, but Proctor creamed him, Nick. The boy's in a right two and eight in hospital. And I am going to personally break Proctor's fucking neck with my bare hands! He ain't hiding behind you or no one else, which is what I came to tell you tonight.'

Nick was intrigued.

'What, Gary slapped the lad? Why?'

Stevie shook his head furiously.

'He didn't *slap* him, Nick, he kicked the shit out of him. That boy is looking at three months in hospital. This ain't just about a slap. Proctor tried to sexually assault him. Tried to get him on his knees. Do you get my drift now?'

'He did *what*?'

Stevie could hear the disbelief in his friend's voice.

'I got it all out of Jerome eventually. I thought he had got a kicking off his mates or something, you know. But I finally got it out of him what had really happened. The boy is in a right state as I said. Apparently Proctor took him to a new warehouse you are buying and told him he would get him a gig if Jerome blew him off.'

'Gary did that?'

Nick's voice was getting higher and higher with disbelief.

Stevie nodded then, utter disgust written all over his face.

'Jerome said no and Proctor attacked him. Tried to force him. Jerome wouldn't have none of it, and fair play to him, who fucking would? He cunted him off, and I tell you now, Nick . . .' Stevie

150

pointed at his friend with a shaking finger, his anger spiralling out of control '. . . that boy is not a spinner. If he said it happened like that then it happened. The funny thing is, Jerome didn't say he was related to me because he wanted to get the gigs off his own back. So that he knew it was because he could really do it, and not because of his family connections. If Gary had known who he was I expect he would have left him alone, but you have to accept that you have a fucking pervert in your circle of associates and it has to be sorted out. And on another note, Nick, me and you will both want this kept quiet for obvious reasons. That is why I am here with you, face to face.'

'Fucking hell!'

Nick shook his head once more.

'I don't believe it. *Gary Proctor*? Are you sure he had the right geezer?'

Stevie was losing patience now.

'Of course I fucking am! This is too serious to make a fuck up, ain't it? It was him all right. Imagine how I felt hearing it all. One of me oldest mates is a fucking shit stabber, and to crown it all a fucking rapist to boot.'

Stevie threw the last of his drink back in one movement and Nick watched him, aware of the menace now emanating from him.

'I could cope with them in the stir – and, believe me, for some of them it was like a fucking busman's holiday. Even on the unit. But that was consenting adults. I ain't having my nephew trumped by that cunt. You want to see the boy. Messed him right up Proctor has, the piece of fucking scum! I mean, who else has he done it to, eh? How many other little boys has he done it to and got away with it, that's what I want to know. Because it ain't something the lads would report to anyone, is it? You got two boys, ain't you, and that cunt is around them, and you didn't know he was a secret fucking lemonade drinker!'

He nodded at the logic of his friend's words.

'Where do you want to take him out?'

Nick wasn't putting up any sort of fight on his man's behalf. This was inexcusable.

'Anywhere, but he is going to pay for this, Nick. That poor little fucker is in a right state, and me sister, well, she thinks he got a kicking from a gang of blokes out on the drink and the hag. I couldn't let on about this to anyone, could I?'

' 'Course not. I'll ring Gary now. He has a little Boxter in Bow. It's quiet and no one knows about it. I'll get him there and we'll be waiting for him together, OK?'

Stevie nodded.

'Thanks, Nick, I knew you would understand, but I can do him on me own.'

Nick shook his head once more and the die was cast.

'Nah, I want to be there by your side to hear what he has to say for himself.'

Stevie grinned.

'Well, it won't be much, will it? Mainly screaming then groaning.' He took out a set of knuckle dusters from his pocket.

Nick laughed along with his friend, but his world that had seemed so safe before the death of Sonny Hatcher now felt as if it had turned upside down.

Tyrell was inside his new home and rolling himself a joint. He actually owned this flat, but like many of his assets Sally knew nothing about it. He had bought many such properties over the years and now had quite a nest egg for his old age. He pulled on the joint and realised he had missed this, missed the freedom of having a puff and a beer when he wanted to.

If he even had a Marlboro Light at home Sally flipped out, fearing it would lead to every other addiction she could think of.

If only she knew.

He hoped she was OK. He had talked to the boys and they didn't seem any the worse for wear. He sometimes thought they understood him better than his wife. At school they had encountered the real world, unlike Sally who shut it out as much as she could. She was more like Jude than she realised, he saw that now. Both of them escaped in different ways. Jude with her skag and poor Sally with her decorating and her needlework and her cooking.

He forced them both from his mind and concentrated on the job in hand. It was a kinger, a six-cigarette-paper dream of a joint, and he was going to smoke it all by himself and then he was going to sleep the sleep of the dead. He had not slept properly for days and it was beginning to show on him. Even his dreads looked defeated.

Tyrell had experienced a terrible shock to his system, he knew that, but he also knew that what was really burning him up was not grief.

He was burning up with the need for revenge.

Gary Proctor was lying in bed watching a video when his wife told him that Nick had called and wanted to meet him at Bow. It was early, but he liked to go to bed and watch a bit of telly when he had experienced a stressful day.

Gary had sore, bruised knuckles from that kid, but he had to give the boy his due, for a skinny little fucker he had put up a fight.

Still, Gary had taught him a lesson about the survival of the fittest he wouldn't forget. He got up and admired himself in the bedroom mirror, then shouted down the stairs, 'Maureen, get me a drink, love.'

He was half-erect from thinking about the boy and what he had nearly got from him. Gary pulled on his penis, enjoying the sensation, and closed his eyes imagining what might have been.

Maureen came in with the drink. Placing it on the dressing table, she said archly, 'Do you mind? The kids could come in and that would be a lovely sight for them, wouldn't it?'

'Oh, fuck off, you miserable old bat.'

Maureen, though, was well able for him and answered sarcastically, 'Pot, kettle and black spring to mind, Gal.'

Then she sneered at him.

'Who'd fucking want you these days? Hardly the answer to a maiden's prayer, are you? I'd rather shag the dog.'

He was laughing at her now.

'Every time I see meself in the mirror I get a hard on, Maureen.'

She rolled her eyes to the ceiling as she said nastily, 'That, Gary, is because you have a face like a cunt.'

She walked from the room and he knew she was laughing at him. Even he had to admit, it was funny. He would store it away for future reference. She was a crack, his Maureen, and in fairness had needed to be considering some of the stunts he had pulled on her over the years.

Gary took time over his hair as he always did. It was his only real vanity. He didn't wonder what was going on with Nick, he would find out soon enough. He assumed it was a bit of skulduggery and he hoped it was a good little earner.

He popped his head round his youngest daughter's door and she waved at him happily. She was eight and safely ensconced in her bed, watching *Law and Order*.

' 'Bye, Daddy. See you in the morning.'

'You can bet on it, princess. I'll make you your brekker, eh?'

She grinned, her face adorable with its gap-toothed smile. He banged on his elder boy's room and got a grunt in reply, but that was par for the course these days. After pecking Maureen on the cheek, Gary left the house wondering what the night would bring.

As he unlocked his car he was whistling happily through his teeth.

Chapter Ten

Nick opened the lock-up garage and walked inside. In the corner was a Calor gas fire which he lit with difficulty. The light here was dim but good enough if you had decent eyesight. It was freezing, though, and they needed some warmth, more than the fire would radiate, so he took out a small hip flask from his coat pocket and two metal shot tumblers. He poured them both a drink and they sipped it as they waited for Gary Proctor's car to arrive. The place was empty except for a few black bin bags.

'Nice and quiet here, Nick, it was a blinding choice of venue.'

'We won't be disturbed, don't worry. Round here even if they heard screams they'd just turn the telly up.'

Nick refilled the glasses.

'I still can't believe it, Stevie. I remember now how he was always giving lifts to those young fellas we worked with. But then I've done it meself, you know, with the raves and that. They're our employees. You just don't think, do you?' Nick sipped at his drink again before continuing. 'Do you think he has done something like this before? Did Jerome say anything about anyone else it might have happened to?'

Stevie shook his head.

'Not a dicky-bird, but then he really don't want to talk about it much. What a fucking perverted viper to have in your nest, Nick!

Can you imagine, if this got out, how it would reflect on you? You know what people are like. He's your right-hand man, ain't he?'

Nick knew his friend was trying to warn him and at the same time justify his having to maim someone he had been friends with for years. But Nick was as up for it as Stevie at the moment, in shock that Gary had been found out this way.

He shook his head.

'Not any more he fucking ain't.'

Stevie was quiet for a few seconds before saying, 'Everyone who was mates with him would be suspect if this got out, and that includes me. I had a beer with him when I was released, and that is what I can't fucking understand. How he thought he would get away with it.'

They looked askance at one another.

'He's got kids, he's married. It just shows you what you don't know, don't it? You think you are on the ball, that you've seen it all, that you are a good judge of character, know who you can fucking trust . . . and then something like this happens and you are left wondering about everyone around you.'

'Do you want me to give him a hammering with you?'

Nick said it matter-of-factly.

Stevie shrugged.

'Up to you, mate, but I'm warning you now, Nick, I am going for blood and guts here. Proctor will be as good as dead.'

He was sorry about his choice of words but knew Nick understood what he was trying to say.

'Look, you shoot off if you want, Nick. I appreciate this but if it all goes tits up I don't want you having anything to do with it.'

He was trying to keep his friend out of a violent situation, warning him how bad this was going to get, and Nick appreciated that.

'I know, mate. What we'll say to everyone is he was a grass. I will confirm the story for you, all right? That way the boy is kept out of it and Gary will be vilified and considered untrustworthy for the rest of his days.'

He shook his head once more.

'I cannot believe I am even having this conversation, can you?'

Stevie sighed theatrically.

'Fucking scary though, eh? I was banged up for fifteen long years with only me right hand for company. It never crossed me mind once to turn elsewhere, and you'd be surprised what some of them in there would do for a Kit-kat or a couple of smokes. I mean, a fucking rapist is bad enough, but a bloke raping another bloke? I mean, what the fuck is that all about?'

Nick was saved from answering by the sound of Gary's car pulling up outside. He knew one thing. He had to see this through to the bitter end. It would not be good for business to do anything else.

This was a scandal they could all live without.

Gino went into the flat with trepidation, he hated scoring here. It was in a dilapidated block and thanks to the number of robberies locally all the flats had metal covers on the doors. This was perfect for Lenny Bagshot's business. It saved on shotguns anyway.

Once inside the flat the door was bolted loudly behind him and a young baby about nine months old came scooting down the hallway in a baby walker. The child was wearing designer clothes and three gold chains. Her ears were already pierced and she wore three sets of keeper earrings.

She smiled widely at Gino and Lenny, who chucked her under the chin. She crowed with happiness.

'She's her daddy's little darling.'

Gino followed the tall young man into the sitting room. The place was like something from a magazine, it was beautiful, and this was what made Gino nervous. This was a room from the TV screen, not the council estate he had grown up on. He was always frightened he would dirty the carpet or break wind. It was impossibly clean in here and that did not sit well in his world. His mum was clean but this place was clinical, like a hospital waiting room.

Lenny's girlfriend was a tall blonde called Harriet, Harry for short, and she was very middle-class and very good-looking. She looked like a film star, or at least Gino thought she did.

Lenny was tall, thin and had blond hair shaved in a number one crop. He dressed well and he chain smoked. Unlike most of the dealers round about he never touched his own stuff. Didn't take drugs period. For him this was just a stepping stone to a better life, and he ran his business with an eye to maximum security and profit.

Lenny was considered a diamond geezer and played up to that. He had a thick rasping cockney accent and joked constantly. Unfortunately the jokes often held a barb. He could get you anything you wanted for money up front. He could also get you killed if you tried to tuck him up.

At least that was what was said on the estate.

'How much tonight?'

'Half an ounce.'

'You are pushing the boat out, ain't you? What, you having a party?'

Lenny laughed at his own wit.

'Are you on it, Gino? Tell me the truth.'

He shook his head.

' 'Course not; it's a mug's game.'

Lenny laughed once more.

'Glad to hear it. Keep away from heroin. It steals your soul, boy, and you never really get it back. You dealing this on then?'

Gino shook his head violently in denial.

'Nah . . . no. It's for Jude Hatcher.'

Lenny was gratified by the boy's discomfort. He liked to frighten them young and then they kept the feeling for the rest of their lives. If this boy didn't dabble Lenny would take him on full-time, but he was sure Gino was on the periphery of H and if that was the case

Lenny wanted nothing to do with him. He could wait, he was patient, he had to be. In his game you watched and waited for your opportunities to arrive. You never went looking for them. But this kid had the makings of a half-decent dealer, so if he didn't succumb Lenny would give him a trial.

'Tell her to be careful, Gino. This is good gear and after the shit she's been jacking up it's liable to kill her.'

Lenny laughed once more.

'Still, if it does, she can visit her scumbag son in hell, can't she?'

Sonny had had a run in with Lenny just before he had been killed. Gino had no idea what it was over but he did know that Sonny had taken it very personally. He stared at the dealer warily. Gino knew that if he was selling on he would be given the hard word from Lenny who would want to cultivate his customers for himself. No one dealt on this estate without Lenny's express say-so.

'Forewarned is forearmed, Gino, my little son. Remember that, won't you?'

He nodded and handed over the money.

Two minutes later he was outside once more and breathing in huge lungfuls of cold night air.

He rushed back to Jude's. She would be eagerly awaiting him and tonight he too wanted to try the brown.

It was time to experience life. As Jude said, you never knew when your time would be up so you might as well enjoy it while it lasted. And he was only going to try it the once anyway, just to see what all the shouting was about.

'Come on, Tyrell, you can't sit in here on your own again.'

'Yes, I can. I can do what I like, I'm all grown up now.'

Louis Clarke laughed out loud. He was as blond as Tyrell was dark and they had been friends since they were little kids. Louis was a ducker and diver. He was handsome, a womaniser, and also the most loyal person Tyrell had ever known.

He had come to Sonny Boy's funeral with his brothers. Even though Sonny had tucked him up in the past, had stolen from his home, Louis had still marked the boy's passing with a beautiful wreath. Tyrell knew the gesture was more for himself than for his dead son but he appreciated it just the same.

'You've had a hard few months and things like this, well, they take their toll, don't they? Why don't you go home and talk to Sally, eh? She's in bits, I bet.'

Tyrell popped open two cans of Red Stripe and handed one to his friend as he sat back down. He was barefoot and all he had on was a pair of track suit bottoms. He would never have slobbed out like this at home, Sal would have had heart failure. It was a revelation being here, really. He could sit around, eat what he liked, and even eat while watching TV. He had actually had fish and chips smothered in salt and vinegar and the stench had made him laugh out loud. In fact, he was looking forward to the boys coming to visit. He would show them how to enjoy a Saturday afternoon properly for once in their lives.

Live dangerously, boys, drop a few crumbs on the carpet, go mad!

He felt the urge to laugh again at his thoughts.

'Tyrell, are you listening to me?'

'Sorry, Lou, I was just thinking how much I'm enjoying being on me own, you know. I can't get over how much I love me own company.'

'You fucking love yourself period, Hatcher! I must admit, though, I thought you would be worried about this business with Sal but you look well considering all that's happened.'

'I feel like I've been let out of school, to be honest. I need this time on me own, need to work things through in me own mind. But fuck all that anyway. Now you're here, I want to ask you a favour.'

'Anything, mate, you name it.'

Tyrell knew that Louis was a true friend. He was honest, loyal and loved Tyrell like a brother. He was the only person he would ask this favour of, and yet he wondered if Louis would say no.

Tyrell took a deep breath. He was fingering his dreads which Louis knew was always a sign that he was agitated.

'This is going to sound so fucking mad . . .'

Louis laughed then. Picking up the remainder of the joint, he relit it and puffed deeply.

'You've sounded madder over the years.'

Tyrell smiled, but he didn't laugh which would normally have been his response. This was serious and Louis suddenly picked up on that fact.

'I want to know what happened to my Sonny Boy.'

Louis looked at him quizzically. His amazing blue eyes had always been his best feature. All his emotions were mirrored in their depths. Tyrell looked into them and hoped his friend would understand what he was going to ask. More importantly, that he would understand why Tyrell was asking him and nobody else.

'But you know what happened to Sonny Boy, everyone does,' Louis told him.

His voice was sad now and Tyrell knew his friend thought he had finally lost the plot. Not only had he left his wonderful wife and gone to live on his own, but he was smoking dope, drinking Red Stripe, and on top of all that growing paranoid about his son's murder. No, he had to stop thinking of it as a murder. Maybe his friend had a point after all. Maybe he was losing it.

'Look, Tyrell, it was a terrible thing to happen to anyone, but you said yourself that you would have done the same thing as that Leary bloke . . .'

Tyrell interrupted him.

'I don't mean Leary, I mean who was behind my boy being there in the first place? My Sonny, God love him, was small-time, a hustler. He wouldn't have robbed a drum of that calibre: had enough trouble getting into a council flat. You've only got to look at his track record, he never actually broke into most places, just nicked stuff while he was there visiting. That place had a state-of-the-art alarm system, the works. There was no fucking way Sonny was behind it, he could not have done it on his own. And I'll tell you something else, the filth must have sussed that out and all. I mean, think about it logically. He was a kid, a big kid. He could never have devised something like that on his todd, he had to have had help. And another thing – the gun. Where would Sonny have got a fucking semi-automatic from?'

Louis didn't want to point out that a semi-automatic gun these days was practically a fashion accessory for a lot of young men.

Instead he tried to talk his friend down.

'Look, man, you're grieving . . .'

' 'Course I'm grieving, but that is neither here nor there. Listen to me and think about what I am saying logically.'

Louis was quiet again. He didn't know what to do or what to say to his friend. But he tried once more to reason with him.

'Sonny died tragically young. You have to let him go . . .'

Tyrell was shouting now. He didn't need platitudes, he needed someone to listen to what he was saying.

'Did you hear what I just said? Do you think that my Sonny, who could barely tie his own shoelaces, could fucking mastermind a burglary of that calibre? Haven't you listened to one fucking word I have said here? Louis, look at me, I ain't a fucking daydreamer, I am a realist, and I know that there was some other skulduggery afoot that night. Where would Sonny have unloaded the stuff from that kind of drum? Where would he even get the idea to rob it in the first place? Think about it. It was not his kind of scene, he didn't have the savvy for the fuckery he got himself into. Why would he have gone big-time thieving? No, there was an agenda at work here and it was not my Sonny's. My boy died through someone else's greed. Can you see where I am coming from now?'

Louis could and wished to Christ he couldn't because he knew that his friend had never had any illusions about his son. He'd seen Sonny Boy exactly as the rest of the world saw him, and had still loved and adored him. Jude was the real culprit here. Most of Sonny's misdemeanours led back to her and her habit.

'So who do you think was part of the show?'

Louis was alert now to the consequences of his reply and Tyrell knew from that statement that his oldest friend was going to stand by his side no matter what.

'Do you think Jude was in on it?'

Tyrell smirked.

'Nah, never in a million years, but someone knows who he was dealing with. Sonny has to have told someone. If Jude knew anything she would have told me, not the filth. She would definitely have talked to me about it. That is why I have to find out the score otherwise I will never sleep peacefully another night in my bed.'

Louis thought about what his friend had said then asked: 'So where do we start?'

Tyrell smiled then, his first real smile for weeks.

'I knew I could rely on you, Lou.'

Louis shrugged, embarrassed by his friend's gratitude.

' 'Course you can, you'd do the same for me.'

But he was worried inside because like the rest of his mates he thought that Sonny Hatcher had finally fucked off the wrong person and paid the ultimate price. End of story. But how could he say so to Tyrell?

'Anything you need I will always be there, you know that.'

It was what his friend wanted to hear.

Lance Walker was in agony, and he wondered when Nick would come back and see him. He thought he would tell him anything he wanted to know now.

It had been over a week and he was still lying on the cold floor, he was still trussed up and he was slowly going out of his mind.

He was in dire pain, his shoulders felt as if they had been pulled from their sockets and his mouth was cracked and dry, the thirst was far worse than the hunger. Twice he had had a bucket of icy cold water thrown over him and he had lapped it up off the dirty floor with glee. Now, though, he had been reduced to licking the walls clean of damp and the mission it had taken him to roll over there had left him shaken and in agony.

The only light at the end of the tunnel was that Nick had always come alone, and that meant he had not told the other members of the syndicate what he knew.

Nick wanted the poke for himself, and Lance could not quibble with that because it was for that very reason he was lying here in the first place.

Nick was clever all right, and Lance had underestimated him. Not a mistake he would make again.

His face was so swollen he had trouble breathing, and the cold of the concrete floor had seeped into his bones.

Nick was a force, and he should have remembered that. Nick was also too clever to ever have anything come back to his front door, he should have remembered that as well.

The stench of where he had soiled himself was now so bad that he wanted to vomit, and his clothes were stuck to his skin from the faeces and urine. Even in his anger, he had to admit to himself that he would have done the same if he had been in Nick's position. But that didn't make Lance feel any better.

He became more determined than ever not to tell Nick Leary what he wanted to know.

Tammy was alone for once and actually enjoying herself. She was sorting through swatches of material for her new bedroom. She had decided to redecorate the upstairs of her house even though it was only nine months since it had been done last. The fact that she had trashed it in a temper with Nick made it a necessity. When Tammy let rip it was a sight to behold. Before and after the event.

This, though, was her forte: decorating and making her home beautiful. It was as if she compensated for some inner emptiness by spending money. Which, of course, she knew deep inside, was exactly why she did it.

Nick's mobile rang. The *Dam Busters* theme annoyed her and she rushed to answer it. Until now she had not realised he had even left it at home. He must have been in a hurry if he had forgotten his phone, he never left the house without it. When she had got back earlier than she had anticipated, her mother-in-law said he had gone out with Stevie Daly and Tammy had been intrigued.

Nick usually guarded that phone like it was worth a fortune, which she supposed it was to him with all the numbers he kept in it. Now she saw a chance to have a recce. It was flashing up Call and that alone alerted her suspicions. Normally, the caller's name flashed up.

'Hello?'

Silence.

Tammy looked at the phone in puzzlement. Putting it back to her ear she said once more, 'Hello.'

The phone went dead in her hand.

The dirty filthy stinking bastard had a bird on the go, after all he had said to her, all the reassurances he had given her!

Well, she would not go through that again, the sleepless nights wondering where he was, the watching and waiting to see exactly what he got up to. No. She could not live like that again. It had nearly brought on a breakdown the last time. He had never admitted anything to her, but she knew. Her face screwed up with anger and pain, she threw the phone across the room.

The land line rang then and she rushed across the room to answer it.

'Hello.'

Complete quiet again.

Tammy lost it.

She had been in this situation before. Well, it wasn't going to happen again, not if she had anything to do with it.

'Listen here, you fucking home-wrecking slut! When I find out who you are, I will rip your tits off . . .'

The line went dead and she sank to the floor, tears already forming in her eyes. It wasn't so much the fact that he had a bird, she could have coped with that, it was the fact he was capable of having sex with someone else.

When he had not been near her for so very long.

She loved sex, and she loved her husband. If only the two could mix. It wasn't a lot to ask, surely? Most of her friends laughed about how their husbands were always after it and they were always trying to put them off. And Tammy joined in the laughter, but it wasn't funny. If Nick was batting away from home then it was serious. Especially if that person had his main mobile number.

He was like her. Normally he had their numbers and rang them. Well, this one must think she was in with a chance if she was daring to ring his home, the one he shared with his wife and children.

Now Nick was *dead*. She would cause so much upset over this that it would take more than a world cruise to placate her this time.

Yet still she cried from the pain, even as she planned how to get even.

As Tammy gazed at the pieces of material and the colour charts she wondered why the hell she bothered with any of it. Then, as usual, she dried her eyes, pulled herself together and started making her plans. Nick was going nowhere, whatever that slut on the other end of the line might think, and neither was she.

* * *

Gary Proctor was all smiles as he walked into the lock-up garage in Bow. His face lit up with genuine pleasure when he saw Stevie standing there.

'Hello, mate, how's it going?'

He assumed that Stevie was here getting a bit of graft put his way through Nick. A guaranteed few quid until he got properly back on his feet.

No one spoke to him and Gary was nonplussed for a few moments.

'What's the matter?'

Nick shook his head sadly at his one-time friend. Then Stevie took back his fist and slammed it with as much force as he could muster into Gary's face. He hit the ground, winded by the blow. He scrambled up quickly, though, shock evident on his face. Gary could have a row, but he conceded that Stevie was the better man.

'What the fuck is all that about?

He seemed genuinely puzzled and for a split second Stevie wondered if he had the right man. But he didn't question his instincts. Instead he bellowed, 'You're a fucking nonce! A nonsense who took my little nephew and tried to get up his arse . . .'

Gary's eyes widened at the words. It was as if a thunderbolt had struck him as he looked at Nick and realised he had had a capture, or a capture and a half as they would put it.

'Listen here, Stevie, I don't know what you have been told . . .'

Gary was babbling now, trying to talk his way out of it.

Stevie began the beating then, as if he couldn't wait to get it over with. Gary went down swiftly under the rain of blows. As Nick watched he wondered what he should do. He knew it would be pointless trying to stop the beating, and he also knew that honour demanded it had to be of a vicious nature. When he saw Gary curl into a ball and cover his head he was relieved that he was not going to try and come back at Stevie and make it all worse for himself.

Suddenly there was blood everywhere, and it was then that he realised Stevie's knuckle dusters were spiked. Stevie punched Gary in the head with such force he had to put his knee on the man's shoulder to prise the duster out of the flesh.

Nick winced involuntarily, knowing it must hurt badly yet accepting that the punishment had to fit the crime and this was a crime of enormous proportions. There were gay men in their circle, openly gay men who still managed to keep their credibility. It was the child chasers who brought on this kind of wrath. In their world it was just not on, it was never tolerated, and that went for men who liked really young girls as well.

Well, for men who liked the girls a bit too young at any rate.

Gary's crime also lay in the fact that he had forced the boy, because that again was never tolerated by their circle.

Stevie was trying to draw breath, his breathing heavy and ragged in the cold night air. Inside the lock-up blood had sprayed everywhere, even on to the ceiling.

Nick pulled him back by the arm.

'Come on, mate, he's had enough.'

'No, he ain't.'

Stevie was puffing and panting but still ready to finish the job properly.

Gary looked at his one-time friend.

'Please, Nick . . . I'm warning you . . .'

The words were faint, hardly audible in the confines of the little garage.

Nick's face went very still.

'What you gonna do? Grass me up about me *business dealings* then?' His voice was dangerously low.

Stevie was watching these proceedings with interest. There was something about Gary's voice as he pleaded with his friend.

'You know I wouldn't do that . . .'

'Well, what you going to do then? What you warning *me* about?'

168

It was the final insult and all three men knew it. Nick changed then. His whole body seemed to lengthen as he drew himself up to his considerable height.

'You'd threaten me, you cunt? After all I done for you over the years? You fuck up and then you would try and nause up my business to stop yourself getting a fucking well-deserved kicking?'

He drew back his booted foot and kicked Gary in the mouth. The man's head snapped back. His teeth were already hanging out when Nick launched himself on to him. Five minutes later it was Stevie who finally stopped the beating. By that time Gary Proctor was a lump of bloody meat. Stevie took his pulse.

'He's half-dead, Nick.'

Nick grinned and it looked eerie by the light of the Calor gas fire. He went to the corner of the garage and came back with a can of petrol which he proceeded to pour over Gary Proctor. The smell seemed to wake the victim up. He stirred, trying to turn himself over to see what was going on.

'You are joking, Nick?' Stevie murmured. There was fear in his voice.

Nick shook his head.

'Am I fuck! This is his drum not mine which is why I chose it for the venue. He can burn to hell in here, I don't give a flying fuck. It was bad enough his nonceing, but to hear that he would try and fuck me up and all, try and drop me in it after what he did . . .'

He lit a match and dropped it on to the prone figure on the floor.

'No one, and I mean *no one*, fucks with me, Stevie. And you of all people should remember that.'

The smell of burning flesh was overpowering. Stevie turned his eyes away from the sight of Gary writhing on the floor as the flames took hold. There was a muffled scream.

'Come on, Stevie me old china, I need a drink. I have a feeling you need one and all,' Nick said in a jocular voice.

They went outside and he locked up. The padlock was big and

heavy and the door steel-clad but Gary's screams were still audible on the still night air. They could see the leaping flames through the grimy windows. Nick looked at Stevie and shrugged.

'Well, he won't be nonceing for a while now, will he?'

In the car he chatted about everything under the sun except the demise of his oldest friend.

Stevie had always known that Nick could be a handful but he had forgotten just how vindictive he could be if crossed. Tonight was a lesson well learned, for all of them.

Chapter Eleven

Nick's head was splitting. He wished he had not had to sit and sink so many drinks to steady Stevie's nerves. In reality he had wanted to get home, find some peace and quiet in which to try and make sense of the night's events. Instead he had come home to a wife like a raving lunatic and his mother frightened out of her life and hiding in her bedroom.

He really didn't need any of it tonight. His life was like a soap opera lately, one crisis after another.

'Tammy, please, it was probably a wrong number . . .'

She could hear the boredom in his voice and knew deep inside that she was pushing him too far, but she could not stop herself. It was as if a devil sat on her shoulder and spoon fed her the irritating words that seemed calculated to send her husband over the edge.

'Don't you dare try and bullshit me, mate . . .'

'Did this mystery woman talk? No. Did their photograph miraculously appear on the handset? No. It could have been anyone, Tammy. You are a fucking nutter! You imagine birds all over the place and yet you know me better than anyone . . .'

Tammy wanted to believe him but she had tortured herself all night, whipping herself up into a frenzy of jealousy. There would be no reasoning with her now. She knew it better even than he did.

'I bet you and her have a right laugh, don't you? Does she know about us? About our so-called life together? Well, answer me then, you dirty stinking rat-shagging low life . . .' Even as she screamed at him she wished in her heart that she could stop herself, but it was impossible.

Nick spoke quietly now through clenched teeth. She saw his hands clench into fists and felt a frisson of fear inside her.

'I am warning you for the last time, Tammy, not tonight, love. I am not in the mood for your histrionics, OK?'

She could hear the dangerous note in his voice, knew that this was neither the time nor the place to persist, but unfortunately the devil was still driving her on. She poked one well-manicured finger into his face, fighting an urge to scratch the skin and provoke a real reaction. Because all she had ever wanted was a reaction from Nick. A fight was better than this indifference. Anything was better than this.

'You know and I know that you are up to something. I know you of old and it's all falling into place now. The late nights, the drinking, all the hanging round with so-called mates . . . and this from a man who if he missed a single episode of *Buffy* was depressed for the week! Well, I am warning you, Nick, you had better tell whoever she is to get on her fucking bike, because when I get me hands on her she won't be capable of shagging anyone's husband let alone mine!'

Nick continued to sip at his hot chocolate, trying to simmer down before he really lost it with her. He was still thinking about Gary Proctor and what he had said, still getting over the cheek of his threat. It just showed that you could trust no one at the end of the day.

All those years of friendship had meant nothing. Gary knew all about Nick's businesses which was reason enough in itself to off him. But it was the principle of it, Nick told himself. Like Lance Walker, he was surrounded by traitors.

Tammy, aware that she did not have her husband's attention, started shrieking once more. Listening to herself, she felt shame and humiliation. But he had reduced her to this and she didn't think she would ever be able to forgive him for that.

He snapped himself back to the present and bellowed at her tiredly, 'You are barking up the wrong tree, Tams. Now will you change the fucking record! At times I feel like having an affair just to give you something to moan about.'

His words shut her up as he knew they would. Food for thought was what silenced Tams. But she soon recovered.

'So where were you tonight then? And what was Stevie Daly doing round here? Making up for lost time, I suppose. He was always out and about years ago – anything with a pulse him. Is that what you were doing tonight, eh? Borrowing him one of your trollops?'

Nick gulped down the last of his hot chocolate.

'Oh, shut up, you stupid woman, I ain't answering any of your questions. And before you start again, Tams, if I hear one more word I am going to walk out of this house and I ain't coming back until you either fuck off or shut the fuck up.'

It was not what he wanted to do but he knew how to scare her. He hated using the power he had over her but at times like this it was all he could do to get some peace and quiet. Gary Proctor's words had thrown him and then he had done something terrible, something so bad he wondered if he was going mad suddenly.

He could still hear that screaming.

It was as if everything was falling apart around Nick, every aspect of his life disintegrating, and he didn't know how to stop it. Sonny Hatcher had started off a chain of events that could only lead to catastrophe. It was as if all Nick's years of skating on thin ice were over. Now he felt jinxed. As a reasonable man he knew that was stupid but at times like this he could almost believe it.

He had felt a rage inside himself tonight like he had never felt before. He knew he could sometimes be formidable, but then he could not have achieved what he had without that kink in his nature. But it had always been controlled violence before, undertaken in pursuit of a clear objective. Now it felt as if he could harm anyone and not even blink an eyelid.

The more he thought about Gary, the more he felt that urge to kill. It was such a shock knowing that Stevie's nephew had been trounced by him and that his oldest friend had had a capture. How could he ever hold his head up if something like this was to become common knowledge? He consoled himself with the fact that Stevie wanted it kept as quiet as he did. But Stevie had a loose lip with a drink in him.

Nick closed his eyes in distress once more.

It was an abortion, the lot of it.

Tammy's voice was sawing through his head and he tried his hardest to tune her out. He had Sky News on low, and watched to see if anything came on about Gary. It would be a gruesome death and therefore newsworthy. Nick knew that much from experience. He kept one eye on the TV as he watched his wife's mouth moving.

She just never stopped going on. It was as if someone had turned her volume up and never bothered to turn it off again. He wished he could take the batteries out once and for all and pictured himself strangling her. It was a picture he had seen in his mind's eye many times over the years and he sometimes thought that perhaps it stopped him from *really* strangling her. Just the thought of doing it calmed him, seeing her mouth moving but hearing nothing was such a wonderful thought.

He stared into her eyes. The strain was showing and finally he found it in his heart to feel sorry for her. He wished he could take her from this room and give her what she wanted because that was the only thing that would reassure her once and for all that he loved her. If he threw her on the floor and fucked the arse off her she would shut up in a second. Because it was fucking Tams needed, not lovemaking or gentle caresses but deep down and dirty sex.

She thrived on it. He wished to God he felt the same.

Since his problem had started years ago he'd thought she would have accepted it by now. He had offered her an out many times in the past, would have agreed to a divorce on her terms, but she had always refused. He knew she loved him, and in his own way he loved her, but not the way she wanted to be loved.

He only wished he could give her what she wanted.

But he couldn't. No matter how hard he tried, he couldn't do it any more.

He wondered who had been on the phone. Whoever it was had caused untold hag and he would like to smack them one in the teeth at this moment in time. He wondered if it was one of Lance's cronies. They would be looking for him by now. He wished it *had* been a woman, it would have made his life easier all round, but of course poor Tammy believed he was getting it up with all and sundry except her.

Why did she make him feel so guilty?

He gave her everything she wanted.

Except, of course, the only thing she had ever been interested in.

He pushed past her and, picking up his car keys, left the house once more. She was still screaming at him as he drove away in his Range Rover.

Nick knew his earlier threat was going to give her a sleepless night. She really would believe he had a woman now, and that he was going there, but he was past caring. He had slept in the motor before, he could easily do it again.

Especially if it meant he did not have to listen to his wife's ranting and raving.

* * *

175

Carlos Brent was surprised to see Tyrell sitting in his flat, if for no other reason than he knew that Tyrell was not into big-time skulduggery. Not on his scale anyway, he didn't rob or thieve.

Tyrell, though, did the dirty work, doors, debt collecting and so on. He also bought debts which was how he had made the majority of his money.

Carlos had sold a few debts to him over the years and, in fairness, he had collected where most people had not. In fact, Tyrell used a network of Rastas with bad attitudes and a penchant for kickings that had made him a legend in his own way. But, so far as serious crime was concerned, he was not what anyone would call a bad man. But that wasn't to say he couldn't be if he wanted to, he had the muscle and he had the connections: he just didn't bother to utilise what he had.

More fool him.

If Carlos had been fortunate enough to have the friendship of people like the Clarkes he would have run the whole fucking gaff in no time.

The Clarkes were legends in their own lifetimes. Vicious and uncompromising, they were behind some of the most audacious and frightening incidents in the criminal world. No one would go up against them, at least no one in their right mind, and Tyrell had the ear of the whole family and was acknowledged almost as a brother to the youngest one. Yet he was still kicking a living, not a bad living admittedly, but not the kind of living he could have commanded with a few words from his cronies.

In short, Carlos Brent thought Tyrell Hatcher was a cunt. But he still gave him his due, his friendship with the Clarkes would see to that.

It was Carlos's particular job to provide iron. He came up with guns for all sorts of people and all sorts of situations. It was what he did, and even if he said it himself he did it very well. None of his guns was traceable, and none of them could ever lead the police back to him. Carlos was far too shrewd for all that.

The only way he could be put in the frame was if someone grassed him up to the police, and that was not liable to happen to him.

He'd made sure of that.

Carlos also knew about Tyrell's son. Even while one part of him loudly sympathised, another part did not really care one iota about the little bastard's demise. He kept that to himself, though, and carried on making all the appropriate noises.

The fact was Tyrell had arrived with his friend Louis, who although not a heavyweight in his own right, had all the right connections because of his three brothers. The other Clarkes were the handful of the year, especially as they tended to work mob-handed. Louis himself had always been seen as a bit of a maverick, but even so was not someone to dismiss out of hand. Particularly when he'd brought his brother Terry with him. So Carlos acted agreeable to the meet even though all he wanted to do was get back to bed and shag his latest amour.

Flora was an eighteen-year-old blonde with large breasts (a must-have as far as he was concerned), long legs and a tight ass. Her only drawback was a particularly strong Bradford accent, but as he did not want to discuss anything of importance with her Carlos felt he could overlook that fact for a while. She was up for it, game as they came, and he was growing tired of listening to Tyrell's catalogue of fucking woes. He'd had more stimulating conversations with strangers in pubs. At least you could fuck off and go home when they bored you.

'It must have been hard, man.'

He tried to put some emotion into his voice but it stayed flat because all he wanted to do was yawn.

Tyrell nodded, aware he did not have the other man's full attention but unable to do a lot about it. Terry Clarke, the youngest brother, had other ideas though and was vocal about what they were.

Terry was naturally argumentative. He was renowned for his belligerent streak and, seeing Carlos's behaviour as a personal slur on him and his family, said sarcastically, 'What's the matter? We fucking keeping you up, mate?'

Carlos was stunned.

'You what?'

Louis closed his eyes in distress.

'Leave it out, Terry.'

But Terry shook his head. He was a big man and imposing. He knew his own worth down to the last ounce.

'Bollocks! We arranged this meet. It ain't like we just turned up on his doorstep, is it?' He turned back to Carlos. 'If you didn't want this you only had to say, mate. We just want the answers to a few questions, that's all. It ain't fucking rocket science.'

Terry had a personal grievance with Carlos but would never let him know that. He had the hump because Carlos had provided the iron that had eventually been used on one of the Clarkes' own workforce in a revenge attack. Now Terry knew that was their line of business, and he knew that it was not really anything to do with Carlos personally, but it still rankled. A gunshot was a bastard of a wound, and as most of the gunshot wounds round and about could be traced back to this prick he felt he had a legitimate reason to take umbrage.

'All we want to know, Carlos, is if you provided the iron that was used by his son? Now do you want me to get Anne Robinson out of bed to ask you or are you going to answer the fucking question now so we can all go home and get some sleep?'

Louis smiled. Terry was a little sod in some respects but you couldn't help liking him. Both men and women did, much to the chagrin of Renee, his long-suffering girlfriend and mother of his five kids. On the downside he had once chased three men through

Rotherhithe tunnel with a machete and he had only been seventeen at the time. Stories like that tended to follow you around and Terry knew this better than anyone.

Carlos was staring at him in dismay but also with slow-burning anger. He was a big man in his own right, half-Spanish and half-Antiguan. He had inherited his Spanish mother's temper along with his Antiguan father's business acumen. He could not in all honesty take this on the chin; he had to come back at the boy and was not really in the mood today.

Tyrell, though, saved the situation.

'As you can see, Carlos, my Sonny Boy's death has caused a stir in our community.'

He was saying to him, Help us out, and get Terry off your back at the same time. He was also giving the other man a mild threat. It was how things were resolved in their world and Tyrell knew the game back to front. It was just strange playing it again after all these years.

When he had been young he had been one of the lads, one of the boys. But he had never been a lover of extreme violence, or any kind of violence for that matter, even though it was an integral part of their world.

Sure his doormen had to have reps, otherwise it was a waste of time having them. Some were armed and he knew that and appreciated it; he also knew most of them had probably purchased their iron from Carlos so he knew the man could help out if he wanted to. This was a compromising situation for Carlos and they all understood that, but he hoped that Sonny's extreme youth would sway the man before him.

Carlos, however, was annoyed now and saw an out. He had almost decided to give them a taste but now he was determined not to give them anything.

'Look, guys, supposing I sold you some firepower tonight, right, and you shot another known associate with it?'

They all nodded.

Carlos opened his arms expansively to thrust his message home.

'Well, suppose this person you shot had brothers and they wanted to know the score and I listened to their sob story. . .'

He nodded at Tyrell.

'No disrespect meant, mate. But suppose, after listening, I told them who I had sold the iron to and they came after you, where would that leave me?'

Terry grinned.

'Fucking dead.'

Carlos laughed.

'Precisely. So why should I break my silence to you lot? I sell the brand, it's up to you what the fuck you do with it, right? I supply a demand, no more, no less. If I didn't sell it to you, some other fucker would. And, I might add, at greatly inflated prices. I am not responsible for the use of any of the purchases made on my premises, and unfortunately I cannot break the confidentiality involved without fear of being seen as the Bertie Smalls of South London. Do you all get my drift?'

Terry sighed.

'He has got a point.'

It grieved him to say so but he had to be fair. He himself wouldn't like Carlos preaching to all and sundry who had bought what. It could cause untold fucking hag for all involved.

Carlos knew he was on to a winner.

'I never, and I repeat *never*, talk about any of my transactions, with anyone. If I did Old Bill would be round here so fast they would burn up the tarmac on the road. I have been banged up and still kept my own counsel as you fucking know.'

He looked at all three of them before continuing. He had done eight months on remand for possession of firearms before getting off on a technicality over the police search through the machinations of a very expensive and eloquent barrister.

'So I'm afraid I cannot under any circumstances change my business practices to suit you lot. I am sorry about the boy but these things happen. I cannot talk about anything pertaining to individual transactions, as I have explained. What I can tell you, though, is that I had no prior knowledge of anything that happened to your boy. People purchase my merchandise. After that it is up to them what the fuck they do with it.'

It was friendly, it was open, and he had just walked away from a potentially dangerous situation.

Carlos smiled disarmingly.

'One thing I will say, though, is look closer to home. I have found in the past that that is often where you get the information you least want to hear.'

'What do you mean by that?'

This from Terry who had never been the sharpest knife in the drawer and was still trying to work out exactly what had been said.

'Just an observation, that's all, from one brother to another.'

Carlos smiled in Tyrell's direction.

He nodded, understanding what the gun dealer was trying to tell him and grateful for the help even though it was something he had actually worked out for himself by now.

The same name was whirling inside every head in the room.

Jude Hatcher.

Nick looked down at the wreck of Lance Walker and sighed. The stench was unbelievable and the sight of his old adversary lying on the filthy floor didn't affect Nick one iota.

Lance had ripped him off, that had put paid to any kind of niceties.

'You look like something from a fucking Hammer Horror.'

Lance stared up at him with sunken eyes.

'Piss off.'

The words were slurred and it was painful for him to talk. It was his sheer hatred that was keeping him alive and they both knew that.

'Fuck you, you're a nonce.'

Nick knelt down on his haunches and looked into Lance's face. He was amazed at the resilience of the human spirit.

'You're as good as dead. You know that, don't you?'

This time Lance didn't answer. He was lapsing, once more, into a coma.

Nick stood up and, walking away from the bundle of dirty rags, he lit another cigarette to mask the smell. Ten minutes later he threw a bucket of water over the man to rouse him.

'I am going out for a nice juicy steak and a bottle of wine. I'll be thinking of you, lying here and dying.'

He was smiling down at him once more. 'You got anything to tell me? If you do, I'll put you out of your misery and I swear that.'

Lance started to cough.

'Bollocks.'

It was final and they both knew that.

Nick sighed, once more, a playful, friendly sigh that reverberated around the dank concrete walls. 'Fair enough. Bye. Lance, don't do anything I wouldn't do, will ya'.'

He walked away, laughing and listening to Lance Walker calling him every name under the sun.

Gino looked at the needle Jude was offering him. He had rolled up his sleeve and even applied the tourniquet to his arm. His vein was bulging nicely and the adrenaline rush at what he was about to do was causing his heart to race.

But it wasn't with excitement, it was with fear.

Now the time had come he was not at all sure it was what he wanted to do. Jude suddenly looked sinister in the half-light of the dirty front room. The skunk he had smoked was making him paranoid and the needle suddenly looked enormous in Jude's small hand.

His teeth were in a terrible state due to his fear of needles and dentistry yet here he was contemplating injecting himself. Where was the logic in that?

'Do you want me to do it, sweetheart?'

Jude's voice was low and gravelly, her eyes misted over from her own large fix earlier. She looked sweeter now; her eyes had lost the haunted, edgy look associated with the need of the next fix that most addicts seemed to acquire after a while on the brown. She looked almost kind in her concern for him. His fear of her was gone suddenly.

She was whispering, talking in reverential tones as she explained her thoughts. 'In my hand, Gino, I have complete oblivion. I am holding the key to all the religions of the world and what they promise you. Why sit on a mountain in Nepal talking to some Lama geezer when you can experience Valhalla in my front room?'

She was smiling at her words, ones that had been said to her too many years ago for her to remember properly. At least she wasn't after his body which had been why she was given her first fix.

'First you get the initial rush, then you feel the gradual relaxation of your body and your mind, then you slip into this other place, Gino, and it's so nice there. There's no bills, no worries, no nothing, except a feeling of complete and utter understanding. Once you visit that place you will want to stay there forever.'

He was smiling at her now, it sounded so good to him.

Oblivion is what he craved more than anything these days. The responsibility he felt over Sonny's death weighed heavily on him at times. He should have taken better care of him, but he had abandoned him when Sonny had started to work on his own. Nothing would have induced him to do what Sonny had done to feed his mother's habit.

Gino's mother had tried to stop her son becoming what she called 'another statistic'; Jude on the other hand had encouraged her son to do whatever it took to make the money needed for her habit.

It could only have been that which had caused his death, could only have been the people he had started to mix with. And he had walked away from him over it, now the guilt weighed heavily.

Now here was Jude offering him an out.

'Close the curtains on the world, son, and relax into a world of your own.'

She pulled his arm towards her and expertly tapped the vein. It was bobbing up clearly. Still smiling, she slipped the needle under the skin.

First she injected the heroin into his blood stream slowly, then she retracted blood, washing it back inside the syringe to clean it out before finally pushing both blood and drug residue back into his body.

Gino watched it all as if it was happening to someone else. Then the rush hit him and he lay back with his eyes closed.

As he lay there Jude went to the kitchen for the washing-up bowl. She threw all the dirty crockery into the sink and brought the empty bowl back, placing it on the floor beside Gino. Not before time either. He started heaving almost immediately as his body tried to reject this foreign substance from his bloodstream.

'Fight it, Gino, it'll be worth it in the end, son.'

He was sweating and vomiting by now. All he could hear was Jude's laughter as she assured him it got easier and easier as you went along.

Angela tapped gently on the master bedroom door.

'Go away.'

She wasn't shouting now, Tammy's voice was almost inaudible, and Angela opened the door and slipped into the room.

This bedroom amazed her, it always did, it was bigger than the whole flat where she had lived as a child. She saw her daughter-in-law curled up on the twenty-two-foot wide bed looking so small and forlorn that Angela felt the first ever spark of pity for her.

'He doesn't mean the half of it, Tammy.'

Tammy's bottom lip was trembling and her blue eyes were red-rimmed from crying. Seeing her mother-in-law in the bedroom without the usual sneer on her face and speaking to her so nicely was the undoing of her.

She burst into tears once more.

Angela sat on the edge of the bed and gently patted her back.

'There now, Tammy. Shall I get you a drink of something? Tea?'

Tammy shook her head and slowly sat herself up. She gulped noisily before saying, between sniffs and coughs, 'There's brandy in the drinks cabinet over there.'

Angela was partial to a drop of the hard so she walked over to the cabinet and poured them both a good measure. In the soft lamplight of the luxurious room he'd paid for she grudgingly admitted to herself that Tammy had a point about her husband at times. Nick, although a good man, maybe, just maybe, might not be the husband of the year. And how could he be, coming from what he had come from? Seeing what he had seen as a child and living through the experiences he had lived through?

Her son, and she loved him dearly, had something missing, a kink in his nature that would always spoil any kind of normal life he might go after.

His father had abused them all, taken the last little bit of confidence they had had and trodden it into the dirt with his filthy mouth and his aggression.

She could still hear him now, beating the kids, terrifying them until, finally, Nick had fought back. On the day he had done that, life had taken on a semblance of normality for them all. Even though, by then, none of them knew what normality actually was.

There was something missing in her son and she had always known that, and over the years the little bits she had garnered, putting two and two together mostly, had given her an insight into her son that this poor girl would never ever understand. She knew him so well, yet she could never let this frightened woman in front of her find out about any of it.

The death of that boy had opened up a can of worms. Only Angela knew that, and she was going to tell *no one*. Dare not tell anyone.

His father had laid the groundwork for her son's life, and she would never betray him by letting it become common knowledge. Nick was strange, and finally admitting it to herself gave her a sense of relief. Her son was strange and he could be dangerous, and it was all down to a drunken Irishman whom she had married while herself in a drunken stupor.

Could she have done more? She knew the answer to that question. And she knew that if she had done something, then this girl would not have had half the heartbreak she had endured.

Angela's own thoughts scandalised her even as she acknowledged the truth of them. But her daughter-in-law's harsh sobbing had finally melted her hard old heart. She had never really liked the girl who had taken her son from her, and she over the years had been frequently harsh in her judgement of Nick's wife as she saw their marriage slowly implode.

But tonight, for the first time ever, Angela had felt a flicker of pity for her. Now, as she held Tammy in her arms and felt the girl's shuddering cries, she finally admitted to herself she could get to like her.

In a strange way she had always liked Tammy. Angela had just resented her taking part in Nick's life. When he had started to do well for himself she had thought he would be better off with a wife who would enhance his newfound wealth and status. She knew, though, that if he had chosen a more upper-class type she herself would not have reigned long in this house, whereas as things stood Tammy had been happy to leave everything to her.

Over the years Angela had convinced herself that Tammy was the reason her son's marriage was crumbling. However, since the demise of that young lad she had seen a different side to Nick. She was warming daily towards Tammy and beginning to see the difficulties of her life.

Even as she felt this disloyalty burning in her gut, the younger woman's wrenching sobs were getting to her. Angela held her tightly, feeling the girl's delicate bones and the slimness of her figure even after bearing two hefty boys. The worst of it was listening to the utter loneliness and desolation expressed in her tears because Angela knew that she was partly to blame for that. She had been there in the background, trying to drive a wedge between husband and wife, from day one.

But it had turned out that they had not needed any help from her and as she had listened over the years to this poor girl begging her husband to do his duty Angela had set her heart against her. But now even she had to admit that Tammy, God love and keep her, had a point.

Her two grandsons, as much as Angela loved them, were slightly suspect to her. The way their eyes differed in shape and colour, their different builds, the way one was curly-haired and the other had hair like silk . . . She pushed these thoughts from her mind. Nick loved them and he would never have accepted cuckoos in his nest, surely?

'Come on, lovey. Drink your brandy, it'll revive you.'

All cried out, but still shuddering with the force of her emotion, Tammy gulped at the brandy, coughing as the rawness hit the back of her throat. The lines around her eyes were more prominent than usual, but despite that she looked very young to Angela. Devoid of make-up you could see her natural prettiness more clearly. When she was all made up it gave her a brittle quality, she looked like a doll. Now she looked like the sweet girl she really was, though she would not see that.

'Did he send you up here?'

Tammy's voice was low and rasping from her earlier shouting and crying. It was also full of hope. If Nick had sent his mother up then it meant he cared, it meant he had come home expressly.

Angela shook her head sadly.

'No, Tammy. But I couldn't listen to you crying any longer.'

They were both quiet for a moment. It had been so long since they had talked like this it felt unnatural, forced.

'He ain't back then?'

Angela shook her head once more.

'He doesn't mean the half of it, love, there's no one else.'

Tammy smiled cynically.

'I wish I could believe that, but I know there's someone, I can feel it inside me.'

Angela sighed.

'He loves you, you know he does. Even if there was someone else it wouldn't mean anything, Tammy. He thinks the world of you.'

She opened her arms wide and gestured around the room.

'Look at your home, girl, he wouldn't give you all this if he didn't care about you. He wouldn't buy you the cars and the watches and everything else if he didn't care, now would he?'

Tammy enjoyed hearing the words even though they had a hollow ring to them. The gifts were purely because he tried to fill her needs and his own conscience with things. Yet she would give the lot up and go back to the council flat they had lived in when they were first married if it brought back the closeness between them.

If Nick would only hold her once more as he had then. It was the holding she craved most, the feeling of being safe in his arms, desired by the man who she loved so much it was like a physical pain to her just to look at him.

Chapter Twelve

Gino was wired. It was 9.30 in the morning and he felt as if he had been hit by a truck. His whole body seemed to ache and he had an incredible thirst. He was also still sick to his stomach and the coffee he had drunk weighed heavily inside him. Jude had advised him to stick to fizzy, sugar-loaded drinks for the thirst because it also tamed the urge to fix for a short time until you could sort yourself out. He filed that titbit away for future reference.

It would be a few days before he stopped eating properly and a few weeks before the weight dropped off him. He was also only a few weeks away from the gnawing pains that would make him literally do anything for a fix.

At the moment, though, it was all still new to him and he was determined to make the most of it and embrace this new feeling with as much dignity as he could still muster. He walked into the dirty bathroom and looked in the mirror. He had black rings under his eyes and his skin was pale and flaky. He was shocked by his own appearance and knew that one look at him would alert his mother to the fact he was taking hard drugs. It was her biggest fear and he felt a prickle of unease as he surveyed his own haunted reflection. He really loved her but her constant moaning drove him mad. Since his father had gone she had relied on him too much. Now she had a new bloke on the scene he had more free time, though.

In fairness, she did worry about him and since Sonny's death had watched him like a hawk. He had promised her time and again that he would not go the way of the majority of teens on their estate. But it was so hard because it was exciting to take drugs. It relieved the boredom and it gave you a certain credibility around the area.

Users were well known, it was a kind of fame really, and like a lot of the youngsters where he grew up it was the only fame he was ever going to have. 'Skaghead' would be his moniker from now on.

He had enjoyed the initial rush, and when he had finally gone on the nod had felt a sort of completeness that really made him feel good. It was like being asleep even though he was aware he was awake. It was awesome. The high had been momentary, but once he had gone on the nod he had never felt such a feeling of complete and utter abandonment before. His limbs had felt heavy and his skin had flushed all over when the chemical hit his brain. Then it was like being in a bath of sticky caramel. Movement was restricted for a while but it didn't matter because there was nowhere else he wanted to go. The feeling was wonderful: no worries, no cares, just being. The effect had worn off within a couple of hours and he had immediately wanted to do it again.

Gino rolled up the sleeve of his John Rocha T-shirt and gazed at the pin pricks in his arm. Smiling to himself in the mirror, he decided to do it once more. Then, as Jude had promised, he would achieve the oblivion he so desperately craved.

It was like she said: what could the world offer that he couldn't find inside his own head?

Nick snuck into the house at 7.30 the next morning to a sight he had never before seen. His mother and his wife sitting in the kitchen talking together: not shouting, fighting or being sarcastic, but actually talking to each other.

It was almost surreal.

He always liked to joke that the last time he had seen Tammy in the kitchen was before her implant operation and that was only because they kept the case of vodka in one of the larders.

After an uncomfortable night in the Range Rover he had hoped to get in, shower in the boys' bathroom, find some clean clothes and be out before Tammy managed to raise her weary head from the mascara-stained pillow. Instead she was sitting here with his mother drinking tea and they both looked less than pleased to see him.

He had scored a double this time. If his mother was on her side, he was well up the proverbial without so much as a paddle.

'You managed to get home then?' This from Tammy.

'Nah, I'm a fucking hallucination. We're all having them today – I thought you was sitting there pleasantly with me mother. Maybe someone dropped some Es in the water supply.'

Tammy wanted to laugh but knew it would be dangerous to do so. Nick had a knack for making her laugh and once she cracked a smile he knew he was back in her good books. She was determined not to fall for it today.

'I could murder a cup of tea.'

He knew she was on the point of laughing and would much rather make her do that than cry, though lately that was not always the case.

'Really, no burglars around then?'

Tammy watched her husband's face pale and she wished she could take the remark back.

'That was out of order, Tammy.'

He wasn't even shouting at her. He walked from the room and she heard him thumping up the stairs.

'That was bad, Tammy, even for you two. Go up and talk to him,' her mother-in-law prompted her.

She shook her head and said honestly, 'I can't. I *want* to hurt him, Angela, that's how I feel inside lately. If I go up there I'll only start a fight trying to find out where he was last night. He will say he slept in the car and I will know he is lying, I'll say so and cause a big fight and then it will all go even further downhill.'

She smiled at her mother-in-law.

'I know what I do, you see? I know I'm silly and I should keep me trap shut like they tell you in magazines. But I can't. I have to say it to him, I have to *know*.'

She got up.

'Might as well get the fight over with now, before he showers.'

She walked from the room, taking her mug of tea with her. In the square entrance hall she saw herself reflected in the full-length mirror. She looked good, she knew she did. Why couldn't he see that?

In the bedroom Nick was already in the shower and his mobile was ringing. Tammy slopped tea all over the polished oak flooring in her quest to get to first it. The *Dam Busters* tone was loud and shrill.

'Hello?'

The voice was feminine.

'Who's that? Is that you, Nick?'

Tammy said quietly, 'It's his wife.'

'Oh, hello, Tammy. It's Gary's wife here, is Nick about? Only Gary ain't come home again . . .'

Tammy was relieved and consequently pleased to hear from Maureen. There was no way Nick's bit on the side was her, she was a right state, consequently Tammy could be nice to her.

'Nick's in the shower. I was just going to jump in with him, you know what he's like!' The lie tripped easily off her tongue as usual. 'I'll get him to ring you back, OK?'

'At least Nick showers, Gary and water don't really mix.'

Tammy laughed.

'I know he met up with Nick last night, ain't seen the fucker since, and we are due to go shopping for a new sofa this morning,' Maureen continued.

Tammy nodded, forgetting that she couldn't be seen.

'I'll get him to ring you.'

'Thanks, love.'

Tammy rang off and stood tapping the mobile phone against her chin as she looked out over the garden. So Nick had come home and Gary had not. Nick had had every intention of staying home, she thought now, and she had sent him out into the night.

But to where, and more importantly whom?

She started to look through the mobile's phonebook for unknown names but realised he was far too shrewd to leave anything in his phone. He would know any dodgy number or numbers off by heart. And what was all this stuff about Gary Proctor doing an all nighter? Who would want to go near him without a massive monetary incentive?

She was curious now to find out what they were both up to.

Lap dancers maybe?

'Had your look, Tam?'

Nick's voice made her jump and she threw the phone at him half-heartedly.

'Gary Proctor's wife just rang. He never came home last night.'

Nick shrugged.

'So?'

Tammy sighed.

'She said he went out to meet you.'

'He did, we had a quick drink, did a bit of business – and what the fuck am I explaining myself to you for?'

Nick started to dry himself and she looked at him in wonderment. To her he was perfect. There was something about the sheer size of him that always attracted her.

'Where were you?'

She hated herself for asking but she had to know.

'I slept in the car. Now, if you ask me one more question I am going to open the balcony doors and sling you over the railings all the while whistling the tune to *Love Story*, my favourite film because his wife dies at the end.'

He was smiling at her, though, and she felt the old attraction flowing once more.

'I do love you, Tams, and I am going to see a doctor, I promise you.'

It was said humbly. But how many times had he promised her that in the past, and how many times had it placated her only until the next big fight?

'What are you doing today?' he asked.

She shrugged.

'Lunch with the girls.'

'No change there then. Will there actually be anyone you like among the bunch of horrors out today?'

Tammy was grinning once more. She loved his dry sense of humour, and when he was like he was now, contrite and trying not to hurt her, she loved him again.

'We all have a lot in common, Nick.'

He laughed out loud now and said loudly as he walked back into the en-suite, 'The only thing you lot have in common is you all started life with brown hair.'

She followed him into the bathroom.

'Where were you really, Nick?'

He wrapped the towel around his waist as he started to fill the sink with hot water for his shave. He had the TV on. She saw it was on Sky News.

'I swear to you, Tammy, that I slept in the Range Rover. I also swear on my mother's life that there is no other woman in my world.'

He locked eyes with her in the mirror and she knew somehow that he was telling her the truth, yet still couldn't let herself believe him.

'Fuck knows, I have enough trouble with you, girl!'

He smiled sadly at her.

'But I have told you before, if you want to go, or you want me to go, then I will. It's all yours, Tams, because I can't live like this any more. It's hard for me, being like I am, not being able to perform. I have swallowed your little boyfriends and swallowed everyone thinking you rule me because I don't do anything about them. But we have to sort this out once and for all, love.'

He was still watching her and she could feel her lips trembling. He turned to her then and hugged her tight.

'Since that boy died, Tams, I hate this fucking house. I hate being in it and having sex is the last thing on my mind. Remember what that quack said in America? He said it was all stress-related, didn't he?'

She nodded.

'So can you imagine the stress I am under now? I see him all the time in me mind's eye. I think I can hear him in the house. I don't even want the boys home for the holidays because I feel nervous around them. I'm terrified something like it might happen again.'

She was stroking his back gently.

'None of that was your fault . . .'

'Well, it feels like it. I have ducked and dived all me life and I have hurt people – really hurt them at times. But he was a kid, Tams, a young boy.'

She squeezed him to her, enjoying the feel of his body against hers.

'I am sorry, Nick, I don't know what gets into me at times. I'm so bloody jealous.'

'I am the one who should be jealous, Tams. You're getting it after all whatever the situation is between us, and I don't cause any hag because I know it's my own fault.'

It was the first time he had ever said anything about her other life out loud.

'It means nothing to me, Nick. They just make me feel better . . . make me feel wanted.'

'But you are wanted, Tams!'

She looked up into his eyes and was surprised to see tears in them.

'I only wish I could believe that, Nick.'

'Believe it.'

'It still wouldn't be enough, whatever you said.'

He sighed.

'Which brings us back to square one then, don't it? Should I stay or should I go?'

Louis Clarke and Tyrell were eating a large breakfast in a café off the Wandsworth Road. It was a real heart attack breakfast and they were enjoying it immensely.

'Look, it might not have gone too well last night, but for fuck's sake, Lou, this is all new to me, ain't it? Why else do you think I wanted you on board?'

'I think you should leave it. I have a bad feeling about it all.'

Tyrell didn't answer. He carried on eating, wondering how long it would be before the pain inside him eased.

'I can't, Lou, but I would understand if you left me to it.'

Louis smiled.

'We need to sort something out here, Tyrell. I think Terry is up for helping us full-time – he said as much.'

Tyrell nodded.

'Thanks, Lou.'

'Shall we go and see Jude then?'

It seemed the logical place to start as far as Louis was concerned but he had been nervous of saying it to his friend.

Tyrell nodded but he was gradually losing his appetite. His biggest fear was that he'd discover Sonny's death could have been avoided, and it was Jude, not himself, who could have made sure of that. Tyrell pushed the terrifying thought from his mind. He didn't know how he'd cope with a discovery like that.

'I just need to sort me blokes out then we can get off. You know Jude, she don't surface with the rest of the world. She'll still be out of it.'

Louis, who hated her with a vengeance, didn't answer. Instead he concentrated on his food and berated himself silently for getting involved with something that could only bring his friend added grief.

But what else could he do?

Louis had seen Jude out of her nut, being taken to a locked ward, and poor distraught Sonny Boy clawing at the ambulance doors as he and Tyrell tried to coax him into their car. She had got off with court fines after shoplifting charges and even assaults because of Sonny and the way he could not cope without her. The boy had done anything he had purely to feed her and her habit. So why was Tyrell so determined to find out the worst about him? God himself knew he had few illusions left concerning the boy as it was.

Louis had a bad feeling about the lot of it. Something was not right about Sonny Boy's death and he for one was not sure he wanted to know what it was.

'Mrs Proctor?'

Maureen nodded, instinctively wary of the two men on her doorstep.

'I might be. Who wants to know?'

The older man sighed.

'Come on, stop playing games, where's Gary?'

She shrugged.

'How the fuck should I know?'

'Well, his car has been found abandoned at Stansted airport and there was over a kilo of cocaine in the boot. So we wondered if he had gone on a little holiday, see?'

She shrugged, closing the door on them.

'I ain't seen him. If you catch up with him before I do, give him my best, won't you?'

They had played this game before.

'Can we come in?'

The policeman's voice was loud through the front door.

'Have you got a warrant?'

Her voice was even louder. She had been playing the game a lot longer than they had.

'No . . .'

'Then fuck off!'

'We can get one.'

Maureen didn't bother to answer. Instead she went upstairs and ransacked the house for anything incriminating. By the time they came back with the warrant she was leafing through the sofa catalogue. She had disposed of anything dodgy-looking by handing it over the fence to her neighbours who, fortunately, had no warrant pending on their house.

Job done.

She would kill Gary when she got her hands on him. It was always the same, he caused hag and she cleared up the shit. As she always said to her sister, 'No change there then.'

'Do you feel better now?'

Gino nodded.

'Told you, didn't I?'

He smiled.

Jude was almost envious of his first foray into heroin. She remembered her own first time, not the guy who had turned her on, he was scum, but that first feeling of belonging somewhere. And that somewhere was inside her own body. The way to true escape did not lie in plane tickets or a fulfilling job, the bullshit that straight people always gave you. The power lay in a needle for anyone who cared to use it.

He was on the nod again, in the twilight zone as Sonny used to say when Jude opted out of reality. She had been on it so long now she couldn't function if the gear was cut too much. The dealer they used cut it with quinine and it was a bastard. But beggars can't be choosers. Jude had to take what she could get.

She still had a thirty-pound bag and was careful not to give Gino too much. The last thing she needed was a dead boy on her hands. But even if he did OD, he was a consenting adult as far as the police were concerned. Once they hit seventeen they were men in the eyes of the law. Didn't need their mummies and daddies down the station any more. So she wasn't too trashed.

Gino would become her new little helper, he would be the next Sonny. For that she needed to guarantee his devotion and this should do it.

She heard a loud knock on the door and went to answer it. Gino's mother was standing there, all thirteen stone of her.

'Is he here?'

Jude shook her head and said in a puzzled voice, 'Who?'

Deborah White stood there with her neat blond bob and her denim jacket, looking down her nose at Jude, and it rankled.

'Who do you think?'

Deborah was obviously not taking any shit today.

' 'Course he ain't here, what would your Gino be doing here?'

She sounded sincere and for a few seconds Deborah White remembered that this woman had just buried a child and felt a twinge of compassion for her.

'Do you know where he might be, Jude?'

She shrugged, wishing this woman a million miles away. Dead would be good.

'Nah . . .'

As she spoke, Gino jerked out of the front room towards the toilet, heaving as he felt the wave of nausea hit him. He was walking like someone drunk, lurching against the walls, the hand over his mouth already full of the yellow bile he was coughing up. It spurted through his fingers. Deborah White looked at her son and her heart stopped dead in her chest.

'Gino?'

She pushed past Jude, knocking her back against the wall.

'Oi, hold up, this is my house!'

It was her voice that did it, Deborah told herself later in the day. The way she acted like she was being wronged when Deborah's son was drugged out of his head and vomiting through taking heroin given to him by this lying scum standing not two feet away from her.

She gave Jude a punch that would have floored Giant Haystacks. She felt the other woman crumple under the force of her blow, and as she went down Deborah's foot seemed to act of its own accord and she kicked Jude in the head with all her might, sorry that she was only wearing bumpers and not a pair of officer boots. For the first time in her life she wanted to take someone's life because she knew that Jude had just taken her son's. He might not die today but he'd be as good as dead once the brown got him.

She ran to the toilet after him. The stench hit her first, and then she saw her son sprawled on the seat, his eyes glazed and his lovely new T-shirt covered in yellow bile. She was trying to pull him up and take him home with her when Jude appeared behind her.

'He had already taken it . . . I took him in. I told him he was a mug, Debbie . . .'

Deborah faced her furiously.

'You fucking whore! You took my boy and you dragged him down to your level. You lost your boy, do you want me to lose mine as well?'

Her voice was loud and by now the neighbours were crowding round the door. There was always a cabaret at Jude's, she was like the local entertainment.

'He's all I've got.'

'I was only trying to help him!'

Jude was all self-righteous now, warming to her theme.

'I lost my boy, that's right, I did. So do you think I would take part in anything like this willingly? I was trying to help him, I tell you.'

'You couldn't help anyone, Jude. You're fucking incapable of doing anything to help anyone except yourself. My Gino loved your boy, and he was a nice boy, Sonny. Despite you and your scummy fucking life, he was a nice kid. You destroyed him like you destroy everything you touch. You're a fucking junkie and junkies are shite in my book. While you kept your shit inside your own front door you was safe from me but now you are in more fucking trouble than you could ever believe possible.'

She grabbed Jude by the throat and pushed her forcibly against the wall, banging her head painfully and repeatedly against it as she shouted at her.

'I don't want to see my Gino outside the toilets renting his arse out like your fucking poor Sonny did to feed your habit. We all used to see him on our way to bingo, flogging his arse for you! You have no shame. People like you never do. We're all fucking working to keep *you* in drugs! The world has gone fucking mad!'

She started to punch Jude again and as she was dragged off, shouted, 'A fucking rent boy, Sonny! It was a disgrace what you did to that boy. Well, you're not doing it to mine.'

Louis watched the scene in shock, unable to believe what he was hearing but instinctively knowing that it was true. Tyrell was holding the big woman in his arms and trying to calm her down. The neighbours were all standing on the landing, shaking their heads and whispering among themselves. Some even had coffee, tea or can of beer in hand, depending on personal preference. It was like a party, only it wasn't to celebrate anything good, it was to witness the final humiliation of his dead son.

Deborah was calmer, crying loudly now as she said to Tyrell between sobs, 'Look at my boy . . . *she* did that. He's out of his nut on skag and *she* gave it to him. Your Sonny wouldn't touch it though God knows she tried to get him on it. I know that for a fact, I used to hear Gino and his mates talking. They all think she's so great, that because they can drink and smoke cannabis round here this is the place to be. I can't fight that, see? My house is boring in comparison, all B&Q wallpaper and *Coronation Street*. But I tell you this, I will kill her! I am taking him home now and if I find out he has been near or by this shit hole again she's fucking *dead*. Because if that's what it takes to keep him off the brown I will do it.'

Everyone fell quiet as she spoke and Tyrell looked at the woman with compassion, knowing that all she said was true.

'Go home, love, I'll sort this out. We'll get your boy back for you, sweetheart, and I guarantee he won't be round here no more.'

'Look at him. Look in that toilet and see what she has reduced him to.'

He turned and looked at Gino, saw him sprawled there, wasted, and felt the urge to clump Jude himself.

'Come on. Let's get you both home.'

He nodded to Louis who went into the toilet and, seeing the state of the boy, placed a filthy towel over his shoulder before picking him up. He carried Gino out of the flat in a fireman's lift, not sure which was filthier, the boy or the towel.

The crowd at the door dispersed slowly as he walked past them. They were all still talking among themselves and there was much whispering and shaking of heads as they saw the condition young Gino was in.

'Show's over, people.'

Tyrell walked the distraught woman out of the door, not even shutting it behind him. Jude was quiet now, feeling her neighbours' animosity and knowing that whatever pity they had felt for her son's death was over now.

Poor Jude was long gone. She was Junkie Jude again.

But she consoled herself with one fact: Gino would be back. Whatever his mother thought, he would be back. The brown had called to him as it had to her, and for all Deborah's big talk about her precious son, he was like all of them on this estate: accidents waiting to happen.

Jude slammed the door in her neighbours' faces as the police arrived on the scene. As usual no one had seen or heard anything and they were glad of that fact. So long as there were no Weapons of Mass Destruction involved they couldn't give a flying fuck what the estate's residents got up to.

Chapter Thirteen

Gino was in bed. He knew something was not right, but as Jude had given him a bigger dose than before he was out of it completely. He could not be arsed to think about what had happened and so retreated further into the drug. He was nodding for England now. Had stopped caring what was going on around him. Tyrell and Louis had settled him and Tyrell watched him for a while, remembering doing the same thing for Jude on many occasions.

This flat was a revelation, it was so spotless and homely. Gino had a much better chance than his Sonny ever did in that respect. Deborah made them all coffee and Tyrell and Louis came and sat in her kitchen and waited with her until she was calm enough to speak. Tyrell knew just how she was feeling; he had felt the same sense of futility so many times during his life with Jude.

He didn't have the heart to tell her that the feeling only got worse, never better.

'What you just said about my Sonny . . . was it true?'

Deborah turned to face him, placing the mugs of coffee on the spotlessly clean table, her eyes still red from crying and her heart sore for the truth she was going to have to tell this man.

'You really didn't know?'

Tyrell shook his head hard, making his dreads move, and she saw what a good-looking man he was. Sonny had looked like him, lighter-skinned maybe but still like him.

'Do I look like I knew?'

Deborah pulled out a chair and settled herself at the table, getting out her cigarettes and lighter and placing the ashtray near her so she could concentrate on the listening men and not have to move again.

'It started when he was about fifteen, not regular then, but I was going to bingo one night and the toilets by the bus station are a known haunt for rent boys. Well, I saw Sonny Boy near there and waved at him like.'

She took a deep drag on her cigarette before shaking her head in sorrow and saying, 'He was a nice kid, I never had a problem with him though there were plenty who did.'

Tyrell knew she was trying to tell him there was no malice involved here but he had already worked that one out for himself. One look at her boy and he understood what her row with Jude was all about.

'Go on, Mrs White.'

She took another pull on her cigarette. Louis saw her hands were shaking and knew that Jude as usual had fucked up another two lives on her merry way to constant oblivion. He would lay money that this woman would never sleep easy another night for worrying about her son, and he would be the same if the boy he had just laid out was his. She knew Gino now had a shortened life expectancy. He would maybe father a child, have a few relationships, but the main relationship in his life would be with heroin. If Jude had got inside his head, that boy was lost.

'The boys there, you can see what they are, bless them. Junkies, crack heads – well, it's like anything really, ain't it?' Deborah shrugged. 'You get used to it. At first it was shocking, you know? Seeing them there in their make up with their funny walks. But eventually they were just part of the landscape. No one really took any notice after a while. But seeing Sonny Boy there . . . it really shocked me.'

She looked into Tyrell's eyes.

'I liked him, cooked him many a dinner here, the poor little fucker. But I told my Gino to keep away from him then. Nothing personal, we all knew how good he was with Jude. People admired Sonny for the way he took care of her. And you know the worst of it all? She was never worth it. The woman is fucking carrion!'

She lit another cigarette from the butt of her last one. Standing up, she said, 'I'm going to check on my Gino then I'm having a drink. Do you want one?'

Tyrell nodded, knowing she wanted company.

'The glasses are in the cabinet by the sink.'

She walked from the room, cigarette still held firmly in her hand. Louis got up, glad of something to do. He found it hard listening to this woman talking about Sonny being a rent boy so he could only guess how much harder it must be for Tyrell. Deborah came back into the room carrying a bottle of cheap Scotch and poured them all a generous measure.

'Was he there much?'

Tyrell could hear the catch in his own voice, could hear the disbelief and the horror, had to swallow down the tears that were threatening to pour down his face. He had never known, never dreamed, that anything like that could have been the case. Why had no one ever told him?

But he knew why. They were too scared.

'Not at first, but later he was there a lot. It was Gino who told me the score, see? I had banned him from seeing Sonny as I said. Didn't want him involved in all that. You see it in the papers, you see it on TV, but we *live* it round here. This ain't a Channel Four documentary showing how the other half live, we *are* the other half! We live that shit night and day. I might not be mother of the year, and I might live in a sink estate, but I do the best I can for my kids. Sonny was on a death wish, mate. I know you don't want to hear it, but he was. She had a hold over him like I have never seen before, and that hold included my Gino. She offered them the chance to be bad boys, and living here, being part of this scummy place, they took it, grabbed the chance with both hands. It was an enticement they couldn't resist.'

Deborah gulped at her drink.

'Gino said Sonny Boy had no choice about it. If he didn't go out on the make then Jude would and Sonny hated her out on the bash, she knew he did. She had had a couple of hidings in the past, and besides she wasn't up to much any more. Didn't get the punters like, especially the state she was in. So he went out with her blessing because that lazy whore couldn't even get her arse in gear to shag for her own skag.'

Tyrell closed his eyes in distress.

Deborah started to cry again as she said plaintively: 'What am I going to do now, eh? Now she's given my boy a taste of nothing. Now he knows what all the shouting is about. He will want it, he's stupid enough for skag. The thieving I could cope with, but not this. I will kill her. I swear to God I will swing for that whore, and I don't care who knows it.'

Louis refilled her glass for her, knowing she would need to soften the edges today.

'I'll keep me eye on him, I promise. Jude won't have him back there, Mrs White. I couldn't help me own boy because I didn't know enough, but I will help yours. I can't say fairer than that,' Tyrell told her.

She nodded. It was what she had hoped he'd say.

'He loved you, Sonny Boy did, I know that much. He talked about you all the time.'

It was small comfort, but it was all she had to offer him.

* * *

Nick was at his club in Bermondsey, a small spieler frequented by known faces. The good thing was no one could get in without either being well known to the other members or else having enough firepower to give Tony Blair an excuse to invade.

The latter, though unlikely, had been tried over the years by better people than the PM, and the place was still standing and holding its own in an ever-changing world.

Stevie was nervous today and this fact was annoying Nick.

Anyone would think he had never done a bit of skulduggery in his life before and he had just come out after doing a big lump. Good job he didn't have to deal with half of what Nick had to deal with on a daily basis. He was only trying to keep his head above water and the shit he had to deal with was astronomical. Now he had Stevie having a heart attack over a pile of shit. In fairness his old mate was still on licence so he had good reason to be bricking it, but Nick was not in the mood for babysitting.

His annoyance came over in his voice as he spoke sharply to his friend.

'They can't trace him back to us. They'll think he was dealing out and had a capture of some kind. The usual for dealers who try and out too much stuff too quickly. The filth will think Gary had open wallet surgery. It happens all the time, bigger firms jumping on the little dealers. There's no way it can come back to us, so stop fucking tarting out and have a drink, for fuck's sake.'

Stevie could see the logic of what Nick was saying but it had all got too heavy for him. He had wanted to spank Gary Proctor, he didn't deny that, hurt him badly, but death had not been on the agenda. He had already done a big lump, unlike Nick who had been lucky enough to live a charmed life. If he had done a bit of bird he might understand why Stevie was so reluctant to go back and do some more.

Not that he had any intention of pointing that fact out in the near future, of course.

'Fucking arsehole bandit! I mean, what the fuck is all that about?'

A young redhead with slim legs and a suspiciously heavy chest came over and smiled at Stevie in a friendly way. Then, looking at Nick, she said in a broad Essex accent: 'Got me wages?'

He laughed. He liked her, she was a good kid. Eighteen but looking twelve without make-up, she had been stripping since she was a fifteen-year-old runaway. He nodded to the girl behind the bar and she passed him an envelope.

'Here you are, love, see you next week.'

She fluttered her eyelashes at him and he winked back at her but they both knew it was a game, he had no interest in her and she liked him all the more because of that. Men had been coming on to her since she had first gone into care as a rather pretty nine year old. She now knew better than women three times her age how to take care of herself.

She smiled at Stevie once more because Nick had assured her he might be up for it. She liked the faces, they normally gave good sex and were always generous. He was looking at her as if he was up for a good time.

Stevie was. He had been good for too long. His wife was a star and he appreciated her waiting for him, but she had the body of a forty year old and unfortunately for her he had dreamed for too many years about the bodies of twenty year olds. This little one was just his cup of tea, and far too good to knock back.

Life was too short for monogamy, he had learned that much in nick. As he started chatting to the girl, Nick grinned. Twenty minutes later they were standing at the other end of the bar and Nick was as far from Stevie's mind as his wife and kids were.

The redhead was a good sort all right, she had done a sterling job of taking that miserable ponce off Nick's hands. He knew Stevie had wanted to hurt Proctor, he had said as much, and Proctor had been hurt. Nick had done the main graft of the night, so what was

Stevie worrying about? He had only given him a slap by their standards.

Nick liked Stevie but he was an old woman in some respects. Still, a lump could do that to a body. They either came out able to hold the world on their shoulders and better for the experience, or else they came out like Stevie, frightened of their own shadow.

But he had wanted Proctor sorted and he had been sorted, the same way that piece of thieving shit Lance Walker had been sorted.

End of fucking story.

Tyrell and Louis went back to Jude's.

Louis felt for his friend, knowing that the utter humiliation was killing him. Louis had heard rumours about Sonny, everyone had. He was a one-boy crime wave and at first it had been seen as amusing. When he had started nicking off his own, though, it had ceased to be funny. It was only Tyrell's standing in the community that had stopped the boy being given a good slap.

But Louis had never heard anything about him being a bender. He tried to imagine how he would feel in Tyrell's shoes and couldn't even get close. But then, he had always seen the boy differently from everyone else. It was what made him a good man. Tyrell had loved his son and Louis respected that.

As they walked inside the flat Jude was standing in the hallway as if waiting for them. One eye was black and her neck was already bruising. She looked like she had been given a good hiding, which of course was the case.

'You cunt.'

Tyrell didn't know who was more surprised at his words, Jude or himself. It was not a word he had ever used to her though he knew it was part of her everyday life like the squalor that surrounded her, the smell she gave off. She was barefoot and he could see the needle marks between her toes and the thread veins all over her ankles. He

211

saw her through everyone else's eyes and all the guilt he usually felt evaporated. In its place was a hatred that frightened him with its intensity.

He saw the shiftiness in her blue eyes that he had never dared to acknowledge before because then he'd have had to deal with the knowledge of what she was really like. He had always given her the benefit of the doubt, but no longer.

'I've been called worse than that, Tyrell.'

He smirked at her and Jude felt the first real prickle of unease.

'I bet you have.'

He took a joint from his jacket pocket and lit it with shaking hands. The smell of skunk was heavy and sweet as it battled with the other odours in the flat.

'So he was flogging his arse, was he?'

She flicked her hair out of her eyes in a gesture of contempt.

' 'Course not. You know what they're like round here, they talk shite.'

But the fear was there, in the minute tremor in her voice, and Tyrell knew he had her on the ropes. All he had to do was deliver the final knock-out punch.

So he did.

'I believe Deborah, Jude.'

She had been banking on his not wanting to believe any of it, but as they looked into each other's eyes he finally knew the truth of it.

Tyrell was a big man, a handsome man, his dreads gave him a dignity that was somehow lacking in the younger West Indian men. It wasn't a fashion statement with Tyrell, it was who he was. He had a wide face, high cheekbones and slanting eyes. He had never appreciated just how good-looking he was, had never cared about anything like that.

Jude shrugged him away dismissively and said in a flat bored voice that was somehow aimed at goading him, 'Believe what you like. It's too late now, ain't it? He's gone.'

She spoke about Sonny as if he was a puppy that had run away, or a stranger who meant nothing, to her.

Tyrell realised then that that was exactly what her son had been to her. He was purely a means to an end, and he had a sneaking feeling poor Sonny had realised it all along.

Louis wasn't prepared for the attack when it took place and neither was Jude. She disappeared under a hail of blows that would have killed any other woman. It took Louis a good five minutes to drag his friend off the now terrified Jude. All the stunts she had pulled on Tyrell over the years had never produced a reaction to match this one. If someone had told her he would raise his hand to her Jude would have laid her last fix in a bet stating otherwise.

Never before had Louis seen anger like it. He knew it had been bottled up a long time. This man's son had led a dog's life and died prematurely. Now it was payback time for Jude because she had not tried to prevent it happening. In fact, had made sure something like that would happen eventually. Sonny never stood a chance of leading a decent life.

He stared at the wreck of the woman before him and her bloody face and sagging countenance did nothing for him now. If someone had told him he would raise his hand to a woman he would have laughed in their face yet he knew that he could cheerfully break her neck now and not lose a moment's sleep over it.

The hate was deep now, ingrained.

'Where did my boy get that gun, Jude?'

He was still panting from exertion as he spoke and Jude, broken and yet still standing, said nastily, 'I *don't* know.'

Her voice set him off once more and when he attacked her again it took all Louis's strength to drag his friend from the flat.

As he pushed him into the car Louis wondered what the repercussions of this night would be.

It wasn't long before he found out.

*　*　*

213

Maureen Proctor stood staring at the second pair of policemen to visit her today. She was unable to take in what they'd just told her.

'Are you sure it's my Gary?'

A PC nodded sadly.

'Is he dead?'

'No, Mrs Proctor, but he is very poorly.'

Poorly?

The word was weird to her. It was one people had used in her mother's day. Coming out of this young man's mouth, it made her want to laugh.

'And he has been beaten up and burned, you say?'

He nodded once more.

'But why would someone do that to my old man? He is an irritating fucker but no one we know would go that far.'

'Would you like us to take you to the hospital?'

She looked at him as if he had grown another head in front of her eyes.

'Do I fuck! I'll drive meself.'

All the way to Billericay burns unit Maureen wondered who Gary had pissed off this time. She was also wondering who to tell first because chances were someone she knew would be aware of who was responsible for the attack. But it was the kilo of cocaine they'd found in his car that really threw her.

Drugs were not Gary's forte, or Nick's, and they'd worked closely on everything. Gary might snort cocaine, he liked the high, but he wasn't up to dealing it. The sentences were far too stiff. He stuck with his other businesses.

Or maybe she didn't know about this move? Maybe he had kept it quiet for the simple reason that he knew she hated drugs of any kind. As she negotiated her way through the traffic she marvelled at all the people she could see going about their lives without having to worry about knocks on the front door, about whether or not their husbands would still be home for Christmas or if they would be visiting them inside for a long time, pretending an affection that wasn't there any more because affection needed human contact and that was impossible now.

Maureen pushed the thoughts from her head. Gary was gravely ill in hospital, not on remand or waiting for bail.

Beaten and burned, though. It sounded like nonce treatment . . . Was he up to something else she didn't know about?

Chances were he was, she acknowledged bitterly. But if he was then it was surely not with Nick by his side. Nick was known as a good family man. He was not even a womaniser. He talked the talk and he flirted, but that was as far as it went. Gary, on the other hand, was like a rutting pig. Had he dabbled with someone else's bird? Or, more to the point, daughter?

The thought frightened Maureen.

She decided to talk to Nick Leary as soon as she could and see what he knew. But not on her mobile. She would ring from a payphone so she could be sure no one could trace anything. If this was over Gary's usual business then she and the kids were home and dry money wise. She would be due some compensation from Nick and would want that sooner rather than later. If Gary died she would need a lump sum and access to his percentages.

She had a lot to think about and Nick Leary, though fair, was not a man to cross. She only hoped Gary had remembered that.

Tyrell sat with his boys and Sally in the lounge of his former home and watched as his sons chatted to one another.

They were good kids. He was proud of them. They were kind, happy, and best of all respectful. He loved them and once he had loved being here with them. Now he felt like a visitor.

It was funny but the room seemed smaller than he remembered and it had only been a week or so since he had lived here all the time. Now he felt as if the walls were coming in on him.

As he watched them he thought of Sonny, and the way he had been living. How could he not have known about it? Why wasn't he aware that something was so drastically wrong?

But then, in Jude's life there was always something going wrong, always something out of the ordinary happening. It was normality for Jude. All her life she had done things that most people would instinctively have seen as wrong. Sonny had grown up with her habit ruling his life. If Jude was stoned then the world was a good place to be. If she was wired then everyone paid the price. Someone knocking the door down at three in the morning for money . . . well, didn't that happen to everyone?

His eldest son had lived that kind of life, one where violence and the threat of violence were commonplace, and Tyrell had let him. But it was the knowledge that Sonny had actually sold himself to buy his mother drugs that was eating at him like acid. Thinking of what his Sonny had done with those men for money, Tyrell hated him for it even as he loved him.

He had seen those boys around the stations in London, had felt sorry for them even as they disgusted him. Had shooed them away from him in case anyone thought he was trying to attract them. He had loathed them and their lifestyles and had patted himself on the back because he'd known it would never happen to any of his sons. They would never *need* to do anything like that, would they? He was there for them, wasn't he?

This new knowledge explained a lot of things to him now, things he had found suspect but had not felt able to question at the time. Like the way Sonny would disappear late at night without any explanation, and the two mobiles he always carried with him. One must have been for business, that was why he always took those calls in private. He must have had a regular clientele.

When Tyrell had been told what had happened to his boy he had never dreamed anything could make him feel worse than that.

But he had been wrong.

* * *

Angela was alone once more. Tammy had left the house to go for lunch. Shortly after that she had gone to her own annexe and made herself a hot milk laced with brandy. She sipped it slowly, her TV tuned to ITV 2. She enjoyed Sally Jesse Raphael, she was an older, more sensible talk show host than the others. Angela particularly liked the strait-laced way she confronted her guests when she thought they were in the wrong.

If only life was that easy.

These people on TV put the world to rights in a few minutes. In the time it took Angela to make a cup of tea they had saved a marriage, exposed a love rat or informed some teenage trollop who the father of her child actually was.

For her it was normally compulsive viewing, making her feel better than those people who used a visual medium to air their filthy washing in the public arena. She couldn't understand the mentality herself. These messed-up people with their dirty lives got paid to make the programme interesting and confrontational. They'd face the baying audience with defiance as if to say, 'Look at me and the fuck up I have made, not only of my life but my children's and their families'.

'How clever I am because now I am a topic of conversation for a load of jobless wonders who in their hearts should know better than to waste precious hours of their lives watching this crap.'

Oh, she was hurting all right.

She was hurting for a son who had been verbally abused all his young life, who had had to stand at the end of the bed and watch his father beat and then rape his mother.

What did these people know of hurt and pain? What did these people know of humiliation, of degradation? What did they know of a young boy who had tried to save his sister from the same fate only to have the indignities heaped upon himself?

217

How could she ever tell her daughter-in-law about all that? How could she ever expect anyone to understand, especially Tammy who lived for sex and for what she believed it stood for.

Sex wasn't about love, not most of the time. It was about keeping people, cowing to people, making them do what you wanted. Sex was a weapon of choice for many men and she knew that from first-hand experience. Angela poured herself a large brandy and gulped it down. The fear was upon her again and even though she knew her husband was lying in a cold grave she still half expected him to come storming through the door at any second. She knew that, at times, Nick expected it too. Such was her husband's anger it still impinged on their lives all these years later.

Angela sighed, knowing that she was going off on a tangent because she didn't know how to fix her own life or more to the point her son's. Didn't know what to do with the terrible knowledge she now had in her possession.

Today, she had been snooping, as usual. She couldn't help it. She had seen something she had never thought to see again in her lifetime. Proof of her son's derangement.

She would have to try to live with the knowledge, yet she wasn't sure that she could cope with it and all that it entailed.

There was a kink in Nick's nature and she had helped to put the kink into place. She knew that better than anyone.

So what was she going to do about it?

There had been a time, not too long ago, when Nick and Tammy's marriage ending would have been cause for celebration to her. She'd howled at the fates that had brought her son and his wife together.

Not any more, though. She was finally seeing poor Tammy and the life she had to live with Nick through clear impartial eyes. And what she now knew terrified her.

Bloody men and their constant craving for excitement . . . why would Tammy want to come home to a house that was empty of all natural affection and love? Angela set no store by all this sex talk. Everyone these days thought they should be having orgasms all over the place and still shagging until their pacemakers packed up with all the excitement. But in its place, which to her was every Saturday night after a few drinks whether you needed it or not, it kept a marriage solid.

Why the hell hadn't her son addressed his problems years before? But then, as she knew from bitter experience, some problems were hard to face up to, let alone resolve.

She opened her little safe and took out the photos. As she gazed at them again she felt tears threaten but sniffed them back. She was harder than Tammy, had had to be.

As she looked around the spacious annexe her son had built for her and saw the beautiful furnishings Tammy had helped her choose, Angela wanted to cry so badly but all the years of keeping her feelings below the surface made it impossible.

When her husband had been at his worst she had been stoical. No matter what happened you never let the outside world know about it. Years ago that had meant the neighbours. Now, though, their nearest neighbour was so far away, you'd need a bus to get to them.

But Tammy's crying had affected Angela more than she would ever have thought possible. As she had heard her sobbing it was as if a steel trap had been lifted off her own emotions and she had been forced to face up to the fact that her daughter-in-law was terribly unhappy through no fault of her own. The long talk they had had together had changed Angela's perspective. That and the contents of her safe.

She had known for a long time that things weren't right between them, and had blamed Tammy and her tantrums and her spending. But inside she'd always known it couldn't have been that one-sided. Nick wasn't his father's son in name only, she reflected bitterly.

Tammy wanted love as well as sex. As the years had gone by and there had been neither from Nick it had twisted and almost destroyed her. Angela knew how that felt only too well which was why, for the moment, she would keep her own counsel about the photographs she'd found in her son's coat pocket just ten minutes after Tammy had left.

Not for his sake – she was done with worrying about her son the moment she discovered them – but for the sake of Tammy, the daughter-in-law she'd never even liked before and now wanted only to love and protect.

Book Two

Be not deceived; God is not mocked: for whatsoever a man soweth,
that shall he also reap.

– Galatians, 6:7

He's mad that trusts in the tameness of a wolf, a horse's health,
a boy's love, or a whore's oath.

– William Shakespeare
King Lear (Act III, scene vi)

Chapter Fourteen

Nick watched his wife as she drank her wine. Actually gulped her wine would have been more like it. But if he could at least get her round to his way of thinking then at seventy quid a throw the bottle would have been worth it. This was an expensive and select restaurant and only Nick could have got the prime table here at such short notice. It was a place to be seen and he knew that would appeal to his wife. She loved being seen with him, and the fact he had brought her here would really please her. All her friends would hear about it and for poor Tams that was what was really important.

He had to set her mind straight on what had happened to Gary. It was important to get her on board.

Nick filled his wife's glass once more.

'Get that down you, Tams.'

She smiled, she was half-cut already. If it was any other man she was having lunch with she would be expecting them to put the hit on her in the next few minutes. But as it was Nick, she did not hold out much hope, though it had been known in the dim and distant past. She could always hope.

'So who do you think did that to Gary then?'

He shrugged nonchalantly.

'Fucked if I know, Tammy.'

She watched him closely. He was lying through his teeth, she knew that much. But she also knew that to anyone else he would look honest, baffled even. Nick Leary was a great actor. In many ways he'd missed his true vocation.

'So your best mate and business partner is found crisply fried in a lock-up and you don't think it's a bit strange like? You don't even want to know who did it?'

He shook his head again.

'That's right.'

Tammy looked at him a few seconds longer before saying brightly, 'I'll ask round the wives then. Between us we can usually get to the bottom of any skulduggery round here.'

He stared at her, aware that other diners were watching the exchange but unable to hear what they were talking about.

'Oh, no, you won't, lady.'

He grabbed her wrist tightly, causing her to wince.

'Look at me, Tams, and read my lips. He was doing a dolly behind me back and he had a capture, all right?'

She nodded, a little bit worried now by the tone of his voice.

Nick looked troubled too, but then that was nothing new. He had looked like that since the burglary. He was going greyer by the day and the frown lines on his face were quickly replacing the laughter lines.

As usual she felt sorry for him. That was another knack he had. Any problem of his had always evoked her pity. Knowing the macho man front he put on, it had to be hard for him living this lie.

She also knew a lot of people including the police would think he had something to do with Gary's accident or that he knew who was behind it.

They were too closely linked for him not to.

But thanks to the unfortunate affair of the burglar, he would be looked upon kindly. It was how their world worked and they both knew that.

224

Nick carried on eating as if he didn't have a care in the world, but then in their world front was everything. And no one could front it out like her and Nick. They were expert at it, had had to be considering the life they lived.

Just like Nick Junior, she either wanted to kick him or kiss him, there was never a happy medium. His oldest friend was half dead, had been horrifically attacked, and Nick looked crushed, yet there was still something not right about any of it.

He didn't look crushed enough.

She was convinced he was in on it all, that there was something more going on than Gary doing a dolly. She ran the facts around her head for a few moments and then said quietly, 'Has this got anything to do with Stevie Daly?'

It was a shot in the dark and she only said the name from instinct. Years of throwing names at Nick to get a reaction had made her adept at it.

She was rewarded by seeing his face pale even more.

'You missed your vocation, Tams, you should have been a filth.'

She laughed then, pleased to have been proved right as he knew she would be. He could always work her and she still hadn't sussed that fact out.

'I'm too short.'

He studied his wife. She was tiny really. It had always been part of the attraction for him, especially when she was co-operating like this. She looked vulnerable, but he knew it wouldn't last because he could see the way her eyes were beginning to change colour. It was so minute only someone who knew her really well would notice it. She was about to start fighting him and he wasn't sure he was able for it.

'So what did Gary do then? It must have been bad. Stevie's a bank robber, not a murderer, there's a big difference.'

Nick sighed.

'Don't know what you're talking about, Tammy. You been watching too many soaps.'

She knew he wouldn't say anything more but there was more to this and it did have something to do with Stevie, so at least that settled her mind a bit.

'This wasn't you, was it?' she said, just checking.

He shook his head.

She wondered what to say next. The drink was taking hold and she was a little bit frightened. She decided to believe him; it was all she could do really. She had to protect herself, her home and her kids, they both knew that.

'Fair enough. But can we expect a knock at the door?'

'If plod asks, I was with you all night, OK?'

She smirked, her blue eyes almost grey now, a steely grey as she realised this was what all the chatting up was for. He'd let her get it out of him. She was learning how he operated but wouldn't let him know that.

Knowledge was power, as he was always saying.

'I see. You need me to corroborate your pack of lies, hence this lunch. I should have guessed.'

'You always were quick on the uptake, Tams, it's why I married you.'

She smiled then.

'So *that* was the reason, was it?'

The hurt was back in her voice and he wondered how long it would be before she got drunk, started a fight, and he could in all conscience take her home. One thing with Tams, though, a message once received was well understood. Whatever happened he had his alibi, they both knew that.

Louis Clarke was drinking a large iced vodka in a drinking club in Clerkenwell, and filling his brothers in on the new information about Tyrell's son. The other men were all amazed by this turn of events and could tell how embarrassed Louis was even to be talking about it to them.

'I feel like a fucking gossip!'

They all laughed nervously.

'Well, you are in a way, aren't you?'

Terry Clarke was red in the face with anger and embarrassment.

'If that was one of my boys, I'd go mad.'

They all nodded, agreeing.

Tyrell was a good bloke, respected and liked. For this to befall him was upsetting for all the men at the table. It was like any disaster when it was too close to home, it made them feel the same could happen in their families. You tried to protect your kids, but whether or not you managed it was another thing entirely these days. The goal posts had been moved and the world was changing by the hour.

'It weren't him, it was that piece of shit that bred him. That Jude. Fucking animal she is.'

'How did he take it?'

This from Colin, the eldest of the brothers.

'How do you think! How would you take it?'

'Definitely not up the arse.'

Terry's voice was laced with innuendo and his brothers all laughed even as they felt guilty about it.

Louis sighed.

'Look, are we going to give him a hand or not? I think he has a point about there being more to it all than meets the eye.'

Colin nodded then said, 'I know Nick Leary, though, and he is as sound as a pound. No way he was involved.'

His tone of voice dismissed any hint of disagreement.

'But who might be up for robbing him? I know he had a bit of trouble with Leo Green a while back. But Leo's not a gas meter bandit. He's just give him a slap and be done with it.'

Terry frowned. Leo Green was a gun and drug dealer. Neither was Nick Leary's forte. He was strictly clubs and raves, fronted by his building business which even on its own kept him quids in.

'What did they fall out over?'

'Leo was dealing out in his clubs. You know the score – get a few youngsters to take in the gear. From what I gather it was shit and one of the kids nearly died. Fucking Es and Rohypnol – date raping, for fuck's sake. What's wrong with getting birds drunk or giving them a bit of coke? Young people today have no fucking class! Anyway, Nick Leary had a word and it all fell out of bed, but Nick ain't someone to mug off, he can handle himself.'

Billy Clarke intervened then.

'But so can Leo. They must have traded off somehow if there was no blood.'

None of them answered and Louis went up to the bar and ordered more drinks. Billy glanced around at his brothers. They looked like clones of one another, and all of them together at one table was an intimidating sight. That was their strength, and they all knew it. No one messed with the Clarkes who always took each other's part. It was a useful business arrangement as well as a good front before the general public.

'What about Leary, though? Do you think Leo Green might have set that up in retribution like?'

Louis shook his head.

'I can't see it meself, but I will mention it to Tyrell. He's in a right state since he found out about his boy being gay.'

Billy sighed.

'Was he though? I remember seeing a documentary about rent boys and a lot of them only do it for money, they don't enjoy it. They ain't benders as such.'

Terry and Colin laughed.

'When have *you* ever watched a fucking documentary?'

Billy flushed.

'You know what Caroline's like, she watches all that crap.'

The other brothers all looked at one another and laughed once more. Caroline was a tall leggy brunette with wide-spaced blue eyes, a body like a supermodel's and a mind like a steel trap. Billy adored her and she adored him and all the brothers had a crush on her in one way or another. After three kids and twelve years of marriage she still looked like a teenager.

Billy took the joking in good part as they knew he would, whereas Terry on the other hand would have kicked off.

'I don't like Leo Green, a fucking tosser he is!' grouched Colin.

'Who's rattled your cage?'

He was the quiet one of the boys, the thinker. Though he often came over like a rambling buffoon he was in fact the brains of the outfit in many respects. They listened to him when he did speak because it was unusual.

Colin gulped at his pint of lager before wiping his mouth noisily and saying, 'Years ago, Leo had a tear up with a geezer who was bringing in dirty films from Amsterdam. Real near the mark they were, couldn't get nothing like it here them days. Anyway the geezer had him over, and do you know what Leo did? This is how snidey that cunt can be – he arranged a holiday in a caravan with his wife and kids, packed up the car, even had the dog with him, then he cut the geezer up in his lorry. The geezer got out by Dartford tunnel, right, and Leo did him with a crowbar. Fucking crunched him, in front of his wife and kids and all.

'When plod came Leo give them this big sob story about how the lorry had nearly run them off the road, how he was an innocent bloke going on holiday with his wife and kids, just grabbed the crowbar because the bloke was going to do his motor with the kids in it. Fucking plod nearly put him up for a bravery award! Well, the bloke couldn't tell the filth what it was really about, could he? Got a capture, went to court and got banged up for threatening behaviour, ABH, you name it! Leo thought it was hilarious. That scum actually used his own kids to get even. Suppose it had all fell out of bed and the bloke had done *him* and then wrecked his car? His kids were babies, he put them and his wife and dog at risk to make a fucking point! Personally, I think he is capable of anything. I have never dealt with him because of it.'

'So you think *he* could be involved in Sonny Boy creeping round Leary's house?'

Colin shrugged.

'I don't know. All I'm saying is, he deals with young boys through his drug peddling, so it's sensible to think he might at least have known Sonny. He deals in guns and all, which is what Tyrell was interested in, weren't it? Where the boy got the iron from in the first place. Leo might not be personally involved, but he might put us all on the right track there.'

'What do you mean, he deals in guns?'

This from Louis who sounded surprised.

Colin said slowly and as if he was talking to a five year old, 'You go to his house and he sells you a gun, that is what dealing means.'

They all laughed once more.

'Very funny. I thought he only dealt in drugs?'

Colin shrugged.

'One of my blokes got a lovely bit of iron off him, he's cheaper than most and all. But knowing Leo, there's a catch to it, has to be. He's a user.'

'Where's Tyrell now?'

Louis shrugged.

'Stoned out of his fucking box. Since he left Sally he's changed. Can't seem to get Sonny Boy out of his mind. But that's natural, I suppose, considering.'

'I don't like that Sally,' Billy put in. 'Caroline said to me that she's cold, and you know my old woman – she's rarely got a bad word to say about anyone.'

They all nodded. It was a measure of the respect they felt for Caroline that the men at the table would listen to her opinion without a second's thought. Unlike their own wives and girlfriends whose opinions were definitely never sought and never really listened to unless they were about the home or the kids.

Their territory as it were.

'I like old Tyrell.'

Billy sounded sad for their friend.

They all nodded in agreement.

'A top bloke, and I think the sooner he gets to the bottom of all this the better off he'll be. The Yanks call it closure.'

Everyone looked at Colin again and Terry said loudly and in a high camp voice, 'Hark at fucking Miriam Stoppard over there.'

They were all laughing once more, but it was forced and the mood turned decidedly sombre. At the end of the day, the last thing they wanted to think about was the abortion that had passed for Sonny Boy's life.

The thought of their own children's futures frightened them now because Sonny had been given access to a good life by his father, and look what had happened to him. None of them wanted their boys ducking and diving, grafting for a living. They wanted them to be straight in more ways than one. And none of them wanted their daughters to marry men like themselves. They didn't want them to have lives like their mothers had, constantly wondering where the old man was, would he be home, would he be nicked? Or what the women all saw as the biggest problem of all: who was he shagging?

They wanted far better for their kids or what the fuck was all the hard graft for?

Jude was starting to panic. Her brown was nearly all gone and Gino was nowhere to be seen. She'd thought he would have unloaded his mother by now, been kicked out of the house and ensconced in Jude's flat for the duration.

If he didn't show up soon then it meant she had to go out and earn a few quid herself and she didn't like doing that. It wasn't so much what she had to do for the money, it was the fact she had to get dressed up and actually leave the flat. Those days were long gone for Jude. She liked to be indoors, away from the world and out of her nut. It was the only way she could cope.

She would have to have a bath as well, and since Sonny had died the bath had hardly been in use. It stank. He had tidied up, washed sheets and done the mundane household stuff. As time had worn on it had been second nature to him. He liked being clean, would spend hours in the bathroom.

Jude also knew that with her bruises she would not be first call for any of the men at the market so all in all she was in a bind.

She couldn't get any more gear through the sympathy vote after the turn out with Gino's mother and she didn't have anything to sell. Even Sonny's portable was gone now as well as his CDs and his Walkman. She could ring up and get a house clearance firm to take his bed and wardrobe, but where would the wannabes sleep then?

She was not going to ask Tyrell for help, not for a good while anyway. Sonny's other mates had given her a wide berth since she had introduced Gino to the brown so she was left with only one choice. She picked up Sonny's mobile and rang the number she had got from Big Ellie. It went straight to answerphone and Jude turned the mobile off with shaking hands. What she was doing was dangerous, she knew, but she was stuck between a rock and a hard place. She had no choice. Nick Leary owed her and this number could get her untold riches. He had a shock coming to him, she was determined on that much.

She would give it an hour and try once more.

In the meantime she would make her way to Verbena's. She was always good for a tap when Jude was desperate.

Even if she did have to listen to her Bible-thumping to get it.

*   *   *

Sally watched her husband as he packed the last of his clothes into the large suitcase they usually kept for holidays. She could not believe that he was leaving her for good. But as she looked at his face she saw the determination there, and was sorry to realise that this actually was the end of their marriage. Once he walked out with that bag, she knew she would never be able to allow him back. Her pride would not permit that. She worried more about what people thought of her and her family than she did about her own happiness. She knew that Tyrell knew that as well and was using it against her and she couldn't blame him, not really.

She was her mother's daughter as he had pointed out many times over the years. It was being proved now because she would not ask him to stay. Inside she wanted to beg him not to go because she still loved him. But they both knew she was more worried about being seen as the deserted wife than anything else.

He looked at her with fresh eyes, and wondered how she had ever snared him. If it had not been for her his eldest son would have lived with him, but Sonny had always known he was not really welcome with Sally around.

It was as if she had been convinced he would taint her boys and maybe she was right. But the world tainted kids. They could come from the best homes and still smoke a bit of puff. Look at Prince Harry.

In the bedroom Tyrell could smell the lavender oil she sprayed on the pillows to aid restful sleep. He glanced at the tasteful pictures on the wall, and knew she was just holding back from straightening the bedspread because his case was on it, and it was rumpled.

Sally's life had been so different from Jude's. She always had everything under control and he had been attracted to that once. Now all he saw when he looked at her was the way she had never wanted his eldest boy messing up her home. It wasn't really to do with the other boys, it was his chaotic life she couldn't stand. If he had been a graduate he would have been welcomed

233

with open arms. Sally was a snob, and the worst type of snob at that.

He only hoped his other sons achieved, because if they didn't she would be the same with them. She was like her own mother in that way: saw her kids as a reflection of herself and worried constantly how other people perceived her.

But he was on to her now and he would make sure his other sons had a better start than poor Sonny Boy. He would see that they knew there was more to life than her constant harping about being the best. His boys would also have fun.

They even laughed quietly, he realised. Why had he never done anything about it before? Because Sally made sure that everyone danced to her tune. Well, it was over now. He was changing the record and they would all dance to whatever tune he decided in the future.

'Can I get you a coffee?'

It was the nearest she would ever get to asking him to stay and they both knew it. If he accepted the coffee she would expect him to try and kiss her, maybe get her into bed. She would say no at first and eventually relent and then it would all be as it was before. He could see the pleading in her eyes.

'Can't. I'm meeting someone and I'm already late.'

His voice was dismissive and he knew he was hurting her but he was past caring. How many times had she spoken to Sonny Boy like that when he had phoned to speak to his brothers? She would cut him off mid-sentence, tell him they were in bed, studying, whatever, and Tyrell had let her. That was the worst of it, *he* had let her because he had not been man enough to tell her where to get off and leave the poor boy alone.

'Well, don't let me keep you then.'

He grinned.

'You won't. By the way, why didn't you tell me Sonny had rung your mobile in Jamaica the night he died?'

He saw the shock on her face.

'The police have your number down as one of his last calls. They spoke to you about it, I'm sure.'

'It was a missed call . . . I told them that.'

But she had not told him and he wanted to get that fact over to her now. She was stuttering and he enjoyed her discomfort because he had waited to say this to her, waited for the right moment.

'According to the phone records the call lasted one minute and twenty seconds, so don't talk your bollocks to me. You did what you always do, didn't you, Sal? You fucked him off quickly because you couldn't stand him interfering with your safe little life.'

She was shaking her head in denial.

'You were all out . . .'

'If I had spoken to him maybe he wouldn't have done what he did. Maybe, just maybe, he was ringing for help or advice.'

She laughed now and said in a hard voice, 'He wanted money. I said to wait till we got home. Did we still have to bankroll his mother's addiction on holiday then?'

She was all self-righteous now.

He pushed his face close to hers and said through gritted teeth, 'You're a cunt, Sal! A nasty, vindictive and jealous cunt.'

It was the second time he had called a woman that in a few days. Tyrell closed his eyes and took a deep breath because for the second time he also had the urge to clump this woman so hard she would never get up again.

'He wanted help, and knowing how you were with him he would not have rung you unless he was desperate.'

'How was I to know what he was going to do?'

Tyrell wiped his nose. It was running and it took all his willpower not to break down in tears.

'He was on the rent, Sal. That boy was flogging his arse for his mother, and I never knew because you made sure I never really had any time on me own with him.'

'You couldn't have got money to him from Jamaica.'

Her voice was dismissive once more. She had recovered herself and he had to admire her for that if for nothing else.

'Oh, but you're wrong. I could have got the money to him through friends. I had done it before.'

He saw the amazement on her face and it gave him a small sense of satisfaction. 'You have never known the half of it, Sal, but you thought you did and that suited you. Well, I'm off. As I said, I have people to see, things to do.'

He dragged the heavy case off the bed and the silk throw fell to the ground. He knew she was itching to pick it up and make it all look neat once more. As he carried the case out of the bedroom he saw his boys and realised they had heard everything that had been said. But he couldn't do anything or say anything about it because he was crying. He was crying for his dead boy. These two were alive and well looked after, he knew. He was going to have to sort his head out before he spoke to them about this.

The revelations of the last few days had destroyed him. He wasn't sure if he would ever be able to mend himself properly. All he did know was that if he didn't leave this house now he would explode.

The handsome boys gazed at him with their big eyes and he dropped the case. Taking them both in his arms, Tyrell hugged them to him. Then, picking up the case again, he walked precariously down the narrow staircase. As he went out of the front door he could hear them both calling out to him, but he shut the door and walked away as quickly as he could.

He would deal with them later when he could talk properly and explain the situation with their mother as best he could. Now, though, he was aware he had to save himself and that was exactly what he was going to do.

Inside his car he lit up a joint and toked on it deeply before he made his way back to his flat and his meeting with Louis Clarke.

Chapter Fifteen

Jude was looking out of the window and trying to calm her nerves. The number she'd tried was still not responding and she was getting more nervous every time she rang it. But: 'Needs must when the devil drives,' and as her devil drove her constantly, she knew she had to see it through to the bitter end.

'The Lord will help you, Jude, if you ask him to.'

She rolled her eyes to the ceiling.

'The Lord couldn't give a fuck about me and you know it, Verbena.'

The other woman wasn't shocked by the words, she expected them now. But she hoped and prayed that one day Jude would see the light and give herself over to Him.

'You're wrong, girl. Now put that phone away and talk to me properly.'

Jude was wired, really sweating, and it wasn't just the need for drugs, it was nervous sweat as well. She could smell herself and for a split second felt a wave of shame. Glancing at herself in the large gilt mirror over the fireplace, she saw a bedraggled woman with dark roots and bloodshot eyes. The reflection depressed her. Jude hated seeing what she was because it pushed home to her the fact that this was it now until she died. Another wave of self-pity swept over her, mingled with self-loathing and the utter need for oblivion.

She had to get out of here, get the money and get back home where she felt safe, where she could convince herself her life was on track, was normal.

'I bet everyone is having a field day round here.'

Verbena shook her head.

'Why would you think that, my love?'

Jude shrugged.

'Not exactly flavour of the month, am I? Now my baby is gone I suppose I won't be welcome here any more.'

Her voice was full of self-pity. She knew what buttons to press, she had been pressing them for over half her life.

Verbena felt her usual sorrow for Jude. It was as if she had a blind spot where this woman was concerned and even she was aware of that fact.

But she could never deny her.

'You will always be welcome in my home, Jude, you know that.'

She smiled and it was a real smile for once. Her faded eyes were dull, but the fact that her ex-mother-in-law still cared for her meant more to her than she had realised. With Sonny gone she had not felt any love in her life recently. Whatever she was, whatever she did, he had always been there for her, had adored her, and she had never realised how much she needed that until now.

Impulsively she grabbed Verbena's hand tightly.

She had lost a son and it had left her unable to leave her home. At times, this had annoyed Jude because she knew if the old woman had been capable she would have dropped off anything she needed and, so, save her a journey.

Samuel had been Verbena's Sonny Boy. Unlike his brothers and sisters he had not been what Verbena would have termed 'a good boy'. He had been her lost sheep, her sinner and she had loved him all the more for it.

Now, though, Jude knew that the death of her son had brought them closer together. Verbena had been good to her, she admitted that. Unlike everyone else who had walked away from her over the years, only Sonny and Verbena had always been there for her.

'What would I do without you?'

For once Jude was being honest, and it came across in her voice.

The older woman shrugged her bulky body, desperate to hug the poor excuse for a mother in front of her. Even though she knew she should not feel any sympathy for Jude her heart felt as if it was going to burst with sadness anyway.

Jude was not a bad person, it was just the drugs that made her do wrong. Verbena knew that because she had experienced it at first hand. Jude had even stolen from her: small amounts of money, the odd ornament. When Sonny had been a baby his grandmother had always searched the pushchair surreptitiously before they left in case a bracelet or ring had gone walkabout there. But having met Jude's family she could see why the girl had turned out this way.

Within five minutes she was opening her purse and giving Jude enough for a ten-pound bag, though they both pretended it was so she could get something to eat. It was a game they had played for many years and Verbena wondered when their strange association would end.

Only, she mused, with the death of one of them. Hopefully it would be her own and then finally she would be able to leave her home.

Once Jude had the money she was gone and the old woman went over to where the photo of her grandson's grave had been placed. She rubbed the picture with her thumb as she thought of his life, knowing that of all the people in her world he would have been the only person to understand why she gave Jude money.

Sonny had inherited Verbena's forgiving nature, and it saddened her that no one else had ever recognised that fact.

Nick had left his wife in a wine bar with her friends and made his way home to get changed and have a few hours' rest while he tried to sort himself out. His mother hardly spoke to him and after a few attempts at conversation he gave up. It seemed that overnight she had taken on the mantle of Tammy's protector. Well, in a way he was glad because it saved a lot of atmospheres and aggravation as far as he was concerned.

He couldn't be bothered to ask her what was wrong, he had enough on his plate as it was.

He loved his mother but sometimes he could understand why she drove Tammy mad. They had never been close, had not even liked each other before this, but it seemed that now Nick was in his mother's bad books and not his wife. He was willing to let that go for a while if it kept his wife sweet. He had enough on his mind without worrying about his mother having a hissy fit. She'd come round when she was over it. There was a bond between them that Angela would never sever, they both knew that.

He showered quickly and lay on the bed. He could lie there in peace as Tammy was out for the duration. He was tired, and knew that a sleep would do him the world of good, but he was finding it difficult to settle. The boy's death had been bad enough, but what he had done to Gary was outrageous, Nick saw that now.

What was wrong with him?

He had not heard anything from the filth yet except a few words at the yard to ask him when he had last seen Mr Proctor, etc. The usual things they would ask anyone. He knew they would not want him in the papers once more. He was a hero of sorts, at least to the public anyway. He had played it schtum and now he had Tammy on board he was more or less home and dry. He knew they were aware of Gary's reputation as they were aware of his but this country's laws required proof, and no matter what they suspected they had to be able to prove he and Gary were up to skulduggery. Nick was far too shrewd for anything to lead back to him. To all outward appearances he at least was a genuine businessman.

He knew they were also under the impression that he and Gary had been tight. Which was exactly what he wanted them to believe. He had made a point of weighing out Proctor's wife with a bundle so Maureen was sweet. In fact, she was over the moon with it all. But then, she would be. Gary had treated her like the hired help for years.

Stevie, bless him, was pleased Nick had done him a favour even though he had not wanted what had happened.

All in all it should be a walk.

At least, Nick hoped so. If they didn't arrest anyone within twenty-four hours of a major offence, chances were the culprit was home and dry. What most people didn't realise was that criminals knew the law and the way it worked better than most Old Bill. They had to otherwise they would not last five minutes on the street. Successful criminals paid out a hefty wedge to barristers and lawyers to find out the score and the best way to beat anything that was thrown at them.

Most justice was about how much you could pay, not how guilty you were, and that had been proved time and time again. Look at the sentences handed out to drunk drivers.

Nick was shaking again. He took a few deep breaths to steady his nerves, closed his eyes and tried to relax, but it was impossible. He saw that boy in his dreams even when he was awake. He'd dreamed about Sonny Hatcher every night, yet he didn't dream once about his oldest friend – how strange was that?

He glanced out of the balcony doors and saw the night starting to draw in. He hated the dark, hated being alone in it. He closed his eyes and swallowed down the fear enveloping him. He saw Sonny Hatcher then as he always did, walking towards him. The boy was smiling and holding out his arms. He looked so young, but then he was very young, a handsome boy with dark eyes and coffee-coloured skin. He actually looked like Nick's nephew. His sister's son was the same age.

He jumped off the bed, his breathing heavy and his heart pounding. He couldn't relax, couldn't rest.

Sonny Hatcher had never done anything wrong to him except to come to his home. Nick had killed him for that. The boy should have used his loaf and kept away.

Gary Proctor, on the other hand, had been a real menace. Nick was only sorry he had not kept his temper and let Stevie deal with it; that would have been the sensible solution, but since Sonny Hatcher he could not think straight.

He sometimes wondered if he was having a breakdown.

It was still early and he knew he wouldn't settle. For once he wished Tammy was there but she wasn't. After getting dressed he left the house, for the first time ever not saying goodbye to his mother. He had to get out, the walls were closing in on him. He needed to be around people.

He made his way into East London and as he drove wondered when all this was going to stop and he could finally get on with his life again. He knew exactly where he was going and he also knew that he definitely shouldn't be going there. It was wrong, so wrong, but he couldn't hold back the urge when it came on him. It came so rarely these days that he had to follow its lead.

This was his first foray since the burglary and he needed the respite tonight more than he had ever needed it before. He had to get all the frustration out of him and this was as good a way as any.

He parked his Mercedes sports in a small turning and made his way up to the tenth floor of a block of flats in Plaistow via the filthy lift. It stank. As he walked from it he hawked deep in his throat before spitting the phlegm noisily over the concrete balcony.

Two young boys were standing on the landing smoking a joint and he eyed them quickly. They dropped their eyes when they saw him looking and he passed them without a word. He banged on a freshly painted red front door.

It was answered by a young blond of about eighteen.

'I wondered when you'd be back round.'

Nick smiled.

'Couldn't keep away, sweetheart, are you alone?'

Big blue eyes drew him into the small hallway. It smelt of Kentucky fried chicken and fried eggs.

'For the moment, yeah.'

Nick took a hundred pounds from his pocket and grinned.

'Turn your mobile off, it's just us tonight, OK?'

'Whatever you want, Nick, you got it.'

He grinned.

'I could have told you that, darling. Now get your fucking kit off and stop poncing about.'

'Are you sure you want to see him?'

Tyrell nodded.

'I got us in to see him because of Colin and that. They're up for doing whatever they can to help. But, Tyrell, are you sure you want to go into all this? Leo is one heavy-duty fucker, you know that.'

'Heavier than you and your brothers? I don't think so.'

Louis smiled.

'You know what I mean. It's only gossip, man. If he had had a run in with Leary it couldn't have had anything to do with your boy, could it?'

Tyrell shrugged.

'It's all I've got at the moment, man. Think about it. What the fuck was he doing in that house with an alarm system like Fort Knox . . .'

Louis sighed. Not that again. He was like a scratched record.

'If Leary was at home the alarm wouldn't have been on, would it?'

Tyrell shook his head.

'It was normally on part-set according to the newspapers, which meant it was on downstairs while they slept.'

Louis nodded but Tyrell could see his heart wasn't in any of this.

'What I mean is, Leary is a handful. He wouldn't need it on, would he, not like Mr and Mrs Average? His attitude would be like ours: who would dare rob us?'

Tyrell laughed.

'That is what I am saying, man, who *would* rob him? Think about it.'

Louis said gently, 'I have thought it about it, mate, and I think the only person who would rob him would be a young boy with no brains and no real knowledge of what he was getting himself into. A boy like your Sonny. He probably did it on the spur of the moment, you know he always needed dough.'

Tyrell finished off his can of Red Stripe noisily then crumpled the can and threw it in the general direction of the bin.

'My Sonny was a lot of things, I don't dispute that, he was just a young boy with no brains to talk of, but there is no way he would have thought of robbing that drum. As we have already established he wasn't exactly the sharpest knife in the drawer. Why Nick Leary of all people? Until that night Sonny had only robbed . . .'

He stopped himself from finishing so Louis finished for him.

'Friends, family and neighbours?'

It was hard hearing it said out loud but it was true.

'But that is what I am trying to say, Louis, he didn't have the fucking savvy for it. He had to have had some help. Maybe Leo knows something.'

Louis knew it was pointless arguing.

'Fair enough, let's get going. Colin and the others will be waiting for us, OK?'

Whatever Leo had to say the Clarke brothers would make sure it was the truth. Tyrell was lucky to have such good friends and he knew it. He got up and hugged his friend.

'I have to do this, you understand that, don't you? I have to have some kind of explanation for what happened.'

Louis nodded but was secretly wondering if his friend might be asking too much.

'I only hope you get the one you want, mate.'

Tyrell pushed his dreads out of his face and said sadly, 'So do I, Lou, so the fuck do I.'

Leo Green was not a happy bunny. He had the Clarke brothers in his home.

In his home.

And, as Colin was just thinking to himself, a very nice home it was and all.

A large detached villa in South London, it had a big garden planted with so many trees the house was not visible from the road. This suited Leo because he needed privacy to carry out his work. The electric gates were a touch as well, and so were the two Dobermanns that prowled his garden twenty-four seven courtesy of a friend's scrap yard. Scrap-yard dogs were the best in as much as they felt no real affection for anyone and respected only the person who fed them. There was no way Lily Law was coming in this house without plenty of warning.

Unlike the Clarkes, of course, who could walk into his bedroom and piss on his sleeping wife without a sound from anyone, least of all him. And that was what galled Leo. As a face in his own right it was difficult for him to kow-tow to anyone any more. He had done his share of boot-licking when he had been a boy, had come down with a severe case of Cherry Blossom-poisoning many times in his quest to better himself. Gradually he had taken out everyone he had ever paid lip service to until now he was at the top of his particular profession. He was the one who gave the orders these days, he was the one everyone listened to in his world, but now he had a far greater force sitting in his smart spacious office and he didn't like it, he didn't like it one bit.

'Any chance of a drink, Leo? My throat's as dry as a buzzard's crutch.'

He jumped from his chair and said apologetically, ' 'Course you can. Beer all right?'

Colin Clarke nodded.

'They'll be here in a minute and then we can get down to it. We ain't keeping you, are we?'

He knew they were but didn't give a toss, and he knew Leo knew that as well.

' 'Course not. I can arrive for me appointment any time I want.'

It was said with bravado. Leo was telling them he was a man to be reckoned with himself.

Billy grinned.

'Fucking *appointment*? Who has fucking *appointments* these days?'

He shook his head as if severely annoyed and said loudly, as if Leo was hard of hearing, 'Doctor's appointment, is it?'

The sarcasm was not lost on anyone in the room and they all laughed.

Leo exploded then. He had talked to Carlos Brent and knew they were eventually going to make their way to his gaff but he was fucked if they were going to mug him off as well.

'Is this about the iron I sold to Carlos Brent that was used on one of your crew? Only once I sell my gear it ain't my responsibility any more. I have franchises all over the smoke, surely you can't hold me responsible for every stray bullet?'

Terry was annoyed. He got up from the black leather DFS sofa and said, 'Who you fucking shouting at?'

Leo stared up at the big man and wondered why, with a house full of guns, he didn't just shoot the fucking lot of them once and for all.

Billy saved the day as he always did.

'Relax, Terry. And you, Leo, get the drinks on the go. The others'll be here in a minute and then we can get down to business.'

The word business was music to Leo's ears.

'Are you definitely on the buy then?'

'Could be. We want a look see, that's all, before we make up our minds.'

As Billy spoke the buzzer sounded and after checking the CCTV Leo let the others into the house. Anyone else would have been searched by his blokes but none of the men in this room would have swallowed that and he had to let them all in blind.

Louis came into the room with his mate Tyrell. Although not as huge as the Clarkes Tyrell had undeniable presence. He was a big, handsome, angry man. This was the old Tyrell from when they were all growing up. He could always handle himself then. As the years had gone on and he had married Sally and become Mr Respectable he had lost it to some degree. Now, though, it was back with a vengeance.

'All right, Leo? Long time no see.'

He nodded at the two new arrivals, his heart hammering in his chest. He had half expected Tyrell to show. Word was out that he was on the want, and Leo respected that.

But right at this moment it was all he fucking needed.

Nick lay on the bed and felt the familiar revulsion sweep over him.

Why did he do it?

The air of squalor was part of the turn on. He knew that and wondered why. The bed was crumpled but then it had been when he had got into it. Frankie catered to a certain clientele and, like Nick, they were not too worried about their surroundings. This place was a world-class dump and the smell was cloying. Already he could taste it in his mouth. He picked up the bottle of vodka and took a long swig, hoping to erase it but knowing it was futile.

On the scratched bedside table beside him there was a piece of mirror, the frame long gone. The white fluffy lines were laid out neatly and tidily – the only neat and tidy thing in the whole place.

He snorted one expertly and then, holding his head back, drew it as far up his nose as it would go. It was not good gear but then he had not supplied it. His nose started to run almost immediately and Nick wiped it with the back of his hand. He looked down at himself and felt the usual revulsion at his own body. It looked puffy and white, and the youth of Frankie made him feel suddenly old and worn out. Yet Frankie was already worn out from overuse, not only of drink and drugs but sexual overuse. It was all just going through the motions for Frankie and that was what attracted Nick most. He pulled the blond head into his lap, and as he felt the cold lips around his member he sighed.

This was what he liked, the image of it all, this was what got him off and Frankie knew how to get him off better than anyone. It was why Nick always came back here even though he swore each time he never would.

Why did the smell of dirt and semen make him aroused? Why did a used and bloodied body give him the erection of a lifetime? Why couldn't he be like other men, have normal wants and desires? Why did his wife, who most men would happily romp with for hours, turn him off?

Frankie's skinny body was a welter of bruises and scratches. As he saw the dirty blond head bobbing up and down Nick felt an overwhelming urge to come. Grabbing the dyed hair tightly, he bucked and shuddered for long moments, forcing himself deeply into Frankie's mouth until he heard the familiar gagging sounds that drove him over the edge.

Nick came like the proverbial train. Smiling, he dressed quickly and was out of the flat in nano-seconds. Frankie was a lot of things but a good conversationalist was not one of them.

Whistling, Nick pressed for the lift. The cool night air felt good on his skin and his breathing was still laboured as he made his way down to his wheels.

In a few hours he would be filled with the familiar self-loathing, in a few hours he would repress his sexual feelings once more out of self-hatred. But for the moment he enjoyed the sated feeling that enveloped him.

And once the guilt came, as it always did, he would also, in a strange and twisted way, enjoy that too.

'So what you after then?'

Leo's voice was neutral once more but it was taking all his willpower.

Terry grinned.

'We want a gun, like the one you sold recently that took out one of my best blokes.'

The sarcasm was lost on no one, least of all Leo. He was glad that he had told his men to leave him alone, and in fairness they had expected him to deal with this crowd of carrion without them.

'I ain't explaining meself any more. I franchise to other dealers like Carlos, you all know the score. Once the merchandise leaves my premises it's no longer my responsibility.'

Colin and Billy stared at Terry in such a way that he knew to let it go. He knew that losing it was wrong but these days all the businesses seemed to overlap and it was getting harder and harder to pinpoint the bad guys.

'What do you want, a hand gun?'

Tyrell nodded and Leo saw that he was going to be the purchaser and acted accordingly.

'What kind?'

'Semi-automatic, preferably Spanish, with parabellum bullets.' He'd read all about the gun Sonny had carried in the newspaper coverage.

Leo was impressed. It made a change to have someone who didn't want to play cowboys for two hours before buying the cheapest model. If he had a pound for every time he had stood there and watched grown men gloving up and pointing guns at invisible targets he would be worth more than Elton John.

He opened a drawer and took out a wad of latex gloves. Anyone who touched his guns had to put them on beforehand; he also cleaned the guns after perusal for extra protection. The last thing they all needed was to leave a print on a gun that was purchased by someone else and then used in a robbery or a murder. It would be a bastard trying to explain *that* one away in a courtroom.

'You know what you want, Tyrell, and I appreciate that, mate.'

Leo was in selling mode now and they all watched as he fell into the role of the firearms expert he was. Love him or loathe him, there was nothing he did not know about guns and gun culture because he was responsible for nearly every firearm available in the smoke. He opened a cupboard and took out something wrapped in chamois leather. Unwrapping it, he held out a handgun to Tyrell. Placing it reverently in his hands, he said quietly, 'This is a semi-auto, Spanish make, good deal. Only a grand to you. It has never to my knowledge been used in connection with anything in this country so it has a good pedigree in its own little way. The beauty of it is, you can also fire single bullets.' He opened the chamber for Tyrell and said happily, 'But if you throw this catch you can take out a room full of people.'

He grinned at the surrounding company and they all grinned back, getting the joke and admiring Leo for making it.

'It isn't heavy, only five and a half pounds loaded, and very comfortable to hold or hide. Terrific little gun. Got a good bang on it, but easy to conceal as well.'

Tyrell weighed the gun in his hand and understood what attracted the younger men to them. It was a powerful feeling, holding something so lethal.

Leo watched his face and smiled, understanding the feeling better than anyone else in the room. He had been a gun fanatic since a boy, and it was only natural he should make it his business.

'There's plenty of these about at the moment. They're brought back from the war zones by British soldiers stationed there. They collect them after any conflict as trophies and obviously they are unaccounted for, ain't they? No one realises they're in their possession, see? Assume they have been taken by the enemy. I have a supplier in the forces who buys them on and they end up in here waiting for people like yourself. The filth hate it when they finally trace them but there ain't a lot they can do. I have even been offered police guns over the years. It's amazing what a hike in the mortgage rate can do for the black economy.'

He opened another cupboard and placed an Uzi in the hands of Terry Clarke. As he had guessed he would, Terry loved it.

Leo poured another round of drinks and waited for them to come to the crux of their problem because they had a problem and he rather thought he was the only person who could solve it.

Chapter Sixteen

Leo was relaxed now, doing what he did best. He had even gone down to the cellar and brought up his best toys though he knew now that he probably would not get a sale. Although he was a wholesaler of guns to most of the other dealers, he only served personally people he knew well or who, like the Clarke brothers, he couldn't refuse. He was known mainly as a drug dealer and also served up most of the coke dealers in the surrounding areas, pavement, street and club, not personally but via a network of up and coming young men who wanted a bite of the coke cherry.

In all he was quite a face in his own right, though not on a par for danger with the men now in his home. They were into so many things it would be hard even to know where to begin, and because they dealt with so many different people it was always impossible to know who else you were actually up against if you fell out with one or all of them. Best not to find out, even if it galled him.

But to talk guns was what he lived for, and Leo was a good salesman for his products. He loved guns, adored them. The feel of them, the smoothness of the metal, even the smell of the oil used to clean them, was to him better than a woman.

The Clarkes were all relaxed now as well, suddenly enjoying their evening listening to Leo enthuse about firearms. He was obviously an expert and talked with such passion that even Terry forgot his grudge. They knew they'd deal with Leo the next time they genuinely needed iron, and Leo knew when he had a captive audience, knew just when he had them in his hand, and was enjoying himself accordingly.

He could sell a gun to the Pope, he knew it, it was what he loved most about his job. Drugs you could sell to anyone who wanted them; guns were a different kettle of fish altogether because unlike a line of coke or an E, you kept them and you used them wisely.

Tyrell held a small Victorian ladies' gun with a pearl handle that Leo had acquired for its curiosity value alone. He saw the beautiful carving crafted on to the handle and visualised it sitting discreetly in a handbag. It was a sweet little novelty that could do a lot of damage.

Unlike Terry he hated the feel of guns while appreciating the psychological power they gave people. Guns were used to intimidate. In a lot of criminal activities fear was the most important factor. Most bank robbers only had guns for show, there was no real intention to wound or kill, they were to frighten people and no more. A gun stopped a have-a-go hero in their tracks. A gun kept everyone still and made them more biddable, all the better for the robbers to go about their business in peace. In drug-dealing guns were used more as enforcing tools, to keep turfs clean of enemies, and because a seven-stone man was Arnold Schwartzenegger with a pump-action shotgun in his hand. It was the law of the street, and the street had never really been Tyrell's territory.

Billy was holding a German handgun and weighing it in his hand. He felt good holding it, it had perfect balance. Leo grinned as he said, 'That's a nine-millimetre, Bill, exactly what you need if you want to iron someone out good and proper. That would blow them away. I can silence that and all because it's a noisy little fucker. The Spanish number would do the job too but not as quickly and neatly. What the Spanish gun has going for it is that if you keep your finger on the trigger it will keep firing, see. There's gas in the tip of each bullet,' he smiled at Tyrell as he explained this, 'and that automatically ejects the next round. Lovely little gun though not a lot of bullets to a magazine. But still, enough to do serious damage if that is what you require of it.'

Terry had found a new best friend in Leo by now. He was enthralled and Colin was watching him nervously. Terry was enough of a handful as it was without arming him up to the hilt. He would be impulse buying like an Essex girl in Lakeside if they weren't careful.

The last thing Terry Clarke needed was a handgun so he decided to remind everyone why they were all there.

'You deal with Nick Leary, don't you?' he asked the gun dealer.

Leo felt his heart sink down to his boots and looked at Tyrell apologetically as he said, 'You know I do, Colin.'

The mood in the room changed then. They all started putting the weapons back on to the desk. Playtime was over and everyone was suddenly remembering why they were really there. The Clarkes waited for Tyrell's reaction.

'I hear you had a run in with him a while back.'

Tyrell's voice was neutral for which Leo was grateful.

'I have run ins with people on a regular basis, it's par for the course in my business dealings.' He made a show of repacking a rifle as he said, 'I was sorry to hear about your boy, but Nick, for all his faults, real or imagined, only did what any man would have done.'

Tyrell knew it had taken a lot for Leo to say that in front of the Clarkes and respected the fact.

'I don't hold any malice towards him, I would have done the same myself.'

Leo knew he spoke the truth.

'What I am interested in, though, is who might have put my boy up to creeping round Leary's home?'

The question stumped Leo, they could all see that much. But he was clever enough to see where they were coming from.

'What are you trying to say?'

His voice was low and guarded.

Tyrell sighed.

'I am asking you, did anyone you know maybe have dealings with my boy, that's all? I need to know if he had any association with someone who might have led him astray.'

'What, are you trying to say he was an innocent abroad then?'

Tyrell shook his head.

'No. But he wasn't as bad as he was made out. At least, I don't think so.'

Leo laughed dismissively.

'Your boy wasn't exactly a fucking angel, know what I mean?'

Tyrell stepped towards him then, menace in his whole stance as he said quietly, 'You watch your fucking trap. That is still my boy you're bad mouthing. You talk about him as if he was a mug.'

Leo sighed.

'If the cap fits.'

It was calculated to annoy and Terry watched bright-eyed as the argument was about to step up a gear.

'I heard he was a nancy boy,' Leo goaded Tyrell.

'You seem to know an awful lot about him, more than I did. Sure you never met him?'

Leo's temper, never far from the surface, erupted then. He faced down Tyrell by shouting, 'All I know is what I hear on the street. Nick was devastated by what happened. But the bottom line is, you have to cream scum and that little fucker got what he was asking for. He's lucky he didn't come in here because I would have shot the bastard without a second's thought.'

Leo was still fuming while he poured himself a brandy and said loudly and with maximum bravado: 'So don't you walk in my house and try and fucking mug me off, Hatcher, because I ain't having none of it! I had a tear up with Nick over something private. I am not discussing it in front of all and sundry. Get that through your thick black head!'

It was the way he said 'black' that caused all the men in the room to widen their eyes and look at each other with incredulous expressions. Tyrell was stunned by the hatred in the other man's voice. He could not believe what he had just heard and neither could anyone else there.

Louis was openly fuming.

'Who do you fucking think you're talking to?'

He stepped menacingly towards Leo who had the nous to step back. He realised he had made the balls-up of the decade and tried to retract the malicious statement as best he could.

Leo didn't like the people he dealt with any more. He saw the young men coming to him, black and white, and all they wanted was firepower. They all wanted to maim, especially the Yardies. They were little bastards, had even tried to tuck Leo up, much to his chagrin. As far as he was concerned he dealt with scum. He decided on reflection, seeing the angry faces all around him, to be honest in his answer.

He looked at Tyrell as he said, 'No disrespect, Tyrell, I know you're a diamond geezer, but over the last ten years nearly all my iron has gone out to West Indians. Fucking shooting each other for fuck all! Black on black they call it. I call it prat on prat personally. Your boy walked into Nick's home and tried to rob him. He had a capture and he died. Sorry, mate, I think he got what he asked for. No more and no less. I apologise to you for saying what I did but I would be a liar if I wasn't honest about it all.

'It's your lot who want the guns, mate, your lot who want the arms, I just sell them, and I am stating a fact. If your boy was armed then I for one ain't fucking surprised, OK? And maybe I am getting racist in me old age but if you did my job, you'd be the same. I have to deal continually with arsehole niggers, and you know what?

They've all got a fucking grudge, an axe to grind or a score to settle, just like you have now. And I sell to them because hopefully then they will shoot one another and clean up the streets for the rest of us. So now you fucking know, don't ya?'

Tyrell stood up then. His eyes, normally so friendly, were almost black with rage as he yelled, 'Is that all you see? Me dreads? I was born here and I walked away from the graft. I run doors. Sure I duck and dive a bit, but it's people like you who cause all the trouble. You think I don't lump *you* altogether at times?'

He looked around the room.

'Sure I do, every time I get a little crew of white boys in one of my clubs looking for a row. But I stop meself because I don't want to be like that. Because I am intelligent enough to know I am viewing a small percentage of the population and pretending it's everyone, and it *ain't* . . . it fucking *ain't*. Most people are basically sound. It just depends who you're dealing with.'

Leo didn't know what to say and neither did anyone else. It was Terry who for once saved the day.

'Calm down, Tyrell. You can't educate haddock, as Mum always used to say.'

Everyone was quiet for a few moments and then the laughter started. Even Leo was laughing though he was not sure exactly why.

Terry turned to him and said, 'I'll take the Spanish piece.'

Leo was glad to change the subject and do a deal for a few quid. Terry took a wad of money out of his pocket and counted out a thousand in used twenties. He knew his brothers weren't happy about this turn of events but he didn't give a toss. He was in love and it was with a small Spanish handgun that could maim, kill and threaten.

Just like Terry.

Leo scooped the money up and stopped himself from counting it. He knew he was not far from a real row and was desperate to avoid it.

'Did you supply the iron that was being used by Tyrell's boy, Leo? There will be no comeback if you did, we swear to that,' Billy told him. 'We just need to know where he got such top-grade merchandise. I can see where Tyrell is coming from. His boy didn't have a twenty-quid shooter, he had a fuck-off piece of weaponry and he would never have got the money together for it on his Jacksy.'

Leo shook his head and said arrogantly, 'No. But, believe me, I wouldn't tell you lot even if I did.'

No one said anything and Tyrell punched him in the head with all his considerable strength. As Leo hit the floor Tyrell said quietly, 'Fuck you, white boy. You better find out who your friends are before you venture out on the street in future because I will make sure someone marks your card.'

He poked the other man in his chest, making him wince as he said gleefully, 'I am your worst nightmare, Leo. I am a nigger with a fucking grudge. And you know what, Dough Boy? That grudge is against *you* now.'

Tammy realised the girl was taking the piss long before the other girl realised she knew exactly what was going down.

Kayleigh Kalibos was married to a large Greek bank robber, and everyone knew that Tammy had slept with him. But as it had been months before, and as Tammy had a selective memory, she had not been bothered by the man's wife joining them in the wine bar for a few drinks. In fact, Tammy had forgotten the whole episode. It was only Kayleigh's needling that had reminded her. Kayleigh, it seemed, had not forgotten or forgiven Tammy for what had taken place. Her husband had pulled a few stunts in his life but trumping Nick Leary's wife had to rank among the most stupid.

Grudgingly she admitted she could see what had attracted him. Tammy had an air about her, she was like a young girl even though she was kicking forty – or so legend had it. Tammy's age was like all her contemporaries' – given only in ball-park figures.

She was on top form today and with all the drink and cocaine inside her actually up for a fight. Her 'friends' realised this and instead of trying to defuse the situation, elected to heap coals on an already smouldering fire. In their heart they all hoped that Tammy would get a good hiding just once and be made aware she was not invincible.

Kayleigh was as drunk as Tammy which was why she was up for a fight in the first place. If her husband knew he would be mortified. He was still frightened that Nick would find out what he had done with his wife and kill him, so the last thing he needed was a public tantrum from his nearest and dearest.

Tammy walked out of a toilet cubicle and smiled at Kayleigh in a friendly fashion. They were in Suzy Snaith's wine bar and she was a friend so they could all cut and snort in full view of the other customers who in any case were like them. It was a place where people went because they were known there and could get out of their nuts in peace. The local plod gave the place a wide berth because it was not worth the trouble of raiding it. Most of the clientele read like a *Who's Who* of the criminal fraternity and were therefore respected in their own way by friends and foes alike.

Fiona and Melanie were busy cutting lines on the granite surface, watching and waiting for the fight they knew was coming. It was like being back at school again. The tension in the Ladies' room was mounting and the air held the electricity only a mix of hormones, vodka and cocaine could generate.

Kayleigh went into one of the cubicles and Melanie said in a whisper, 'Let's unload her, Tams. She's out for a row, you don't need it.'

Tammy laughed as Melanie knew she would.

'Fuck her!'

This was said loudly as Melanie also knew it would be.

Tammy was already breathing deeply, anger boiling up inside her at the thought of Kayleigh trying to get one over on her.

She was out with her mates and had to keep her reputation as the top girl in their crew. Plus she needed to let off some steam. Nick was using her as usual, and even though she would allow herself to be used it didn't mean she wasn't upset about it all. Her life was looking like crap again. She had nothing really. Her husband was no good to her, she had broken up with her toy boy waiter, and her sons were asking if they could stay on at their private school for the next lot of holidays.

All she really had was Angela, and what use was that for a woman who wanted to have fun? She knew her friends wanted her to fight this scrubber, she knew it was wrong to fight Kayleigh, but it was the answer to her prayers tonight because if she didn't lash out at someone she would crack, Tammy knew it.

Cocaine always did this to her in the end. Her high lasted for a while and then she became depressed, bitter, seeing slights where there weren't any and convincing herself that everyone was talking about her. Coke paranoia caused more fights than whisky and brandy mixed.

Suddenly, Kayleigh was the cause of all her troubles and Tammy wanted to smack her one so badly it was almost tangible.

Kayleigh came out of the toilet unsteadily and, as she checked her make-up, accidentally jostled Tammy who was just about to snort a large line of cocaine. It was all that was needed. Tammy brought herself up fast and smacked the bigger woman in the face with all the force she could muster.

Kayleigh, weighing in at eleven stone, was knocked backwards by the blow. Despite her diminutive size Tammy could fight, due to the fact that she actually liked fighting.

Kayleigh, though, was well able for her and as she had about three stone on Tammy the fight soon spilled out of the toilets and into the wine bar itself. Men and women moved quickly out of the way of the brawling pair. Kayleigh picked up a bottle of wine from one of the tables and as she held it aloft, ready to bring it down on Tammy's expensive hair, a large man called Greg Peterson quickly snatched it from her and, with three of his friends, finally separated the struggling women.

Suzy Snaith was shouting, 'Get them outside!'

Dragging the kicking and swearing women outside was a hard task and it took the men a good five minutes.

'I'll teach you to shag my husband!'

Tammy laughed.

'No, love, it should be *me* teaching *you* to shag your husband, surely?'

That was the trigger for the fight of the century.

Kayleigh came out of her captor's arms like a lunatic and Tammy was ready and waiting for her. Stabbing her stiletto heel into her own escort's foot, he yelped and she flew from his arms and met Kayleigh head on. Both of them continued the fight with glee.

The men knew it was pointless trying to separate them now and in all honesty those long false nails and professionally whitened teeth looked intimidating even to them. They decided to leave the two women to it.

The police arrived five minutes later.

Tyrell sat outside the public toilets in his car. They were on the estate his son had grown up on and he had passed them many times without a second's thought. They were situated by the car park next to the local high street.

He saw that the place was teeming with young boys and fought an urge to vomit. He was watching to see if there were any boys he recognised from seeing them with Sonny.

It was after eleven and other than the local Tesco's which was open twenty-four hours the high street was all but deserted. The toilets, however, were a different matter. Cars were pulling up and driving off at an alarming rate. It was a whole new world to Tyrell and he was shocked that such things even went on here. He thought it was confined to Soho and places like that. Vice centres. He didn't know that this went on in nearly every public toilet in the country.

As he lit himself another Marlboro Light a gentle tapping sound made him jump. He turned to see a blond boy in his early teens smiling at him.

Tyrell opened the window quickly.

'What do you want?'

It was only then that he realised the boy was touting for business. The shock nearly rendered Tyrell speechless.

Did he look queer?

But then, after seeing some of the men who had been in and out of the place tonight, he wondered what *queer* was supposed to look like exactly. Most of them had looked like normal family men.

'You new round here?'

The boy smiled in a friendly way. His teeth were crooked and Tyrell put him at about fifteen, or maybe younger. He was slim, skinny even, and dressed like one of the refugees you saw shunting round Piccadilly.

He was obviously homeless.

Tyrell took a deep breath.

'You worked here long?'

The boy nodded and then started to open the passenger door.

'Come on, mate, I am fucking freezing. You up for it or not?'

Tyrell made a split-second decision and let the boy get into the car.

'Where do you want to go, mate?'

'What do you mean?'

Tyrell's voice was puzzled.

The boy grinned and said, 'Fuck me, you *are* new. We can't shag on a public road under the street lights, can we? Let's go to the park.'

Tyrell started up the car, every inch of his skin crawling with the fear of getting caught out by Old Bill.

He would never live it down.

But he pulled away without incident and the boy proceeded to direct him to an appropriate spot.

Nick could see how drunk and stoned Tammy was, and knew the policemen could see it too.

'I fucking love him . . .'

She was trying to kiss her husband and he was trying to keep her away from him.

'Thanks for keeping it quiet.'

The policemen looked at him with pity. Tammy was battered and bruised but obviously the victor, her high spirits told him that much.

'Are there any charges?'

The elder patrolman shook his head.

'Just take her home, mate, she's doing our heads in.'

Tammy was half-lying on a plastic seat in the station house, trying to stop herself from falling asleep. DI Rudde came out then and called Nick through to an interview room.

'All right, Nick?'

He nodded.

'Who was she fighting with this time?'

Nick's voice was tired-sounding and Rudde guessed rightly that he had had enough for one night.

'Kayleigh Kalibos. Her husband has already been and picked her up and I can tell you now, I would not want to be in her shoes when he gets her home.'

Nick knew Kayleigh's husband would be terrified of a comeback from him and that Rudde was also aware of the fact.

'Heard anything more about Gary?'

Rudde shook his head and said sagely, 'More to that than meets the eye, but from what I can gather they can't get a trail anywhere. Still, you know Gary. He had a finger in so many pies it was only a matter of time before he got burned.'

'You can say that again! He tried to tuck me up a few times but even so I'm sorry about what happened to him. I weighed his old woman out, had to really, he did work with me for years.'

Rudde tried to change the subject. 'By the way, Tammy had some grade-A cocaine in her possession. I've sorted it but she has to be told, Nick. I can't get her off if it happens again.'

He sighed.

'If the papers got hold of that there would be a field day, you know the score, especially after all that's happened.'

Nick nodded once more.

'It hit her very hard, you have to understand that . . .'

The detective smiled his understanding. Nick knew that like everyone else Rudde secretly wondered why he did not give his wife the slap of the century.

'Well, I'll leave her in your more than capable hands. By the way, Nick, a word to the wise. Sonny Hatcher's father Tyrell is snooping around, thinks someone put his boy up to robbing your drum. Expect to see or hear from him at some point, OK?'

Nick was shocked and Rudde could see it.

'He's like any father, mate, just trying to make sense of what happened. He don't bear no malice towards you, I know that for a fact. All I am trying to do is warn you so you can be prepared for him.'

Nick smiled.

'I appreciate that. Now I had better get my dear wife home.'

They could hear Tammy laughing raucously and the sound seemed to make Nick's face even paler and more troubled. Rudde had never been afflicted by marriage which was something he was very grateful for. The more he saw of it at close hand, the less he liked the idea of being in lumber to someone for the rest of your days.

'She been on the lash all day?'

Nick nodded. Wiping a hand across his face, he sighed as he said sadly, 'I know what everyone thinks but Tammy has a lot on her plate, you know. A few drinks and a bit of gear soften the edges for her.'

Rudde didn't answer. Instead he watched Nick Leary leave the room to the sounds of his wife retching half her guts up, and marvelled once more at his own good fortune in not being the marrying kind.

Chapter Seventeen

The boy's name was Lomax, William Lomax, and he went under the nickname Willy. Tyrell decided he would call him Lomax, or plain Will. Under the circumstances he didn't think he could bring himself to say that nickname out loud.

'What do you want then?' the boy said.

Tyrell was parked up by the local park under the shade of some overhanging trees. It was dark and in the dimness he could make out the figures of men and boys all along the park railings. It was something he had never thought to see. Some had wandered into the bushes through a gap in the fence and he realised once more that there was a whole underclass here of which he had no knowledge at all.

But then again, why would he?

Unless you had reason to look for something out of the ordinary you would not necessarily know it even existed. He had known that this kind of thing went on, it had just never occurred to him that it went on night after night all over the country in such numbers. His son, his Sonny, had once been like this little boy beside Tyrell, selling himself to strangers for a few pounds.

It was disgusting, it was shaming, and most of all it was so squalid and demoralising that he wondered if Louis Clarke was right and ignorance could be bliss. To think that the boy he had loved and cherished had been reduced to this and worse, and his own father had never once had an inkling, amazed Tyrell even as it broke his heart.

'Look, mister, I ain't got all night. If you just wanted a wank we could have stayed at the cottage.'

Tyrell looked at the unkempt boy beside him once more.

'Cottage?'

The boy grinned.

'The bogs . . . toilets? Where you picked me up.'

He laughed louder then.

'Is this your first time?'

'I don't want sex from you.'

Tyrell's voice was shaking with emotion and the boy took it the wrong way. Willy Lomax assumed he had a new boy on the block here. Placing one grubby hand gently on Tyrell's thigh, he said throatily, 'Come on, don't be silly. You'll be all right.'

Tyrell stared at him then. The boy saw how the man's eyes looked him over and with the experience of long practice he smiled once more and caressed his groin, finally going for the zip of Tyrell's jeans.

His hand was slapped away much harder than he had believed possible. The stinging sensation brought tears to his eyes and Tyrell felt a moment's shame for taking his feelings out on a boy.

'Look, mate, I ain't staying here for all that, I don't do the pain stuff.'

He was unlocking the door and trying to get out.

Tyrell stopped him by grabbing his arm gently and saying, 'I don't want sex, son, I just need to know about a boy called Sonny Hatcher.'

His words stopped the boy in his tracks. He had blond hair that was cut below his ears. Tyrell supposed he was quite a nice-looking young man, but his grey eyes already had the look of someone who had seen and done too much. The atmosphere in the car grew charged. He felt the boy's fear and said in as friendly a voice as he could muster, 'I'll pay you for any information you give me.'

The boy was still hesitant.

'And I'll pay you well.'

He relaxed back into the seat now. Taking a pack of ten Benson's from his pocket, he lit one and after a deep leisurely puff, said, 'He was a mate, that's all. What do you want to know?'

He blew out the smoke noisily and Tyrell relaxed.

'How long did you know him?'

Lomax shrugged.

'A year or so. He wasn't round the cottage much after a while, he seemed to know who to pick up like. Did you know him?'

Tyrell nodded.

'Nice fella, old Sonny, had a hard life.'

The boy pulled on the cigarette again.

'How much you giving me?'

'Depends how much you tell me.'

'What do you want to know?'

Tyrell pulled out two fifty-pound notes and said quietly, 'Everything you know about him basically.'

'There's a café round the corner. Throw in an all day breakfast and you got yourself a deal.'

Suddenly, the boy looked what he was: a nice little kid. Tyrell started up the car, glad to get away from the people around him, shadows who sneaked around in the dark with young boys and tried to convince themselves they were doing nothing wrong.

Jude was stoned.

As she lay on the sofa and felt herself going on the nod she placed her cigarette in the ashtray and left it burning while she followed the feelings inside her head and body. She had finally got enough money for her dealer by doing three blow jobs one after the other. She had not used a condom for any of them.

She could still taste the salty bitterness after half a bottle of vodka. But she had what she wanted now and just wanted to relax and let the good times roll.

She had Fleetwood Mac on the stereo, 'Albatross' on low. The guitar strains had always helped mellow her out and as she lay back even the stench of her own surroundings was gradually receding as her mind and body were taken over by the high. This was the only time she could think about her Sonny Boy without feeling anger. But whatever happened she would be making sure she got full compensation for her Sonny Boy's demise.

Nick Leary was a known face, for all his prancing about on TV and his interviews in the newspapers. Well, he owed her, and she was going to see that he paid her in full. She knew, for example, that it was his mate, Gary Proctor, who had brought her boy to that house. She also knew that Nick Leary would pay well to keep that information quiet because now Gary Proctor was dead and all. Sonny had liked Proctor, had said he was an all-right bloke. Maybe he was? It was too late now.

She was scared, she knew what her Sonny had told her and she knew how to use the information but the fear of taking him on overrode everything else. Now Proctor was dead, and she was going to have to front up Leary; he was the hero of the hour and she would make him pay for that.

As she melted into the furniture she heard a noise and, opening her eyes, saw Gino standing by her seat. He was already well on and she smiled dreamily at him. Even when he picked up her bag of brown from the table and started to burn himself a fix she didn't say anything. He was back, that was all she was worried about.

No more being on her own, no more outings for money, he could take over that role now. As for his mother, Jude would cross that particular bridge when she came to it.

* * *

The café was an all nighter and so it was quite busy, but they managed to get a table in the corner and Tyrell ordered the boy a large breakfast with a side order of chips and bread and butter. He also ordered two mugs of tea and two cans of orange Tango. He took the Tangos from the fridge and collected his change from the twenty-pound note he had given the owner.

'I don't want him in here for long, right?'

Tyrell looked at the man in surprise.

'What do you mean?'

The café owner, a large overweight Turk with crooked white teeth and a whiter apron, said: 'I don't encourage them, they normally use the burger van off the high street. This once I'll swallow because he's with you, but tell him not to venture in after tonight. They ain't welcome. And a word of warning – they're all thieves. If you're new to this then you remember that for the future and all.'

Tyrell didn't know what to say. It was only when he realised that the man thought he was pimping his companion that he understood what was meant.

'You got it all wrong, mate. I'm only getting him something to eat, he's got something I want.'

He regretted his turn of phrase immediately.

The other man raised his eyebrows, looking Tyrell over as if he was so much dirt that had been brought in on someone's shoes.

'I worked that one out for meself, mate! Each to their own.'

Tyrell was annoyed now and whispered angrily, 'Do I look like a nonce to you?'

The café owner grinned.

'I don't know, mate, what do they look like?'

The Turk wandered into the back of his café and Tyrell wondered what the fuck had made him say that. He decided to retreat before it all got out of hand and because his fuse was growing shorter by the minute.

Embarrassed, he sat down and lit himself a cigarette. He saw the boy properly for the first time by the fluorescent light of the café, and was shocked by what he saw.

His skin was grey, spotty, and filthy; his fingernails engrained with dirt. In the warmth of the café his clothes were already giving off a rancid smell. Did people want these boys for no other reason than that they were rotten dirty? Tyrell saw people looking at them curiously and stared them down. In his heart he was embarrassed to be seen with such a boy, and ashamed of that fact. After all, this was what his own son had been doing for a living, and by the looks of it this poor little sod had no choice in the matter.

Perched on a plastic chair, the boy now looked even more unkempt and vulnerable. Smiling awkwardly, he said to Tyrell, 'He don't normally let us in but I had a feeling he might if I was with you.'

Tyrell nodded.

'He said as much. Said you usually use the burger van off the high street.'

The boy smiled again. His teeth were yellow and thickly coated with scum as was his tongue.

'It's cold tonight and I wanted a warm up.'

'Will you stay out all night?'

Willy nodded and said honestly, 'Most of it. As it's a Friday we get a lot of men on their way home from clubbing or the pubs. The straight-acting ones are easy, you know. They just want it quickly before they jump in a cab home.'

Tyrell didn't know what to say.

'Why do you want to know about Sonny?'

He didn't answer but instead lit another cigarette and the boy picked up the packet and held them out as if to ask permission.

Tyrell nodded his acquiescence and lit the cigarette for him, glad of something to do. He didn't like to see the boy smoke at his young age but considering the circumstances didn't feel he had the right to moralise about it.

It was getting warmer in the café now and Tyrell slipped off his leather jacket, placing it over the back of the chair.

Willy smoked the cigarette. Popping his can of Tango, he sipped at it noisily and then asked: 'Are you Sonny's dad?'

Hearing the word 'dad' he felt an urge to cry, and nodded.

'I thought so. You don't smell of Old Bill. He used to talk about you a lot – about your house and his brothers. You were on holiday a while ago, weren't you? He said you were going to take him to Jamaica with you next time.'

'You seem to know a lot about him.'

Willy shrugged with the arrogance of youth.

'He was me mate, helped me out a few times when I was in trouble. I stayed at his mum's once but to be honest I prefer it on the street.'

'Why was that?'

Willy shrugged again and turned his mouth down sadly.

'To be honest, his mother was a bit too much like mine, if you get my drift? I like me own space anyway. Too much mug-bunnying with that lot, you know?'

Tyrell knew exactly what he meant, the addict's incessant self-justifying monologue, and wondered at a child who had the sense to keep away from Jude even though he was living on the street and selling his body. Wonders, as far as Tyrell was concerned, would never cease.

'Don't you get scared, Will? Don't you want a better life than this?'

Willy Lomax looked at him with the eyes of a thirteen-year-old pensioner and said honestly: ' 'Course I do, but smack and that ain't my scene. I get meself a little nest on the street and I bed down there. I ain't queer, I just do this to get a few quid so I can eat and have a drink now and again. I used to use glue but it's a mug's game, ain't it?'

273

Tyrell was saved from answering by the food and tea arriving.

Willy Lomax attacked his food and sipped at the scalding hot tea, gulping it even though it was burning his mouth. Then he put the mug down and heaped in five large spoons of sugar. After building himself a large chip sandwich and wolfing it down, he seemed to relax a bit.

Tyrell watched him in amazement.

'This is fucking handsome.'

Tyrell smiled now as he said, 'It sounds it.'

Willy closed his mouth and tried to eat daintily. He liked this big Rasta with the white smile and gentle demeanour. Sonny had told the truth about his father, he had said he was a cool guy and he was.

'How did you find out? We all expected to be talked to after he died but no one came near us. We assumed that no one knew.'

It was Tyrell's turn to shrug now.

It was strange that the police had not picked up on it, but in a way that was a Godsend. It was bad enough his boy was vilified all over the place without it also coming out he'd been a rent boy.

Tyrell was ashamed of his thoughts once more. He was more worried about how it would reflect on him and admitted this to himself even though he knew it was wrong. Poor Sonny had never had a chance. He must remember that and not let anything alter his love for the boy. But the guilt would be with him till the day he died. It was now even more important he should find out what had really happened. It was the last thing he could do for his boy and maybe, just maybe, he might find peace for himself as well. Tyrell needed to know that there was someone else to blame as well as himself.

'I heard he had regular customers.'

Willy nodded, his mouth once more full of food. He swallowed noisily before saying carefully, 'He was lucky like that. Kept himself spotlessly clean, see, always used a rubber and invested in a mobile for customer use. He advertised in the local paper.'

Tyrell was convinced he was not hearing right.

'He what?'

His voice was louder than he had anticipated and people stared at them once more. A tall man with a bad comb-over, straggly beard and milk-bottle glasses was staring at Willy and Tyrell saw the hunger in his eyes.

'Had your fucking look, mate?'

The man turned hastily away.

Willy laughed. 'He's always down the cottage, hangs around the bridal suite. He likes full penetration, see. But I'm a bit too old for him now.'

Tyrell could not keep the shock out of his voice.

'*You* are too old?'

Willy sighed.

'I don't do the bridal suite any more these days. It's good money but it fucks you up big-time inside.'

Tyrell was shaking his head in disbelief.

'The bridal suite? What the fuck is that?'

Willy Lomax laughed again.

'You got a lot to learn, mate. The bridal suite is the disabled toilet. You got more room to move in there, see?'

A cold gust of air hit them then and Tyrell saw the man walking past the steamy window, his head down and coat pulled tight around him.

Willy placed a grubby hand gently on his arm.

'There's worse than him about, believe me.'

'Finish your food. Do you want another cup of tea?'

The boy nodded and Tyrell signalled for two more. The café owner brought them over almost immediately, and by the time Tyrell had calmed himself down and the boy had finished eating the café was nearly empty. The small portable TV was on the boxing and the man behind the counter was watching Audley Harrison with interest. Normally Tyrell would have joined in, sinking a few beers and cheering him on, a good fighter and a good man. But tonight the boxing held no interest for him. It was comforting, though, having the noise of the commentators in the background.

Tyrell was still reeling from the news that his son had advertised in the newspaper for men. It was unbelievable to him even though he knew this boy was telling the truth and had no reason to lie.

The boy seemed to understand his predicament and said casually, 'What else are you wanting to know, mate?'

Tyrell looked at him and said, 'I don't know, son. I suppose I want to know why he did it? What got him into this kind of life? The usual things parents want to know about their kids. The whys and the wherefores.'

He sighed heavily.

'To be honest I don't know what I want to know any more. I'm frightened to know in some ways.'

'You want to know if he had anyone pimping him, don't you?'

Tyrell nodded, dreading the answer.

'Well, he didn't. He was all right on his own, but he was good mates with one of the other black boys, Justin. He showed Sonny the ropes like, but he went missing a while back.'

'What do you mean, went missing?'

Willy shrugged once more.

'Just missing. In my world that happens a lot. People move on, arguments start. He was a runaway like me but he was already well into the grind, you know, from a little kid. And he got to be mates with Sonny. Well, he was mates with all of us really, but him and Sonny were close. He was the one who told Sonny to get a mobile and advertise in the paper. That way you go to people's houses sometimes and it's more comfortable, see. Plus you can have a nick up.'

Willy grinned as he said that.

'I get asked back to places even now, especially by the old blokes. They like to see you washing and all that. I love it because then I can have a bath and clean meself up. It's still a crap life, but Justin and Sonny, they had it sewn up. Hung around together.'

'Where was this kid living?'

'Now that I can tell you because he used to let me crash there sometimes.'

Tyrell waited for him to talk. Instead Willy smiled at him.

'You want more money?'

He nodded.

'I will give it to you but not in here, not in front of him, OK?'

He nodded in the direction of the café owner.

Willy nodded.

'I'll trust you, seeing as how you are Sonny's dad.'

Tyrell felt an urge to laugh at this little boy acting like a man, but supposed the boy had had to learn to talk himself up in his game.

'He lived above the baker's in the high street. It's a rat house, but he had his own room there.'

Tyrell was nonplussed.

'What the fuck is a rat house?'

Willy grinned.

'Sorry, it's street jargon for a sort of legal squat. Someone rents a flat and then they sub-let it to all and sundry. Some people only rent the rooms for a few hours a day or the odd night. I'm sure I don't have to paint you a picture, do I? Anyway it's gone now and so is Justin.'

Tyrell shook his head once more. There was a whole world out there and he had honestly believed that he knew all about it, the bad as well as the good. Now it seemed he had not even seen the tip of the iceberg.

Willy's cheeks were pinker, and he was starting to look almost healthy. Tyrell guessed rightly it was the warmth and the full belly that was doing it. The boy yawned noisily. The heat was taking its toll and it occurred to Tyrell then that the child in front of him was whacked out.

277

'Do you want to sleep at my flat tonight?'

Willy looked shocked and said immediately, 'Really?'

Tyrell wasn't sure if he was doing the right thing but he couldn't leave the boy here and needed to know a lot more than he had already heard. But he wanted to do it gradually, give himself time to digest the information. He sensed that the boy would be easier to talk to in a neutral environment. Every time the door went he stared at it and Tyrell supposed he watched for Social Services as well as the police.

'Only for one night, though. I have some of Sonny's bits there that I got him in Jamaica. He won't need them so you can have them. But I want you to think of anyone you can who might know more about my Sonny and how he got into that house in the first place, OK?'

'Sure. Can I have a bath?'

'Have what you fucking like, son, but don't think anything funny, right, or me and you will fall out big-time. And don't even think of skanking off me because if you do I will be annoyed, OK?'

Willy Lomax laughed aloud.

'Makes no odds to me really, the sex bit. It's just me job, ain't it? And as for stealing, I ain't that stupid.'

He sounded offended and Tyrell didn't know what to say after that but when they left the café together somehow they were easy. He wasn't sure if he was doing the right thing bringing the boy to his flat but reasoned that at least there he could talk to him properly and, as Willy had said, he could have a bath and a decent night's kip.

Tyrell found that in a funny way he liked this odd little boy with the faded grey eyes and lust for living.

In the car he put the heater on because the boy was shivering.

'You going down with a cold, son, do you want me to get you something from the chemist's?'

Willy shook his head and said loudly, 'I better warn you, I'm HIV.'

Tyrell didn't answer for a few moments then, taking off the handbrake, he drove them both towards his flat.

Tammy was unconscious in bed and Nick was on his way into East London once more. As he parked he knew that what he was doing was wrong but couldn't stop himself. All the time he kept away it made his life easier, but once he dipped his toe into the water again he was hooked once more. It was something about the squalor and the risk of being found out. It was so dangerous he couldn't resist the thrill.

He walked into the block of flats and made his way as usual up to the tenth floor in the lift. The grinding sound was like a love song to him, even the smell of it got him hard. This was all part of it.

The door to the flat was opened by a tall man in tight leather trousers and no shirt. His beer belly hung over the waistband and he had tattoos all over his arms and chest.

'Where's Frankie?'

The man coughed as he said belligerently, 'Who wants to know?'

Nick looked at him warningly then, grabbing him by the throat, dragged him down the long narrow hallway and into the lounge where he threw the man on to the brokendown sofa.

'Get your stuff and fuck off.'

The punter did not need to be told twice. He scrambled around for his clothes and Frankie sat there giggling in an overstuffed armchair as the man ran from the flat in terror.

Nick smiled back tightly as he pulled out a pack of Durex and a bottle of red wine from inside his Aquascutum raincoat.

Frankie said throatily, 'You think of everything, don't you?'

Throwing a wrap of cocaine on to the table, Nick said happily, 'Let's have a party, eh?'

Chapter Eighteen

Willy was lying in the bath, wondering if he had died and gone to heaven. Tyrell's flat was warm, well decorated and smelled of skunk. There were good sounds coming from the CD player and the remains of a large joint had been left in the ashtray. He had also seen a Sky Plus remote control. If this was heaven, then the sooner he died the better.

He checked his body over, completely confident now that Tyrell was not going to come on to him. Even though he looked straighter than a ruler, Willy knew that men who looked harmless could be more dangerous than the ones who, unfortunately for them, looked like the stereotypical nonce.

He had lain there in the warm water and waited for the excuses to start: such as he needed to use the toilet, or wanted to talk to Willy, maybe bring him a beer. It was all just a ploy so as to see him naked then start on him.

But not a thing. Tyrell had not been near or by. If he had approached Willy, he would have obliged of course. What other choice did he have? He had had a feeling this man was OK, though you never really knew. If he was an abuser maybe that was why Sonny ended up at the cottage. Willy had learned at a young age never to judge a book by its cover. People could look so squeaky clean they should be on television adverts for breakfast cereals when in reality they deserved to be on Wanted posters.

For all he knew it was Sonny's own dad who had started him off on the rocky road. Maybe Tyrell Hatcher was in fact a nonce, but Willy's shit detector was telling him he was safe. This man did not have an ulterior motive like so many others did, as he knew to his cost.

In Willy's case it had been his mum's boyfriends. All she had ever done was get drunk, and he had had more uncles than a lottery winner on a council estate. He had learned young what to do to stop them hurting him, learned how to keep them sweet and get a few quid from them so at least he would come out of it with something more than a sore arse and a sense of smouldering anger that even he had sense enough to know would one day explode on to an unsuspecting public.

The thing was a lot of them looked normal. They didn't look like nonces and they didn't sound like nonces, which of course was their armour. If he accused them no one believed him, least of all his mother. They would tell her he was just after attention, or else lying because the uncle was about to accuse him of stealing from him, tell his mother how Willy had been found out so now he was saying all these bad things to get them in trouble, make them *go away* from her even, and his terrified mum would then decide to believe them because it suited her.

His uncles could give her money aplenty, and drink, and laughter. He couldn't give her that.

And then the uncles would wait a while and start it all again, because they knew they were safe, she didn't believe her little boy, she *didn't want to*. She preferred her safe little life with the man and his money so she turned a blind eye to it all. Or rather, a drunken eye.

He had never felt safe in his life till he had hit the streets. Oh, he knew all the ruses nonces used by then, had had to learn them the hard way. It was how he'd survived. He would rather be in a cold shop doorway than anywhere near his mother's house. At least anything that happened to him now was because he allowed it to happen, he was in control to certain extent.

But it had all left its mark on him and Willy was glad in one way that he had HIV. At least he knew he would be out of it all soon and then nothing would ever bother him again. He was fourteen years old and already he was finished with life and all the people he'd met. But tonight was like a holiday for him. He had a full belly and a few quid and he did not have to use his mouth for anything but talking.

What a touch!

He could hear Tyrell moving about in the lounge and carried on checking himself over. He was bad lately, breaking out in rashes and sores. He needed to get to a clinic and get to one soon, but Willy was always frightened that they would involve Social Services. That thought scared him. Knowing his luck they would send him home again. The Terrence Higgins Trust was supposed to be good so he would try them soon. Until then, he was going to get out of the bath and have a nice cold beer and hopefully watch a bit of telly.

It was strange to feel normal, which was exactly how he felt now. Normal.

This was what Sonny had yearned for all his life, Willy knew that and had empathised with him. But he also knew that Tyrell's wife was not the most accommodating person in the world. Still, she did not seem to be around tonight so he would do what he had always done, make the most of what he had.

Wrapping himself in a nice warm towel and sitting on the toilet, Willy started to cry. He was only crying because he was hurting, he was under the weather and sleeping out in the cold had made him ache. He was not crying because he was sad or anything. He told himself that over and over again.

*　*　*

283

Nick Leary had left Frankie's place and driven back to Essex and then, because he was still buzzing, he'd decided to call in at the pub. There was a lock-in as usual and a few of the regulars were in such high spirits they were having piggy-back competitions in the bar.

His presence made everyone subdued at first. Gary Proctor's death had caused a stir as he had known it would and no one had as yet had the guts to ask him about it outright. He knew that no one would either, not unless he brought it up first.

Everyone was scared of him. It had afforded Nick comfort in the past to know that merely raising his voice could send shock waves through his so-called friends; now all it did was depress him. He had finally learned that he actually had no real friends. With his lifestyle they were a luxury he could not afford.

He had already sent the grassing rumour round though if it had come from any mouth but his it would have been dismissed out of hand.

So all in all he was set like a jelly.

Albeit a lonely jelly. But that was the price you paid for his kind of life. He knew none of the people around him would understand about little Frankie, that was a secret he would have to keep. Would kill to keep, in fact. Image was everything in their world and once that image was tarnished it was time to leave the party and go home on your own.

Nick walked purposefully to the bar where drugs were openly lying around and the drinks were being poured over-generously. He enjoyed the obvious fear of not only his bar staff but the clientele as well.

Everyone had heard about Tammy's tear up and he knew it would be a topic of conversation for years to come. Tammy, God love her, was a legend in her own lunchtime. And that was how it should be: she was so over the top she should have been a transvestite by rights.

But at least it had given everyone a new topic of conversation. Gary's demise would only be talked about again once when it was time for his funeral. Nick wasn't going to go, and he would let everyone know he wasn't going. Grasses didn't get buried like normal people. They got planted alone, with no fanfare and no interest.

He was scowling as he looked around the bar and saw all the usual suspects. Turning to his old friend Joey, he said loudly, 'Have you been fucking repossessed, Joey, and not told no one? Because to my knowledge you ain't been home for months.'

He smiled then and sniffed loudly and everyone sighed with relief. If Nick was snorting then it was OK for them to do it too. As if reading everyone's mind he snorted a line quickly and that set the seal on the night.

Joey wiped a hand across his face. Even though he was still nervous, he said jokingly, 'You put the fuck right up me then, Nick.'

But as he looked into his old friend's eyes he saw that he was not just drunk and stoned, Nick was at danger level once more. He wanted a fight and he would make sure he got one.

Joey had not seen him like this for years. This was like the teenage Nick who had fought and scrapped to get to the top. Well, he was at the top now, why did he have to keep ruining it for himself?

And what was this with the cocaine? Nick had never really been into all that, hated it in fact because he had never liked not being in control. But lately he was coked out more often than not by eleven in the morning.

He had always said, 'If you sell it, leave it alone.' They had seen too many mates go under through dealing while under the influence. It made you stupid, made you either paranoid or over-generous. It made you forget your priorities, they had seen that with other people over and over again.

Joey took a deep breath and said as casually as he could, 'Sid Haulfryn is in here, Nick, popped in to see you like. Wanted your new mobile number but I wasn't giving it to him.'

He thought he should tell Nick before anyone else did. Sid and Nick had fought a war on and off for years. One minute they were bosom buddies then a frost would set in over some imagined slight and it was the Cold War all over again. They had been mates as youngsters and still had a funny sort of one upmanship going on between them. When it didn't get violent it was amusing to watch.

Both of them were big men and both were into exactly the same things.

Both of them were arrogant too and unable to admit it when they were wrong.

Nick grinned.

'Where is he then?'

He looked around the bar and, catching Sid's eye, shouted, 'Who let that cunt in?'

It was said in a friendly but warning voice, and Sid took it in the manner it was intended. He walked over to Nick.

Sidney Haulfryn was a big man. He had long dark hair tied back in a pony tail and a deep pleasant voice that belied the fact he could fight like Mohammed Ali on speed.

'Hello, mate.' He held up his arms as if to say, What you going to do about me? His love of flashy jewellery was his undoing, his fingers were always heavy with gold and diamonds. It annoyed Nick who thought that any ostentatious show of wealth without good reason was like giving Lily Law a warrant in your own handwriting. Despite all that he was inordinately pleased to see the other man. He was a good joker was old Sid and so Nick conveniently forgot their usual antagonism.

He could do with a laugh tonight and, love him or loathe him, Sid was a crack. As his old mum would say, he could make a cat laugh.

The Graft

Nick was so genuinely pleased to see him he hugged Sid in a friendly manner, pleasing him no end and also pleasing most of the people in the bar. Because if Nick didn't like someone then they didn't like them. It was how it worked in their world and no one knew that better than Sidney Haulfryn.

Sid had a hidden agenda, of course, and he knew that Nick was sensible enough to realise that.

Nick waved towards the barmaid.

'Get us a drink, all of us.'

He grinned.

'Everyone in the fucking place, let's have a party!'

The juke box was turned back up to full volume and everyone relaxed, ready for a good night. As no one had any regular kind of job to go to tomorrow, and as their nefarious business dealings could be done at any time of the day, a night-long party was no problem for any of them. It was all about socialising and being seen to be seen. Plus more deals would be done here tonight than in the City the following morning. It was their world and they all loved it this way. Except Nick who was starting to see it all from a different perspective.

Sidney Haulfryn was pleased by his welcome. He had wanted to talk to Nick for a while and it looked like this would be a golden opportunity.

'I was talking about you the other day. So fucking funny you are, Sid.'

Nick was laughing as he said it.

'Here, Nick, you want funny? How about this? You heard the one about the bloke in the sex shop in Soho . . . he wants to buy a blow-up doll. The bloke says, "Do you want a Christian one or a Muslim one?" And the geezer says, "What's the difference?" And the man says, "The Muslim ones blow themselves up!"'

Nick started to laugh and didn't stop. He was literally roaring with laughter and Sid, who knew it had been a funny joke, also

287

knew in his heart that it had not been *that* funny. He watched in disbelief as Nick started to cry with laughter.

As the noise grew louder and louder he said gently, 'Give over, you twonk, it wasn't that funny!'

Nick was wiping his eyes now. They were real tears, Sid and Joey realised. Joey looked at Sid and shook his head almost imperceptibly.

'You all right, Nick?'

Sid was genuinely worried and Nick knew that. It just made him feel even worse than he was already feeling.

'Nah, I ain't all right, Sid, I ain't all right at all. I can't seem to get me head together lately, you know?' He wiped his eyes and then snorted another line before saying, 'This whole thing is shit, see? It's all fucking shit.'

Tyrell had locked away or nailed down anything that could be stolen. Even though he'd felt bad doing it, he knew you could not trust people who were completely boracic and amoral. He had learned that much from his own son. It was only sensible to remember who he was dealing with here. Lives like Willy's were a series of dramas and tragedies; he knew that better than anyone, having lived with Jude. But he had taken a liking to the boy, and knew it was because he'd spoken kindly about Sonny, had seen him as a friend, which these days was a touch in itself. Everyone else talked about him as if he was shite.

Willy came into the lounge. He had changed into a Bob Marley T-shirt and a pair of Sonny's old jeans. Tyrell had packed them with his things when he had left Sally's. Sonny had liked to keep his good stuff at their house in case Jude sold it while his back was turned.

Willy Lomax looked almost respectable now and he knew it. The feeling of clean skin inside clean clothes also made him upset in a funny way. It had been so long since he had had a full belly and a relaxing time that he wondered if he was dreaming it all.

'You look much better than you did earlier.'

Willy shrugged, his trademark 'me against the world' shrug, perfected by the time he was nine. Tyrell grinned.

'Right little hard man, ain't you?'

Willy took that as a compliment and for some reason this made Tyrell want to laugh. 'Sit yourself down, mate. And listen to me – if you try and con me I will be annoyed, do you understand me?'

Willy looked into this man's eyes and saw danger. He also saw the kindness and generosity underlying it and smiled easily as he said, 'Never in a million years. You're a top geezer, and I am having the time of me life.'

Tyrell knew that the boy spoke from the heart, and also knew that he would get the truth from this child, no matter how bad it was.

He had a feeling that it would be bad but had braced himself for that. All he needed now was to hear it.

Nick and Sid were deep in conversation, and Sid was surprised at what he was hearing. He had heard about all Nick's troubles and guessed Nick knew that much. But he was being so open and honest about them it was painful to listen to him. This was not the man Sid knew and actually, despite the gossip about them, liked. This man was vulnerable, frightened and depressed. Sid would lay money on that being the correct diagnosis.

Cocaine was making Nick talk. It wasn't the usual coke-induced mugbunnying that heralded a large intake of narcotics and alcohol, it was an honest and truthful unloading of his personal demons. It wasn't the usual line of chat of a well-known hard man, either.

'Look, Nick, you got to let this go, mate. That boy is dead and no matter what happens, or what you say, nothing will bring him back.'

Nick nodded.

'I know that, Siddy, no one better. But I feel that since it all happened my life has changed, see? I feel like I'm being dogged by bad luck.'

Sid laughed.

'Tell me about it! Sounds like what happened to me after I married Carol. One cunt of a woman that was.'

Nick didn't laugh as he would have done usually. He was deadly earnest and Sid looked once more at Joey who half smiled at him as if to say, See what I mean? There was no doubt Nick Leary was well on the way to a nut farm if he didn't get himself sorted out soon.

'Have another line, guys. Joey, get a few wraps out of the downstairs safe, eh?'

He smiled placatingly.

'You just had a line. Have a rest, Nick, for five minutes. Give your nose a chance to recover.'

It was said in jest but Nick pushed his face close to Joey's and ordered him: 'Don't fucking lecture me! Just go and get the fucking coke.'

People were watching the little tableau and Joey, red-faced and awkward, rushed to do as he had been told. Sidney could almost feel the man's embarrassment.

'That was a bit harsh, Nick, weren't it?'

Sid kept his voice low so as not to be seen disrespecting him. Nick scowled at everyone around them as he answered.

'Look at them, fucking carrion the lot of them! And see that Joey? He's the worst. He hangs on to me coat tails and I see him all right for his booze, his poke and his fucking gear . . .'

But Sid couldn't hear him talking down about Joey and said as much.

'Joey's a good mate to you. He's loyal and he loves you like a brother. You shouldn't mug him off like that in front of people.'

Somewhere in Nick's drug-fuelled brain he knew that Sidney Haulfryn was telling him the truth and a spark of shame washed

through him for his own meanness. Joey had kept the building
businesses going since Gary's death, the building work and the
clubs. He had helped Nick over so much and he had indeed mugged
him off.

He broke wind loudly and said drunkenly, 'You are right, so
fucking right.' He was maudlin now and, taking his arm, Sid walked
him through the pub and out into the car park.

'Come on, you need some air.'

Outside Nick sat on the wall that surrounded the car park and
took deep breaths to try to steady his racing heart.

'You need a holiday, Nick, for at least a month. Can't you fly off
to your villa in Spain and try and get your head together? Put the
last few months behind you, eh?'

It was said with kindness and that was Nick's undoing.

'I killed that boy, Siddy! I killed him and I knew what I was
doing, see? I hit him as hard as I could and I kept hitting him . . .'

' 'Course you did. Anyone would have done the same.'

Sid was talking him down again and wondered at something so
mundane in their world getting to Nick Leary so badly. They
crunched people for a living. He and Nick had been nose to nose
themselves many times over the years. So what was the big drama
about this boy? He was a thief, he was carrion, he would probably
be out mugging old ladies now if Nick had not put him out of the
game.

He was on the verge of breakdown over it, though, that much
was evident.

'Why don't you go home, Nick? Try and sleep, get yourself back
together.'

He stared at Sid for a while then said suddenly: 'What brought
you here tonight?'

Sid shrugged. His black hair was shining in the light coming
from the pub. His huge shoulders made him look suddenly
intimidating. Nick was afraid of him for a moment. It was coke

paranoia. Even though he knew that, he still felt the full shock of his own fear.

'I want me money, Nick. I want the money Proctor owes me for the drugs I supplied. It's ten grand and I ain't swallowing me knob over it. He got it in both your names, and you know and I know you used him so if anything went tits up there would never be any comeback to you. Well, there is now.'

Nick nodded.

'In truth, I had forgotten about it. You'll get it.'

It was said with all the contempt he felt. Ten grand was nothing to him and Sid should have known and respected that fact.

Sidney did.

This was the Nick he knew, arrogant and quick to take offence. There was hope for him yet. Siddy smiled in the darkness, thrusting home his barb quickly and neatly.

'I heard he was nonceing young boys, is it true?'

Nick was alert now, all his other worries forgotten.

'Who told you that?'

'A little bird told me. Actually it was a little bloke.'

Nick could hear the accusation in the other man's voice and knew Sid was feeling him out, fishing for the whole story. This was what he had been frightened of, people finding out about all that shit and then putting two and two together and making five.

He coughed loudly. He was thinking on his feet because he knew that if this man decided to pursue his suspicions the chances were he would find out more than he'd bargained for.

Their world was far too small for Nick to allow something like this to take hold. He had to nip it in the bud now while he still had the chance.

'I found out he was trying it on with the boys we use for the clubs. It was me that done him in the lock-up. But that is between me and you, right? No one else knows about it.'

Siddy grinned even as he heard the threat in his old friend's voice.

'But people do know about it, Nick, and they applaud what you did. Stevie couldn't keep his trap shut, see? He told the boy's father in confidence and you know old Mackie – he might as well have put it in the *Romford* fucking *Recorder*. No one else would want it put about that their own son had been vandalised by that piece of shite, but Mackie couldn't keep it to himself. The man's a cunt. Anyway, I thought I'd let you know because chances are you'll be getting your collar felt at some point. I assume you've already put yourself out of the frame? You have a tame filth, don't you? That Rudde ... I hear you and him are practically bum chums.'

Sid laughed at his own wit.

Nick relaxed. Though Mackie was due a visit now, and he would get one he'd never forget.

'You want a trade off, don't you? I might have known. I get to keep me ten grand and you keep your trap shut if I get Rudde to do you a favour, isn't that it?'

'Always quick on the uptake, you, Nick.'

'What do you want then?'

'I need a few names, that's all.'

'You like to kick a man when he's down, don't you, Sid?'

Siddy grinned.

'I could say the same about you and poor old Gary Proctor, mate.'

Tyrell had brought in a bucket full of ice and placed a few cans of Red Stripe in it. On the black ash coffee table he had put out crisps and nuts. He had also rolled himself a large joint of skunk. He had a feeling he would need it once this boy told him the whole nine yards.

They both cracked a beer and Tyrell watched as the boy sipped his and watched the TV surreptitiously out of the corner of his eye.

'Why ain't you at home then? Sonny said you had a big house and two other kids.'

The question was asked in all innocence but it still made Tyrell feel bad.

'Never you mind that. I want some answers. I have kept my side of the bargain, it's time for you to keep yours.'

The boy picked up a bowl of Doritos and started to eat them.

'It's Justin you need to talk to but he's disappeared off the face of the earth. He used to knock about with a boy called Kerr, or so I heard anyway. Kerr works out of the Cross and also out of a rat house in East London. A bloke picks them up a couple of times a week from the station and they rent the rooms from him. This bloke brings in the customers, see, you don't get any say.'

Tyrell guessed rightly that this boy had been a frequent visitor there before the HIV had grabbed hold and made him look so ill.

'He's a piece of shit, that bloke. Right rough, you know, and you can never tell what's going to be going down there, if you'll excuse the pun.'

'How do you mean?'

The boy lay back to make himself more comfortable.

'What can I say? You could get lumbered with two or three at the same time there, but at least the money's good.'

He could see the shock and the horror on Tyrell's face and said hastily, 'Sonny never went there. At least, not that I know of anyway.'

He knew it was what Tyrell wanted to hear. So did Tyrell, who knew the boy was lying.

'Who was the bloke who picked them up? Do you know his name?'

'It was just Mr P. But he was a hard old fucker. We was all scared of him, he was one of them straight-acting heavy blokes. He would make us all do what he wanted but didn't give us any money or anything. It was as if he was getting us the work so we had to give him whatever he wanted for free.'

'Where exactly did he pick you all up from, and what days and times? Also write down the names of anyone you remember who might know anything about my Sonny and his other dealings. Anything, no matter how small. It could be important, right?'

Tyrell wanted to see this man for himself. He knew when he did it would probably open up a whole new heartbreak for him. But he had come this far, he might as well see it through to the bitter end.

Chapter Nineteen

Tyrell had covered the boy up with a quilt. He watched him sleep for a while, wondering at a child of that age who had two parents yet no one to call his own. How did people give birth to a child and then completely forget about them? It was beyond his comprehension.

This boy had a good sense of humour and street smarts that belied his years. Considering all that had happened to him Tyrell marvelled that he still had that small spark of decency inside him.

Willy had cared about Sonny Boy in a way no one else would understand. He had tried to sanitise the story he had told to save Tyrell's feelings and Sonny Boy's reputation. It had been terrible to listen to, let alone think about now Tyrell was alone and Willy Lomax was sleeping. It was shocking and it was frightening.

Real life was not what everyone thought it was. At least Tyrell knew that now if nothing else. Creeping from the room, he left the boy to whatever dreams or nightmares he commanded while sleeping.

He blamed himself for this, but he also blamed Jude. She must have known what was going on. No, he corrected himself, she *did* know what was going on. Even after all that had happened he still wanted to believe the best of her. It was hard admitting that it was his own mother who had sent Sonny to his fate.

Why had he not seen her for what she was like everyone else had? Why had he given her the benefit of the doubt all the time? Why didn't he go round there now and break her fucking neck once and for all?

He knew one thing. Next time he saw a street child he would not be so quick to dismiss them. This had been a learning curve in more ways than one.

He looked at what Willy had written down for him. The boy had nice handwriting and that had surprised Tyrell, but apparently he had not done badly at school when he had bothered to go. Since the onset of his HIV he had taken to reading when he could not work because of the intense tiredness he experienced.

What a different life he could have lived with different parents, a different home, a different set of values.

Willy had gone to his backpack and shown Tyrell his reading torch, displaying it proudly like it was some kind of precious gift, which he supposed to the boy was probably the case. Willy owned it and Willy, God love him, did not own much. It was a large yellow workman's torch, possibly stolen but the batteries must have been expensive for the boy on his kind of money.

Tyrell's own boys used torches to play with, to scare one another by turning them on under their chins and making faces at each other in the dark. They would never see these torches as an integral part of their lives, depend on them for light and comfort while they slept out in doorways. Willy had said the torch enabled him to reach into other worlds, such as J.K. Rowling's and Terry Pratchett's. He liked to lose himself in fantasies where people always solved their problems, made sure that right was done and evil cast aside.

If only life was that simple.

The child in Willy was still uppermost even though people had done their best to trample on his innocence, snatch it from him.

How could Sonny have been a part of all this too and his own father not even realise?

So many men were fathers, had brought kids into the world, yet so few seemed to be a proper daddy, the man who was always there for his kids, no matter what. Tyrell had believed for a long time that he had been there for all three of his boys, but he hadn't.

Not really.

If he had been a more complete man he would not have had to bury his eldest and then find out that he had been a part of society most people walked away from. Tyrell included.

His mother had always said, 'We are all guilty of something even if it is only laziness or ignorance.' He had never understood what she meant till now.

He knew one thing, though, he was going to see this through to the bitter end and he would get the truth of it from Jude, no matter what it took. If he had to batter her brains out on the floor then he would.

She would have the full SP. She always did. It was how people like her survived.

Gino was listening to Jude avidly, taking in all she was saying. He knew she was trying to help him on his way and he appreciated it. Her voice was hoarse from too many cigarettes and too much booze. He had arrived with a bottle of cheap vodka, and the cheaper the better as far as she was concerned. She didn't want smoothness or flavour, her only interest in alcohol was to get as far out of her box as she could. Mixed with the brown it usually mellowed her out, but not tonight.

She knew she had to grab Gino as soon as possible, get him under her influence before he started to try and think for himself. That was the last thing she needed. At least with Sonny there'd been the blood tie to keep him under her thumb.

His death had been a real inconvenience and no one seemed to see that except her. It was all right for Tyrell and everyone else, they had their lives settled. Or they thought they did. Not one of them gave a monkey's for her and her needs.

As she watched Gino trying to make everything all right, she smiled. Picking up the mobile the police had not got near, she once more dialled the number.

This time the phone was answered.

It was her turn to switch off now. The unexpected was always worse than the expected. No one knew that better than Jude.

Pink Floyd were belting out 'Shine On You Crazy Diamond', and Nick was listening to them. He was alone, in his Range Rover, with a wrap of coke and a bottle of Scotch, wondering how his life had come to this.

He started up the motor. It was chilly now and he had watched his own house for too long. Tammy didn't know about this. When he went on the missing list, even after he had seen his Frankie, he often parked up and watched the house. His mobile had been going all night but he had ignored it. In fact he was sick of the sound of *Dam Busters*.

It had been funny once, hilarious even, now it depressed him.

He drove on to his property. The lights were all on. As usual it looked like Battersea power station. He switched off his phone and watched as the dogs all came up to greet him, their stumpy tails wagging. Getting out of the car, he stumbled and cursed himself silently for driving while so full of drink and drugs.

The front door opened and Tammy stood there in all her glory, a scowl on her face and her mouth already going into overdrive. He wondered then why he had not bought the attack dogs he had been offered. It would have been like a dream come true to see them rip his wife limb from limb. But it was like anything in life: the more you desired it, the further away it seemed to be.

He walked into his home and his fate.

He had made a decision at least. He was going to sort all this out once and for all. It was what he had been dreading, but it needed to be done. Maybe then at last he could get on with his life and put what had happened behind him where it belonged.

Willy woke up to the smell of eggs and bacon. Stretching himself lazily on the couch, he saw that the BBC breakfast news was on low and a cup of steaming tea had been placed on the coffee table for him.

It took him a few minutes to remember where he was.

Sitting up, his blond hair spiked on his head and his eyes still full of sleep, he saw the smiling face of Tyrell and envied his dead friend for his closeness to this man.

'All right, son?'

Willy smiled amiably.

'Never better. That breakfast smells fucking handsome.'

Tyrell went back into the kitchen. The last thing he'd wanted was a cooked breakfast but he knew the boy would want one, more to the point need one, so he had slipped out and bought the supplies ready for his waking up.

Now, though, the smell was getting to him too and he was actually looking forward to eating. He had originally planned to take Willy to a café but after the experience of the night before had decided against it. He felt embarrassed to be seen with the boy. Even though he knew that was wrong, he was man enough to admit it to himself.

But he would have to venture out with him eventually whatever he felt because he was going to take him to the Cross and ask him to try and find Justin. He would also enlist the help of the Clarkes in finding this Mr P because he would need all the help he could get there.

Once more Tyrell asked himself if he really wanted to know all that had happened in his son's life, and once more the answer was yes. He owed it to his dead boy not to turn his back on a single unpalatable fact, the way he had done while Sonny Boy was alive.

Billy Clarke had not seen Nick Leary for a long time, and was relishing the prospect of seeing him again. He had always liked Nick for some reason. He knew that he was a bit of a stiff in as much as he had made his money over other people's bodies, but to Billy that was part of their way of life. He was aware that someone would try and do it to him one day and consequently was always ready and waiting for them to try.

He would give them a run for their money, and he had a feeling that Nick Leary was waiting for the exact same thing and was as well provided for such an eventuality. It was the nature of their game, their lives. You took off those who had what you wanted, then you protected what you saw as yours.

But Nick had always had a certain coldness about him that had worried Billy and many other people of his acquaintance. It was an innate distance in him that told you he would stop at nothing to get what he wanted – and from what Billy heard it had got him an eight-bedroomed farmhouse with indoor pool and stables. What it had not got him, however, was peace of mind or happiness, but then they were luxuries people like them could never afford.

As he made his way into Essex Billy marvelled at how much it had changed over the years since he had been a regular visitor. Those days were well in the past, thank God, but he had had some memorable fights as well as fucks in Southend before he had married and settled down to the usual two point four kids. He knew those days were well behind him. It was good to look back with nostalgia, though, and as he and Nick went back such a long time it should be a pleasant visit.

Or so at least he hoped.

Nick Leary would have to talk to Tyrell, they were all agreed on

302

that one. It should give him the closure he so desperately needed but Nick needed to be well briefed on what he would be taking on because Tyrell was a mate to Louis, a good mate, and Louis loved him like a brother.

Now Billy had to put the hard word on Nick Leary and didn't want to. He hoped for Nick's sake he would listen or Billy had no option but to bring in his brothers, 'The Heavy Brigade' as they were known locally.

He wondered how Tammy was. He had shagged her many years ago and hoped she had never felt the urge to confide this in her husband. He had liked old Tammy, and felt she got a rough deal from Nick even though in fairness you never heard about him with other women. Another reason people didn't entirely trust Nick. With money came spare, and the spare in Essex was par excellence as far as Billy was concerned. But he had a feeling that the coldness he had seen in Nick many years before extended as far as his marital bed.

Tammy needed love, she thrived on it like most women do.

He wasn't sure Nick was even capable of feeling the emotion.

'You have to do it, don't you, Tammy?'

She laughed.

'Do what?'

Nick walked away from her and into the kitchen. As usual lately his mother left the room as soon as he entered it. Following her into the entrance hall, he shouted, 'What the fuck is the matter with you?'

Angela turned at the bottom of the stairs and looked at her son for long moments.

'Hester is coming over later to pick me up. I'm going to stay with her for a while.'

The mention of his sister's name threw Nick for a few seconds.

'What – you're going to stay with *Hester*?'

He sounded as if he had not heard her right and this made Angela smile. She nodded. Nick was lost for words, just stood and watched her climb the stairs. Then he shouted spitefully, as loudly as he could, 'Well, fucking stay there, and don't come back!'

Angela didn't answer him.

He went back to the kitchen. Cutting a few lines on the granite work surface he snorted two, one after the other, to stop himself shaking with the anger that was threatening to envelop him. He could feel the buzz arriving in seconds. Then, going down to the cellar, he picked up a case of Smirnoff Black Label vodka that had fallen, miraculously without breaking one bottle, off the back of a lorry.

As he picked it up he saw that someone had been rifling through his private papers again. He knew Tammy kept a lead on what he was doing, he expected that much but it still annoyed him. And he was already irritated that his mother was going to Hester's. He rarely saw his sister because his mother had hardly opened her mouth to her since she had married her husband Dixon. The big black man had set off something in his mother that had lasted for years. Now though the miserable old bag was going round there after all the years of strained gatherings at Christmas and New Year. The two-faced old cow.

When he went back into the kitchen it was to see his wife snorting a line herself and then going to the large American fridge for a bowl of ice.

'If you can't beat them . . .' Tammy said gaily.

He hugged her to him then.

'You are one argumentative bastard, Tams.'

She grinned.

'I know, and that is all part of me charm.'

He poured them both large vodkas.

'Thanks for getting me out yesterday anyway.'

He shrugged.

'What was it all over?'

He knew, and she knew he knew, it was the game they played.

'Oh, this and that. Too much gear, too much booze, and that prat has a mouth like a docker's auntie.'

'She can have a row though, Tams.'

She grinned again, and he wiped the cocaine from under her nostril as she said confidently, 'Not any more she can't.'

He laughed at her. She had perfect comedy timing and in another life could have made a fortune in the movies or on stage. Her whole life was one big pretence in any case. She could not distinguish between reality and fantasy any more. Though it was getting like that for him as well these days.

'Will I have to put the hard word on her old man?'

It was a loaded question.

' 'Course not, Nick, stop being a wanker for five minutes. Give yourself a day off, will you!'

He had to admire her front. Only Tammy could do what she did and still front it out as if she was the victim.

'Do you know what is going on with me mother, you two being so close and all?' The sarcasm was not lost on Tammy but she answered him anyway. Knowing she had to box clever, she smiled sweetly and said, 'You have got up her nose, probably the drug-taking and the drinking, but even I was taken aback to think that poor old Dixon is preferable company to us two! She has hardly opened her mouth to their kids, has she?'

Nick nodded sagely. 'She completely ignores Dixon. Even I keep quiet about them in case someone puts their foot in it round here by asking too much about them. It's the one thing I never understood with her, Tams, why she is so racist?'

Tammy shrugged. 'It's an age thing I think, Nick. What does it matter now anyway? If she goes for a while it'll give her a chance to calm down. We've all been hit by what happened in one way or another.'

He nodded then, seeing her point of view.

'Do her good to get away. I think she gets lonely here, misses all her old mates and that.'

The buzzer that heralded an arrival at the front gates broke into their conversation then and on the CCTV camera Nick saw Billy Clarke's face smiling at him.

'All right, Billy boy! Don't get out of the car until I come on the drive, the dogs are loose, OK?'

'Just let me in, you tosser.'

Nick was laughing as he pressed the button to open the gates.

'What's he want?'

Tammy's voice was wary and Nick knew why that was, though as usual he didn't let on. One day he was going to try and find a man under the age of seventy she *hadn't* slept with.

'We'll soon find out, Tams, he'll be here in a few minutes. Cut another couple of lines and I'll go and greet our guest.'

She smiled and did as she was bidden.

King's Cross was busy as usual on a Friday afternoon. Commuters swarmed round Tyrell. Everyone wanted an early shoot on a Friday, and the place was buzzing with all sorts. The smell of Kentucky and McDonald's vied with travellers' damp coats and the rubbish thrown carelessly underfoot.

There was also the smell of rent boys and prostitutes. They were both out in force, and as Tyrell listened to the boy beside him he was in shock at what he was hearing.

'That boy over there, right? With the green shirt and black jeans. His name is Thomas, and he grooms for some of the older boys. He makes friends with the younger kids and introduces them to the bigger boys for a bit of gear. He's a heroin addict, see, a lot of them are. He's HIV as well. It was him who told me what was wrong with me a while ago. I thought I just had a cold like and couldn't shake it off.'

Willy blew his nose before continuing.

'Now the boy he's talking to is called Kerr and he's a dealer. He will know where to find Justin, they're good mates.'

Tyrell looked at the tall black boy with the new dreads and the sneaky look of a child dealer. He was forever peering around him, watching and waiting to see who was on the horizon. Tyrell had grown up with boys just like this Kerr, chancers who would sell their own grannies for a few pounds to put something in their arms. It was like looking at a negative of Jude.

Dealers who were also users were a dangerous breed. They cut the fuck out of everything to make the maximum money regardless of who they might harm in the process. Keeping the lion's share for themselves just hastened their own slide down the slippery slope. Eventually they scoffed all the gear, left themselves in enormous debt and ducked and dived until the main supplier caught up with them.

And they *always* caught up with them, it was what they did to protect their own livelihoods. A scar across the face and the kicking of a lifetime were the least you could expect if you failed to pay your bills on time.

Tyrell was suddenly depressed. It was like looking in a window and knowing that you were observing your own life, except he was observing the daily dealings of his dead son instead.

'Walk back to my car and put yourself inside in the warm, OK?' He passed Willy his car keys. 'I am going to have a word with little Kerr. You'll be OK?'

Willy nodded happily. If Tyrell was asking him to sit in the car then he wasn't leaving him here, which meant Willy might get another night at his flat.

He hoped so, it was great there.

Tammy had left the men to themselves. As she went Billy was shaking his head at his friend's liberal use of cocaine.

'You want to grow up, Nick, at your fucking age. You sell the fucking stuff, you don't snort it! Where the fuck is the profit in that, I ask you?'

Nick laughed.

'Don't tell me you've fucking hit the wagon, Billy? Is this the same Billy Clarke who snorted so many amphetamines in his youth he put the price up because they were scarce! Fucking Billy the Dyson Clarke!'

'As you said, that was in my youth. We're past all that now at our age. Look in the mirror, mate, you look fucking dreadful. If I met you and didn't know you, I would think you were in your fifties not your forties.'

Nick looked in the mirror above the fireplace in his lounge and grinned even though he knew what his friend said was true. He looked terrible. His blue eyes were red-rimmed through coke and lack of proper sleep, his jowls were hanging down like a Bassett hound's and his skin was dough-coloured. He looked like the kind of man he had always despised. He still made a joke, though, as was expected of him.

'Why do you care, want to be me boyfriend or something? Stop fucking nagging, you old tart, and tell me what brings you here?'

Billy sighed heavily.

'Not good stuff, but I'm here as an emissary like.'

Nick rolled his eyes to the ceiling at this turn of phrase and said resignedly: 'Who sent you?'

'No one. Me and me brothers have a bit of a problem and hope you can help us solve it.'

The mention of his brothers did the trick as Billy knew it would. He hated using them as a lever with an old pal but Nick in his state needed to be told exactly how important this errand was. And judging by the way he was carrying on, he would need a reminder as well. Thank God he had come alone. Terry would have been on it with Nick in minutes and ended up having a row with him. Or worse than that, nipping off with the ever-delectable Tammy.

Within five minutes of Billy's being in the house she had practically shoved her threepenny bits in his face. She would never change, old Tammy. But in fairness she still looked good. Nick was sobering up quickly now and due to the cocaine was paranoid as well.

Before he could answer Billy his sister Hester arrived to pick up their mother. Nick hurried to tidy away any signs of drug-taking before letting her in. Hester had not been in this house for many years. Her falling out with their mother had caused a family rift of Olympic standards.

Angela had never accepted the fact that her daughter had been in love with the big black man who had known her daughter since school. It was not that she was racist, as such, but she did not believe in mixed marriages, at least that was how she explained it to herself.

Dixon's mother, a thin Jamaican woman with a serious work ethic and prematurely grey hair, felt exactly the same way. Consequently, they had married and lived a life without family around them. Both mothers unaware that they were so alike in their thinking it was uncanny.

Hester loved their mother, she had fought for them all their lives against the drunken Irishman she had married. It had broken her heart when Angela had turned her back on her and her children without a second's thought.

Nick knew it must have taken a lot for her to come here today. He also knew she would be rejoicing inside because finally her mother had wanted to see her. The fact she had her husband Dixon with her now spoke volumes. Nick and he got on like a house on fire. Grabbing his brother-in-law's hand firmly, Nick cried, 'Hello, mate, come in, come on in. You know Billy Clarke?'

Billy happily shook hands with the tall black man. They had worked together many times and had also been friends as boys, growing up on adjacent estates.

'All right, Bill?'

It was the usual form of address, not a question.

Hester, tall and naturally blonde, was plumper than she had been as a girl but it suited her. She was what was called years before 'voluptuous'. As far as Dixon was concerned, she was sex on legs.

'You got the old dragon then, for a few weeks?'

Dixon grinned.

'So it seems.'

Hester kissed Billy on the cheek, and Billy being Billy could not resist squeezing her to him and copping a quick feel.

'I'll go and get Mum's bags, but before I do, what's happened?'

'I don't know, Hes, but I tell you something, I'll be glad to be rid of her miserable boat-race for a while.'

As Nick said it his mother walked into the room, hat and coat on and her make-up perfect from the thick face powder to the cupid's bow lips.

'A nice thing for a mother to hear, Nick Leary.'

He looked shamefaced and Billy and Dixon wondered at the power of motherhood. The hardest men in the world could be scared of their own mothers.

'Well, if you won't tell me what's wrong, what the fuck am I supposed to do?'

'I'll tell you what you do, Nicholas Leary, you walk your poor mother to the car.'

He rolled his eyes at the ceiling once more and followed her out of the room. Everyone wanted to laugh but no one did. By the car his mother waited until Nick had opened the door and settled her inside before she said quietly, 'You want to know what's wrong with me?'

He nodded, just stopping himself from shouting at her.

'Look in my safe. There's something there of yours, and when you see it you'll understand why after today I never want to clap eyes on you again. Never – do you hear me?' Angela pushed him away from her as if to touch him made her feel sick and then said, 'I'll send for me bits when I decide what I'm doing.'

She shut the car door on him then and he stood on the drive surrounded by his dogs, wondering what had made her go like this. Angela sat staring straight ahead, not allowing herself even a glance in his direction. Shaking his head, Nick walked back into the house. She was finally off her trolley. That was all he could come up with to explain such mad behaviour.

Tyrell walked slowly around the station, watching Kerr as he did his rounds. He saw him slipping packages into small grubby hands and chatting to other boys. Waiting his chance, he followed at a distance until the boy walked out of the station and around the corner.

As Kerr looked round to check for traffic, Tyrell grabbed him firmly by the top of his arm. Squeezing him tightly, enough to hurt but not to mark, he whispered, 'You walk with me, Kerr, and if you try anything I will punch your fucking lights out, you hearing what I am saying, boy?'

Kerr looked up into the man's face. He was frightened and it showed. It was only then at such close quarters that Tyrell saw how young this boy was. Distance and his height made him look a lot older.

'Who are you, man? What you want with me?'

'I am Sonny Hatcher's dad, Kerr, and I want a little chat with you.'

The boy stopped struggling then and walked sedately beside him back to where the car was parked. But Tyrell still kept a tight grip because he knew now that you could not trust anyone.

Anyone at all. Even those closest to you.

Chapter Twenty

Tammy didn't even realise that her mother-in-law had left the house, she was too busy getting ready to go out. In her heart of hearts she was embarrassed by the events of the day before and, being Tammy, had decided to get all her cronies together again and front it all out.

Every time she thought about that fight she flushed with shame. This had happened to her a lot over the years. She would wake up the day after a big tear up, think about what had happened and want to die there and then in her bed, always vowing it would be the last time she drank or drugged.

Now she would have to go back to the wine bar, make her apologies by ordering the most expensive wines and murmuring a few noises that sounded contrite, and then it would all be over and she could get back to normal.

No way would she be barred, they wouldn't dare, but she felt she should make all the appropriate moves for appearance's sake. That was the upside to being married to Nick Leary: no matter what she said or did it was quickly forgiven. Nick's name got her whatever she wanted, and a lot of the time whoever she wanted.

She would go out looking like she was too expensive for everyone around her, which in truth she was. The jewellery too was part of her armour against the rest of the world, like the cars and the house.

She opened her jewellery box and saw the array of diamond rings, bracelets and watches. There was not a piece of designer bling she did not own. Yet it meant nothing to her. She remembered back to when she was first with Nick, when he had still loved and wanted her, and the little diamond ring he had bought her with his wages off Romford market.

It was a diamond chip really, but it had meant they were engaged.

Her mother had got out a magnifying glass to look at it, for a laugh, but it had not been funny and Tammy remembered Nick's face then. He had been angry and embarrassed because at the time it had cost and meant so much it wasn't right to mock it. 'So much' meant something very different today. She had everything a woman could want, materially at least. Yet she wasn't happy, and knew in her heart she never would be happy, not in the way other people were, and now she was at a stage where even *things* didn't make her happy any more.

At least not for long anyway.

The next ring she'd been given had indeed been a rock, and she still had it, still wore it in fact, even though she could never insure it because it had been kited. She'd had the satisfaction then of seeing envy in her mother's eyes at the life she was getting for herself. Her mother had resented the houses, the cars, and Tammy's whole way of life, and somehow her resentment had made it all worthwhile.

So how was it, all these years later, that her mother ran a poxy little bar in Marbella with her toy boy and Tammy now envied *her*? At least her mother was getting a regular rogering, but then so was she, except hers was no longer coming from the man she'd expected it to come from. From the man she loved. The man she had married. In fact, she often wished Nick was a womaniser like her friends' husbands. That would at least have been a normal worry, something she could have coped with.

She put the TV on and looked on her Sky Plus for the *Will and*

Grace she had taped. She loved them and their humour, liked their uncomplicated world. She could watch the same episode over and over again, and Nick, though he moaned, loved the programme as well.

She often fantasised about living like they did on American TV where everything was always neatly resolved and fun, and they all dressed phenomenally well and had great apartments and enjoyed their lives. They ate huge amounts of food too and never put on weight. It was the business as far as she was concerned.

If only Tammy's problems could be solved in half an hour with a few great one-liners and a laugh, how much easier life would be.

Well, she had the one-liners, but unfortunately they were of the narcotic kind.

She could hear the low rumble of her husband talking downstairs and smiled. Billy Boy was all right, she liked him, and he had been pretty good in the kip if she remembered rightly. Tammy smiled slightly at the memory. He'd been into oral sex. Well, so had she. It had been quite memorable in its own little way.

Then she immersed herself in the programme as she applied too much make-up and snorted too much cocaine. Looking in the mirror without the usual smile she displayed to the world Tammy saw the signs of ageing: the deep grooves by the side of her mouth caused by her discontent and the crow's feet that looked more like vulture's feet to her at the moment. She forced the smile she knew would banish the look and maybe convince herself and her world that she was happy for a little longer at least.

Going to the fridge integrated into her wardrobe, she poured herself a shot of vodka. Knocking it back, she quickly poured another.

Was this always to be her life now she wondered. Then she laughed. The coke was getting to her, she could feel the buzz and along with the buzz she could feel the idea of taking a long holiday coming over her, and had a hunch she would be going on it alone.

Suddenly she didn't want Nick cramping her style, depressing her, and their villa in Marbella was empty. They hardly went there now. It had been a retreat for her and the boys once, but the boys got on her nerves when Nick wasn't around because he had always been the one to keep them amused. For some reason her own kids got on top of her. They wanted more than she was willing to give, and if Angela had really gone on the trot then what was she supposed to do when the holidays came round again? The nanny was fucking useless in most respects. James especially walked all over her. They couldn't stay at school all the time though, could they? She would have to look into it. They seemed settled enough there and she really didn't have the energy for them any more.

She would use the excuse that her nerves were still in tatters after the terrible event, when in reality she never gave that boy more than a fleeting thought. But it really was time for a change of scene.

She was always running away from her problems, and they were always problems she had caused for herself, and as Nick tried to point out it didn't matter where she ran or how far because *she* would still be there.

But she was going to learn to look out for herself more. That was her trouble, she was always looking out for everyone else. It was time she started to be selfish, time she started looking after *number one*.

Now Tammy had made her decision she felt better inside. It was about time she put herself first.

Happy now, she planned her holiday, conveniently forgetting her sons and her life in England. And the worst of it all was she was actually starting to believe what she'd told herself. Even in her worst drug-induced fantasies she had never gone that far before.

Kerr was in the flat with Tyrell and Willy. He had been so glad to see Willy at the Cross that somehow it had eased the fear inside him.

As they had left the station a man had approached them and Tyrell Hatcher had growled at him and seen him off like a Rottweiler. The look on his face as he had cursed at the nonce made him seem a different man from the one he was now. Kerr envied Sonny for having had him as a father, a role model, though it hadn't saved him in the end.

Tyrell Hatcher seemed like a good man. Now as he gave them both beers and smiled at them with his expensive white teeth, Kerr felt himself starting to relax.

He was still flying, and Tyrell guessed that fact.

The boy had the sunken eyes of an addict. They looked so deep and so beautiful, when in fact it was just the result of the heroin he'd taken. It was what made people trust addicts, those eyes, until they got to know them properly and realised that it was the drug that made them look like that, nothing to do with their own personality.

'You coming down yet?'

The boy nodded, ashamed to admit he was an addict.

'You got more?'

He nodded again, looking at Willy who shook his head to assure him Tyrell wasn't after anything.

If the four-minute warning went off this boy and all his kind would just make sure they had a fix in case they survived it. In a way Tyrell envied them. Everyday worries did not intrude on their lives like they did on everyone else's.

He said sternly, 'You want to fix, you go for it, but you don't get so blasted you can't talk to me, right?' He was pointing at the boy with one finger, warning him he knew all the dodges. Tyrell had been there and done that with Jude. He knew his case and he wanted the boy to understand that. Junkies were born liars, they lied about everything, it was second nature to them.

'You try and bullshit me and I'll give you the biggest clump of your fucking life, right?' He poked his dreadlocked head into the boy's face to bring home his point. 'I am talking massive hurt, do you understand me?'

The boy nodded once more. He believed him and that was all Tyrell was interested in. With addicts you had to be a greater force than their drugs; if you achieved that you were halfway home.

Willy patted the seat on the sofa next to him and Kerr sat down there gently, as if he was frightened to make a noise. Willy understood that. He knew it was a long time since this boy had been in a straight place where there was food in the fridge and a TV that worked. Where you were not terrified by every knock on the door or any new faces. He had felt the same himself.

He wanted to tell Kerr to relax and everything would be OK, but he couldn't, Tyrell had taken on the mantle of the man in charge and so he should. It was after all his drum. Willy had no intention of fucking things up for himself. He was hoping for a few more nights in a place where he could read in peace and a man didn't want *anything* from him.

Kerr sipped at his can of Red Stripe. He was pleased the man had given it to him, it was a friendly gesture even though he could see Tyrell was obviously used to getting his own way. Sonny had talked about his dad a lot and Kerr saw that he had actually underplayed his father, unlike most of his acquaintances who boasted endlessly about their backgrounds, good or bad. Kerr had liked Sonny Hatcher and no one had thought he would die the way he had, but how was he supposed to explain that to the boy's dad?

Kerr decided it was up to him to take some kind of control so he said quickly and nervously, 'What are you after, man?'

Tyrell was still getting over his amazement at this boy's youth. He was big for his age and from a distance looked older, intimidating even. Close up you could see the youth shining out of him. But the boy still had the look of a junkie, that nervousness and furtiveness.

Tyrell knew the boy had priced up everything in his flat as a matter of course and was filing it away for future reference because that was what addicts did. They always had their mind on the future, and the future for them consisted of getting money in whatever way they could. They did not care who they trampled on in the process.

Was that how poor Sonny had ended up in Nick Leary's house?

Tyrell took a deep drink from his can of Red Stripe and said coldly, 'Where's this Justin then?'

He did not bother with any preliminaries, dwelling on Sonny's death. He knew the best way to keep this boy in place was to fire questions at him and not give him any time to think about the answers.

'Who wants to know?'

It was said with bravado. Before Tyrell could answer, Willy said simply, 'Tell him, Kerr. Just for once do something that's right, eh?'

His words carried more weight than all the punches or threats in the world, and both Kerr and Tyrell were aware of that fact. But Kerr shrugged as if he had no idea what Willy was talking about.

'No one 'as seen him for a long time.'

Kerr had the English black boy talk, he said 'arks' instead of ask, and 'behint' instead of behind. It was an accent that irritated Tyrell who was a real Jamaican Englishman. He wondered if boys like this even knew Jamaica was part of the British Commonwealth. He doubted it very much. This boy had no passport, British, European or otherwise. But how the fuck did he think his family got over here in the first place? Tyrell knew it was unfair to be angry with him but he couldn't help it.

Willy was listening and nodding as Kerr explained the situation.

'What do you mean, no one has seen him? Has he left the area? Gone away, got nicked, overdosed? What?'

Tyrell knew all the things that happened to junkies.

'The last time I saw Justin he was with Sonny, it was a couple of days before he died.'

'Do you think he knew what Sonny was going to do?'

The boy shrugged. He was dressed in the baggy trousers that were so popular these days. They hung low down on his hips and Tyrell wondered if he knew the fashion came from a prison in America where the majority of the prisoners were black and on Death Row, and where they were not allowed belts in case of suicide so their trousers hung off them.

It was this kind of thing that had sent him mad with Sonny. This was not what they were supposed to be about. He pushed the thoughts aside and lit himself another joint.

'What – you fucking stupid boy, with your stupid Attica trousers and your stupid fucking talk? Answer me, for fuck's sake, you think I got all fucking night?'

Kerr didn't answer, just sat on the sofa staring down at his can of beer.

'Well, answer me, boy, you a fucking retard or what?'

Tyrell was getting fed up with pussy footing around everyone, especially these kids. They were adult enough to ruin their lives, why couldn't they just answer a question?

Willy, though, answered it for Kerr when he said simply, 'He's scared, look at him. He's terrified.'

It was only then that Tyrell realised there were tears dropping from the boy's chin on to his hands, clasping the can of Red Stripe as if his life depended on it.

Billy looked at Tammy as she breezed into the room ready for her outing. Her mobile was glued to her ear and she was wearing the equivalent of the crown jewels if they had been made in Essex. A diamond-encrusted Rolex, Gucci diamond earrings, and at her throat a choker that had cost more than a four-bedroomed detached house. Her hands sparkled with rings, and she was wearing a plain black dress with high-heeled Jimmy Choos.

She didn't realise just how astonishing she looked. The jewellery ruined the beautifully cut dress, though both men knew it would be pointless telling her that. Nick walked over to his jacket that was lying on the chair and put on his sunglasses for a joke, holding up his arms as if blinded.

'Fuck me, Tammy, where you going – the Oscars?'

But he knew this was her armour against the world, and in fairness it was a small price to pay to make her happy even if it never lasted longer than it took for the novelty of whatever new toy he bought her to wear off.

She was thrilled by his reaction and it showed.

Billy looked on in amazement at the way they interacted with each other. She kissed her husband goodbye lingeringly while he could have been kissing a maiden aunt. It suddenly occurred to Billy then that Nick was almost sexless. He chatted birds up, talked to them, said all the right things, but no one had ever actually seen him play away. And Tammy was a bit of all right if she shut her trap; he personally had fucked worse over the years. Some right old boilers had danced on his ample hips, and yet here they were, her on her night out – well, day and night out – and wearing enough tom to finance the Cuban economy, and Nick wasn't even batting an eyelid.

She was also half-drunk and stoned yet he was going to let her drive?

'You all right driving, Tammy?' Billy prompted.

She smiled over at him as she answered gaily, 'I've driven while worse than this, mate, but I'll cab it back.'

She was taking their new Mercedes sports. Would pull up outside the wine bar in it and make her entrance.

Billy didn't answer her, he didn't know what to say. He didn't like women drivers at the best of times. The thought of a head on with Tammy Leary did not appeal to him at all.

She left in a cloud of perfume and smiles and Nick rolled his eyes as he said honestly, 'She is a fucking nightmare. She's going back to the wine bar where she got arrested yesterday for having a tear up. The tom's all part of her act.'

He was explaining himself and they both knew it.

'Now then, where were we?'

Nick was pouring yet more drinks even though Billy still had his from earlier. 'Not for me, mate, I'm still drinking this one.'

It was said in such a way as to be critical but friendly. Nick had the rushes from the coke and could hear his heart beating in his ears. His hands were shaking and he was consciously trying to act normal. He wished Billy would go so he could sort himself out and see what the fuck his mother was going on about.

He kept looking at his watch. He wanted to get out soon. He had an appointment and was determined to keep it whatever Billy Clarke thought.

Hester and her husband Dixon were worried about Angela. She was smiling at the children, and the kids were loving it. Yet in all the years they had been part of her family, Angela had avoided them whenever possible. It wasn't so much that she was racist as she didn't believe in mixing the races; no amount of talking could convince her that Dixon was as English as she was.

But for the first time today she was all over them.

It was unexpected, that much was for sure.

Now Nick, he adored them, especially his niece Ria. He was always telling her how beautiful she was, how clever. All three kids adored him as much as he adored them. He was a good mate of Dixon's as well, and he had helped them over the years although their mother didn't know that.

Dixon opened a bottle of brandy and poured his mother-in-law a small glass. She looked like she needed it and accepted it gratefully. Tactfully, he then left the two women alone, taking the kids with him to the local park.

When they had gone Angela said, 'You've a lovely home and a lovely family.'

Hester knew how much it had taken her mother to say those words and respected that fact.

'Why are you here, Mum? What happened with you and Nick?'

'Nothing happened, I just wanted to see you all. Can't I see me grandchildren without being interrogated?'

It was said in fun, but they both knew there was no joy in any of it for her.

'Mum, with respect, you have seen my kids only a dozen times in sixteen years and even then Nick forced them on you.'

The two women stared at one another for a while.

'You love Nick, don't you?'

Hester smiled widely, she was so like her father it pained Angela to look at her.

' 'Course I do, Mum. He's been so good to us over the years. He helped Dixon and me get settled, he loves the kids, he is a really good man.'

Angela smiled once more. She wanted to ask her daughter why he never invited them to parties at his house, and why he never invited them to his villa in Spain, but she didn't.

Why ask the road you know?

It was because of her, and now that knowledge shamed her. She had begged him not to let them into her life and he had loved her so much he had agreed. Keeping his sister in the background, keeping them apart. To make matters worse, she had a sneaky feeling her daughter was aware of all this and, being the good woman she was, kept it to herself for fear of finally severing the tenuous link that kept them together.

'I'll ask you once more, Mum. Why are you here? What's happened with you and Nick?'

Hester knew it had to be catastrophic, nothing less would have brought her here, but she wouldn't push it too far. Her mother would tell her in her own good time.

Nick was the golden boy, her mother's baby. She had lived with that all her life and now it didn't bother her so much. She loved Nick, always had and always would. She knew what he had suffered at their father's hands and even at the hands of this woman sitting before her now, looking for all the world like the average mother.

She had suffocated her son, uncaring about anyone else in the world and when she had still been drinking heavily she had forced her son to take her side no matter what. It had been awful and she respected what Nick had achieved against all the odds. And the strange thing was this woman had been the cause of most of the trouble and upset, but no one could say that out loud.

She had been the instigator of most of her husband's spite; she would goad him into his terrible rages and there had been a time when she had been a part of it all. When she would make her husband lash out because of what she would say or do.

Yet Nick still saw her as some kind of saint. For herself all she had ever wanted was her mother's approval, nothing more and nothing less.

'Have you rowed with Nick, or fallen out with Tammy?'

Angela shrugged.

'Nothing, I just needed a change, that's all. Now stop asking me questions and tell me what's been happening? Carl was telling me he has taken ten GCSEs. Clever boy him, like his father.' Angela smiled.

'Dixon spends a lot of time with them. Carl isn't naturally the brightest bulb on the Christmas tree, this has been hard graft for him and he has worked for it. If he gets good grades we're going to get him a motorbike. Well, a trail bike anyway.'

Angela nodded.

'And don't forget little Ria is having her Holy Communion soon. We're having a party as usual.'

Dixon had become Catholic so they could get married in church. It amazed Angela that this little family were so tight together when she knew money must always have been a problem. Why did you never appreciate the right child? Why did most women always see their children so differently from everyone else in their lives?

Hester saw that her mother was miles away and shook her head sadly. She would not get any answers today.

'I'll make a cup of tea, eh? Do you want a sandwich, something to keep you going before dinner?'

Angela smiled then, a real smile.

'I'll help you with the dinner, lovey, I like to cook. Which was just as well in Nick's house – Tammy couldn't boil a shagging egg but she'd ruin it.'

They both smiled now. The truth was that Tammy could cook, when she bothered, she just didn't bother any more. Hester couldn't wait to find out what had happened. If her mother was rowing with Nick it had to be serious. She had stood by him through everything and anything, and it had never been her Nick's fault.

Angela would tell Hester what had happened in her own time. She had waited this long for a visit from her mother and she was not going to spoil it now.

'So you've never had any dealings with Tyrell Hatcher then?'

Nick shook his head.

'The name doesn't ring a bell, no.'

Billy lit another cigarette as he wondered what Nick was really saying.

'He's my little brother's best mate. You remember Louis?'

Nick nodded, remembering a tall boy with a nice smile.

'Yeah. And?'

He was getting belligerent now. He poured himself yet another drink as he said through gritted teeth, 'I ain't apologising for what I done, Billy. You get up in the night and you find that little cunt in your house and you tell me you would get his fucking family pedigree before you outed him? Is that what you're trying to say? I never had you down as a social worker.'

Billy was annoyed.

'Don't be silly, you know I don't mean that.'

Nick laughed.

'Do I? What am I, a fucking mind reader now?'

Billy Clarke had heard enough. Walking over to where Nick was standing, he said deliberately, 'You want to lay off the fucking gear, mate. I have seen too many of me mates go down that fucking path. You're paranoid, you're acting like a cunt, and you ain't treating me like one, you hear me? I am here as a friend, I want to sort this out. Tyrell wants to know what brought his boy into your home, that's all. He don't hold nothing against you personally.'

'Is that so, Billy? Big of him.'

Billy closed his eyes and swallowed down his anger.

'Listen to yourself. Look around you. You have more than most people could ever imagine, Nick, and you are fucking it up by shoving it up your nose. Well, that's your prerogative, ain't it? But I think you should see Tyrell because that poor fucker has had to deal with not just the death of his son but the life the poor little bastard had to live with his junkie mother.'

'Junkie Jude?'

It was said with so much hatred that Billy said quietly, 'How do you know her then?'

Nick swallowed hard before he said, 'I read the papers, mate. They're local, and she is renowned for her lifestyle. It ain't my fault Hatcher left his son with a piece of shit like her, is it? Maybe he should have looked out for him a bit more, eh? Instead of trying to find out what made him go wrong now, he should have tried to fix it before I had to fucking bash his boy's head in.'

'Listen to yourself, Nick. This ain't Tyrell's fault. And look how we all turned out. Look at my poor mother – we were nearly the death of her. You can't always blame the parents. You don't know how your own boys will turn out yet. There's lots of different kinds of junkies and you don't seem to be doing too bad yourself.

You've snorted the equivalent of Escobar's pension scheme and I've only been here a couple of hours, what the fuck is all that about?'

He had gone too far now and he knew it, but anger had got the better of him.

Nick looked into his old friend's eyes and suddenly the anger left him. He started to cry then, cried openly, and seeing him Billy felt bitterly embarrassed, but it also told him how badly the night of Sonny Hatcher's death had affected his friend.

'I didn't mean to kill him, see? I didn't really want him dead, not really. I was just frightened, that's all. Just frightened.'

Nick Leary sank down on to the sofa and with his head in his hands cried loudly, the noise echoing in the silence of the large, imposing house.

Of all the things Billy Clarke had expected, this was not one of them.

'What you crying for, son?'

Tyrell's voice was lower now, kinder. The boy was not making any noise and this was what scared Tyrell the most. He was just sitting there crying in complete silence.

Willy tapped him on the arm and motioned with his head for Tyrell to go to the kitchen. 'Let me talk to him. I'll burn him an armful, see if that straightens him out. His head's fucked. Let me talk to him, eh? You're scaring him and I think he doesn't want to tell you what went on.'

Tyrell left the room, grateful for the boy's advice. In the kitchen he relit his joint and puffed on it deeply, wondering how his life had come to this.

He had two rent boy runaways in his flat when he should be back at home in his nice house. But he knew that would never happen now. He would never go back there. Too much water had flowed under that particular bridge.

Yet it still seemed amazing to him that in a few short months everything in his life had changed for the worse. His eldest boy was dead and nothing would bring him back, Tyrell knew that, but he had to know what the boy was doing in Leary's house that night. If he could only get the answer to that question he knew he could start to live again. It had to be because of someone else. Someone had to have sent that boy to his death and when he found out who . . .

Tyrell didn't finish the thought. Instead he toked once more on the joint and wondered how long it would be before Willy calmed the boy down. He would sort out what he was going to do next when he found out the score there and not before.

It was like the old riddle: How did the man get out of the room with no windows and no doors? Well, the answer was: The same way he got in there.

Chapter Twenty-One

Billy was driving back to London, and as he drove was thinking about two men with no real understanding of the world they lived in. And he was wondering at the way Nicholas Leary, bad man personified, had crumpled over the death of a burglar. A creeper, the lowest of the low in their world, a gas meter bandit, a council house insurance man – call him what you wanted, the kid was just a thief. And yet it was a broken man he had just left, a broken man now reliant on a bit of gear and a pint of vodka to get him through the day. This was Nick Leary who had, according to urban legend, killed before. But that had been for a just cause in their world, and so was killing Sonny Hatcher. Fucking hell, even the filth thought he was in the right this time and how often did that happen?

Billy had also heard a rumour that Nick had recently taken out his own right-hand man, Gary Proctor, and knew there was more there than met the eye. There was something about Proctor he had never liked, he was far too slippery for Billy. Had too much to say for himself, had way too much front, but that front was usually backed up by Nick Leary.

Billy could only assume that Leary had had a business run in with his number one and it had resulted in the man's demise. Quite rightly so. They couldn't keep anyone around in their world who knew too much about them and their precarious business dealings and was starting to get antsy. That was the unwritten law. Nick had outed him fair and square, Billy should imagine.

So why was the death of a mere burglar taking over Leary's life?

He could understand it from Tyrell's point of view. Billy knew that there was nothing Tyrell could find out about his boy that would make what he'd done right, he just wanted to know what had caused him to be there in the first place.

And, he had to admit, Tyrell had a point.

Where did Sonny get the gun? Were the dogs at the house that night? How did that boy get past all the CCTV and everything else on there?

Billy himself would be hard pushed to creep up on Nick Leary and he had years of experience on Sonny Boy Hatcher. It would have had to be like a military operation, and from what he had heard about Tyrell's boy he was not the sharpest knife in the fucking drawer. In fact, he was a bit of a div by all accounts. Followed the leader.

His own middle boy was like that, his Jason. He was a lovely kid and all that, but he had to take his socks off to count and his reading amounted to comic books and porn magazines. You allowed for it eventually. Everyone wanted to have the next Einstein. Unfortunately now and again you got the next Boris Johnson. If one of the other boys told his Jason to jump off a bridge, then jump off a bridge he would. You still loved kids like that, you just tried to look out for them more. Jason would work for his dad, that was a foregone conclusion. He was going to be a lump, so Billy would use the boy's plusses. Jason would be a heavy, there was no shame in that in their world.

Now his eldest boy, Damien, he had the brains of a fucking dictator him, and Billy would see to it that he became a lawyer. The boy was up for it. He could argue his way out of anything and enjoy it while he was doing it. He would go far that one, and good luck to him and all. You could rob more money with a briefcase and an amiable personality, everyone knew that.

Now, though, after the visit to that house, he thought Tyrell had a point about Sonny's being there in the first place, and despite himself even Billy wanted to know what the score was. This had Gary Proctor written all over it, but did Nick realise that? Because Proctor would need someone behind *him*. Like poor Sonny Hatcher he could never have dreamed this one up on his lonesome.

Yes, there was more here than met the eye, and Billy for one was intrigued. He would make sure that when they finally had the meet all the boys were there for it. He had a feeling that Terry's personality disorder would come in distinctly handy at that meeting because if any two men were completely alike yet completely different it was Nick Leary and Tyrell Hatcher.

It was weird how similar they were emotionally while streets apart in every other way. That boy's death had fucked up too many heads. The sooner it was all put to bed the better.

Jude was in her element. Gino was well able for what she asked of him. In fact, he was showing off. As she lay back on the sofa and waited for the rush she knew was coming, she was smiling.

Gino had gone out, got the money for some scran and come back like a conquering hero. She had made a point of letting him know how clever he was, how much she relied on him. He had preened and puffed himself up with pride.

Now he was burning the brown. He had an old tablespoon full of heroin and had added water gently, burning it from beneath. As it bubbled away Jude saw the glint in his eye as he contemplated what was to come.

He had the right personality for it, there was no doubt about that.

Her Sonny, on the other hand, had hated it all, yet he would move heaven and earth to get it for her. Now Gino, who loved it, would be scoring for both of them.

She had on a Pink Floyd album, Animals, and it was playing 'Pigs on the Wing'. She loved this track, could listen to it over and over again. The flat was like a tip but she ignored it. It was all part of the game so far as she was concerned. Who was it who said life was too short to stuff a mushroom? Well, whoever it was had a point. Life was also too short to keep cleaning up, and going out and doing the same repetitive job day after day.

That was for mugs, as far as Jude was concerned.

The loud banging on the front door startled both of them and she pulled herself up from the sofa with difficulty.

'Ignore it, Gino, they'll go away soon enough.'

But seconds later the banging resumed.

Gino was too involved in what he was doing now to notice. As he gently pulled the liquid into a syringe the front door was kicked off its hinges. They heard the wood splitting and both jumped up in fright.

Jude was white-faced. Thinking it was Old Bill she automatically distanced herself from the boy and the loaded syringe.

'Throw it all out of the window, you fucking moron!'

Her voice was high with fright and Gino, rooted to the spot with fear, stood there and watched in amazement as his mother and three of his uncles burst into the room.

His mother's rooms were lovely. Nick had never really appreciated that until now, but then he rarely ventured into them. But in fairness to old Tammy they were out of this world, better than anything Mum had ever had in her whole life before. Not that she would ever admit that, though now they were like best mates maybe he was wrong about that as well.

The annexe was all done in cream and russet tones, and the picture window in her bedroom had heavy brocade curtains that would not have looked out of place in Buckingham Palace. She had done Mum proud, old Tams, and in fairness it must have been hard at the time because Angela Leary had ridden Tammy's back from day one. All those years Nick had dreamed of a truce between them and now it had come about he wanted it back as it had been before. He looked in her wardrobes and saw with relief that some of Mum's clothes were still there, so she must be thinking about coming back. He was annoyed with her but could not imagine his life without her in it.

Truth be told, he adored her. Always had and always would. He had protected her from his father and eventually taken over the mantle of caring for them all, so in a way he had taken on the role of husband in early life.

But what choice had he had? Should he have stood back and watched her being beaten to a pulp? Let his father demoralise and terrorise both him and his sister?

He had been seven when his father had first nonced him, and in that first act his father had ruined him as far as physical affection was concerned. He could only find solace now with faceless, uncaring people who used him as he used them. The guilt and the self-hatred was what he craved these days, that was the real turn on for him.

He had found peace, as the years had gone on, by bettering himself, by having a bigger house or a bigger car, having money had been a salve at one time. It had reassured him that he was *somebody* no matter what he felt inside. No matter how his mind tried to destroy all he had achieved, he knew, every time he looked around him, that he had made something of his life. The memory of what his father had put them all through was still vivid, like an open wound and he lived with it every day of his life. Yet the more he achieved the worse he felt inside, how had that come about?

He wished he knew what was going on in his head. All his years of working had left him able to harm someone, maim them and justify it to himself. Yet Sonny Hatcher had been his Achilles heel.

All the feelings that his father's treatment of him had engendered could not hold a candle to the guilt he felt over that boy.

Every time his father had touched him the bile had risen inside him and he had wanted to vomit it all away once and for all. He had saved Hester, though. He had to remember that, cherish that fact, otherwise what was it all about? How would he be able to get through the days, let alone the nights, if it had all been for nothing?

His mother had not been herself since the turn out with Gary Proctor and he wondered if that was what was bothering her.

When she'd calmed down and he'd explained it to her, she would be all right once more. She knew him better than anyone and she had stood by him through all sorts. Not that anything had ever been proved, of course. Nick Leary was whiter than white and he intended to stay that way as well.

But his mother wasn't stupid, she knew the score, and had decided long ago not to delve too deeply into his various dealings. The clubs were all legit, the building firm was straight, he had every right to live in his fuck-off house, had paid for it fair and square. He wasn't afraid of a bit of hard graft, a bit of hard collar, and Mum knew it. Had actively encouraged it all his life.

Nick wasn't going to live like his father, from hand to mouth, wondering where the money for the next drink was coming from. Was he fuck! He had given them all a good life and Mum knew it. She'd enjoyed the fruits of his labour so it was a bit late now to start being finicky.

Nick lifted the carpet up and laid it back gently. Her safe was under the floorboards and unless you knew where it was it would take forever to find it. He had had all the safes fitted by a little firm from Belfast, the thinking behind that being it would be too far to come and burgle him from there.

Now, though, Nick opened his mother's safe with trepidation.

Inside there were a few photos and a mobile phone.

It was the phone that threw him.

It had recently been charged up, and had eleven missed calls logged on it. Picking up the photos he felt his heart catapult itself up into his mouth. He saw himself smiling away, could remember when the photo had been taken. He had been so happy that day.

Frankie looked happy as well, they all did. It was a good photo, but if Nick had not been so drunk it would never have been taken.

But it had been taken and he had made sure that Gary got all the prints and the negatives of it, and Gary had done just that because he was in the photos as well and none of them wanted this kind of evidence lying about. Nick had forgotten about it then, he had never dreamed that the photo would be seen by anyone else in the world, let alone his own mother.

She also had his old phone, the mobile that he used to call up Frankie and his other amours. The phone that had once been his link to his other way of life, a life that Tammy and his mother would never understand. And why should they understand, he didn't understand it himself half the time.

But the need was always there, it was like a cancer inside him, growing silently and waiting to erupt and when it did he was always unable to resist what it offered him.

He looked at the missed calls and sighed. These photos meant a divorce, at the very least. One thing was for sure: Angela had not shown any of it to Tammy. If she had then the world as he knew it would be well and truly over by now.

Willy called out to Tyrell and he went back into the lounge, full of trepidation. The boy had obviously sorted himself out. He looked more relaxed somehow, and Tyrell, thanks to Jude, knew all the signs of a good fix. He didn't hold it against Kerr though because he knew how hard the demon drove. All he felt now that his anger had dissipated was sorrow.

What a waste of a life.

But it was pointless saying that to this boy because he wouldn't listen. Anyway Kerr was not his problem, he was someone else's. All Tyrell wanted from him was information on his son. And he would get it if he had to beat it out of him.

But Kerr didn't do any talking, it was Willy who told Tyrell what he needed to know.

'He's scared because Justin was supposed to go with Sonny that night, but the bloke who was going to pick him up didn't show. He assumed like that it was all off, so you can imagine how he felt when he heard what had happened.'

'Well, why didn't he tell anyone? Why didn't any of them tell anyone about it?'

Tyrell knew as he was asking the question what the answer would be.

For the first time Willy looked annoyed and said sharply, 'He sleeps in shop doorways, or crashes where he can, and you know that TVs get sold when you haven't got electricity and newspapers aren't really our bag unless it's to pad out our clothes if we're sleeping outside on cold winter nights. Or maybe it's because those things are for people with lives to live. Unfortunately, Mr Hatcher, that is not us. We have enough trouble just getting through the day.'

Willy pulled open another car of beer with a snap.

That 'Mr Hatcher' said it all as far as Tyrell was concerned.

'And anyway, who the fuck was he going to tell then? The Old Bill? Get himself put in the frame for something he didn't do. Get real!'

Tyrell sat down on the sofa, half ashamed now. He looked at the terrified Kerr and sighed.

'So who was going to pick him up then?'

Kerr shrugged.

'The geezer from the rat house.'

'What's his name?'

'Don't know. P.'

'What does he look like?'

'He's old.'

'Where does he hang out?'

'All over.'

Tyrell was having trouble keeping his temper. He had had longer conversations with answering machines.

'Where is this Justin now then?'

The other boy shrugged once more and Tyrell felt his hands clenching into fists.

Willy, sensing his impatience, said quietly, 'Get a pen and paper and we'll go through it all, eh?'

He was motioning Tyrell to go back to the kitchen. Once out there with him Willy said sadly, 'He's a bit backward, can't you tell?'

Tyrell's patience was nearly drained as he looked at this young boy who had stayed in his flat, had eaten his food and drunk his drink, and was now trying to be the go-between for him and Benny from *Crossroads*. It suddenly occurred to him that he might just be being taken for a ride.

'Just take it slowly. He's frightened in case he gets it wrong, that's all. I think he's talking about that bloke who picks up the boys for the nonces. Sounds like him anyway. But you have to remember that Kerr is only thirteen and has been on the streets for a good while so we ain't talking Brainiac status here, you know?'

Tyrell nodded.

'Let's get back in there, Willy, and see what else we can gather from him. Find out if there is anyone else who might have something to tell us.'

Willy smiled now.

'That is exactly what I was going to say. Maybe we should go round to the rat house and be done with it?'

'You aren't scared to do that any more then?'

Willy shook his head. He had flat out refused before. It was what Tyrell had wanted all along and the boy had refused point blank to go there, had had to be careful, he'd said. He had to live on the street and even after all this was over, that fact alone made it easy for him to go missing. Who would notice he was even gone? Who looked out for street kids?

Tyrell had respected his thoughts on the subject because he would not put this child's life in danger any more than he would one of his own sons'.

'You've been good to me the last few days, Tyrell, and I want to pay you back. But I also want some kind of justice for Sonny Boy. He was a good mate, you know.'

Tyrell didn't know what to do so he ruffled the boy's hair.

'You're a good kid, Willy Lomax.'

Tyrell's mobile was ringing once more and he glanced at it to see who was calling before he rejected the call.

'Listen, can I trust you here with him for a few hours until I get back?'

Willy nodded, and Tyrell saw the relief in his eyes.

'I will talk to him, OK?'

Tyrell picked up his jacket and as he reached the front door, remembered he didn't have his wallet. From his bedroom he could hear Willy talking and what he heard made him smile sadly.

'He ain't a bad bloke, Kerr, so you try and remember what you was told, OK?'

Willy was clearly trying to get as much information as possible.

Tyrell popped his head back round the front room door then.

'Shall I bring you two back a takeaway?'

Willy nodded happily.

'Hamburger and fries for me.'

Tyrell was already gone but Willy knew he had heard him, knew he would bring back something nice. He was all right was Sonny's dad, but Willy had an awful feeling that when he got to the bottom of his son's death he wouldn't get any kind of relief from the knowledge, would just create further nightmares for himself.

But he couldn't say that, of course, because the man didn't want to hear it.

Nick looked at the caller numbers on the phone from the safe, and the more he checked them the greater his fear became. He had hidden this particular phone along with a lot of other stuff after the burglary. That was of course the downside to being in his business. Lily Law was the last person you wanted perusing your private and personals.

Even though he had had the weight of the law on his side then he would not have put it past them to have used it as an excuse to turn him over. And a search warrant would have been a disaster that night. He would not be the first person who had lost their liberty like that, and he would not have been the last.

He glanced down at the photographs once more and tried to imagine how his mother felt, seeing them. It was obvious they were all into something sexual because they were in various states of undress. Why the fuck did he let them take the photos in the first place? They looked so young, so very young, and so very vulnerable.

It wasn't as if he and Frankie were an item, though, was it? Or any of the others in the photograph. In fact, he would be hard pushed to remember their names. But there was one person in the photo his mother would have latched on to and he knew she would have made the connection. So now on top of it all he had to try and placate her, because she was just the type to blow the lid off everything if she was upset enough.

As much as he loved her she was a fucking nuisance in some respects. Like Tammy, she was a bastard for snooping. He knew that Tammy, for all her acting the prat, knew what he was worth down to the last penny. She also worked out the Euro rates for the

Spanish dealings in nano-seconds and could run all his businesses while still spending her life in wine bars and restaurants.

She pretended to everyone that she had no head for business, but it had been her idea for him to deal in the first place and the money from it had set them up for life. His mother knew all about it, how could she not, she snooped as much as her daughter-in-law did. But this little lot would be the equivalent of a bomb going off in all their lives. Especially Tammy's. How could he explain Frankie or any of the others? Frankie had at least had the sense not to want more from him, not to fall in love with him and he was so glad about that fact. For all Tammy was and for all their fights he would not let her be hurt for the world. She had not asked for anything from him except his love and she had that although she didn't believe it now.

If his mother and Tammy were now bosom pals, and she had actually left the house to go to Hester, poor Hester who had shamed them all by marrying her black man, was she going to blow the lid on all this?

He stared down at the photos once more, the sickness enveloping him.

His mother might have stood by him through thick and thin, but would this be one step too far as far as Angela Leary was concerned?

It was Gary's fault as usual. He never could leave anything alone. Now thanks to him Nick had to go and sort out Mackie. He only hoped he got there in time to shut the fucker's mouth up. Permanently.

This whole mess was all Proctor's fault, had his greasy finger-marks all over it. Just like every other fuck up over the years. Nick should have sorted him twelve months before when he had realised just how far the man had sunk. If it got out now it would cause untold ag.

He stood up and decided there was no time like the present. He would go and put the hard word on Mackie himself.

* * *

Louis Clarke and Tyrell were in the Beehive in Brixton. It was busy in there and they had to talk close to each other's ear to hear what was being said. This suited them, though: it was hard to overhear conversations in noisy pubs.

'Billy went to see Leary.'

Tyrell nodded slowly.

'And?'

'Talk to him, Tyrell, he is well poggered over it all. Billy said it has made Leary go on the drink and the Charlie. And from what I heard about Leary, he was straight like that before. Anyway, Billy is setting up a meet.'

Tyrell nodded once more and sipped at his lager.

'I know how he feels. I went like that meself afterwards.'

Louis didn't know what to say to that.

'He is full of guilt apparently. Thought it was a grown-up, see, because of the ski mask and the weapon. Anyone would.'

Tyrell knew his friend was trying to make it all easier but he wasn't. In fact, in a way he was making it worse.

'I just want to hear from his own mouth what exactly went down that night, nothing else. I ain't got no argument with him.'

Louis nearly said it wouldn't matter if he did. Nick was more worried about the Clarke brothers than he was about Tyrell Hatcher. He just wanted his friend to get it over with and maybe then he could get on with his life. Or what was left of it anyway.

'Is that kid still at your flat?'

Tyrell smiled.

'I got fucking two of them now. This younger one, Kerr, is a right fucking dick but he knows more than he's letting on. I left the other kid with him. I think he'll get more than me out of him. I think I frighten him.'

Louis laughed.

'It's the dreads, they'd scare anyone. Come on, drink up and I'll get us another one.'

Mackie lived in Basildon, and he was not a liked man.

He was a drunken, argument-prone bully with no interest in anything other than football, 'filling his boots' as he so nicely described his sex life with a string of girlfriends now his wife had gone, and drinking himself into oblivion.

He had no interest in his son Jerome other than as a topic of conversation in the pub. He had systematically threatened all his neighbours over the years and consequently enjoyed their discomfiture when he bumped into them while going to or from the local pub.

He did not disappoint this fine Friday evening. A neighbour's daughter had got married that afternoon in Basildon register office. The girl, a pretty blonde with a belly full of arms and legs and a new husband who worked for the Post Office, was getting out of the wedding car. Mackie stood staring at them from his garden, enjoying the uneasiness he was obviously causing.

In the close everyone else's house was pretty and cared for. His, however, looked like it had been bombed regularly by the Luftwaffe ever since the Second World War.

'Who you fucking looking at?'

This was directed at a man walking past on his way home from work. It was a nightly insult and he hurried on his way.

Yet when Nick Leary pulled up a few minutes later in his Range Rover, Mackie was all smiles for him. He was a bully, but he only bullied people he knew were scared of him. Nick Leary did not fall into that category, and as Nick had helped his boy out Mackie owed him even though it galled him to admit that much to himself.

It didn't matter that his son had no time for him, it didn't matter that Stevie had come out of prison and had not been told the half of it by his sister about the way Mackie had treated her. As far as he was concerned, it was always everyone else's fault.

He was sensible enough to know, however, that Nick Leary was big-time while he himself was strictly small. And his mouth was causing him trouble as usual.

Nick stood outside the gate and looked his home over with undisguised contempt.

'Fucking hell, Mackie, this is a bigger shit hole than I imagined.'

Cars were pulling up all over the road now as the guests arrived back for the reception. Nick smiled at a couple of them and they smiled back, relieved that whoever was over at Mackie's was not going to start a fight with them. Some of his less than salubrious guests had been known to provoke the occasional spat amongst themselves or with innocent passers-by.

Nick stood and stared at the other man, knowing it would make him nervous. No one knew how to play the game like Nick Leary. And for a few minutes he found he was enjoying himself.

'You coming in, Nick?'

'Fuck off. If the inside is anything like the outside I'd need tetanus and typhoid jabs at least before I chanced your fucking front room.'

Mackie had to laugh even though he barely had a laugh in him. 'So what you after then?'

He knew exactly what Nick Leary was after but needed to hear the words from him. Mackie knew he had opened his big trap too far and had a sinking feeling that Nick was here to shut him up. Stevie had warned him to keep it quiet but he had not been able to resist talking about it.

Mackie's real name was Fergus McDermot, not a good name to grow up with outside Glasgow and consequently he had taken a lot of stick for it over the years.

Mackie was what everyone called him now. A friend who was going into the wedding called over, 'All right, Mackie.'

The mother of the bride nearly passed out with fright in case he took it as an invitation to join them all.

Nick looked around him at the nicely dressed wedding guests arriving and then said quietly, 'On second thoughts, I think we will go inside, Mackie.'

They disappeared into the house and Nick kicked the front door to without closing it. Then, standing in the cluttered hallway, he said loudly: 'How many times have you been warned over your fucking great big trap?'

Mackie didn't answer. His eyes were glued to the claw hammer sitting neatly in Nick's hand. It had been hidden up the sleeve of his jacket but now he held it comfortably in his right hand.

Mackie had a sinking feeling that his Nemesis had finally found him.

Chapter Twenty-Two

Jude squinted at the policeman through tired and bruised eyes. She could see the way he was looking at her and knew he couldn't wait to leave her in the casualty department and get on with his own life. She had taken a battering but, like everything else in her life, that was secondary to getting out of this hospital and back home to see if there was any of the brown left untouched.

Gino, his mother and uncles were long gone by the time the police arrived, and Jude had not offered any kind of explanation for her state. In fact, she wondered if it was the Whites who had rung the police in the first place. This was just routine to Old Bill. They dealt with cases like this on a daily basis. Junkies were forever fighting among themselves after imagined slights or ripping off each other's gear.

The young PC stared at her for a few moments more before he said, 'If you're sure you'll be OK?'

Jude didn't even bother to answer him. She was going to pick up some methadone first, in case of emergencies, and then she'd get herself back home. She had managed to hide her kit before the filth and the ambulance had arrived; now she just wanted to pick up her gear and get on her way. She also needed some food. If she ate something it might still the queasiness in her belly. She hoped the script would not be too long coming, because she could sell the methadone on and then if need be buy more brown.

She wondered if anyone had tried to find it. Her front door had been kicked in and on her estate that meant someone would take the opportunity to rob her. But they would be wasting their time. Anything saleable had been gone this long time.

'What you got that for, Nick?'

Mackie's eyes were like flying saucers at he stared at the claw hammer and Nick smiled lazily, enjoying his fear.

'Oh, ain't you heard? It's the new Basildon fashion accessory. You take it and you crunch through people's heads with it, see? Smaller than the ball-peen, of course, but just as deadly.'

He was balancing the hammer between his hands, playing with it.

'It's a good little weapon actually. If you're caught with it, you say you just bought it because you was doing a bit of do-it-yourself. And I am doing this myself, aren't I?'

He smiled again and Mackie felt his breath leave his body as fright took hold.

Nick shook his head reprovingly before continuing, 'You couldn't even let your own boy have a bit of peace after his ordeal, could you, Mackie? Anyone else had that happen to their son, they'd have swallowed it down and kept it in the family, but not you. You used it to get drinks in the fucking pub! Did you mention me by any chance while telling your tale? Only I heard about it from Siddy Haulfryn.'

Mackie was pasty-faced now. Nick knew his name may not have been bandied about, but Mackie would have left no one in any doubt who the saviour of the McDermot family honour had been.

This was one dangerous fuck.

'I wouldn't do that, Nick. I know the score . . .'

Mackie held up his arms in supplication.

'Please, Nick, I have learned me lesson, mate. No need to go to all this trouble, is there?'

He was panicking and it just made Nick more angry with him.

'Get upstairs, Mackie.'

'What for?'

This was not what he had been expecting.

Nick sighed dramatically.

'Walk up the fucking stairs, now, and don't get any hopes or dreams going that you are capable of talking your way out of this because if you try it will be the worse for you, see?'

He stepped towards the other man who moved quickly to the stairs. Nick followed him slowly.

'This place fucking stinks!'

Mackie didn't answer as he watched Nick checking all the rooms over.

'This is your bedroom, I take it?'

The room was filthy, with grey stained sheets and the smell of old socks and takeaways, mingling with the stench of antique farts and lager. But what it had going for it as far as Nick was concerned was the large window that overlooked the front garden. This was to be a statement of revenge and that window suited him perfectly.

'Get in here.'

Mackie walked into the room slowly. He was sweating profusely now and Nick was deliberately stretching things to make it all the worse for him. Mackie was a bully, it was time he had a taste of his own medicine. He was also such a coward he didn't even try to do a runner like a normal person would.

'Come on, Nick, this has gone far enough. I won't say another word, I was out of order . . .'

Nick silenced him with a look.

'Too right you were out of order. Your boy was nonced by Proctor and *you* told the whole fucking world about it! How is that going to affect him, eh? And then to add insult to injury you bring *me* into it and I was doing you a right fucking *favour*.'

'I didn't mention your name, I swear, Nick.'

'You might not have said it out loud, but I bet it wouldn't have taken Basil fucking Rathbone long to suss out who you meant, would it?'

He shook his head in disbelief.

'You're scum, Mackie. You are pond life. Fucking vermin. Now stand in front of that window.'

Mackie stood there shaking and for once it was not because he needed a drink.

'You got a fag?'

Mackie nodded and looked down. As he felt in his trouser pocket for his pack of Samson tobacco Nick took the opportunity to whack him three times over the head with the hammer. He went down as Nick knew he would, but in fairness to Mackie was up again in no time.

It was then that Nick with all his considerable strength picked the other man up and threw him unceremoniously through the bedroom window. Mackie's scream as he went through the glass was like an animal's.

Nick walked sedately down the stairs and out the front door, leaving it open. He had touched nothing in the place.

Mackie was lying awkwardly but fully conscious on the over-grown grass of his front garden.

'You want to take more water with it, mate.'

Nick was laughing as he said it.

Then, after hitting Mackie twice more in the face with the hammer, he took out a thick plastic bin bag from his sheepskin jacket pocket and deposited the hammer carefully inside it. In the Range Rover he checked himself over in the mirror. Blood had splattered him and he had a pack of baby wipes handy to tidy himself up with. He wiped his hands and face carefully before driving away.

He would go to his yard and change his clothes then get rid of everything, hammer included. He had other fish to fry this evening.

He had no fear of retribution from Mackie or his mates or from the police. The neighbours would have seen nothing, that was how it worked in their world. Plus he had finally shut Mackie up, got shot of him: that alone would get them all on side. Mackie was looking at a few months in hospital at least, and if he walked again he would be lucky. But knowing Mackie he would buy Nick a drink in a few years to celebrate his Invalidity Benefit payments.

Nick knew his enemy, all right, it was what had kept him on top for so long.

Tyrell picked up a bucket of chicken and some fries and went back to the flat. It was later than he had thought and Willy was watching the cartoon network on Sky Kids. The lights were all off and Kerr was nowhere to be seen.

'Where's the boy?'

Willy shushed him and that was when he saw that Kerr was asleep behind the sofa in a tattered old sleeping bag. Tyrell realised that it was Willy's, the one he tied up and carried about with him all day.

'Did he talk?'

Willy smiled.

'Most of it's down there.'

He pointed to a pile of pages torn from his notebook. As Tyrell glanced at them he thought again how neat Willy's handwriting was. This was a clever kid who through no fault of his own had no future to speak of.

The smell of the chicken woke Kerr up and Tyrell smiled at him as he said, 'Tuck in, mate, I'll get some plates from the kitchen.'

When he came back with the plates and the condiments neither of the kids had moved.

'What's the matter?' he asked.

349

Willy looked at Kerr and grinned.

'We were waiting till you got yours.'

It was the law of the street: whoever provided the food got the lion's share.

'That's all right, I ain't hungry.'

And in truth he wasn't any more.

He'd looked at Kerr's wiry hair when he'd turned on the overhead light. The boy was walking alive with all sorts of vermin and Tyrell made a mental note to make sure he outed the carpets at the soonest possible opportunity.

But he also saw that the boy had tried to tidy himself up and guessed that was something to do with Willy because he was quite fastidious in his own way. Tyrell gave them both a Diet Coke, knowing they would rather have a beer, and poured himself a large shot of Bacardi and Coke, drinking it down quickly and then making another immediately.

He had a feeling he would need to anaesthetise himself before he read the notes. It was strange but the closer he got to finding out about poor Sonny, the less inclined he was to know any more.

That, he supposed, was human nature.

Kerr ate as if his life depended on it, in great big bites washed down with guzzles of Diet Coke. But Tyrell also noticed that he had placed some of the paper serviettes on his lap and knew it was to save the carpet not to protect his clothes. He was watching the silly cartoon of the Cramp twins with avid interest. Once more Tyrell marvelled that a woman somewhere had given birth to this child and thirteen years later this was his idea of a holiday. Where was the love, where was the care, and more importantly where were the fucking parents of these kids? Didn't they give a damn what happened to their offspring? And was the care system in this country so bad that these kids would rather risk life and limb on the streets than go into it?

He glanced at Willy. He had HIV. Slowly but surely he was dying and he had not even lived yet. Just like Tyrell's Sonny Boy, Willy's life was over before it had even begun.

The underbelly of society frightened Tyrell, as it did most people. And if you didn't know about it you didn't have to deal with it. He wondered now how he would react with the rest of world after all this was wrapped up and put away.

He couldn't answer that question yet so, settling in the armchair, he started to look at the notes Willy had made. It was strange but he didn't mind the boys being there. In fact, they were so quiet and respectful he forgot they were after a while and lost himself in the terrible story written down so neatly by Willy.

Angela couldn't sleep. It was nothing to do with the bed or the fact that she felt strange in her daughter's house.

It was because of Nick.

The room she was in was lovely, all muted colours and pretty prints, but she felt her heart racing with terror because her own son had done something terrible and she knew what it was.

The dinner had been gorgeous, and she had sat and watched the family happily interacting. Carl had a fantastic sense of humour, and little Ria, she was a darling. They all were in their own way. But it was Dixon who had surprised her most. He had poured her a glass of wine after dinner, cleared the table with his wife and loaded the dishwasher, all the time chatting with the kids and being *interested* in them and their lives.

When her other grandsons were home from school, Nick and Tammy hardly saw them. It was as if their lives were too busy for there to be space for children or anyone else come to that. Yet none of them really did anything. Poor Tammy filled her days up with the gym and her lunches because she couldn't stand being in her own home.

A home most women would kill to possess.

And then there was Angela's Hester. Well, she was a truly happy woman. Later, when the kids had gone to bed, Angela had caught her and Dixon having a quick cuddle in the kitchen. How different this house was from her son's, and how different from her own house when they were growing up.

Yet it was Nick who still had her heart. Even now, she realised. Hester was a good girl, none better, but from the moment Angela had given birth to her son, he had ruled her heart and mind. Even after what she had found out, she was still worrying about him, and knew in her heart of hearts that she would always worry more about him than anyone else, even herself.

Frankie saw Nick at the door and grinned.

'Can't keep away, can you?'

'No, I can't, where can we go?'

'In the bedroom, I was just going in meself.'

Nick walked into the room and noticed it was tidy for once.

'You got a cleaner now then?'

Frankie grinned.

'Have I fuck. It's been a slow day, that's all. Now, what can I do you for?'

It was said with sly innuendo but Nick wasn't listening, he was already cutting a few lines on the dressing table. He knew he should not be here, that he was taking a big chance once again, but he couldn't help it. Frankie was like a drug to him and they both knew it.

Especially Frankie who saw this man as a meal ticket that, if treated properly, could feed them all for years.

'Come on, get your kecks off, I'm in a hurry.'

'Ain't you always?'

Nick didn't laugh, he was too busy snorting.

Kerr was talking to Tyrell now and answering his questions about the notes Willy had made. Willy got them all a drink and Tyrell was once more amazed when both boys said they wanted hot chocolate. He had expected a row with them for his Bacardi.

Willy had made him a Bacardi and Coke, nice and strong, and Tyrell sipped it slowly. The alcohol was needed by this time. They had put Kiss on now, and the music was soothing in the background. Tyrell glanced at the TV screen and watched 50 Cent 'Pimp' strutting his stuff. Give him Bob Marley or Eddie Grant any day.

'So Justin could easily be in this rat house then?'

Kerr nodded.

'He could be, but like I say, man, no one's seen him since . . .'

His voice trailed off.

Tyrell said gently, 'Kerr, just tell me what you know. Don't be afraid, OK? I will not blame you no matter what I hear, I promise on Sonny's grave.'

Kerr looked at Willy, who nodded sagely.

'Did Sonny go to the rat house with Justin?'

Kerr nodded again.

'He started to go there a lot more often in the last weeks before he died.'

Tyrell dropped his head down on to his chest; this was so painful to listen to.

'Have you ever been there?'

Kerr nodded, ashamed and embarrassed to admit the fact.

'But they didn't like me, see? They could see I hated it there so they stopped taking me. The big man said I was useless and laughed at me.'

It was said deadly seriously and Tyrell took a deep breath before saying, ' 'Course you didn't like it, mate. No one would.'

Willy and Kerr looked at one another strangely and Tyrell, picking up the signals from them, said: 'What's going on?'

'Tell him, Kerr.'

The big boy waved his arms as if warding off evil.

'You have to tell him, Willy, you promised me.'

He took a deep breath before saying, 'You sure you want the truth, Tyrell?'

He nodded, wondering what they were going to tell him next.

Willy wiped his nose with the back of his hand before saying loudly, 'Sonny went to the rat house a lot because the man who took him there liked him and Sonny liked the man.'

Tyrell was looking quizzically at the boy as he took in what he was saying.

'You what? What are you trying to tell me?'

Willy licked his lips nervously before he continued.

'The man he was seeing . . . we don't know his name, but Sonny was going out with him like . . . Kerr said they were together a lot. Sonny told him all about it. Said he was going to get a flat to live in and money to keep himself like.'

Tyrell was still staring at the two boys in astonishment.

'What are you on about? Are you telling me my Sonny was with an old bloke *through choice*?'

Willy nodded.

'Yeah, he met him when he was still new to it all. They like them new, the older men. And from what Kerr said they got on really well and Sonny was mental on him, said he was in love and that this man loved him and had promised to take care of him always.'

Tyrell heard the words but was convinced he was having aural hallucinations. This had to be wrong, there was no way his son was like that. They had to have got it all wrong. It was bad enough finding out his boy had flogged his arse, but to find out he actually *liked* it?

Was willing to accept money. To be kept.

He looked at Kerr. The boy didn't have it in him to make up something like that, Tyrell's sensible side was telling him that much. If this was true, though, he had never known the boy he called his son. Could never really have known him.

He just thought he did.

'Tyrell?'

He looked up at Willy, and then his eyes were stinging with tears and for all the world it felt like he was going to die of grief all over again.

'Kerr says he saw the man with Sonny a few times. He didn't see him close up or nothing, but he knew they weren't hiding it. At least, Sonny wasn't.'

Willy watched all the changing expressions on Tyrell's face and then without being asked started to build him a joint.

Tammy had had what was for her a good night. Now, though, she was home and the house felt completely empty. It was strange but all the time Angela had been there and a thorn in her side, she had never felt like she did now, coming home to this enormous place and being completely alone.

How had Angela stood it?

She had spent half her time here on her Jacksy, and it must have been horrible.

As Tammy walked into the kitchen the sheer size of it was enough to make her nervous. She walked over to the cellar door and pushed the bolt across. It was nearly 2.30, early for her but she had cabbed it home because no one who was anyone was out. Her mates had been excited about the day before and had made all the right noises. They all bored her rigid in the end.

She made her way upstairs after part-setting the alarm so it was on downstairs. She hoped Nick would not set it off as usual when he finally strolled home. In the bedroom she stripped off her clothes and left them on a chair, then she dumped all her jewellery on the dressing table including her wedding and eternity rings. Putting on a silk kimono-type dressing gown, she poured herself another iced vodka and put the TV on. She climbed into the big comfortable bed and opened the bedside cabinet to get out a bottle of Night Nurse. There was nothing like it to send you to sleep when you had coked yourself out. Tammy had trouble getting the lid off and her language was ripe as she wondered aloud how old people managed to get the stuff out of the bottle in the first place. She swigged the bitter green fluid straight from the bottle, hating the acrid taste as it coated her mouth like oil, then finally she lay back to watch TV.

As usual she lost herself in *Will and Grace* and *The Golden Girls*. She didn't know what she would do without her Sky Plus. She taped all the soaps but it was these comedies she loved most. She was just drifting off when she felt Nick climb into bed beside her.

She turned to face him, feeling the familiar size of him in the bed. As she cuddled into him she froze, then sitting bolt upright screamed out, 'Who you been with?'

Nick was lying there looking at her as if she was mad. She could see he was out of his head and that for some reason made her madder than ever.

'I can smell you, Nick. You've been with one of your fucking whores!'

She was out of the bed now and he knew this could turn into an all-nighter if he wasn't careful. But she was right, he could smell himself now. It was so strong, why had he not noticed it before?

Tammy was crying as she shouted at him.

'Who is she? Do I know her? Is she one of me mates?'

'Don't be so paranoid, Tammy. I swear to God there is no other woman in my life, on my mother's life.'

'What's wrong with me, Nick, why can't you make love to me any more?'

She was always so dramatic. He wondered what film she had taken that phrase from. He jumped from the bed and went to the en-suite bathroom. Turning the shower on, he said nastily, 'I have been in these clothes since this morning and what you think is the smell of another woman is actually from where I was lifting gear to store with Billy Clarke. It's sweat, love, that's all, and when I have had this shower I am going back to that bed to sleep, all right? One more word out of you, Tammy, and I am going to punch you one.'

'You fucking lying wanker!'

She was in the bathroom now, wide awake despite the Night Nurse, running on pure adrenaline.

'Where you been? I want to know once and for all, Nick.'

He stepped from the shower. He had soaped himself quickly and now, feeling cleaner and less guilty, walked back into the bedroom and poured them both a drink.

'If I tell you where I was, you have to swear you won't tell your mates, right?'

She nodded, but he could see the cynical expression on her face.

'Come on then, let's hear it. It must be bad if you need another drink to tell me about it.'

'I done Mackie tonight, with a claw hammer.'

His words stopped her in her tracks as he knew they would.

'You what?'

'Remember when Stevie came round here a while back?'

She nodded, frightened now of what he was going to say.

'And you know Mackie's married to Stevie's sister?'

She nodded once more.

'Well, Gary Proctor tried to nonce their boy – that's what Stevie wanted to see me about. We sorted it, but instead of keeping schtum about his boy being raped, Mackie was telling all and sundry. So tonight I shut the fucker up once and for all because we done Gary, see? That was why he died.'

Nothing Tammy had thought to hear could have had more of an effect on her than her husband's shocking story. And she knew it was true. Nick was telling her the truth for once.

'Gary raped a boy?'

Her voice was shaking with shock and revulsion.

Nick nodded tiredly.

'As good as. Didn't know who he was, see? The boy didn't say about Stevie being his uncle because, bless him, he wanted to get a DJ's job on his own merits, not because his uncle was a certified bank robber. So now you know why I smell like I do. It's sweat and a bonfire. I done Mackie with a claw hammer and there was blood spattered all over me clobber so I burned it at the yard. I threw him through his bedroom window, Tammy. He's probably crippled. At least, I hope he is anyway.'

Nick grinned then.

'I don't know what kind of birds you hang about with, Tammy, but if they smell like this then I pity them.'

There was no answering smile.

'So you really did Proctor then?'

'You *know* I did. But it was with just cause, as I have just explained to you. Now can we get into bed and go to fucking sleep because I am knackered?'

He looked so cold and unmoved standing there, it occurred to her then that he really was a dangerous man. That was his rep but until tonight he had also been her husband, her other half. He looked frightening now. She wondered if it was because for the first time in years they were in the house alone. Their fights had been subdued or even stopped by his mother's intervention. Now she was gone it was just them and the thing Tammy had always wanted was not making her as happy as she had believed it would. In fact it made her nervous because it had finally sunk in that Nick didn't love her at all. He didn't love anyone.

He didn't know how to.

She climbed into bed with him but didn't try and cuddle him this time even though she knew he would let her. He liked a cuddle did Nick. Years before when they had had a sex life he had cuddled for England, and it had taken a while before she realised it was because he lost his erection quickly and would talk to her and make her laugh to take her mind off it.

Now, though, for the first time ever, she knew that if he came near her she would push him away.

Chapter Twenty-Three

Tyrell sat in his kitchen after a sleepless night. The boys had slept like logs, were still asleep. Every now and then he popped his head around the door to check on them. Kerr snuffled in his sleep and it reminded Tyrell of Sonny. He had snored quietly as well.

It was thoughts of Sonny that were keeping him awake. He glanced at his watch. Nearly six o'clock. He was going to slip out soon and do a bit more investigating on his own. The traffic was getting louder and more frequent now. The day was beginning for so many people, all going about their lives hopefully without the knowledge about their closest relations that he had. Every time he had tried to close his eyes he was tortured by images of his son with that man. What kind of monster bought himself a young boy? What kind of man dragged a young boy down into the gutter?

And maybe more to the point: what kind of young boy *wanted* it to happen?

Tyrell poured himself more coffee and sipped it lazily as he dragged on his cigarette. Normally he liked this time of the morning, liked the feeling of a new day starting. Today, though, he wished he could lie down and never get up again.

He tried to picture his other sons sleeping, tried to visualise their little heads on their pillows and their chests moving confidently in and out as they dreamed only of good things. Why was it some people seemed to be blessed while others seemed to be put on this earth only to be hurt or to hurt others?

His mother believed in God, he was a certainty to her, a woman who had never left her own home for years. Even her beloved grandson's burial couldn't move her from that house. She was a good person, meant well, needed her family around her. He never wanted her to know what he had found out about her Sonny Boy, he was sure it would be the end of her. She would understand it less than he did, and he was trying hard.

If it had been with a boy his own age, Tyrell could have taken that, it would not have bothered him. But knowing this big love affair came about through rent-boying just didn't wash with him. There was more to it all than Kerr and poor Willy Lomax knew, he could feel it.

'Are you OK?'

It was Willy, standing in the doorway.

Tyrell nodded, wishing the boy out of his life even as he felt responsible for him.

'Do you want some coffee?'

The boy shook his head. Instead he picked up Tyrell's cigarettes and lit one. 'I prefer tea in the mornings.' He laughed as he said it. 'Hark at me! Anyone would think I had a choice in the matter.'

'Well, you have this morning anyway.'

Tyrell put the kettle on and dug around in the cupboard for tea bags, all the time wondering when the boy would go away again and leave him alone.

Willy sensed his feelings and said gently, 'We'll be gone by this afternoon.'

Tyrell closed his eyes tightly before turning to the boy and saying lightly, 'You're OK.'

Willy raised his eyebrows sceptically.

'Honestly, Willy. Anyway, I want you to come to the rat house with me. Give me the lowdown on who goes in there.'

Willy shrugged and puffed on his Marlboro Light.

'Whatever.'

Tyrell could see how hard it was for the boy to act as if he wasn't bothered about what happened to him now, but he could also see the relief in his eyes at the thought of another night or two in the warmth.

'Do you want some breakfast?'

Willy nodded happily.

'Then make yourself something. I have to slip out for a while.'

Tyrell picked up his coffee and as he left the kitchen, said quietly, 'And clean up after you, right?'

' 'Course I will. Can I make something for Kerr?'

Tyrell raised his eyes to the ceiling. As if he would say no. Why did the boy check everything out like he did? He answered tersely.

'Of course you can, don't be daft. I'm hardly going to say no, am I?'

Willy shrugged once more, his 'I am hard' trademark shrug, and said stoutly, 'You'd be surprised.'

Tyrell left the room then before he lost his temper.

But he knew in his heart what was wrong with him. He didn't like the fact this boy had lumped him in with all the other people who had used him in his life.

Nick was feeling good. He didn't know why or how considering all he had drunk and snorted over the last few days, but he did. He was high, naturally high, and jumped from the bed eagerly before wandering downstairs to the kitchen in search of breakfast. Tammy was already up and that surprised him. In the kitchen she was reading the *Daily Mail* and sipping black coffee. He opened the fridge and saw that there was hardly anything in it except beer and fresh orange juice.

'Ain't there any food?'

He was annoyed. He would have cooked for himself, would not

have expected Tammy to do it, but now there was nothing even to cook.

She shook her head.

'Your mum normally shops on a Friday, and in case you ain't noticed she ain't here any more.'

He swallowed back the angry retort that was dying to escape from his mouth and instead poured himself a livener.

'Bit early, ain't it?'

The vodka was swallowed down quickly and expertly and for some reason this bothered Tammy. She was the one who did all the mad things in their marriage, not Nick. He was the sensible half of the partnership usually and if he stopped being sensible anything could happen. She glanced round the kitchen. Like the rest of the house it looked grubby. Well, she wasn't cleaning it, she wouldn't know where to start. It was a far cry from the early days of their marriage when she had scrubbed and cooked to her heart's content. But she had been happy then, so happy.

Tammy observed her husband and realised she was still frightened of him. He was over the top now and it had taken her a while to see that. Recently he had turned into a male version of her. Last night had shown her just how far apart they actually were. This was a Nick she didn't even like.

It had been hard enough for her the day before. Suddenly she had not wanted to be in the wine bar, didn't want to listen to all the empty talk around her, even coke couldn't lift her mood. She had drunk so much it had stopped having any effect, and listening to those stupid bitches telling her how great she was had paled after the first two hours. Funnily enough the only bright spot had been Janine Aldridge actually having the nerve to tell her she was going over the top too often and should sort herself out before it was too late.

Janine had had to sort herself out big-time, and she had. There was a time when she had been in Tammy's shoes, and she had worn them out. Her husband had been a player and Janine the player's wife. Simon Aldridge had been murdered getting into his car one fine Sunday afternoon. He had been taking his boys to football practice but two shots to the back of his head had put paid to that.

Once the shock had worn off Janine had changed beyond recognition. From the Queen she had become the Queen Mother and actually found she enjoyed it. Once the pressure was off, she said, the need constantly to obliterate her own way of life was gone and she had retired gracefully to bring up her kids and live off her husband's ill-gotten gains. She'd told Tammy last night that you knew when you had torn the arse out of something when it stopped feeling good, be it love, drugs or marriage, and Tammy knew exactly what she meant now.

She had torn the arse out of everything around her and nothing made her feel good any more. She didn't even want her husband at this moment, though she knew from experience that could change.

She watched the fleeting expressions on Nick's face and decided she didn't want access to his private thoughts today. She had a feeling they would not be anything she wanted to hear. Normally she wished that the Japanese would build a computer that read people's minds. Now, even if it was on special in Argos she wouldn't want it. Janine had opened Tammy's eyes to what was going on around her and she didn't like what she saw, but she knew that only she could change it. Janine had shown her the future and Tammy was considering her position. She wouldn't do anything just yet. She would do what she always did, let circumstances take over and then go with the flow. But she had an odd feeling that circumstances were changing rapidly in Nick's life, and what affected him affected her.

All she could do was wait and see how things worked out for them both.

Nick left the house an hour later and Tammy still had not left the kitchen. She was watching *The Golden Girls* again and wondering what to do with the rest of her day. She might take Janine Aldridge up on her offer of lunch. It was funny but Tammy actually liked her. Which was more than she could say about most of her other mates.

Sally looked at the clock and gritted her teeth. The boys were in their bedrooms and the usual sounds of Saturday morning were coming down the stairs: music, laughter, and the occasional shout of excitement. She could already feel a headache coming on. Until Tyrell had left she had never realised just how much he had done with them. By that she meant, of course, how much he had taken them out and left her to do her incessant cleaning.

She glanced at the clock once more. It was after eleven and Tyrell was over an hour late picking them up. No call, no nothing, and she couldn't raise him on his mobile. It was ringing but not being answered.

She wondered if it was because he was with another woman. She couldn't help wondering if it was Jude. She hated Jude with a vengeance as she had hated Sonny though she could only admit that to herself now.

She tried Tyrell's mobile once more and her call was rejected on the second ring. Now her anger was spilling over. When he finally turned up he would regret that for the rest of his days. Black-Eyed Peas were screeching out 'Shut Up' over and over again and the boys were singing along to it at the top of their voices, their laughter at the lyrics overriding any fear of her. Sally had already planned a nice calm afternoon, cleaning and ironing and watching the *Coronation Street* omnibus on ITV 2. It was her Saturday afternoon treat because none of her friends was even aware she watched the programme.

The music was still pounding out and the man she loved was still not answering his phone when Sally forgot her usual dignity and reserve as she ran out into the hallway and screamed: 'Turn that fucking music down!'

Then, seeing the blue vase with the yellow roses on it that Sonny had bought them one Christmas sitting on the hall table, she picked it up and launched it with all her might at the kitchen door. The sound of it smashing was almost cathartic.

Two handsome dark heads looked round the top of the stairs and she could see the shock in her boys' faces as they stared as if they had never seen their own mother before.

Louis Clarke was with his brother Terry on their way to meet with Tyrell and look this so-called rat house over. They were meeting for a drink first at Wapping Wall in the Prospect of Whitby. Tyrell was going to fill them in on what was going on and they were to try and talk him into meeting with Nick Leary. Billy thought it might make life easier for them all. He wanted a day and time set and he wanted it over with, it was all getting on his nerves.

As they walked into the pub Terry glanced around him through force of habit. He had had so many tear ups the chances were he'd meet someone who knew him and had to watch his back in any new place. He was not disappointed. A tall man with reddish hair and an easy smile said to him: 'All right, Tel? How's tricks?'

To which an irate Terry answered sharply, 'I am a bank robber, mate, not a member of the Magic fucking Circle!' He pushed the man out of his way and walked purposefully to the bar. Terry hated over-familiarity and this geezer had crossed the line.

Terry didn't even know him really, why would he want to talk to him?

The front of some people never ceased to amaze him.

Louis winked at the bloke and said quietly, 'Ignore him, he's got the raving hump today.'

The man, though, who was with a couple of friends was not to be lightly placated and answered back loudly.

'He wants to take care because one of these days his brothers ain't going to be enough to keep someone off his back.'

Louis glanced over at Terry who, mercifully, was too busy looking down a dark-haired woman's cleavage to hear what had been said. Stepping towards the man, he grinned.

'Are you on a fucking death wish, mate? Only your pals don't look like they want a piece of him so you'll be on your own.'

The man looked around and saw the truth of what was being said.

'Now finish your drink and leave us to ours, eh?'

Louis sighed. He had a feeling that this was going to be a fore-taste of the rest of the day. Terry was up for anything, and the trouble with Terry was, he usually got it.

Jude was completely alone and it felt wrong. Gino was locked away at his mother's house and she knew she was not going to get to him. None of the other boys had been near or by for a while and she had the terrible feeling she was finally, and irrevocably, on her own.

Even her neighbours were blanking her, and that was a first because usually they would have talked to her just to get the gossip about what had happened the night before. She was completely on her Jack Jones and knew it. Sitting on the sofa, she lit a cigarette with trembling hands and poured a stiff vodka into the glass of orange juice she already had.

The place was still mashed up from the day before but she didn't notice it. The methadone was kicking in.

She picked up Sonny's mobile and stared at it for a few seconds. Then she carefully dialled the number she had got from Big Ellie.

The phone was answered on the first ring and this threw her. She had not expected that to happen.

'Hello.'

The familiar voice made her go clammy with fear.

'Who is this?'

'It's me, Sonny's mum.'

Her voice sounded much stronger than she felt. Her hands were already shaking and her nerves, already in shreds from the brown stuff, were on their last knockings.

'What do you want?'

The voice was colder than an Arctic breeze and Jude swallowed deeply before saying, 'Money.'

The line went dead and she sat back on the sofa, terrified now by what she had done. But she would keep with it. Sonny Boy had told her everything, and this was just the first number on a long list of men she was going to fleece. She was starting with a little fish and making her way up to the big one. It had actually been easier than she had first thought. Now the initial fear had worn off she felt quite pleased with herself.

After the last few weeks of worry, she almost felt like laughing at the fact that she had been so frightened of blowing apart a world that her son had not only embraced but had also enjoyed. The men who had enjoyed it with him owed her, and she had to make sure they understood that. If she could start with the small fry she could work her way up the chain to the big pay-off.

That had been the idea when Sonny had robbed that bastard's house. Well, Proctor was dead and gone but the others were still alive and kicking and she knew that it was the right time to play her trump card.

Sonny Boy had always told her everything and she had filed it all away for future reference. Most people would have seen Sonny's actions over the years as wrong, but she had seen him for what he was a long time before he had known it himself. As far as she was concerned, if he could turn his little foible into an earner all the better. She had sold her own body before now, even giving a few blow jobs when necessary to top up her income support. But unlike Sonny Boy, she had not enjoyed it. As he had once said, job satisfaction was half the pleasure of a job well done.

She had kept her trap shut to Old Bill, expecting to have been given compensation long before she had had to resort to this little game.

The filth would have loved to hear her side of the story, but fair's fair, or so she had thought. Wait till it all dies down, but not any more. Life was too fucking short and her needs were too immediate to keep up this bollocks any longer.

The silent calls should have alerted them all to the fact she was on to them. That alone should have brought her in a few quid. Not a fucking brass Razoo though, from any of them, and they all had a hefty wedge. Well, fuck them now, she was after her insurance money on her boy and she was going to get it.

'You look fucking terrible, Tyrell.'

Terry laughed jovially.

'That nearly rhymes, don't it? Terrible Tyrell. Makes you sound like a Rumanian despot.' He pulled a face and pretended to twirl an imaginary moustache. Tyrell grinned back. When Terry had a lightning change of mood like this he could be funny, could be a laugh, and he needed a laugh.

The dark woman with the humungous breasts was still at the bar and Terry was working on buying her another drink. Tyrell and Louis knew it would be pointless trying to remove him from the pub just yet.

'How about another, love?'

Terry turned to the barman and said sotto voce: 'Stick a quadruple brandy in that port, would you?'

The woman was laughing good-naturedly.

'Just the port will do, thank you.'

Terry rolled his eyes at the ceiling. Tyrell and Louis both knew this might be a long one. He could spend hours cracking a bird and then take her outside, give her one and be hard pushed to remember her name within hours. With Terry it was all about the thrill of the chase. He was chasing this one big style, and in fairness she was gorgeous. In another life Tyrell might have gone after her himself. Still, it was fun watching Terry at work, he really was a master.

'Here, Tyrell, have a guess what? Leonie here is a Jack the Ripper! Why am I not surprised?'

He was thrilled and so was she. A match had just been made in shag heaven as far as Terry was concerned. A stripper was his dream woman.

'Have another drink, my sweet. I think this could be an interesting couple of hours, don't you, guys?'

Louis laughed. Terry after a bird was a sight to see, and he was always after birds.

He said to Tyrell, 'We are in lumber now, mate, he ain't going nowhere till he's cracked it.'

In a way Tyrell was glad of that fact. He needed to psych himself up for it all tonight. He had a feeling it would go downhill from here. They would be far better off under cover of darkness anyway. According to Willy it was lively on a Saturday night in the rat houses.

Tyrell had texted his boys, explaining he could not pick them up today, and they had texted back saying it was fine. He couldn't see them today anyway. It would be too hard trying to act normal with all that was going round in his head. So now he had a long afternoon stretching ahead of him and as Terry was driving he could have a few drinks. He might use the excuse to go and take care of another bit of business that needed to be sorted.

When he finally saw her again Jude was going to get the shock of her life. In a way he was frightened to see her in case his feelings got the better of him and he totally flipped. The hatred he felt for her now was obscuring everything good that had ever happened between them. She had served her own son up on a plate, Tyrell had no qualms about admitting that to himself now. She had thrown their son's life away to feed her addiction, and he had let her. He had stepped back and let her because it made his life with Sally easier. Two women, so different and yet so alike. Two women who always seemed to get what they wanted.

Well, not any more.

He would have another couple of drinks first and see how he felt then. This new lifestyle was very seductive. He could fall into a face's routine very easily. You just took care of business and then enjoyed the fruits of your labour. And as far as Tyrell was concerned, not before time either.

Jude was in a good mood. She had found a bag of brown under the sofa. It must have been knocked off the table in the fracas of the day before. It was a good sign as far as she was concerned. It meant that things were looking up, that everything could only get better. At least she hoped that was what it meant.

She had a knack for making things into what she wanted them to be. It had stood her in good stead over the years. When her life was at its lowest points she always managed to fight her way back to the top. For Jude that meant getting some gear and forgetting whatever she had done to others in the meantime.

Sonny had loved it when she was on top. He would sit and brush her hair for hours, telling her how much he loved her and listening to her stories about growing up and her first loves. He had been really good like that. He was the only person who'd still wanted to talk to her, be with her. Over the years any friends she had made soon disappeared, her habit had seen to that. She had borrowed money, used them in any way she could, and eventually stolen from them. No one took that for long. Sonny on the other hand had given her just what she wanted without a murmur and before she had the chance to take it. Even his birthday money was not sacrosanct yet he had never mentioned it if she stole it from him.

Jude was feeling sad now, at what she had lost. No one realised just how much they had done for each other. Now he was gone, and he would never come back, and those men owed her. They all owed her for that.

When Sonny had caught his big fish she had been inordinately proud of him. A boy who was so naturally sensitive and kind had to have homosexual leanings, it stood to reason. So she had only pushed him to follow his natural inclination. Or that at least was what she told herself over and over again.

But he had been such a good-looking boy, such a lovely boy. Why *should* he sell himself cheap? She knew the street better than anyone and had steered him in the right direction. And Sonny had wanted to be steered.

She was justifying what she had done to herself and deep inside she knew that. Jude wiped the tears from her eyes with the back of her hand, remembering how they would sit together and watch *EastEnders*, discussing the storylines as if the characters were real people that they knew. They had had the time of their lives together, why didn't anyone see that except her? Sonny had been happy here with his mum, happy doing things with her. Her life had been blighted when her son had died, why did no one see that? Why didn't they understand that what she had had with Sonny was a special bond that transcended the usual mother and son relationship?

He would have killed for her, that was how much he loved her. How many women could say that about their kids, eh?

She turned around as she heard someone come in at the front door. She had left it ajar in case Gino managed to escape his tormentors. Turning round with a big smile on her face, she said gaily, 'Just in time!'

But the smile was wiped off her face as she saw who it was. Her heart stopped in her chest as fright took hold.

'Hello Jude, long time no see.'

The voice was just as she remembered it, but now the man she had scored off for all those years looked dangerous somehow.

She thought of all the times she had scagged from him, and even though she had expected him to be annoyed, she had never in her wildest dreams expected to feel this fear. He was weighing her up as if she was so much dirt and his nose was wrinkling to show the utter distaste he felt for her and her lifestyle.

His own home was like an operating theatre in comparison, he wouldn't even sit down in her house in case he soiled his expensive suit.

She still thought though, that he had come to weigh her out in some way, either with money or the brown.

She had just not expected him so soon.

None of the others she had rung had even bothered to answer her call; maybe this was an omen for the future. Jude, like all junkies, lived in a world of hope.

Lenny stared into her face, trying to intimidate her and achieving his objective. 'You think you can make a few phone calls and everyone will come running, do you? Well, I am here to tell you, Jude, that you are wrong.' She looked into his eyes, saw the hate, saw the disgust and this prompted her to forget just who she was dealing with. She pointed a dirty finger at him, her anger outweighing her fear now. 'You fucking owe me, as much as the others, if not more. It was you who pulled my Sonny into the world of baby boys. He was twelve when you started him on the road, introducing him to your so-called *mates*. Would you like people to know about that, Lenny, eh? You might be a respectable dealer but nonces are a different breed and everyone knows that, and you, Lenny, are a nonce.'

The words were spoken with all the venom she could muster and in fairness to him she knew she had hit a nerve. Lenny Bagshots saw himself as a man of means, a face on the rise and as a good family man. His aberration, as he put it, was nothing to worry about. As long as it stayed a secret it could not impinge on his other life. He knew other, like-minded men who felt exactly the same. The trouble with Sonny was, he had been a loose cannon and as the time had gone on he had embraced his lifestyle a little bit too openly.

Now this piece of shite was trying to screw him.

Well, better people than Jude had tried. Her son was a prime example; he had tried to pull too many people down and he knew in his heart that she was probably behind her son's skulduggery. Junkies always needed money. If they won the national lottery they would still not feel they had enough. Their eyes were always on the fix they couldn't afford, never on the one they actually had in their arms at the time.

It was this that had been her son's downfall and if she had been any kind of a mother she would have been ashamed of what she had done to him. She had served that boy up to him as quickly as he had served her up the brown. He had bought him really and he had bought him off a woman who had no love for her child.

He walked towards her quickly and she backed away from him.

This made him laugh and he said sarcastically, 'Frightened you have I, Jude?'

She nodded, her eyes were large, opened to their widest and for a brief second he saw the girl she had once been, a long time ago when the brown had been in her future.

'Well, you be frightened and listen to what I am saying, right?'

She nodded, allowing herself to relax a tiny bit.

But he was on her in seconds and she felt the full force of his contained anger and violence. As he punched her to the ground he was saying in a low, controlled voice, 'You think you can threaten me, do you? You think you are woman enough to try and play me for a cunt, Jude?'

He had her hair now and he was speaking into her face as she hung limply like a rag doll. 'Didn't your Sonny's death teach you nothing, woman?'

She stared into his eyes and said in quiet hatred, 'He was set up!'

He laughed once more and then, throwing her to the ground, he commenced with the good hiding she knew she deserved. Finally spent he said roughly, 'And we all know who set him up, don't we? You pushed him into it all and you know you did. Getting him to ask people for money, people he had not seen for years. It was all about you as usual, wasn't it? All about you and the shit you pump into your arm.'

She lay on the floor, a crumpled heap but still he saw there were no tears, no real fear in her.

'You're scum, Jude, nothing more and nothing less and your son was just the same. He might have had a chance without you hanging on to him like a fucking leech. He might have had a different end, who knows. But as it stands, Jude, he's dead and, if you're not careful, you might be joining him sooner than you expected.'

She pulled herself from the floor and despite his anger he admired her for taking what he had doled out without a word of complaint. 'You owe me, Lenny, whatever you think. You fucking owe me and you owe me big-time.'

He walked up to her. Grabbing her chin tightly in one hand, he said through gritted teeth: 'I owe you nothing, lady.'

He smiled to see her terror.

'Like the song says: "*Nothing* at all".'

He pushed her across the room and she landed awkwardly on the sofa. Lenny Bagshots went over to her and threw an ounce of brown on to her trembling body.

'That's it, that is your compensation. I had nothing to do with what happened to your boy but I know a man who does.'

He kicked her in the ribs as a parting shot.

'Oh, by the way, Jude, you want to shut your front door in future. You never know who might be coming in to see you.'

It was a threat and she knew it, but once he had gone she could relax. He had been first on her list. Now she had gradually worked her way through it. She would get what she wanted, no matter what they thought.

Grinning now, she picked up the bag of brown. Happier than she had been for days she got up off the floor and poured herself a drink.

She would celebrate with a large armful of happiness.

Chapter Twenty-Four

'Bit of all right, old big tits, eh?'

Tyrell and Louis laughed at Terry's lecherous way of talking. He was a real entertainer when he wanted to be. In another life and with another upbringing he could have gone on the stage and done stand up. But Terry had something that no other comedian had: he was literally capable of killing someone in the audience if they didn't laugh loud enough or he thought they were taking the piss. There would have been no heckling when Terry was on the stage. His lightning mood changes would never have suited a legitimate job either.

Billy always said he should have been born in America and worked for the Post Office there. It would only have been a matter of time before he was picking off his workmates with a high-velocity rifle. Everyone always laughed when he said that, especially Terry who took it as a compliment.

It was now after ten and they were finally going to pick up Willy. Terry had had the cheek to take the bird outside and, as he put it so nicely, trump her in his car. Leonie, a chancer who felt she had hit the jackpot, was definitely going to be on the menu for months to come. He had got her phone number and her level. She was just Terry's sort. It would take a while before his erratic behaviour and his jealousy started to frighten her, when he was demanding to know where she was every five minutes and who she had spoken to. At first she would enjoy the constant attention, his petty jealousy. It would be a while before she realised just how possessive he actually was. Then she would go the way of all the others, try and stop seeing him, try and reason with him.

But you couldn't reason with people like Terry Clarke. He owned her now, until he was fed up with her. If she got another man Terry would turn up at the house and threaten him, hurt him, make sure he knew the score. He would expect to see who he wanted, when he wanted, and she would be expected to wait patiently on her own until he turned up. He would actually enjoy terrorising her and any new man who dared enter her life. Then, one day, another woman would grab his attention and Leonie would be forgotten overnight. Then and only then would he deign to leave her life.

For now, though, Terry was happy and ready for a night's work. Tyrell was nervous of Willy being in the car with them. Terry changed with the weather, from laughing his head off to manic depression in seconds. No one who couldn't watch their own back ever went on a job with him, and that included his own brothers.

He seemed to take to the boy, though. As Willy climbed in the car Terry smiled at him in a friendly fashion and said, 'All right, Geeze?'

The way he said it made Willy smile. Like most people when they first met Terry, poor Willy Lomax liked him. Tyrell devoutly hoped nothing happened tonight to change that.

As the boy only had a location, not an address, they made their way to Plaistow. Willy, a little shrewdie in his own way, directed them as best he could. Eventually, just after 11.30, they were outside a tower block, parking the car.

Terry turned around in his seat. Looking at Willy, he said, 'Now you think it's here, right?'

He nodded.

'It looks right, yeah.'

'Is he coming with us to make sure we got the right gaff?'

Louis looked at Tyrell who nodded.

'Once we get there, though, you come back to the car, right?'

Willy nodded happily.

'Here's a punter now, see.' He pointed. 'I can tell them a mile off.'

They all looked out of the car and saw a tall bald-headed man getting out of a Lexus. Hardly the kind of car you would expect to see around this area. The man locked his car and looked around him furtively before sauntering towards the flat's entrance. He was well dressed, obviously a ducker and diver, going by the car and his clothes.

Terry's voice was incredulous as he said loudly, 'What? Are you telling me *he* is a kiddy shit-stabber?'

Lewis and Tyrell closed their eyes in distress as they realised he was about to go off on one. Terry was scandalised and disgusted. Yet they both knew the chances were they would be glad of his muscle at some point in the evening.

Willy laughed.

'You'd be surprised just who these people are, mate.'

Terry looked at the boy with interest.

'What, honest, they look like him?'

Willy just stopped himself from saying, And you, and Tyrell, and all the people you drink with in the pub. He guessed rightly that this was not the time or place to give the hard man a lesson in the seamier side of life. Instead he just nodded.

'They're like the CID then? Coppers in disguise, dressed up as real people?'

This made Willy laugh and Terry laughed with him.

'They look like normal people, Terry, because that's how they get away with it for so long. But some of the boys up there are over sixteen, they just look younger, so it's not illegal as such.'

Terry digested this information for a few moments. Then his mood changed once more and he was suddenly ferocious.

'I don't know what's worse. This is fucking mental! We going up to sort these fuckers out or what?'

He was really annoyed now. He had seen it with his own eyes. Until then he had never really believed it was possible. Had never believed normal-looking people like him could be nonces.

He could have drunk in a pub with that bloke.

He would have let him in his house.

He thought they all looked like, well, like nonces. Old blokes in dirty raincoats, with grimy fingernails and greasy hair.

This geezer looked like one of his own!

It did not occur to Terry that his own sexual appetite had kept them all in the pub for the best part of the evening because his appetites were normal. He liked birds, what man didn't? As far as he was concerned the fact that he pursued women constantly made him more of a man. It was all about boundaries for Terry.

His boundaries and his guidelines, of course.

As far as he could see anyone who liked young boys had to be a perverted lunatic and as such should be taken out of the ball game and redistributed around the planet, preferably in easy-to-bury-sized pieces. They didn't need prison, paedos needed to be wiped off the face of the earth. Like any cancer, you nuked it as best you could, and if it came back you nuked the fucker again.

'That's it. Come on, let's get up there.'

Terry was up for it now, incensed and feeling inexplicably upset. He liked the little blond boy in his car. Why would anyone want to hurt him like that? He was a little fella, a nice little fella who had had a few bad breaks. If Terry had seen him out begging he would have given him a score, he was like that. Fuck the grown-up tramps with their cans of Tennant's Super, they could get a fucking job, but the kids always got a few quid off him because they were after all *kids*.

He got out of the car quickly and took a short-handled sledge-hammer from the boot. It was a tool he had used often over the years, and it did the job as far as Terry was concerned. Louis and

Tyrell got out after him, and Willy stayed inside watching and listening to them all talking.

'Calm down, all right?'

Terry pushed his brother away.

'I *am* calm. Calm as I can be with all this going on around me.'

He was in a state of high tension and both the men with him knew that this was not a good sign. Terry could explode over the tiniest thing.

'What you going to do with that then?'

Louis pointed to the weapon in his hands.

Terry sighed heavily and said with undisguised sarcasm, '*Well*, I was going to smash the front door in. What were you two thinking of doing then? Just shouting out, "Let us in, we're a load of nonces on a fucking pervos' night out. Bring on the little boys"?'

Tyrell had to admit he had a point.

Terry, though, laughed as he said quietly, 'This, boys,' he weighed the weapon in his hands to demonstrate his point, 'is what is called the element of surprise. It will do to whack open the front door and then whack around a few heads and all if need be.'

He looked at Tyrell.

'You want to know who runs these gaffs, right?'

Tyrell nodded.

'Well, this guarantees we find that out. They ain't exactly going to roll over while sipping a cup of tea and chomping daintily on cupcakes, you get my drift?'

Willy leaned out of the car window then.

'He's right, guys. If I was you, I'd listen to what he's saying.'

Terry grinned at him.

'Come on, son, let's get this show on the fucking road.'

Willy followed them happily. He felt safe beside the big man holding the sledgehammer, had already sussed out that Terry was the only one here with any inkling of exactly what they were dealing with tonight.

* * *

Jude fixed herself a good armful and lay back to listen to a bit of music. 'Trick of the Tail' was playing low in the background, a Genesis track from her happier days. Before the brown had taken over her life completely. As she lay there her eyes were glazing over and her body was relaxing to the point of coma.

She would start nodding soon.

It was the nodding she loved best. What she craved more than anything or anyone in the world. The music was moving inside her body now as the heroin hit her bloodstream. She closed her eyes tightly and enjoyed the colours there. Vibrant greens and pinks, eventually settling to creamy whites and electric blues. This was what it was all about, this was her dream state.

As the nod took her over she saw her Sonny running towards her with his arms open wide and she smiled then. She smiled and tried to lift her own arms up to welcome him into them. But they felt like lead and she knew it would be a while before she could move, before she would even want to move.

She was gone now and stayed as she was, with her eyes closed and her body totally relaxed. She couldn't move now if a SWAT team decided to hold their Christmas party in her front room.

Tammy was drunker than she had been in ages, and it was the first time she had not been out on a Saturday night in years. There was still no food in the house, still no husband to talk to. Not that she wanted to talk to Nick anyway, but he was the only other company in the house now he had driven his mother away.

All her plans for meeting Janine had died the death after she had got on the brandy at lunchtime. One drink had turned into nearly a whole bottle and now she was out of her brain. She was also up for a fight, or failing that a takeaway.

Tammy laughed at her own thoughts.

Going into her mother-in-law's rooms she decided to have a look in her fridge, see if Angela had left anything edible in there. She was not disappointed. There were a couple of sausage rolls and some Scotch eggs. Angela loved a snack while she watched the telly and her fridge had a good quantity of chocolate in it as well.

Tammy stuffed a sausage roll into her mouth hungrily. She would regret the food tomorrow, especially the pastry, but at this moment in time it was like manna from heaven. She was drunk hungry and knew it was pointless trying to ignore it.

She sat on the floor, not caring about the crumbs going everywhere and the fact that she was too drunk to get back up again. Burping loudly, she looked around the room. There were photos everywhere, all of them of the boys and Nick. None of her, she noticed, or poor Hester and her family.

'Old golden boy Nick.'

Tammy could hear her own voice echoing around the room. This made her laugh for some reason. Pulling herself off the floor, she leaned on the dressing table to keep herself upright. She saw that Angela's safe had been opened and walked over to it.

Pulling back the carpet, which had not been replaced properly, she opened the safe easily. All the safes in the house had the same code. For all his so-called class, Nick was a cheapskate about some things.

Tammy was worried now that if her mother-in-law had cleared her safe she would not be coming back. She wanted Angela back, and wanted her back soon. She picked up the photographs that were lying in the steel box. Seeing Gary Proctor's face she wondered fleetingly what on earth a photo of him was doing in her mother-in-law's safe. Looking more carefully, utter shock hit her.

Tammy stared at them for long moments, taking in each detail of the individual snaps, unable to believe what she was seeing. She retched then, and brought up everything she had eaten on to the expensive carpet. She was still retching when she was empty of everything, even the booze.

And that was how Angela found her.

Terry and the others watched as Willy went back to the lift. Once he was in it and out of sight they nodded to one another to start the evening's entertainment.

The front door was half-wood and half-glass, but it was reinforced safety glass. It would keep out the average burglar but not a large man with a sledgehammer. Taking back the weapon, Terry crashed it through the lock with all the force he could muster. The door burst open on its hinges and the three men walked inside, shutting it calmly behind them. This was not an area where anyone would be calling in Lily Law.

The whole place was in pandemonium. Terry watched in disbelief as teenage boys and girls ran out of the rooms that led off the hall, their clothing in disarray, emaciated bodies shining in the dim light of the naked light bulbs.

But it was the smell that hit the men first. The acrid stench of old carpets and ancient bin bags. No wonder they called them rat houses.

A large man, the bloke they had seen parking the Lexus, came out of one bedroom dragging on his trousers. He saw the three of them and was almost relieved. His big fear was that it might have been the police, but he could try to talk or buy his way out of his dilemma now.

Terry grabbed him by the throat and used him to batter open the front-room door. Inside the cramped space were three men, all well into their fifties and casually dressed. Tyrell and Louis guessed that they had not long arrived and were waiting for the next available boy.

'Who runs this gaff?'

Terry's voice brooked no defiance. Lexus man, however, didn't answer him, he was too scared. Terry smashed his head once more into the doorjamb, splitting it open.

Then, looking around him, he shouted: 'If you lot don't answer me you are going over that fucking balcony, one by one. Now . . . who runs this fucking gaff?'

The balcony door stood open and Tyrell could see a couple of young boys out there. He guessed they must be freezing. The bald-headed man from the Lexus pointed to one of the men on the sofa.

'It's him . . . he runs it! His name's Gordon Winters.'

The man tried to get up but Louis and Tyrell were on him in seconds.

'See, you know it makes sense.'

Terry's voice was quieter now. He pushed the man away from him, straightening up and sounding almost friendly.

'Don't fucking try and leave the flat, any of you, right?'

He stared around at the youngsters and the men who were all in shock.

'I have got the right hump, and if I have to go looking for any of you . . .'

He left the sentence unfinished, motioned to Tyrell and Louis.

'Give me him here.'

Terry grabbed Winters from his brother and unceremoniously pulled him out on to the balcony. The man was terrified and, convinced he was going to die, put up a valiant fight. The two young boys already out there cowered down on the floor.

'Get in there, you little fuckers.'

The boys ran as fast as they could into the flat, wondering what the hell had been unleashed on them this night.

'Come on, guys, let's hang him over the balcony. See if he can remember enough to get us going on our way.'

Terry was enjoying himself, that much was evident. Especially to Gordon Winters, the man now trying desperately to evade his captors.

The three men hung him over the balcony without difficulty. Winters had stopped fighting. Instead he was begging for his life.

'I'll tell you anything! Please don't do this . . . please . . . I only work here, it's just me job . . .'

Terry was laughing now.

'You call *this* a job? You having a fucking laugh?'

He shook the man then, making him feel even more frightened than he already was. It was a long way down.

'Shut up, you fucking nonce, and talk to me pals.' He looked at Tyrell and Louis as he shouted, 'Ask away, guys. But be quick 'cos my arms are getting tired and we don't want to drop Gordon on to the pavement, do we?'

The man started crying. He was broken, they all knew that.

Tyrell saw one of the men inside getting out his mobile. Nudging Louis, he went back inside and removed it from him.

'You dare try anything like that again and see what you get.' Tyrell stared around him. 'You lot move one muscle and you'll regret it for the rest of your days.'

No one moved.

'Outside that front door are more of me mates and you lot don't want to meet them, believe me.'

It did the trick.

Tyrell walked back on to the balcony. The cold air was refreshing after the stuffiness of the flat. Terry hauled Winters back over the railing and the man slumped down on to the floor. His teeth were chattering with cold and fright.

'Don't wind me up, Gordon, because if you do you are going back over and this time we won't pull you back, OK?'

The man nodded quickly, eyes bulging out of his head with fear. Tyrell started the questioning then and at first the man was happy to answer anything he was asked.

Lenny Bagshots walked back into Jude's flat quietly. He saw her lying sideways on the sofa and crept up behind her.

You never knew with Jude, she might be playing possum. But he could see enough to know she had no knowledge of who was there. He knew that thanks to the brown he had left her she would never know anything again. For once the heroin she had injected was pure, and he knew her body could not cope with that.

If he had a pound for every time he saw a warning on local news broadcasts going out to junkies about pure heroin when it hit the streets, he would be a millionaire. New dealers often made the mistake of undercutting their gear and consequently caused the deaths of many customers without realising it.

Most junkies got shit. Lenny cut his stuff with everything from quinine to strychnine. If they ever got the dream needle it killed them.

He smiled as he looked at her dead body. Poor old Jude, she had finally got what she wanted. He felt her face. She was still warm, but cooling fast. She looked at peace, which he guessed was probably a first for her. He was glad she had been greedy, it had saved him from having to finish her off himself. He wanted this to look like any other OD.

He walked into the bedrooms and started searching through everything. He knew what he was looking for and was determined to find it. He also wanted anything else that could alert the police to the fact that he had a closer relationship with this family than he had ever let on.

He stared around at the squalor of Jude's life. The chaos she had lived in amazed him. Lenny was a dealer but it was just a step on the ladder for him. He didn't even care that he had taken out one of his best customers; there were plenty more where she came from.

Gino included.

He was in and out in under fifteen minutes, though now he was carrying a Pound Stretcher carrier bag, containing two mobile phones, Jude's and Sonny's, and a pair of leather gloves he had used so that he did not leave any fingerprints. Carefully, he pulled the door closed behind him. He couldn't lock it properly, but it looked closed enough to keep people out for a while.

Whistling, he made his way home. His girlfriend wanted to watch *Love Actually*. They had a snide copy and he had heard it was a good film.

Jude was now as far from his mind as the moon.

And that, as Lenny would tell himself later, was exactly how it should be.

Angela sat with Tammy for a long while on the bedroom floor. She had come back because she didn't know what else to do. If she had stayed at Hester's any longer she would have spilled the beans and even after all this she was still protecting her son.

But she knew she couldn't protect him from Tammy any more. She had a right to know what was going on.

Holding the distressed woman tightly to her, Angela murmured endearments until she calmed down.

'Come on, Tammy, come down to the kitchen and let's get you sorted out, eh?'

She stood up unsteadily. The two women were leaning against one another now for support. Tammy was visibly shaking, her sobbing loud and unrestrained.

Angela walked her slowly down to the kitchen. As they passed through the entrance hall she glanced around her. The house that she had once loved, that she had allowed to become her prison, was now making her nervous and jittery.

In the kitchen she put Tammy on the leather Chesterfield by the big fireplace. She curled up on it, clutching at one of the tapestry cushions and holding it in front of her belly like a child. Angela put the kettle on to make one of her endless cups of tea. She didn't know what else to do.

'This is why you went, ain't it?'

Tammy sat up and threw the photos on to the table.

Angela barely nodded. She couldn't look at the poor woman whose life had just been destroyed.

'Where did you find them, Angela?'

She snorted in derision.

'He'd left them in one of his coats. I found it down in the cellar... you know his heavy brown leather jacket? The one he lived and died in until that burglary?'

She poured water over the tea bags in the cups.

'Well, I was going to hang it up, that was all.' She had been snooping as usual. 'They were in the inside pocket...'

She turned to face Tammy.

'They fell out, I wasn't nosing about.'

It was important to her that Tammy realised she had found it all out by accident. This was the end of the line for them, she knew that much.

'That's why he never had any time for me, ain't it?'

Angela didn't answer her now, unsure what to say.

'Did you know about it?'

Angela stared at the girl before her and at that moment Tammy was a girl again, a girl like she herself had once been.

She wondered if Tammy would have fought for her sons as she had fought for Nick. Looking into her eyes and then remembering the photos she had found she made a decision and hoped against hope that she would not live to regret it. 'It's not his fault, Tammy, not really.'

Tammy sniffed loudly, wiping her nose with the back of her wrist, reminiscent of a child crying over nothing. With that simple action Angela was brought back in time and the sight she saw was a sight she had forced from her mind over many years.

'What do you mean it ain't his fault, because it fucking well ain't mine? They are children in those photos, young boys...'

Tammy's voice was louder now, and the utter contempt in it was like a physical blow to the old woman trying desperately to find the words that would explain her son's sexual preferences.

Suddenly, Tammy thought of her sons and she said in a whisper; 'What about me boys? Has he been near me boys?'

All the motherly concern missing from her for so long was now flooding her brain. She half rose from the chair in a panic.

Angela pushed her back down none too gently. 'Hush, don't be letting your imagination run away with you.'

Tammy stared up into her face earnestly and then it all fell into place for her. 'That's why you lived with us, ain't it? You were protecting him and at the same time you were protecting us.'

Angela walked to the worktop and poured two more large brandies. She placed one in her daughter-in-law's hand and, sitting down heavily, she sighed before saying, 'Nick had a kink even as a child. He was eleven when a neighbour first accused him. I didn't believe her, of course, my big handsome lad doing something like that to her little boy. And he *was* a little boy, no more than seven. I put it down to a boyish prank, see.'

She took a large sip of brandy.

'What had he done?'

Angela shook her head, 'You really don't want to know. But what you do need to know is what my husband and his friends did.'

She finished off the brandy quickly, then wiped her eyes on a piece of kitchen roll before saying, 'I couldn't stop it, you see. Those days his father was drinking all the time, he hated us all, it's why I don't see much of my daughter. She forgave me but I could never forgive myself.'

She took a deep breath before continuing slowly.

'They were children, *my* children and I couldn't help them.'

As the memories she had suppressed for so many years flooded her mind, the history she had rewritten, and which she almost believed, was crumbling in the face of her daughter-in-law.

She poured more brandy before saying to the dumbstruck girl

before her, 'They were vicious to him, hurt him so much and if I tried to interfere they would turn on me. It's not all about grooming that they talk about now, this was brutality, and that was all they could enjoy. Nick, well, Nick never knew any different, did he? Poor Nick. For some reason he started wanting it, he liked the money, he liked the affection, he was doing something right for his father for the first time ever. He was being *good*.'

She laughed sadly. 'Can you imagine how that made me feel?'

She wiped her eyes once more, but the tears had stopped now.

'That bastard destroyed any natural feelings Nick had and when he was older and he fought him back I thought that was an end to it all, see. He beat his father nearly to death and it all stopped then. It was over.'

She stared at her daughter-in-law with tired eyes.

'You have to believe me. I didn't realise he had gone on to the same kind of life as his father. You see Nick has always been what he wanted to be, has always had the strength to make you believe that he was the person you saw before you. But he isn't, he doesn't know who he is any more.'

Tammy was trying to take in what was being said to her.

'This is fucking mad. Are you trying to tell me Nick is a fucking nonce, a proper kiddy fiddler not just a fucking queer?'

Angela nodded.

'It was Gary who liked the older boys, the teenagers. Nick liked them much younger, see. He used the older boys to gain access to younger, more tender boys. Look *closely* at the photos, Tammy.'

Tammy picked up the photos and stared at them, then gradually she realised what she should have been looking at instead of her husband's smiling face. It hit her. The room in the photos had ripped and dirty Thomas the Tank Engine wallpaper on the walls; it was so dilapidated that unless you looked closely you wouldn't notice it. And there were kiddies' toys strewn all over the small single bed that they were all happily posing on.

'Now you know why he was terrified of being found out all these years. Now you know why he let you sleep your way across Essex and the East End of London without a murmur.'

Tammy's brain was struggling to absorb it all yet, in her heart of hearts, she knew it was true. In a way, she realised, she had half guessed it many years ago.

'Why are you telling me all this now, Angela? You could have saved us all years of unhappiness and heartache if you had told me before or made him get help. He listens to you, no one else but you.'

Angela poured yet more brandy, but it was not helping either of them. It was just something to do.

'Nick had many accusations over the years. In my heart, I knew they were true, but I didn't want to believe them, see. No mother does. So I did what I had always done.'

'What was that?'

'I played the game. Until now, of course.'

Tammy stared at the floor, her first instinct of protecting her children was long gone. This was damage limitation now. She started to cry once more only this time it was quiet, more restrained sobbing.

Holding her tight in her arms, Angela looked at the doorway to the hall, and said clearly, 'I know you're there, Nick. Come and talk to the mother of your children. You owe her that much at least.'

Chapter Twenty-Five

Gordon Winters lay on the balcony and realised he was in for a hammering from the big man with the mad eyes and the clenched fists.

The black bloke didn't look too good either.

Terry had completely lost the fucking plot. This place was doing his head in and he was being very vocal about it. Terrified kids were sitting there listening to him rant at them and wondering where all this was going to end.

Winters was watching from the balcony as Terry stood in the front room and harangued all the people in there. Every now and then, in Winters' world especially, you came up against a force that nothing and no one could harness. He knew that writing out the mathematical formula for nuclear fusion would be far easier than calming down this man who had invaded his home.

And this *was* his home, he only rented it out to pay his bills, but he knew that these three guys would not understand that because none of them shared the same sexual peccadillos as him and his friends.

Tyrell and Louis had stayed on the balcony with him.

'Did you know Sonny Hatcher?'

Winters smiled then, a slight smile but Tyrell saw it nonetheless. It was a smile that said he'd known him intimately and Tyrell had to contain himself once more. There was plenty of time for revenge when he had found out all he wanted to know. He shook his head slowly as he looked at the man.

'He came here then, did he?'

Remembering what was going down, Gordon Winters started desperately trying to justify himself. He pointed one tobacco-stained finger towards the window.

'None of them in there is under sixteen, you can check that. They might look under sixteen but they ain't.'

Tyrell kicked him hard in the legs, containing his anger with difficulty. Unlike Terry, he could control his urges and he was glad of that fact now more than ever before. It was one of the reasons why he had never tried for the big time: you needed to be constantly on a short fuse to live in that world, or, more to the point, survive in it.

'Did *my* Sonny Boy come here or not?'

It was the *my* that finally made the other man understand what he was dealing with here.

He nodded.

'Look, mate, you don't want to hear this but he loved it here, he was *always* here. He would even tout for us; younger runaways were his speciality.'

Louis walked away then. Going inside, he shut the door on Tyrell and Winters, leaving them out there in the cold alone. Somehow he knew that Tyrell would not want an audience for what he was going to hear next and in all honesty Louis didn't want to hear it, either.

Terry was on the phone to Billy, and Louis guessed from the conversation that their brother was on his way.

Tyrell could hear his own heart beating in his ears now. He remembered his mother saying that was what happened to her when she tried to leave the house.

'Who brought him here?'

The man shrugged.

'I can't remember, to be honest.'

He was lying and Tyrell knew it.

'Do you want me to get my mate back to ask you these questions?'

He had a feeling that Gordon Winters, like anyone with half a brain, would be far more scared of Terry Clarke than he would be of anyone else.

And so he fucking should be.

Winters sighed, trying it on, fronting it all out.

'Get who you like, mate, he ain't the only person who scares me.'

Tyrell understood what he was trying to say.

He now knew that whoever was behind all this was obviously a well-known face. Was someone to be reckoned with. And after the way Terry had carried on this person had to be very dangerous indeed.

Tyrell decided to front it out himself. He had nothing to lose and everything to gain. 'Well, I am Sonny's father and I ain't going nowhere.'

It was said gently but with a dangerous edge to the words. He was trying to appeal to the other man's better nature. That was assuming he had one. If he didn't they'd have to terrify him into talking. And if he didn't start talking soon Tyrell would happily kick the knowledge from him.

The other man was quiet for a few moments as if weighing him up. Then he got to his knees on the cement floor, wincing at the pain in his legs from where Terry had gripped them while dangling him over the edge.

'Look, mate, no one *made* him come here, he *wanted* to be here. When I found him he was on the pavement, selling his little arse round the fucking cottages. Like it or lump it, he was safer here in the long run.'

He was getting his bit in before he crumpled, Tyrell understood that.

'Who was the man – the older man he was caught up with?'

'I can't tell you that. I wish I could but I never knew him personally. This ain't the kind of place where you ask names, know what I mean?'

Tyrell took back his fist then and, grabbing Gordon's shirt, pulled him forward as he smashed it into his face with all his might.

He felt skin and bone crumple under the force of it.

'Once more, Gordon, answer the fucking question!'

The man was bleeding profusely now. His nose was flattened and his eyes streaming with tears.

But he still shook his head.

'Please, it's more than my life's worth . . .'

People amazed Tyrell sometimes. This man actually expected him to play the *white* man, be the good guy, let him *off*.

Feel his pain, as they said these days, and respond to it.

Which was exactly what was wrong with the world nowadays, a nanny state had seen to that. This man had no conception of what he had done to Tyrell and his blood. Didn't really see he had even done anything wrong.

This was the way of things now and it scared Tyrell. You could pick up your girlfriend's baby and swing it round a room by its leg, and if you said you were suffering from stress, you walked away from it. Kick your wife to death, just say she was a nagger, and who cared any more? Be a bully-boy twelve year old, torture your elderly neighbours, and when they came back at you, finally snapped, maybe hit you with a walking stick or went after you with a bread knife, *they* were the ones breaking the law.

No one was ever held accountable for their own badness any more.

And even more scary was the fact that these morons believed it really *wasn't* their fault, that *they* were the victims in it all, and then they were let loose on society once more without so much as a slap on the wrist.

No one took any responsibility for the damage they inflicted on the innocent.

It was a whole new ball game.

Yet a villain like Terry, who was a borderline lunatic in other ways, would no more harm a child or a pensioner than he would cut off his own arm. It was all to do with having *some* kind of moral code. However wacky it might be, the point was, he still had an idea of how to behave. So did his brothers and so did Tyrell. So did most of the people he had grown up with, though they were not the most upstanding members of society in some ways, granted.

But Sonny Boy had looked for an easy way out. He was just the kind people like Gordon Winters prayed for. He was weak. Jude had brought him up to get money in any way he could. Not earn it like everyone else, oh, no. And people like this Winters, well, they fed off these kids like a lion off a carcass, and when they had had enough discarded it in favour of a newer, fresher one.

Yet, if you robbed a bank you would get twenty years in jail, but if you mugged an eighty year old, by the time the social workers and psychologists were finished making excuses for you, the old lady should not have been there with her pension in the first place. There was no cause and effect any more.

No one ever saw the consequences of their own actions, felt sorrow for what they inflicted upon complete strangers. Because it was all about them and *their* needs and *their* wants. This man had introduced his boy to this place and this life, and as far as he was concerned he had done Sonny a big favour. Saved him from the squalor of the public toilets.

Tyrell looked around the narrow balcony and saw a piece of wood. It looked like it had once been a chair leg. Picking it up, he poked the man hard in the face with the end of it, leaving Winters in no doubt now about what he was capable of.

'Your life is worth fuck all to me, right? And at the moment it is me you have to answer to. If your memory is so short you have already forgotten hanging over that fucking balcony then you deserve all you get. Because I will throw you over there meself without a second thought.'

Tyrell brought the chair leg down across Winters' shoulders with all the strength he could muster then, and in his state that was considerable.

'You better talk, cunt, because the way I feel now my mate in there won't be in it if I start, you hear me?'

Gordon Winters was caught now. This man really was on the edge. He knew he had to decide who he was going to protect. And, like most people, he decided it was going to be himself.

'You'll let me go, right? If I tell you I walk away, yeah?'

Tyrell grinned.

'We'll decide that when you start talking. And I warn you now, I have a built-in shit detector, you hear me?'

Gordon Winters knew when he was beaten, and he knew he was beaten now. This dreadlocked man with the black eyes and the vicious demeanour was suddenly scaring him.

'I had nothing to do with what happened to him, you have to believe that.'

This time the chair leg hit him on the side of his face. The cold made the pain worse because it was freezing outside now.

'What – you mean the burglary?'

Winters was on a roll. He wanted to get it all over with as soon as possible.

'Of course, what else?'

'Well, if you weren't behind it, you must know who was?'

The man nodded then and Tyrell relaxed a little.

'So someone did send him to that house?'

Winters nodded once more, his bloodied face a picture of self-pity and subdued anger.

'A bloke called Gary Proctor sent him.'

The name stunned Tyrell for a few seconds but he soon recovered.

This was turning out even better than he had hoped. He knew there had to have been something behind his boy's destruction and finally he was going to find out what it was.

Nick came into the kitchen, and his mother saw that he was drunk.

Drunk and frightened.

He walked towards his wife and tried to put a hand out to her. Tammy threw her arm out and struck him with such force he was almost knocked off his feet.

'You bastard!'

There was so much hatred in the words that Nick didn't know how to react.

She glared at her husband and, hawking deep in her throat, she spat at him. 'No wonder you never wanted me.'

It was always about her, never about anyone else. His old animosity rose once more, even as his fear at her knowing terrified him.

She pointed at the photos on the table. 'Bit too old for you, ain't I?'

She was breaking before his eyes and in a small part of his brain he was genuinely sorry for her.

'A fucking nonce. A nonce under my roof, and I never knew.'

She was talking to herself now. 'You're as fucking bad, lying for him, letting him think it was all *normal*. You hated your father and yet you brutalise little kids. No wonder you became a hard man, who would ever have believed it, eh? Nick Leary, a fucking kiddy shagger. You scumbag fucking piece of dirt.'

Tammy was out of the chair in seconds and as she launched herself at him he shoved her hard in her expensively enhanced breasts. She flew across the kitchen, hitting her face on the Aga and landing awkwardly on the stone-flagged floor.

As he walked towards her, Angela stood between them. 'That's enough.'

He laughed then, a harsh sounding, sarcastic laugh.

'Get out of my fucking way, woman. You're another one, a fucking leech hanging on to me all me life.'

He shoved her out of his way and, going to Tammy, he pulled her up from the floor. Tammy looked at the man she had loved all her adult life. But she knew him now, really knew him and she realised then with a jolt that she felt nothing for him. It was as if someone had flipped a switch and any feelings she had had were gone. It was like being released from prison. All those years she had wanted him, needed him so much and yet suddenly he was nothing to her any more.

'What are you going to do then, Tams?'

His voice was quiet, almost normal and, looking at him, you would not believe that he was exactly what his mother had said he was. A child molester, a nonce.

She could really see him now, see the slackness of his mouth and the paunchiness of his body. She could see him for what he was. Finally his guard was down and his acting would never fool her again. It was a liberating experience and she savoured it, savoured the little hint of fear in his voice as he asked her the question. Then instead of answering him she said softly, 'What was Sonny Hatcher doing in those photos? He is a lot younger looking but I can see it's him.'

It was as though a bomb had exploded in the room.

'Was he one of your little friends and all?'

Nick stared at her.

'Making up another story, eh? Well, I ain't your fucking mother so it will take a lot more than a few well-chosen words to shut me up, mate.'

Her anger was taking over now and it was obvious to all three of them that her fear of him was gone.

Nick smiled then. It was a smile that showed off the handsomeness of his features. It made him look almost benign. Then he walked away from her and, picking up the brandy bottle, he put it to his mouth and half emptied it in a few swallows.

'You killed that boy, didn't you? He was *meant* to come here that night, wasn't he? By the looks of that picture you knew him well, knew him very well.'

She wiped her face with her hands, wiping the blood from the corner of her eye where she had hit the Aga.

'I got rid of him the same way I get rid of anyone who stands in my way.'

It was a threat.

'So you two better think on, hadn't you? Because you are both starting to aggravate me.'

He was goading her once more and the coldness in his tone shocked both his mother and his wife.

'How did you think you would get away with it all, Nick?'

He pulled on the brandy once more and said cockily to his wife, 'But I *did* get away with it, didn't I?' He was deadly serious. 'What are you going to do now then, Tams? Grass me up?' He grinned again. 'I don't think so. I know you better than you know yourself.'

He picked up the phone from the table and held it out to her. 'Here you are, Tams, ring the filth, go on. Bring it on, girl! Go for it. But remember, if I go down, I take you both with me, because you would be finished around here. Remember that. All your so-called mates would be in their element, seeing you brought so low. I ain't just a murderer, I am a fucking nonce, girl. You would be a fucking laughing stock.' He knew in his heart that she would not do it. Tammy didn't have finer feelings or any kind of principles. All she knew was how to look after number one and she was an expert at that. She had had to be.

Nick was ranting now. 'He was like you, Tammy, my Sonny Boy. A fucking leech! Always wanting me, but I hadn't wanted him since he was a kid. I used him like I used you. He got me what I wanted and I paid him for that but, like you, Tams, I shoved a mercy fuck his way and kept him sweet. He actually thought we would play happy families, see, and I let him think it, like I did with you, and I wiped him off the face of the earth and that is what I will do to you if you push me, see?'

Nick looked sinister now, his face twisted angrily with aggression and defiance. 'I was *protecting you*, Tammy. You, the kids, me *mother*. I was protecting you all from him and his fucking hanging on all the time.'

The two women realised that he actually believed what he was saying. He was now trying to justify what he had done and his wife and his mother exchanged glances as he stood between them looking for all the world like an innocent man.

'What about the little kids then, son? How do you justify them?' Angela pulled him round to face her and she slapped him with all her might across the cheek. 'What have I bred? Listening to you just then it would have been so easy to forgive you like I've always forgiven you. But now I know you are nothing. You are scum, son. And Tammy doesn't need to phone the police, because I will. I will do it and gladly.'

The cocaine had made him aggressive and, smiling at her, he said gently but viciously, 'I was more worried about you finding out, Mum. Do you know that?'

He flicked his head towards his wife as he said louder, 'Now her, I couldn't really give a fuck about. But you? Well, I was always a mummy's boy, wasn't I? You saw to that, didn't you? But Tammy was only ever a means to an end, and like the fucking albatrosses you both are, I have had the pair of you hanging round my neck for the best part of my life. Is it any wonder I like the uncomplicated, *innocent* world of children?'

Tammy felt the brandy rising up from her stomach and she ran to the sink and retched until her tummy was empty. But the sickness was still there.

Angela's voice was loud as she said, 'You used us all, that was why you wanted me here in the first place, isn't it? You knew Tammy didn't want me here yet you insisted. Telling me you had bought the house for me—'

'It got you here, didn't it?' He was laughing once more. 'I have fuck all on my conscience where you are concerned, Mother.'

Nick looked at his wife. 'Or you, for that matter. I gave you the world on a plate and you know I did.'

'What about the little kids? Aren't they on your conscience then?' Tammy's words were low and bitter. 'The little kids you've destroyed because you are a fucking weirdo. What about Sonny Hatcher? Is he on your conscience?'

He shook his head sadly.

'I loved Sonny, as a matter of fact. He was everything I had ever wanted in a lover.'

Tammy laughed then. 'Till he grew up and you murdered him.'

Nick started to walk around the kitchen once more as he spoke. 'Gary Proctor was filling his head with shit behind my back, Sonny was always after me for more and more money and I had had enough of it. I had what I wanted in a rat house in London and I tell you both now I ain't ashamed of my preferences. That is what you can't seem to get on board. I *like* what I do, I get enjoyment out of it. I love my life!'

'You need help, son, and the police will make sure you get it.'

He shook his head as if she had said the funniest thing he had ever heard.

'Fuck off, Mother, and take that sick cunt with you.'

'Your father always said you were bad, rotten to the core and he was right, wasn't he?'

Nick's eyes were stretched to their utmost now.

'Back to him, are we? Ask poor fucking Hester how she feels about him, Mum. Ask her about her feelings for once. Like you, she can't bear the thought of anyone finding out the truth of it all.'

It was strange but even in her heartbreak she knew he genuinely loved his sister.

He was pouring himself a brandy then as he said, 'I liked my life, Tams. Whatever you might think I kept this shit away from you. I bankrolled the lot, Sonny included. I let you do what you liked, Tams.'

'We were just a blind no more and no less, Nick.'

It was the truth and he couldn't deny it. He knew his life was over now. The life he knew anyway.

'Sonny was going to blow us *all* wide open, and so he had to be sorted. With Gary, I set him up. He thought he was going to rob me and get money from the insurance company, see. It was so easy. Murder is much easier than people think, you know.'

He was talking matter of factly now. 'No one is who you think they are, Tams, me mother is proof of that, ain't you?' He was looking into her eyes now. 'It was better for all of us if Sonny was gone, see. I regretted it, but it was better for everyone. I swear to you both that I didn't really want to do it, but what else could I do?'

Tammy looked around the beautiful home she had never really appreciated, saw poor Angela's face, saw the disgust on it and knew it was mirrored on her own.

'You are nothing but a child molester.' Angela said it quietly and with conviction. 'You are your father's son all right.'

'Am I?'

He smiled once more at her, snorting through his nose with his laughter.

'Well, you always wanted him more than you wanted us, so don't try and come the old fucking soldier with me! You would still shag him when he wanted you to and his mates as well.'

He turned to Tammy as he said loudly, 'She was worse than you in her younger days, old holy Joe, she'd fuck him and his mates, it was like our whole lives were about sex and sexual innuendo and she was as bad as him because she let him do it to us.'

He grinned once more and his gaze was almost malevolent. 'Remember, Mum, remember the Friday nights?'

'Stop it! Stop it will you, Nick!'

There was something in Angela's shrill and frightened voice that Tammy picked up on. Shaking her head at what was being said to her she instinctively knew that he was telling the truth.

Realising she believed him, he deflated in seconds. Then he said to her sadly, 'Ask her about how she would comfort me. Go on, Tams, ask her. Ask old holy Joe there what she would do to me.'

He turned and stared at his mother then. 'You remember, don't you, Mum?'

Tammy felt sick once more as she watched them.

'If I am a pervert what does that make you, Mum, eh? Answer me that.'

Had she known all this on some deeper level? Deep in her heart. She remembered him at the christening of his son, James, taking the pats on the back and the ribald comments. Even though he knew most people were asking the same question he was. Who the hell was the real father? Tammy, by then, had been round the turf of Essex more times than Frankie Dettori.

Yet he had swallowed it so that no one would ever find out that he liked young boys. Kids. He was also telling her that his mother had abused him as well.

What the fuck was happening here?

'Give me that phone, Tammy. If you won't ring the police, I will.'

Nick's head shot up and he looked her in the face.

'You wouldn't?'

His voice was low.

She laughed then, an utterly sad and broken laugh.

'Try me, Nick, see what I am really capable of.'

He pushed the phone away from her.

'Don't do this, Mum. You need to think about what you're doing, this is just a knee-jerk reaction, nothing more.'

She tried to grab the phone from him but he had picked it up and was now standing, holding it behind his back.

'I do not need to think about anything, I know what has to be done and I am going to see that you pay for everything you've ever done!'

'But I am your son, you should be helping me, Mum, protecting me like I've protected you.'

She shook her head then, walking towards him, she said quietly, 'Not any more, Nick, you're on your own. Now give me the phone.'

He was backing away from her towards the granite island that housed the summer cooker and the chopping board. When his back was against it, he said in a low, babyish voice, 'Please, Mum, don't make me do this . . . please!'

'Look at yourself, a fine thing for a mother to have to look at, eh? Me son, the queer boy.'

Nick closed his eyes in distress at the vitriolic words.

'Come away from him, Angela, come away now.' Tammy's voice was loud in the room but the man and the woman ignored her. This was a private battle and they both knew it. One of them had to give.

'I want that phone and if you don't give it to me I will walk out to the hallway and phone the police from there.'

She shook her head at him in derision.

'Because, son, no matter what you say or what you do, I am going to tell them what you are.'

It was said with finality and as she turned away from him he took the large boning knife from the expensive beech block that housed it and stabbed her in the back with it. Then, with Tammy's screams ringing in his ears, he walked from the house.

Chapter Twenty-Six

Billy Clarke walked into a scene of pandemonium. He looked around the scruffy flat and was in turn disgusted and fascinated by what he was seeing. It was like something from a television play, something you knew went on but never believed you would see for yourself.

Now, though, they were all seeing it and real life was a bastard when it was so in your face. A classless society? Well, there was no class of any kind in this fucking drum, that much was for sure. His wife, though, would have known all about this kind of life. Caroline was interested in other people, especially the ones no one cared about.

The underclass, she called them.

She was a diamond like that, had educated him in many ways and he loved her for it. And she was absolutely right in what she had said to him: no one seemed to care about these kids, least of all the man who professed to be looking after them.

Terry was grilling the Lexus owner. For some reason the man really seemed to annoy him and Billy could see why. He looked like one of their associates, looked like any normal grafter, and he had obviously done a bit of bird. You could see that by his tattoos and his general demeanour.

Billy walked from the room, leaving his brother to it.

In one of the bedrooms he saw a young girl of about fifteen. She wasn't even pretty, God love her, not that that should have made any difference, of course, but in all honesty it did to him. He understood about chasing youth and beauty, they were what most men desired. If it wasn't most films would never be made, all those lovely girls flashing their threepenny bits all over the show. Somehow a young bird always spelled renewed youth to the man screwing her. Luckily most men were happy just looking at pictures of them in the paper or dreaming about them when they rogered the old woman.

These people, though, to them it was a form of control. His wife knew all about that, too. She had explained to him once that rape was not really a sex crime. It was using sex to subdue or *destroy* someone.

It was the weapon of choice, if you liked. The worst thing that could happen to anyone. Billy finally realised that he was staring at the poor girl and probably frightening her. He told her to get dressed but she just stared back at him and he saw she was stoned out of her box.

He walked back into the front room and said to Terry in anger 'The cream of fucking society in here, eh?'

His brother shook his head in disgust.

'Look at this cunt. He is masquerading as a fucking *person*, a grafter like us. He works for Liam O'Halloran. Wait till I tell *him* this sorry little tale.'

O'Halloran, another local lunatic, would be honour bound to bounce his man round the pavement when he found out about this.

'Imagine getting your rocks off with this lot, Bill. It's like a fucking nightmare, ain't it?'

Terry clumped O'Halloran's man without any ceremony in the face. Not knowing how to react to a situation like this, they were all caught between anger and shock.

Louis stayed quiet, just watching his friend through the dirty window as he laid into the man on the balcony outside.

Watching and waiting in case Tyrell needed his help in any way.

Billy loved his brother Louis. He wasn't cut out for all this really, he was like Tyrell in that way, they were both too nice. You had to have a deep-seated anger at the world to succeed in their business, or in Terry's case just be a bona-fide loony tunes. But Louis was a grafter, in his own way he got things done. Billy remembered him and Tyrell as kids, one so blond and the other so dark. They had loved each other like brothers. When Tyrell's boy had died, Louis had taken his friend's grief as his own. Billy respected that. You needed family, but a good friend was as important at times. You could tell them things you could not tell your own flesh and blood.

He heard a smacking sound and saw Terry had lashed out once more. The man with the Lexus was openly terrified and Billy glanced at him without a flicker of remorse. He knew Terry wanted to hurt this scum and as far as he was concerned his brother could go for it.

A young boy with longish red hair and mascara was sitting on the sofa watching it all.

'What you looking at?' snarled Terry.

The boy turned away quickly, his fear almost tangible.

'What's your name then?'

He looked at Terry and stammered, 'F-Frankie . . . Frankie Watts.'

He had a girlish voice, quiet and put on. Billy imagined he had practised it over a period of time to get it just right.

It cut no ice with him.

'How old are you?'

'Seventeen.'

He looked all of twelve, with his skinny body and baby face.

Terry looked at his brother again and held his arms up as if to say, See what I mean?

'This place is mental, Bill, I can't take it all on board.'

Billy nodded, knowing exactly how he felt. This was too far out for them, too fucking weird.

'Let's get out of here, this place is giving me the fucking creeps.'

Billy had had enough now. He walked out on to the balcony; he needed to hurry Tyrell up. He honestly didn't know how much more of this he could take. It made him want to go home and check on his own kids, make sure they were OK.

The cold hit him but he liked the clean feel of it in his lungs. After that flat it was almost like ambrosia.

'All right, Tyrell?'

He nodded.

'You getting anything useful?'

Billy was lighting a cigarette, something he only did when stressed. Tyrell held his hand out for the smoke and Billy gave it to him gladly.

'This is sick, Billy, you won't believe any it, I tell you.' Tyrell looked down at the man cowering on the floor. Freezing and bloody, he was finally broken. 'Tell him! Tell him what you told me.' Tyrell kicked him none too gently in the ribs as he spoke.

The man looked up at him and Billy could see his broken teeth. From the way his arm hung crooked and bleeding he knew Winters had felt the full force of the chair leg more than once during the course of their conversation.

Billy was impressed with old Tyrell. Had thought when it finally came to it he might have shit out. And who could blame him? Who wanted to know the truth about their own kid when it was as ugly as this? He had expected to take over from here, to mete out the punishment for Tyrell, and would have done it gladly. The man needed to know that whoever had taken his boy down was wiped off the face of the earth.

Winters was stuttering in fear. He knew who Billy was and was terrified all over again.

'Tell him!'

'It was Proctor . . . Proctor and Leary and their mate Rudde. It was Rudde who brought them here in the first place.'

Billy looked at the man and said in a high, incredulous voice: 'Rudde? Peter Rudde? The filth?'

Tyrell nodded.

'Tell him everything.'

Winters was gabbling now, trying to get it all over with as quickly as possible.

'It was Rudde who tracked them down for us. He looked in the station books, kept an eye out for the runaways and the homeless kids, then Proctor passed the names and details on to me.'

'What about Leary, where did he fit in then?'

The man sighed heavily.

'Nick was always here – still comes, in fact. Him and Sonny . . . well, I don't have to paint you a picture, do I? But Nick likes the kids, Lenny Bagshots provides them.'

Billy's eyes were open to their widest. If this man had told them Gandhi himself had been in this flat he would have found it easier to believe than what he was hearing now. 'Fuck off! That's bollocks . . .'

Rudde he could cope with, but Nick Leary?

'No, it ain't, Billy. You ain't heard the half of it yet.'

Billy didn't answer Tyrell. He couldn't. He had been to Nick's home, had spoken to him . . . Nick Leary was one of them. He was a face, a diamond geezer.

Billy was reeling from the news.

But he knew deep inside that this scum Winters was telling the truth. He didn't know how but he knew. He had thought Nick cold and sexless the last time they'd met. Seen how he blanked his own highly desirable wife. Now here it was, the missing piece of the puzzle, and he knew it to be true as surely as he knew his own name.

'Nick Leary lured my boy to his house that night to finish him off, get him out of the frame.'

Tyrell let his words sink in. He knew how Billy was feeling, had felt the same himself. But Winters wasn't lying.

'It's Peter Rudde who keeps this place from being trounced as well. There's a big network of them, see. They all work together. Sonny had threatened to expose Leary.'

Billy Clarke was still in shock but he could see the pattern here. Rudde was Nick's tame filth, everyone knew that. They'd even had villas built side by side in Spain. Nick had paid for them, of course, and Rudde's wasn't a patch on Nick's place, but it explained a lot.

The old saying was so true: Keep your friends close, but your enemies closer still.

The man on the ground was whimpering now. Fear and cold had kicked in and he just wanted this over with once and for all.

'I told you the score, now please let me go. I told you everything you asked of me.'

Tyrell stared down at him for long moments. This man had had intimate knowledge of his boy, his child.

This man had fucked his boy.

This man had taken rent from his son here and allowed him to be used by the likes of Nick Leary and now he wanted to walk away as if nothing had happened?

Leave him here and he'd corrupt other young men, use them until the next new kid on the block hooked his attention.

Tyrell stubbed the cigarette out on the man's cheek.

Then, grabbing him by the neck, he lifted Winters bodily in the air and threw him over the balcony with all the force he could muster.

Angela was on the floor. Tammy was kneeling beside her, feeling the sticky blood soaking into her silk dressing gown as it ran like a river from the woman's body. The knife was poking out of her back, the black handle trembling as she tried to breathe. She was making a choking sound in her throat, a bubbling noise, and it was making Tammy want to be sick. She held a hand over her mouth to stem the flow as she started heaving once more.

Angela was grabbing at nothing now, her hand clutching at empty space.

'Oh, Angela love, please be all right. You have to be all right.'

Getting up, Tammy ran into the hallway and picked up the phone.

She was going to be sick again.

Really sick.

But she dialled 999 first. Screaming and shouting, she tried to explain what had happened, but fear had overtaken her now and she was incoherent.

She finally threw up all over the entrance hall floor.

Peter Rudde was sitting in his house eating a microwave meal for one. He liked Iceland's ready meals. They were not only cheap, they contained no GM ingredients. Rudde was funny like that. Liked to take care of the pennies *and* his health.

He was watching *The Shield* on Channel Five, his favourite programme, and drinking a nice cold beer. He had a forty-two-inch flat-screen set and he loved it. He liked the TV programmes on Saturdays as well. Providing no one decided to commit too heinous a crime he had an easy night of it ahead.

He finished his beer and went out to his state-of-the-art kitchen during the commercial break. Putting his plate in the sink, he opened another Grolsch. Then he went back to the front room and settled himself once more in his chair.

His phone rang just as the storyline was hotting up. Rudde answered it without interest. In seconds he was turning down the volume on the TV and saying, 'You are joking?'

Putting down the phone, he started walking around the room, saying, 'Oh, for fuck's sake!' over and over again.

But he had to pull himself together. He was dressed and out of the house in less than fifteen minutes. He knew that whatever else happened tonight, nothing would ever be the same again for any of them.

Willy was still sitting in the car and waiting patiently when he saw a body come out of the dark sky and land with a thud on the pavement. He guessed that Tyrell and his friends would not be long now.

He was right.

They bundled into the car and drove away quickly. Willy had seen the other man go inside and realised he was with them when he followed their car.

Terry was laughing his head off. He was high on adrenaline now he was out of that place.

'You fucking finally crossed the line, Tyrell. You realise that, don't you, man?'

Louis answered for his friend.

'We all realise it, Terry, now give it a fucking rest.'

And for once Terry did as he was asked without a row.

The paramedic had injected Tammy to calm her down. Now she was holding on to Peter Rudde's arm as if her life depended on it. She was still babbling away and he was shushing her.

'Please, Peter, you have to help us . . .'

He saw the WPC watching them with interest and snapped, 'Why don't you go and make this woman a cup of tea, love? Do something constructive for a change?'

She went out of the bedroom quickly. Her boss wasn't the friendliest of men at the best of times and everyone knew he had formed a close relationship with this family after the tragic burglary that had caused so much interest in the media.

Now there had been a fatal stabbing in the same house, and he seemed to think it was a revenge attack, or so he had insinuated when he had got there.

But if that was the case, why was the wife walking around without a scratch? Hers, though, as a WPC, was not to reason why, and she knew it. It had been explained to her enough times.

'Are you sure that's what he said?'

Tyrell was getting annoyed now as he snapped, 'I am hardly liable to forget it, am I?'

Billy finally took umbrage then.

'All right, keep your fucking hair on! I have to make sure, don't I?' This was a living nightmare as far as he was concerned. 'I'm sorry, Tyrell, but this is all fucking doing my head in.'

It was Tyrell's turn to be stroppy now and he said with heavy sarcasm, 'You don't fucking say?'

He picked up a joint from the ashtray and relit it before continuing.

'None of this is easy for me, you know. I found out things tonight that no one should ever know about their kid.'

He looked meaningfully at Willy Lomax and they all realised he was only telling them the half of it for the sake of this boy. But he continued talking and his anger was unmistakable.

'Now I am sorry if you all think Leary and his cronies are the dog's knob, but I want him. I fucking want him . . .'

He leaned forward in his chair and they could all see the hatred in his eyes.

Terry grinned.

'And you'll get him, sunbeam, don't you worry about that.'

'But we have to find him first.'

It was Billy speaking once more. The brothers all knew that his was the voice of reason. He was a man who never made any kind of move without thinking it through thoroughly. It was his sensible head that had kept them all out of prison for so long.

He picked up his mobile and started to ring round. Twenty minutes later they left the flat. Willy watched them go, aware that none of them even remembered he was there. He put the TV on and hoped against hope they'd resolve it all sooner rather than later. He picked up Tyrell's joint and smoked it slowly, savouring the good weed and laughing at the cartoons.

His little holiday would be well and truly over then. He would be back on the street before he knew it and wanted to savour the warmth and easiness of this life for a little longer.

It was strange but if he'd been anywhere else he would have seen the light, realised he was on his way out and blagged the place. He would have gone long before he was asked and taken half the place with him. He would need all the money he could get once he was back on the street.

But he would not do that to Tyrell. He liked him too much and Tyrell had been good to him. But Willy did sort out his few belongings and pack them neatly, in case he had to go on the quick like.

Nick was pacing around the room, mumbling to himself. The young man watched him in earnest, not knowing what to do. He had not seen Nick for two weeks, and had been wondering when he would be launched out of this flat in Barkingside.

He liked it here, liked the area.

But he knew he was only here for as long as he was welcome and had thought maybe he was not welcome any more.

Now here was Nick, but he was a different man tonight. He looked frightening, half-demented, and the boy assumed he was on drugs. He was certainly drunk anyway, he could smell the drink on him from here.

'Can I get you anything?'

Nick looked at him finally, looked right at him, and the boy was pleased about that.

'What you got?'

'Depends what you want, Nick.'

This was said with a leer and Nick closed his eyes in annoyance. The boy tried to make amends. It was something you learned quickly on the streets, how to adapt to other people's mood changes. Especially if they held all the trump cards, which invariably they did.

Nick took a small wrap of coke from his pocket and the boy's eyes lit up.

'Shall I get you a drink, Nick? How about a Scotch?'

He nodded, then grunted at him to hurry up. When the lines were cut the boy brought back drinks for them both. Nick snorted two lines, one after the other, and downed his drink quickly. Justin snorted a line then, but only after asking Nick's permission by raising his plucked eyebrows.

This boy was beautiful.

'I was going to pack my bags and leave, I hadn't seen you for so long.' The words were said with as much feeling as Justin could muster.

Nick looked fleetingly at him, and seeing him for the money-hungry little piece of trade he was, said nastily, 'Don't push me, Justin. I had another one just like you and I soon got rid of him.'

The boy didn't say anything else. He knew what Nick was talking about.

Nick started to cut more lines on the table top. Justin sat back in a chair and wondered, not for the first time in his young life, where the night would end.

Nick could feel himself coming up once more. Coke was great like that, it made you feel that you could take on anything or anyone.

And he needed that feeling now, more than he had ever needed it before.

* * *

Lenny Bagshots was shitting himself and everyone could see it, including his girlfriend who picked up their daughter and walked deliberately from the room. She went into the master bedroom and turned on the TV. Whatever happened she wanted no part of it. She just wanted to keep her daughter and herself safe from the men who had literally invaded her home.

She turned up the volume and, cuddling her daughter to her, watched *Kill Bill* with vacant, frightened eyes.

She heard her boyfriend shouting from the front room and turned the volume up once more.

'Who told you that?'

Lenny was playing the wronged party so well it was almost laughable.

Tyrell looked at him and sighed.

'Gordon Winters, and he has the photographs to prove it apparently. Now you'd better tell us where Leary might be or I am going to kill you stone dead.'

It was said with such quiet conviction Lenny believed him. He looked at the Clarke brothers, all standing in his home and all looking like they wanted to be anywhere else in the world but where they were. Terry looked like he was just waiting for the word to pounce, and knowing him he was. Lenny knew it was all over then. He knew they were on to him, and he also knew once the word got out, and it *would* get out, he would be finished in every way.

That is, providing they left him alive.

Nick was like a cat on a hot tin roof, he just couldn't settle down. He was a bundle of nerves, and every time he thought about his mother he felt the familiar terror envelop him like it had after Sonny Boy.

How could she even have contemplated grassing him up? He could have taken it off Tammy, because she would have had good reason to do it. But he knew no matter what, she wouldn't do it because she looked after number one first and foremost. But his mum? After all he had done for her? The way he had cared for her, the way he had loved her? And she would have put it all on the line without a second's thought. He knew she had meant what she had said, he had seen it in her eyes. He had known there would be no talking her round this time, not like before. She wouldn't believe what she wanted to believe any more.

He had known then and there that those days were gone and he had to look out for himself. Which was what he had done. He had not stabbed his mother, she was already dead to him, he had stabbed a fucking grass. He wasn't worried about Tammy, though, she would know to keep her trap shut. He had made sure of that years ago. She would not put her lifestyle on the line even for her newfound best friend, his so-called mother.

Peter Rudde would sort that out, and Nick would call in every favour he had ever been owed. There was a dirty great big network of them, and he knew who they all were. Rudde even recruited from the CPS files via a mate there, from prison files and court documents too. They tracked down like-minded men because the bigger the network, the less chance they had of being found out.

Nick had blackmailed some of them over the years to get where he was, whether it was for planning permission, bigger overdrafts, or even just an extension on his club licences. 'Use what you got,' his mother always told him. Well, he had taken the advice and look where it had got *her*. He liked his little men, felt happy with them. And he had loved some of them, really loved them.

His phone rang and the sudden noise made him and Justin jump.

Nick answered it quickly.

'Open up, Nick, it's me – Rudde.'

The words were music to his ears. He switched off his phone and smiled, his first real smile.

'Get in the bedroom. And no matter what, you fucking stay there, right?'

Justin did as he was told without a murmur.

Nick went to the front door quickly, pleased that his friend had finally turned up. If anyone could help him it was this man and this man alone.

When he opened the front door, though, it wasn't Rudde standing there, it was the Clarke brothers and Sonny Boy's father.

Nick Leary's capture had finally arrived and they all knew it.

Chapter Twenty-Seven

Tammy sat by the hospital bed and held on to her mother-in-law's hand.

She had taken Rudde's advice and gone in the ambulance with Angela. She had also taken his advice to keep her mouth shut.

For the time being, anyway, if Nick had gone on the missing list then she would wait until she knew the score before deciding what she was going to say. At the moment she wanted to see what happened to poor Angela. She was serious but stable. Tammy stared down into the older woman's wrinkled face and wondered at a woman whose son had accused her of abuse and yet who lived her life quoting her good friend Jesus morning, noon and night.

Her mother had always been suspicious of holy Joes, said they were normally bigger bastards than everyone else and Tammy had to give her brownie points for getting that much night.

But she still didn't want Angela to die. She sat patiently by the bed, waiting for the next drama to unfold. Something told her it would not be long before it did. Nick, she decided, had reached the end of his road. All that was left now was for her to wait and see what he did. Whatever it was, she hoped it did not reflect on her.

If necessary, she would tell the truth about Angela's injuries. Until then, she would bide her time.

* * *

Nick felt his stomach acids rise into his throat and swallowed them down with difficulty. He realised that Rudde had served him up on a plate and in a small recess of his mind he couldn't blame him. He would have done the same.

It was bad enough seeing Billy Clarke, his old friend, standing there, but the real frightener was seeing Terry. His reputation was such that even a bully like Nick was wary of falling out with him.

'You perverted cunt, been out on any dates with skateboarders lately?' Terry's voice was low and his intentions were crystal clear to anyone within earshot. Tyrell saw that Nick wasn't even going to try and deny anything, which made their job so much easier.

Nick's eyes, he noticed, kept darting to the billiard balls that had been placed inside a thick nylon sock. When they connected with his forehead he crumpled like a deflated balloon. Tyrell then kicked and punched him back inside the flat.

Justin listened to the commotion with an ever rising terror, but he still didn't make a sound.

Verbena looked at the policeman with tired eyes.

'Are you sure it was her?'

He nodded.

'She overdosed some time yesterday, she was found this morning by a friend of her son's.'

'Gino? It would be Gino, he was good to Jude.'

The police officer didn't answer her, he didn't know what to say.

The boy was as out of it as Jude usually was, but he wasn't going to pile on the shit. This poor woman had enough to contend with.

'Can I call anyone for you? Get someone to come by?'

She shook her head. 'That's OK. No one will really care but me.'

It was said simply and honestly and he couldn't deny the truth of her statement. Jude's neighbours were already breathing a sigh of relief, and the few bits she had had in the flat had already disappeared.

'I'll be on me way then.'

She nodded, smiling her beatific smile on him. 'Thank you for letting me know.'

'She had you down as next of kin at the hospital, love.'

She smiled once more, pleased at this proof of Jude's love for her.

Alone then, Verbena sat back on her comfortable chair and thought long and hard about the girl who had come into her family like a firework. All noise and bright colours.

She remembered her before the brown had taken her over so completely. Then, picking up her phone book, she looked slowly through it for Jude's mother's number. She knew she wouldn't bother coming to the funeral, knew she would not even pay for it, but she still felt she should alert her to the fact of her daughter's death. She had a right to know; she was her mother after all.

At least Jude would be with her Sonny Boy, she would be happy with him beside her. She consoled herself with the thought even as the tears overwhelmed her and the shuddering of extreme grief encompassed her body.

Nick's forehead had split open and the blood was running down into his eyes.

Tyrell watched him closely, strangely detached from what was going on. The smell of the blood was heavy in the room and the Clarke brothers all made ribald comments egging him on to even more extreme violence.

The carpet was soaked and the walls and ceiling were also drenched with the drying, brown, blood stains.

Nick, by their standards, had to be hurt, and he also had to feel his hurt. Tyrell was aware of this and even agreeable to it now. Sonny's death demanded it, his lifestyle forced this retribution.

Every time he hurt Nick he thought of Sonny, and then he thought of this man with other little kids. It became easier then.

Where the cut-throat razor had come from he didn't know, but guessed rightly that it was from Terry. The feel of the blade as it sliced through the skin and jarred on the bone was like nothing he had ever experienced before. But Tyrell was on a violence high, for the first time in his life he was getting off on someone else's pain. Each blow or slash brought him closer to peace and even though, on one level, he knew what he was feeling was wrong, he savoured it.

Each blow was for his boy, each grunt of pain was pay back for taking his boy and using him like an animal. Each moment he heard this man's pain was like a balm on a festering sore.

Nick's mouth was taped up with black, electrician's duct tape but his moans and screams could still be heard in the room.

He was unrecognisable as a human being, and he sounded more like a wounded bear now than a man.

Terry watched it all bright-eyed. He loved retribution, and this kind, righteous retribution, was the best of all. He almost felt saint-like in his devotion to seeing this man die. He was scum and scum had to be eliminated. For the first time ever he saw the world through Terry Clarke's eyes. Something he had never thought would happen.

Billy Clarke and the others egged them both on, but somewhere in Louis and Billy there was a voice saying it was too much. Maybe not for Terry, but for Tyrell; he had after all turned his back on this kind of servitude whereas they had all embraced it as a job.

As Tyrell slashed him again, Nick made a gurgling sound and they all knew that his mouth was filling up with blood and puke. It seemed to last for an eternity and Tyrell watched him in fascinated silence as he fought to stay alive.

Nick was unconscious now and, taking the cattle prod from his pocket, Terry thrust it into Nick's body, causing his bleeding carcass to leap off the floor from the strength of the current.

'Wake up, you fucking nonsense!' Tyrell was laughing in hysterical excitement but he knew in his heart of hearts that Nick Leary would never wake up again.

Hester walked into the intensive-care unit and took her place beside Tammy. Grasping her sister-in-law's hand, she smiled sadly. 'Is she dying, Tams?'

Tammy shrugged. She didn't know what to say.

'I hope she is.'

Tammy was shocked at what she heard. 'Stop it, Hess.'

Hester smiled gently. 'Nick did this, didn't he?'

Tammy nodded, her eyes filled with tears.

'Then I hope she dies, because she wouldn't want to live knowing he had harmed her.'

She wiped at her own eyes with a tissue but there were hardly any tears. 'They had a strange relationship, Tams. Unless you lived our life you couldn't understand any of it.'

Tammy understood a lot more than Hester realised but she wasn't going to let on about that. She had always known there was something not right between Angela and her daughter but she had put it down to the fact she had married a black man. Now she saw that Angela had known Nick's preferences for boys had erred on the Caribbean side. Sonny Hatcher proved that. All that time her daughter had thought she had never cared for her or her children when, in fact, Angela had been protecting them; as she had protected her own boys by chaperoning them constantly. It suddenly occurred to her that she would have to explain their grandmother's attack to them and the thought of that frightened her.

Whatever her husband had accused his mother of, she would never breathe a word of it to another soul. She knew her sons had been safe with her. She had to believe that or she would go mad, especially as she had virtually given them to this woman without a backwards glance. She wondered what their reaction would be to all that had happened?

Hester looked old suddenly and unkempt. The years had not been kind to her, yet Tammy knew that Hester's husband adored her and for some strange reason that knowledge made her feel inexplicably sad.

She knew she had never really been loved. Even the kids had only loved her when they were tiny and vulnerable.

Over the years, her indignation at her husband and the boredom of her marriage had changed her. From the happy-go-lucky girl she had been when first married, she was now an unhappy woman who chased meaningless sexual encounters, trying to convince herself they were great love affairs.

What would happen if Nick was caught or, worse, got off with what he had done? She had to think, and think clearly. She knew every deal he had ever done and she knew where the money was placed. She had made a point of knowing over the years in case he had ever got a lump through one or other of his nefarious dealings.

Nick was wrapped in a tarpaulin on the front-room floor of the flat and they were all sitting around smoking quietly.

The violence of the attack had finally hit them and they saw the blood all over themselves and the room.

Going to the kitchen, Terry looked in the fridge, took out some milk and started to make everyone coffee. The thick, latex gloves he wore washed easily and he leaned over the sink under an old gas geyser and washed himself as best he could. The others followed suit. Cleaning up quickly and efficiently.

They still looked bloody, though. Their clothes were covered in it, especially Terry's and Tyrell's.

While the kettle boiled, Terry nipped down to the car and took out the bag of shirts he kept in the boot. He always carried spare clothes. With his unpredictable temper, he never knew when he might need them. He prided himself on always being one step ahead of any skulduggery he might encounter in the course of an average day. He also kept a nice, ironed shirt hanging up in the back of his car in case he decided to visit one of his amours. Terry Clarke thought of everything.

Inside the flat, they laughed at his black bag full of clothes and he basked, like a kid, in their appreciation and their humorous ripostes. He had really enjoyed it all, in a funny way; it had made him aware of how lucky he was.

Rudde was alone now, and the pain in his rectum was so acute he felt he could pass out. The bastards had held him down and violated him with a broom handle. Leaving him bleeding and terrified they had told him they would be back after they had seen Nick. Then Kerr had made him phone Nick and left him there.

He knew they spoke the truth. They would be back all right. He had seen Tyrell Hatcher in a new light.

Now he lay on his bed and waited for them to return. They had tied him up like a chicken and he lay there uncomfortably and terrified as he contemplated what their final savage act would be.

Whatever it was it could not match what they would do to Nick Leary and he knew that deep inside.

Tammy was at home and, in the pool house, she opened the safe she had had fitted when Nick was away on one of his Malaga weekends with the lads.

She had copies of every document he had ever possessed as well as his insurance policies. She would be a very rich woman if her husband died or disappeared. She hoped it would be the former.

Nick could never come back. But she knew how sneaky he could be and she had to make sure that everything was taken care of. If necessary, she would serve him up without a second's thought.

She tried Rudde's mobile once more, in case he had news of her husband, but it rang until it went to voicemail. There was no way she was going to leave a message on it. She was using one of Nick's mobiles so she wasn't too trashed about the call being logged. She heard her landline ringing and knew without a doubt that her mother-in-law was dead.

Sitting on the floor she felt a flicker of sadness run through her. She was finally, irrevocably, on her own.

Getting up she walked sedately back to the hallway and looking around her she felt a small thrill at the knowledge that this was all hers.

Verbena sat in the darkening twilight listening to the radio and thinking about Jude. It was funny, but her heart was lighter than it had been for many a year.

Jude had cast a pall over her family, she had known that, known how much they had all despised her, also known that Sonny had loved her very much.

She looked at the photograph of her own dead son and smiled at it, as she always did. She had once entreated her dead child to watch over Sonny, and now asked him to look out for Jude as well. This made her feel so much better.

Hearing a soft tap on the door, she knew it was the reverend and she plastered a huge smile on her face ready to greet him. She had rung him earlier, had not even bothered to talk to Tyrell, she didn't want to talk about Jude with the family just yet, they wouldn't understand.

The reverend, like most people, had had no time for Jude, even with his Christian spirit, but she knew he would say all the right things even if he didn't really mean it. And she needed to hear them now, more than she had ever needed anything in her life.

Jude, to her, had always been the lost sheep. Well, now, finally, she had been found and nothing or no one could ever hurt her again.

* * *

The shadows on his bedroom wall had lengthened when Peter Rudde heard the sound of a key in his lock. He felt his bowels loosen immediately. The pain had subsided a little but he was aware that it would soon be returning and it would be far worse than anything that had gone before.

The men walked into his bedroom and, in the dimness, he saw their changed clothes and hyper stances. He knew they had taken care of Nick.

He closed his eyes on the thought of what Nick had gone through; he knew he was due more of the same.

Billy and Tyrell laughed as they held up a length of rope and some handcuffs. 'You are going out like a sex-game Peter, me old mucker, and all your photos of little boys are going to be left out for your colleagues to find. Now, I wonder what they will make of that?'

His photographs were of bondage and when he knew that they had found them his fear was tenfold.

It took them twenty minutes to hang him from the butcher's hook they had screwed into the bedroom ceiling, and another five minutes of pulling on his legs and choking him before they were finally convinced he was dead.

It was Terry who decided to finish the job by pulling down his trousers and shoving a shard of broken glass inside his rectum. He stood back to admire his handiwork, the laughter as usual not far from the surface. He started singing Lou Reed's 'Hanging Around' and even Tyrell laughed.

'Well, this cunt has certainly had a walk on the fucking wild side tonight, eh lads?'

They left the flat, locking up carefully behind them.

They didn't want him found just yet. Popping the keys back through the letterbox, they made their way back to the van they had purloined to transport Nick Leary in comfort to one of his building sites.

* * *

When Tyrell finally got home he had managed to get a takeaway for himself and Willy Lomax. Roadside cheese burgers and chips, but it would have to do, the smell had made him realise that he was starving.

Giving the food to Willy to set out on plates, he smiled at the boy and said, 'Build a kinger, son, eh. I am going to have a shower.'

In the shower, he scrubbed his body clean of the night's events. As he put his head under the shower the clean hot water mixed with the tears he knew he had to shed for his child. The child he had never really looked out for, not properly, not as he should have.

He felt like a new man now. Felt that he had at last got retribution for what had happened to his son.

Dressing himself in jeans and a T shirt he went into the lounge and wolfed down the cheese burger and chips like a man starved for weeks. Cracking open a can of Red Stripe he swallowed it quickly. The meal was over in five minutes.

Willy watched him surreptitiously, afraid of this new man he was seeing. Tyrell had anger washing out of every pore, even in repose his face looked harder than before. He was frightened of him now, seriously frightened, and he didn't know why. Tyrell glanced at Willy as he lit a joint and, seeing the boy's face, he put the joint back in the ashtray and said quietly, 'You OK?'

Willy Lomax barely nodded. This was the man he had come to know and love. Not the man who had walked in smelling faintly of blood and sweat and with wild, red-rimmed eyes.

'Hey, little man, what's wrong?'

Tyrell remembered that Willy had probably seen the man go over the balcony and he sighed inwardly. Without this kid he would never have found out the truth of the situation his son had found himself in. Was he grateful? He didn't know. What he did know, however, was that this boy looked whiter than ever, looked ill. He was ill, he had HIV, for Christ's sake.

'Do you need a doctor, little man?'

Once more Willy shook his head.

'Are you frightened?'

He didn't answer.

'Are you frightened of me?'

Willy nodded then, his eyes like flying saucers.

'Oh shit, Willy, you ain't got to be scared of me, mate.'

His voice was so soft, so caring that it was the undoing of the young man sitting alone and frightened on the comfortable sofa. He burst into tears. It had been so stressful, all his life it had been so stressful, and he wasn't able for it any more. He was going soft and he knew it.

Tyrell went to him and put a strong arm gently across his shoulders, frightened of making contact like that with the boy, frightened it would be misconstrued. But Willy grabbed the arm as if it was a lifeline and sobbed like he had never sobbed before. He cried for his own life, for Tyrell's life and for all the boys and girls he had met over the years trapped in the same kind of world as his. He cried for his mother who he had loved so much and who had never wanted him from the moment of his conception.

Tyrell held him while he cried and gently rubbed his back, making low, hushing sounds to try to calm him.

Finally, spent, Willy looked up into Tyrell's face and said, 'Thanks, mate, thanks for looking out for me.'

Tyrell pulled the red head to him and hugged him tightly, as he hugged his own boys, as he had hugged Sonny all that time ago.

'Thank *you*, little man, for helping me out like you have. Now, come on, let me make you a nice hot chocolate, eh? I know it's your favourite and I will even watch the Cramp twins if it will cheer you up, OK?'

Willy smiled then, a sad little smile that broke Tyrell's heart.

'I wish you'd been my dad.'

Tyrell ruffled his hair, he didn't know what to say. After the brutality of the last few hours this boy was like a breath of fresh air.

'So do I, son, so do I.'

He was surprised to find that he meant it.

Tammy lay back in the Jacuzzi and sipped at her gin and tonic.

She had always liked room service and the little waiter had been a dream boat. The hotel was expensive, and so it should be. She needed pampering at the moment. But even she knew she had to be as good as gold for a while. She wondered, once more, where her husband might be and how the upshot of everything was going to affect her.

Poor Angela, what a way to go, murdered by her own son.

She looked down at her body and, for once, she didn't criticise herself. She wasn't bothered about any of it any more. She had other things on her mind.

She would pick the boys up from school tomorrow. She would not, could not, stay in that big lump of a house on her Jack Jones. She knew that much. In fact, she decided she might get herself a live-in housekeeper.

They could all swim and just chill out. She would organise herself. She wasn't stupid, was she? In fact, she had a feeling that once this was all over her real life might just begin.

She closed her eyes and tried to blot out, once more, the sight of her husband as he stabbed his mother in the back.

It was funny, she had used that expression so many times over the years and now he had actually stabbed someone in the back. Her husband was a nonce, a bona fide, card-carrying fuck-ing child-chaser. What the fuck would she do if that all came out?

What would her so-called mates say? In reality, she realised that she didn't really care.

After the events of today it seemed to put everything into perspective. The strangest thing of all was she also felt liberated. As if her possessive love for her husband had never existed.

Nick had always been a big strong lad, had prided himself on his strength. As he lay in a water-filled hole, dug for a cement footing, he regained consciousness. It took a monumental effort for him to drag himself to his knees, but he did it. The pain was like white fire threading its way through every part of his body and his mind was jumbled, confused. He was acting on the instinct for survival that every man has inside them regardless of race, colour or creed.

It wasn't enough though. Dropping forward on to his face he landed in the watery mud and that was how he finally died. His last thought was of a photo of him and his mother smiling together as he collected a football medal. The photo had stood in his mother's bedroom for years.

Willy was asleep at last and Tyrell tucked him in so he would be nice and warm. Going into his bedroom, he sat on the bed and put his head in his hands to steady his shaking.

It was shock and he knew that. He was in shock at all that had happened, not only today but over the last few months.

Jude was dead, Rudde had told him that, actually expecting him to be grateful. He knew his mother would take it hard but he couldn't do anything about that, could he? She had always seen a different Jude to everyone else, as he had done himself for a while. He hoped sincerely that Jude had found some kind of peace. She had never known true peace, not like others had. Jude's life had been one drama after another and he hoped that now she could finally sleep properly. She had been so beautiful once, especially when she had been carrying Sonny Boy, and he was sorry that her son and her husband had never been enough for her.

Now he had two broken marriages behind him because he knew that, no matter what, he would never go back to Sally again.

A bomb had exploded in his life and that bomb's name had been Jude. The reverberations of that bang had caused ructions for nearly twenty years and now it was all over and he hoped that, finally, they might find some calm and some peace. Especially poor Jude, and his handsome Sonny Boy.

Once more, he cried.

Epilogue

Tyrell looked good and Sally could not help noticing it while she sat with his mother. She did it frequently these days, but only because Tyrell spent so much time there. She also observed how close he was to his sons.

Why had she never valued that before? Appreciated that fact for what it was, instead of finding fault with him all the time. Why had Jude and Sonny Boy always seemed to loom so much larger in her life than the good man she'd actually been married to?

Now Jude was dead, as well as her Sonny Boy, the victim of her own greed. She had finally scored a decent armful and it had killed her. Too late, though, to have been any good to Sally. If only she had known what was going to happen, she could just have waited for them both to disappear, and by now she would be his sole love. But she had not done that. Instead she had tried to make him choose and in the end he had chosen, but it had not been her.

Tyrell walked purposefully out into the kitchen. Even his walk was different. Everything about him was different these days.

The boys had noticed it too.

They didn't talk to her like they had once before. They still treated her as their mother, were still *respectful* to her, still *loved* her. But now all their private thoughts were kept for their father.

Sally followed her husband out to the kitchen, ignoring her

mother-in-law's warning look. Verbena had advised her to stop throwing herself at him, said he needed time to heal. But Sally couldn't do that, it was not in her make up.

He was expecting her. She knew that because he was already facing her, leaning against the cheap worktop and smiling that strange smile he seemed to have developed in the last few months.

It was as if he was there all right, but also as far away from her as he had ever been, all at the same time. She just couldn't get close to him at all, and that saddened her.

'What do you want to talk about this time, Sal?'

His tone was neutral, but loaded with insinuation. She had the grace to feel embarrassed. She could hear her sons' chatter coming from the lounge, knew they were talking once more about their brother because that was what happened frequently nowadays. Their grandmother was keeping his memory alive for them, making sure Sonny was never forgotten. The place was like a shrine to him and Jude.

Sally smiled and tried her hardest to look non-confrontational, whatever that meant. It was something she had read in a women's magazine and since she wanted her marriage back on track she was willing to try it. Willing to do anything. She wanted this man back where he belonged: in her house and in her bed. No matter what it took or what the personal cost might be to her pride, she wanted to make it all as it had been before.

Tyrell folded his arms across his chest and said quietly, 'Come on, Sal, I ain't got all day.'

He had been expecting this, she saw that now. Had brought her after him so she would not have to hunt for another excuse to be out here with him. Something she had done a lot lately. Was she that transparent?

'Come on, the boys want to get going,' Tyrell pressed her.

She looked humble, contrite. He could see the pain behind her eyes, and still it didn't move him.

'Please, Tyrell, please come home.'

It was the nearest Sally had ever come to begging and they both knew that.

He looked at her but didn't answer.

She saw the heavy dreads that framed his face, saw the sadness in his brown eyes, saw how the weight had dropped from him, leaving him even leaner. More attractive, more sexy than he had ever been to her.

Why was it you never knew what you had till it was gone from you? Until you had driven it away?

And in her heart she already knew she had driven this man away when with a few kind words she could have kept him by her side for the rest of her life.

He had changed beyond all recognition. It was there in his face. This was still Tyrell but a different one, a harder, more complex man. All of a sudden she knew it was pointless trying to talk him round, his mind was made up and she would never be able to change it.

He was still watching her, and she could see the cynicism in his eyes, in the set of his mouth.

In his whole demeanour.

When he didn't answer her she knew it was over. And the knowledge hurt her so much, she thought she might die from it.

Gino smiled at his mother and she smiled back. It had taken a while but they had come through it together, as Deborah was forever pointing out to him. He could smell the dinner cooking, frozen fishcakes and mashed potatoes. He felt an urge to be sick, but swallowed it down. Once he had eaten he could go out, and the first place he was going was to the big flats nearby.

The big flats were the tower blocks. He lived with his mother in a low-rise building, built before the Second World War when there had still been plenty of space and greenery around.

Gino was going to score a bit of gear for himself over there and chill out big-time. His girlfriend Abby was his blind, she was as up for the brown as him.

It was a perfect arrangement.

He liked the brown, liked how it made him feel, liked the fact he could get off the estate without having to get on a fucking bus. It was his world now, and Gino was grateful for it.

Jude might be gone, but her memory lived on.

He was proof of that.

Tammy lay by the indoor pool. She looked around her at the beautiful empty house and counted the days until she could get the boys from school and go to Spain. She sipped at her drink which was as strong as she needed it to be. She was still in seclusion after the murder of her husband and mother-in-law. Her friends had actually been good, rallying round her, even if it was only to find out what was going on.

Nick had been found face down in the footings of one of his buildings, beaten to death. No one had been arrested for the crime and she knew that no one ever would be. No one knew why it had happened.

Except Tammy, of course, and she wasn't telling *anyone*.

What they guessed was their business, of course, but she had buried her dead in separate graves. In separate cemeteries even. It was the least she could do for Angela.

She wondered how much Hester knew, and how much she had guessed. But whatever it was she had not argued about any of the arrangements.

Nick was gone, and Tammy didn't miss him at all. Why had she lived her life in his shadow for so long? It was pitiful really how much she had depended on him. Wanted him. Needed him.

All those wasted years and all the constant wondering where he was when all the time the man she thought she knew, believed she loved, was a hollow shell, not worthy of her love or anyone else's.

Rudde was gone, hanged himself apparently, though no one seemed to know why. He had destroyed the photographs first, though, and made her see sense. Tammy had a lot to thank him for. Not that she would bother to go looking for him, of course.

And now here she was with more money than she knew what to do with and a sexy new slim figure, thanks to all the worry.

But it was all over, that was the main thing.

Finally, it was over.

The funny thing was, she was off men. Didn't want anything to do with them these days. And after spending more time with her boys she had actually learned to enjoy them and their company.

If only she had found out years before what really mattered in life, how much happier she would have been. But she knew now, and was determined to make sure she never forgot her priorities again.

Willy Lomax was grinning widely. When Tyrell and the boys picked him up from the halfway house he had some good news for them all for once.

He had been allocated a flat.

He finally had a home of his own and this little family who had adopted him so readily would be his first visitors.

They were going bowling today and he was just grateful that they let him be a part of it all.

He was dying, and he knew it.

But he wasn't dead yet!

As Tyrell said, you had to make the most of every day, and that was exactly what Willy was doing.

Justin smiled at the punter with every ounce of charm he possessed. He knew that was a considerable amount.

The man, a commuter in a crumpled black suit and a sweat-stained grey shirt, walked towards him with a sheepish grin. He was in his fifties, married to a social worker with a hectic hairdo and a constant sniff. Consequently he was up for a bit of fun and games. He had seen the boy earlier, and let his train go in case his assumption proved to be correct.

It was, and he was over the moon. They left the station together a few minutes later. The old rat house might be gone but a new one had opened up just as quickly around the corner.

Justin could find a rat house like other boys found cricket balls.

Tyrell watched the three boys as they bowled each other out. He watched everyone else as well now, something he had never done before. He looked around him all the time for men who were alone and watching the youngsters at play.

He felt a million years old now. Felt as if Methuselah was a babe in arms in comparison to him, now he knew so much about the world.

Jude was gone, her own victim, and Sonny had gone the same way. Tyrell had buried her, and had done her proud because he knew his mother expected that much from him. But he had seen her off without any kind of emotion whatever. He was past all that. He only cared about these three boys now. That was it until he had mended himself, and he wasn't sure how he was supposed to do that.

Louis said he just had to wait, be patient until it didn't hurt so much any more, and Tyrell had a feeling he was probably right about that. One day he would be ready to be with someone again, but it would never be Sally, he knew that much. He wanted someone who was softer, didn't want to own him and his life. Sally had made sure he had lost precious time with his eldest son. Well, he had been given a steep learning curve lately and he knew he had learned a lot from that.

But he also knew that in a way he had been lucky.

So many people didn't see what was happening right under their noses, but he did now. In fact, he was a fucking expert. Maybe, just maybe, if he had known all this before he might have been able to look out properly for his Sonny Boy. But that was something he would never know for sure.

Terry Clarke came into the Princess bowling alley in Dagenham then, a very unlikely visitor, and Willy's smile grew even wider. Terry had taken to this boy, even when he had found out about his illness. Now he met up with them once a week and they all had the time of their lives. Tyrell saw a side of Terry then he had never guessed at before. He also knew that Terry popped by to see Willy on a regular basis on his own even though it was never discussed.

Wonders would never cease.

Tyrell grinned happily at Willy and his sons, glad that he had this chance to be with them and enjoy them. Glad that if nothing else he had learned one thing. You couldn't protect your kids properly until you understood exactly what you were supposed to be protecting them from.

Then, and only then, could you actually keep them safe.